Draconian Aria

Draconian Symphony, Book 2

Benjamin Dempsey

Draconian Aria

Printed in the United States of America

First Movement - Scherzo

1

The Angel Fermata

Draco

"Hey, serving boy, you blind?" Lascivus clanged her glass against a hollow bottle. "Almost out of mead here, kid. Hop to it."

"Yes, m'dame," the waiter, a mustachioed Iranian in a plum tuxedo, bowed to veil his contempt and excused himself to the kitchen.

"You shouldn't be so condescending to the wait-staff, princess, less they pass water or worse into your cherished bottle," I warned.

A decade and a half ago this woman tried to kill and eat me. Instead I coerced her into helping me kill an abomination from my past. She then rescued me from a formless void I accidentally trapped us in when I slew the rest of my family. It turned out she was the devil's own daughter, and I was made to pay off my debt doing Hell's dirty work.

"He so much as looks at my booze wrong I'll put knots in his intestines." With a chuff she drained the last of the bottle, her glass untouched.

"Mother, please, you're being embarrassing," our daughter hissed, eyes darting about anxiously.

During such dirty work I surrendered my body to Lascivus so she'd have enough strength to break us out of mad elf jail. From that union bore twin fruit, and after a rather embarrassing escapade involving an accidental curse, I agreed to marry her. A bit old fashioned for the 31st Century but I couldn't resist the perks.

The sparsely populated restaurant fed some 13/8 jumble as they listened to the string quintet on stage. Here could be seen a young couple quietly blushing, there an old couple hooting over raunchy stories, and off to the side took place either a business meeting, a conspiracy, or a surprisingly well-organized free-love convent that sat scrutinizing a spread of charts between their pasta bowls. The five of us, Lascivus, the twins, my living sword, Drakkengard, and I, sat around a square table. Lascivus sat to my left, Drakkengard to my right, and the kids opposite. The succulent aroma of tender meats and rich sauces made a most pleasing olfactory tapestry.

"Loosen a little, Sis. They wouldn't throw away our wads if we burnt down the kitchen," our son Lach mimed, slapping money against his hand and flashed his incisors.

"Yes, how did you get that money again, Father?"

"Let's just say someone owed me," I brushed off her concerns and helped myself to a few more slices of beef.

As per tradition, our children hadn't been named until they'd taken breath and their hearts beat. That was a bit of a superstitious exaggeration. They'd had pulse and all from the start. It was just hard to detect. A harmless defect found in most cambion's it seems, at least that was my minion Dr. Vengai-Ra's call —Cambion is what they call the union of a demon and a human, well, probably human.

Nonetheless after several years they'd both gasped and the only strange thing left about them was the eyes they'd inherited from me, which weren't too striking in this day and age. So sure enough, at that time, our children were named. I named our daughter Cicula, and Lasivus named our son Lach. Now, they were deep into their teenaged years, and brimming with piss and vinegar as they say.

"Yet do we really want to be *that* family, tolerated only for wealth? Bad things happen to those families when they fall on hard times," Cicula warned.

"Do you think that likely to happen any time soon?" I locked eyes with our daughter as I poured gravy over my plate. "Have you heard something? Who are these conspirators? Is it the Milkman?"

"Not everything has to be about rumors and portents, Father. What ever happened to being prepared? If the world ended tomorrow, where would we be?"

"Off world, ideally."

"Just chill already, Sis, I mean yikes. Your paranoia's going to get you killed one day," Lach cackled.

"Not before your lack of it drags you down, Brother." Cicula glared at his feigned innocence expression. Our son just laughed and stuffed his mouth with a turkey leg.

The waiter's return interrupted their little spat, and he brought Lascivus's booze, a whole crate of it this time. He clearly wanted as few excuses to call upon them as possible.

"Your mead, m'dame."

"Thanks, Sebastian."

"My name is Mahdi."

"Shut up and piss off, Bastion."

"Gladly." He about faced and strode off before she could complain more.

"Oh, you got sassed," our son brayed, his ponytail tossing about from his laughter.

"Can it, brat, else I'll make you and sword-bitch go five rounds in the snow."

"Make?" Drakkengard cocked her head at my wife. The shapeshifting sword had been a part of my life for as long as I've been me. Frankly I'm just not myself without her.

"Wait, is sending me on a playdate with Dad's sword meant to be punishment? That makes no sense to begin with." Lach looked from his mother to his half eaten turkey leg, as though the bird bone might divine an insight into her mind.

"You back talking me, boy?" Lascivus tossed and caught a bottle of mead from the crate.

"No, no, just trying to figure which of us is the mad one."

"You're all mad from where I'm sitting, the whole bally lot of you." Our daughter stabbed a chunk of roast pumpkin from the platter, placed it on her plate, and began methodically slicing it with her knife.

"Bally? Didn't that go extinct already?" Lach gnawed on his turkey bone and reached for a baked potato.

"Clearly not, since I just said it," our daughter huffed, going for the pumpkin.

"Maybe what you just did was unnatural-like. Let dead words rest, Sis, no need to drag up their corpses."

"Oh, piss off."

Cicula flipped her knife around, eyes alight, and lunged for her brother. He only needed to make even a slight allusion to necromantic craft to rile her up, so frequent was his needling. I had no clue regarding her grudge against the undead, but for one so close to god's mayhap it's just professional rivalry. My daughter's craft was that of a summoner, an art taught to her by someone she insisted was just an imaginary friend.

I pinched my brow. A metallic clang rang out, and both Cicula's knife and Lach's turkey bone were driven into a golden-delicious apple. Drakkengard stood between their chairs, holding both the kids by the wrist. They were half out of their chairs already, and glaring at each other in opposing scorn and mockery. In the corner, a woman in white giggled.

"Can you two broods calm your humors and just get along for a while," I chided, but softened my tone as best I could. "You want to tear each other's hair out at least wait till we're home. No requisite to ruin a good outing." Drakkengard let go of their wrists, and the two of them sat back down, one with a huff and the other a laugh. Drakkengard returned to her seat at my side.

"Thank you. Also you, Drakkengard."

"Always, Master," Drakkengard smiled and refilled my wineglass. Lascivus snorted and took a deep swig of her mead.

"Aww, I would have liked a bit of show with the meal," she slurred, eyes unblinking. Ye gods, the cask of mead was disappearing fast. Though not so fast to convince me the slurring was authentic.

"Maybe someone will try to rob us before we get home. That'll get you a show," Lach brayed. The boy bore no malice, he just thrived on chaos and conflict. Much the opposite of my daughter.

"It ain't the same," Lascivus scoffed. "There a pit fight near here? Coliseum maybe? Actually I could really go for some high stakes charioting right now."

"I don't think Londinium ever had a coliseum. You're out of luck." I shrugged. In the far end of the room, a newcomer entered through the restaurant door. Lascivus's nostrils flared.

"Is that some *thrice*-damned peace-dove I smell," she spat venomously. "Or did a putrefied basilisk just crap its guts out and try to breed with 'em?"

I closed my eyes and took a deep breath. "A nice meal, that's all I wanted. A nice family-thing meal to lay a little anchor down." I took another deep breath, smelled smoke, and opened my eyes again.

The newcomer made a beeline for our table. She was a young looking woman, with tan skin, strawberry blonde hair, white halter top and faded jeans. Even when she got closer, it was hard to make out the color of her eyes, a sort of cream perhaps, indistinguishable from the whites. The strange woman reached our tables and leaned back, one hand in her pocket. With her queer milky eyes it was difficult to tell where she was looking.

"Rather than packing this tension into boxes and stacking it like I've half a mind to, how about you just say what you want with us?" I implored the woman. "Maybe bugger off in a hurry if you're feeling generous."

"Don't you know what she is?" Lascivus hissed, eyes slitted and fangs bared. I could taste the faint tang of miasma coming off her.

"Rude, although I think you insulted her earlier so that makes two of you." I wiped my mouth with a napkin. The kids watched. Lach tensed and tried not to grin.

"She's a peace-dove, a bleach-feather, a miserable piece of shit, a— "

"Be you Draco?" the woman interrupted. "He who consorts with demons, wed to the family of the serpent and doer of the devil's work? Murderer, pillager, thief and sinner of countless other crimes? Son of no man and— "

"Hold up there!" I jerked my hand, cutting her off, and stood. Lascivus and Drakkengard also rose.

"That rap sheet sounds far too grandiose for me. I'm just a debt collector for my father-in-law," I took a deep breath. My left hand twitched. *And then there was music.* Am I being framed?"

"You plead innocent, mongrel?"

"Who the hell do you think you are law-basher? You trying to start something coming in here with—" Lascivus fell silent. A second later, she fell over, face first onto the table, and a long, golden needle protruded from her neck.

The strange woman caught my fist two inches from her face. My magick flames licked her cheek unheeded.

"Be not afraid, she isn't dead. Despicable though she is, she's not my quarry today. No, today's price is on your head."

Drakkengard leapt toward her, contorting in mid-air to whip a sharpened leg at the woman's flank. A bright flash blinded me, and then nothing.

2

Harmonious Hemlock

Cicula

After a loud metallic clang came silence. I didn't let go of my breath until my vision returned. It could have taken a few seconds or a few minutes.

Mother lay face down on the table, unmoving. Lach stood beside her, regarding her body with unworried curiosity. Father's blade had fallen to the ground, unmoving. No trace remained of him or the strange woman, nor anyone else in the building. They all seemed to have evacuated at the first sign of trouble. This was not a venue accustomed to violence. Cops would be here soon. My breath quickened and my skin ran cold with sweat.

"Huh, she ain't dead after all." Lach's voice snapped my attention to him. He prodded Mother in the shin with his foot.

"Are you sure?" I swallowed, and swallowed again. Absently I reached for the nearest glass to wet my throat and gulp it down. I gagged, my tongue and throat aflame with sour and bitter flavors, and dropped Father's wine glass on the floor.

"For sure I'm sure. It's like when you pinch a cat." He jerked his thumb at the golden needle in Mother's neck. It was so narrow as to be just a faint glow unless you squinted. My sight blurred, and I had to steady myself against the table.

"What the hell was that? What just happened? I don't- why?" I clutched my chest and forced my breathing to slow.

Lach shrugged. "Mom's out, Dad's gone, and his sword's gone to standby-mode." He picked up Father's blade and pressed his finger into its edge. The digit came away with a thin white pressure line but no blood. "She can't even hold an edge if he's not here, huh? Neat."

"Neat? Neat?" Father's just been abducted and you're distracted by how neat it is his sword is now useless?"

"Chill, Sis. Focus on my voice. Our old man probably has this down. I bet he'll be back in just a few minutes."

"What if he isn't? What if he's dead already? What if he's been imprisoned for all eternity in a crystal prison or something? What if he's being brainwashed and is sent to hunt the rest of us down?" I slammed my fist into the table. The small thing made a quiet thump, and I held back a wince.

"Well that'll be a thing that happens, I guess." Lach shrugged again, and turned his gaze to the half-finished food still on the table.

"Look you tickle-brained puttock, we can't just stand around here all day. We need to do something."

"Such as?"

"Get Mother some help, for one. Then figure out where that woman took Father." I bit my lip.

"Why do we have to do it, though?"

"We can't just assume anyone else gives half a rat. We should go see Grandfather, he can help." I looked my brother up and down. He wore one of those stupid sleeveless red things he likes, the ones that show off his shoulders and cling to his chest muscles. How utterly contemptuous.

"Look, you have all the gross biceps, so you get Mother and carry her into the kitchen. I'll bring Drakkengard. There should be some materials there to send us to Hell. We can figure out our next step there, and for fucks sake don't bump that needle. You might paralyze her for life or some such rubbish." I took Father's sword from Lach. She was too heavy for me to wield, but not so heavy that I couldn't carry her to the next room.

Lach gave me a puzzled look as he lifted Mother. He tossed her over his shoulder like she was too drunk to walk.

"Since when were you such a dutiful kid?"

"Just shut up and follow me." With Drakkengard in tow, I glanced about the room's exits then headed to the egress marked *kitchen*. It was barred by a simple pair of swinging doors, and I pushed right through.

"Hey, you can't come in here." It seemed the chef didn't leave. Perhaps she didn't hear the ruckus. She was a stocky woman, with her black hair up in a bun. She pointed a quavering finger at the sword in my hands. "What's that? Some prop? I told Victor to stop trying to make this a theme dive. People want food and quiet, not fang-shee. Get it out of here."

I ignored her and found a clear space on the floor. Lach came in just a moment later, carrying Mother, and the chef's eyes narrowed.

"She's not got food poisoning has she? I tell you for sure she didn't get it here, and what are you doing bringing her in here for? Get her to a hospital if she's sick, you'll contaminate everything."

"Put her here, it seems to be a good spot." I pointed to a part of the floor not too cluttered by sacks and crates like the rest of it.

"What? No! I said get her out!" The cook yelled and charged toward us. Lach placed Mother face-down on the floor, with less gentleness than he should, and stood up. From the pocket of my petticoat I pulled out a cigarette and my holder.

"Shut her up, would you?" I took out a brass lighter and light up.

"The quick way or the fun way?" Lach glanced around the kitchen and pocketed an apple.

"Quick. I need her blood, not her underwear you miserable letch." I rolled my eyes, and looked about for something to draw with, sucking in a mouthful of smoke.

You could hear the clang of the chef's assumptions shifting lenses. "Wait a minute," she said, drawing herself up. "You're a bunch of rotten hooligans aren't you?" Lach walked toward her, smiling and with arms spread. She seized a knife from the counter beside her and brandished it with surprising confidence.

"I warn you kid, I know how to use this." She brandished her knife. The way she held it reminded me of some soldiers I'd seen in films, blade horizontal and off-hand held at the ready. Lach just laughed and stepped into her range.

"No," he said in amusement. She lunged. Lach leaned to the right and lifted his arm so her blade passed right by him. "You don't." He brought his fist down against her skull with a crack. She went limp, and the knife clattered from her hand. Lach halted her fall, stuck his foot out, and the knife sank blade first into the heel of his boot. With remarkable balance he lowered the chef to the floor while reaching back for his outstretched foot to remove the knife. It came away clean, having failed to penetrate his thick soles.

"Right, where do you want her and how much blood do you need? She'll only be dazed for five." He dragged the chef by the scruff of her apron toward me. Rather than carve the sigil with a cleaver, I decided to just pour out some flour while my brother took care of the noise.

"Just there is fine. I don't need much blood, a nice cut along the back of her arm should be sufficient."

"Has anyone ever told you that you talk like a psychopath?" He scanned his nails for dirt.

"Shut the hell up and make that woman bleed already, unless you want to offer your own. Cambrion blood's a bit volatile for such a small job though. I might accidentally send us straight through the underworld to some far-off exotic plane of existence."

"Yeesh, calm your tits. Alright, say when." He held out the chef's arm over the edge of my circle and pressed the tip of her knife against the side of her arm.

"Hang on, just need to finish up with this." I finished pouring the flour in a ring around Mother and redirected the sack to make a small pile either side of her head. With my finger, I spread these piles in a simple pattern outwards till they join with the circle's edge, then channeled my magick into it, weaving the pattern of my will into the established boundary.

"Alright, go," I said. He cut the woman's arm in a confidant slash, right down to the elbow, and held her arm up as her blood dripped down onto the flour below. On the fifth thick drop the circle started to blacken and smoke, and the thick smell of miasma filled the air.

"And we are live, please make sure not to touch the circuit without properly grounding yourself or you will be shocked and might even die," Lach chattered aloud to himself, dropping the woman's hand and pushing her away with his foot. "Sorry it had to be this way, hope you don't get an infection. We ready?"

The circle erupted in a gout of hellfire, and Mother vanished.

"That was meant to happen, right?"

"Of course. Now come on you big baby and step in." I took another draw of my cigarette, picked up Father's sword, and stepped into the opened portal.

3

𝕰mpty 𝕳ouse 𝕰legy

Lach

We dropped through the hole into the receiving room of our family residence, in the inner circle of *Violenti*. It was no surprise when the old man decided to move here, the Victorian trappings let him feel like a dandy and the flaming metal heads had an underground fighting ring just down the right. Meanwhile, it sat far enough from Grandpa to please his paranoia without needing to trek all the way across the underworld whenever work called. I'd have preferred Bolgia IX myself, more surprises there.

"Alright, so do we just stick her in the bedroom and call a doctor or what?" I stretched my arms behind my head till they cracked and glanced at Mom's prone body. Actually, so long as the parents were out of commission, was there anything I wanted to do they'd normally stop me from doing?

"Just move her to the couch for now. I want Grandfather to have a look at her first, but I'm not sure how we can get her to Pandemonium without raising a raucous."

"Don't you mean a ruckus? And who would care? Just another unconscious."

"No I mean shut up. As for why, in case you haven't noticed the only daughter of the underworld's keeper is kind of a big deal." Cicula leaned Dad's sword against the wall and took a drag of her smoke.

Sometimes I got the feeling she only took up the habit so she could pose about looking all mysterious and gloomy with her cigarette holder in hand like some reverse grip conductor's baton. Or maybe she just think's Mom's made drinking too mainstream in this household. I don't pretend to get her.

"We should just dump her in a wheelbarrow and stick a tarp over it." I grabbed the apple from my pocket to snack and glanced at the paintings on the wall. They were mostly solemn looking people or vaguely religious. One of them's supposed to be Granma, but I've no idea why the dude who painted it thought a Middle Eastern wind demon would look like a red-headed white chick. Maybe she felt like losing her tan that year. I guess the snake's meant to be Gramps before he took over down here or something. Actually if that is the case it means it's a picture of my grandparents naked and wrapped around each other, which is kinda not cool.

"Are you even listening to me?"

"Huh? Sorry, I wasn't listening," I forced myself to look away from the old-people-intimacy and turned back to my sister.

"Forget it, just take my word for it that trying to smuggle her across the Bolgia is not a good idea."

"Well, I'm out of ideas." I shrugged and dropped myself onto the ground by the couch. "Can't you just summon him? You're the big-shot god-speaker."

"Don't you know anything? It's almost impossible for him to even leave Pandemonium."

"So? You're good. You could do it."

"Shut up."

"Are you two squabbling again?" A familiar velveteen voice echoed through the room. The space distorted around us and a cold chill filled the air. I grinned.

"Speak— "

"Don't say it," Cicula growled at me.

"—of the Devil,"

"And in he walks," Grandpa finished, stepping through the doorway as our surroundings solidified into his frosty castle.

"Do you two have to do that *every* time?" Cicula rolled her eyes and took a hissing draw of smoke.

"My dear, no. Never. That's a saying for a reason, you know. After being chief resident here so long I may as well be its genius loci. Letting people make their own way to me, well that's just politeness." He wore one of those cherry pink suits of his, and his hair had been slicked back save a single curl down his forehead. Who was it that did that again? Ubermensch? No, Elvis.

"That's, well, kinda not cool." I shrugged. "And what about all those stories you hear about people escaping? You could have just whisked them back to your feet at any time?"

"I'm not a heartless tyrant." He spread a hand like that proved anything, "*Quid pro quo* can take many forms, *exempli gratia* a good breakout provides an opportunity for my staff to demonstrate competence or lack thereof, identify any holes in security, provide entertainment for the citizens and raise morale of the other debtors. Enough about me and this realm's twisted spaces though." He turned to Mom on the couch and creased his brow. "Which *persona non grata* did this to my daughter?" He walked over and touched her back, his hand just below the needle.

"Some woman. She had weird white eyes and mentioned a price on Dad's head. I think she was a bounty hunter or something."

"What's this about your father?"

"She took him. At least I think she took him. There was a bright light and they were both gone. Mom was left like that."

"Also, Mother called her quite a few strange phrases which I gather where not quite flattery, though the language was odd."

"Such as?"

"*Peace-dove* and *bleach-feather* stood out. I don't remember what else." Cicula popped her holder out of her mouth and studied the finished cigarette, unsure what to do with it. An ash tray slid out the wall with a click. She looked to Grandpa, gave a slight shrug of her eyebrows and disposed of her dog-end.

"So what's with the needle? Who was that chick?" I tapped the floor with my foot where I sat, and looked to the ceiling. Five lanterns hung from the room's corners. A good omen. I smiled.

"It's an anti-demon seal. The technique was designed for the possessed, but it's been modified to disable one in the flesh. It is a human method, a curious choice for our culprit." Gramps stood up and straightened his tie, his mouth curved in a slight frown.

"Why?"

"Your mother of all people can tell an angel in proximity. This makes things problematic."

"An angel? From the overworld? If it was an assassination attempt on Mother would make sense, but why would she want Father? Surely there are worse sinners presenting a more urgent case."

"I'm afraid there is another element you aren't seeing. As you said before, your mother is 'kind of a big deal'. Speaking strictly factually, the last time an angel struck against her it triggered a series of events resulting in all-out war against the angelic host the likes of which had not been seen since my rebellion. It was all terribly messy. If word gets out about this, it could cause quite a scandal."

"Can't I at least ask Bifrons? I can trust him," Sis said. Bifrons was this skull-headed demon she'd struck an affinity with a while back.

"Not even your most trusted oath brothers," Gramps chided.

"Okay, so *ixnay* on the *gelanay*," I said. "Is Mom going to be alright though?"

"The seal is radiance based but subtle. While the ambient miasma here and in her body will slowly neutralize it, rushing things could trigger a volatile reaction."

"So can you just dispel it? You're the big strong guy. You could just break the thing."

"Our culprit is a cunning one. There's no telling how complex this seal is until you're already cutting into it. If you underestimate it, you might set off lethal countermeasures. If you overestimate it, you might try to treat venom that isn't there, and poison her with your own remedy. If I devoted all my best resources to removing the seal, there would still be a point one percent chance of harming my daughter in the process. Alternatively, if we just leave it the magick should dissipate on its own. That might take a week or it might take a year, but no significant length of time."

"So that's it? You'll just hide sleeping beauty away somewhere so no one finds out the state she's in until the thing wears off?" There was an odd tine of anger in Cicula's voice that seemed to take Grandpa by surprise, or at least he acted like it did.

"Why yes. She'll be well taken care of. In fact, without those inhibitive substances she's so fond of imbibing her body will be better equipped to wear away at the foreign magick."

"Wait a minute."

"What?"

"Are you saying that when Mom wakes up, she'll be sober?"

"Yes."

"Y'know, I don't think I've ever seen her sober." I turned to Cicula. "Have you?"

She shook her head.

"Oh come now, children. A bit of blood-toxin doesn't fundamentally change a person. She's just a bit more overwhelming without that liquid courage clouding her mind."

"Man, I don't care it just feels weird to think about. It's like seeing her naked. Not the demon way, or the normal way for that matter, some third totally bizarre naked most people aren't even capable of."

"I think you'll find most people have at least one more facet of vulnerability they cover up for shame."

"Oh yeah, what's yours?"

"Perhaps a better question for you to ask is what is yours?"

"Enough of the pseudo-psychology," Cicula butted in. "So we lock Mother up in the highest room of the tallest tower until she wakes up entertaining the grand progenitor of all hangovers. What about Father?"

"That our mysterious hunter took him rather than trying to slay him right there suggests he's alive, for now. Finding out where will be difficult. Most forms of seerage have probably been obfuscated. I'll get some people I can trust to look into it, but don't expect any results. For now the question shifts to whom and why. What do you think?"

Cicula frowned, stuck another smoke in her holder and lit it. "Father really shouldn't have come under the classification of a menace that needs to be removed, all things considered. He's morally questionable for sure, but he's not tried to conquer the world or anything. If someone was willing to make a deal to have him removed from the picture, it was probably for personal reasons."

"Excellent deduction, child. So what is the next step?"

She took a puff of her smoke and blew it to the ceiling. "Find out who the half-mad bastard pissed off this time, I suppose. It could be work related, or something he did in his spare time. Of course there's no telling how long ago it happened. For all we know the one paying for this has spent the last twenty years gathering up whatever it is an angel can be bought with to get revenge for something Father did as a teenager."

"That an angel can be bought at all is a curiosity in itself. Short of a supremely holy artifact or the soul of a saint it is difficult to imagine what else could sway them. Unless it is a fallen angel after all."

"I suppose." Sis lit up another smoke. "All we can do is work backwards until we find something. Even if it happened a while ago, it's possible some clue can be found amongst those he's had dealings with recently. Someone else asking about him or some such."

"Do you know where he has been recently, however?"

"He's mentioned bits and pieces here and there, when he's actually around. I don't think he's quite kept receipts for everything though." She looked down from the ceiling to Grandpa. "If we could ask his retainers that would save us some hassle."

"Alas, I am afraid Ko and Vengai-Ra are busy on another errand for me right now, and pulling them away from that task would jeopardize something in which I have some measure of investment in."

"So as long as your daughter's going to be fine, you don't care what happens to Father, is that what I'm hearing?"

"Child, being a ruler is not so simple that I can drop everything on short notice. I do what I can for all my people, not just those I have close ties with. "

"That's your story and you're sticking with it, I suppose."

"Once those two have finished what currently occupies them I'll be sure to send them your way, naturally."

"Naturally," she parroted.

"So let me see if I have everything straight," I chimed in, rising to my feet. "Dad's been abducted by what Mom identified as an angel, though this one isn't acting angel-like. Mom is out of commission for an uncertain amount of time. Dad's sword is out of commission so long as he's gone. The two people Dad works with most can't be reached for an uncertain amount of time."

I sighed with frustration and with hands on hips continued, "The only lead we have is going everywhere we remember Dad talking about of late, and seeing who he pissed off at the time. From there, figure out if they could have paid off a not-very-angelic angel to do this thing for them. You can't just launch a full scale investigation, since if word gets out they'll take this as an act of war, even though Mom's gonna be fine and most of them don't give a rat's ass about Dad."

I stuck an accusatory finger toward Grandpa and said, "You can't do it yourself for obvious chains-of-god reasons, which you can't blame anyone for forgetting about since you strut around like you own the world. So, the two of us are going to go on a wild goose chase while Dad goes through who knows what. Have I got that right?"

"More or less. Do you have a point, Brother?"

I pinched my brow. I could almost see it, almost project these fractal curves past what's observable and grasp the full chaos at hand. There was something amazing in these ripples, but I still couldn't hold where the rain came from. I opened my eyes and laughed.

"Alright, I'll take this dance."

"Hang on, there's one thing you overlooked. Grandfather can't leave Pandemonium, but what about Grandmother?" She turned back to Grandpa, who shrugged.

"She is a capricious being, and prone to being quite contrary. I'll talk to her. She has a right to know what's happened to her daughter and son-in-law, but there's no telling what she might do either way. She may help you; she may hunt the culprit herself; she may cry havoc, or she may even obstruct your efforts just for the novelty of it."

"Well, that's that. The screech owl is the wildcard on the table." Ten bucks said she never even hears about this.

"I suppose we'd better head home and start making preparations. Have you any advice?" Sis asked. "Perhaps a final punch line to the absurdity of it all."

"Try not to offend someone without good reason, and always keep more firepower in reserve. Good luck."

The room distorted again. The scenery rippled outward and changed back to our house in *Violenti*. After a few moments, it solidified, and we were standing right back where we started. Mom, however, was left behind with Grandpa.

"Well I suppose that's that. Come on. We should gather what we want to take and try to think of anything useful. I'll meet you in the library in two hours."

"Whatever you say, Sis." I unfocused and let my gut drive for the meanwhile. Time for the next part of my chaos apple seed pilgrimage.

4

Herbology Half-Step

Cicula

I made quick retreat to my room down the long, vacant halls, and shut the door behind me. With the sound of its lock's click I took a deep breath, and another. Familiar paintings and statuettes had transformed into the decorations of a stranger. My cigarette holder weighed heavier than it should and all my muscles ached. This was ludicrous, everything about this was ludicrous. Who were we to be charged with this ridiculous task? Just a pair of spoilt rich kids is who. I shoved a chair out of my way and sat on the edge of my bed. For several minutes I remained still but failed to resume any semblance of harmony. I resigned to ugly pitifulness and drew my legs up to my chest.

"Ia— " No, I ground my teeth to cage my tongue. I would not beg for Ianus, not even now and not ever. That cruel little imp of a mentor could stay a memory. I took another breath and let my limbs relax. I needed to gather my things, as Lach should be doing right now. Dear Brother, had I not already browbeat you into going along with this my courage might fail me. Pride is a funny thing, telling you *I changed my mind* was somehow scarier.

And yet, every time I unbundled my nerves they seized up again. Someone better should be doing this, there had to be someone better. No, stop it already. If I couldn't stop myself from not starting I'd just force my idiot self into compliance.

I got off my bed and opened one of the drawers. Paper, chalk, ink, and a few other supplies stared up at me. I took them and arranged them in a neat pile beside me. Once I'd emptied the drawer I slid my hand across the bottom and located the hidden panel. It came off with a bit of leverage from my fingernail, revealing my other supplies. Did father know I had these? Did he even care?

I needed to dam these thoughts before I drowned. What I took from my trove was a single cigarette, but it was not just tobacco I'd rolled inside it. I had to stand up again to get the other item back from my desk. I loaded the stick of plant matter into my holder and lit up. The distinctly different smell hit me as strong as ever as I breathed in. In a cross-legged position on the floor, I sat and smoked, letting the ash fall where it willed onto the varnished wood floor. An ash tray sat on my desk, a brass mechanical one that matched my lighter, but I'd sooner run a triathlon than get up to bring it over right now.

The murky white fog didn't eke into the corners of my brain until the last draw. My troublesome self sat isolated, reduced to something more manageable. I scooped myself out and set me aside to squirm out of mind. Just to make sure, I took another cigarette of mixed substances from my trove and lit it as well, to smoke while I gathered my things.

A bit of mind altering chemstuff made it easier to see the wisps. Wisps were to gods what plankton was to mammals, not complex thoughtform but rudimentary psycho-emotional reactions that just barely qualified as the same kind of life. They were pretty rare in the underworld since most demons treated them as ambient snack food, but over the years our house had picked up a decent population of the ephemeral things. They had more than enough volatile emotions to subsist on. They drifted like invisible floating bunnies of hope and torment.

First, I changed into some different clothes—some undergarments more appropriate for unexpected athleticism, a good pair of slacks, a blouse with breezy sleeves, and some practical lace-up boots. I slipped onto one finger a metal false nail of dull sheen. It was a useful tool that aided summoning. Once that was done, I set about stocking my little sub-space pocket. Of the scarce things Mother taught me, it was this simple, practical bit of magick for which I was most grateful. Into the micro-dimension went my drawing supplies, some practical knives, a spice rack's worth of ritual supplies, and finally my trove. At first I only placed a few cigarettes, but after a moment's thought I dumped the whole lot in it. Better safe than useless.

Now set, I locked my room behind me and headed to the library to wait for my idiot brother. The anticipated wait went undelivered, since he already awaited me. Clad in his usual slacks and sleeveless top, he rustled his ponytail in idleness. He looked out of place surrounded by all this literature. No, that was too generous for Father's collection. There were plenty of combat manuals, smut, low brow comedy and lower brow romance on these shelves. Where was I?

"Did you even gather anything?" I ran a hand through my hair.

"I gathered my thoughts, my wits, and some extra poise. Also some tiny dice I've never seen before, but they turned out to be candy. Want one?" Lach held up a small bag.

"Oh forget it. Have you at least put some thought into how we're going to backtrack Father's footsteps?"

"So here's my thinking. He's got all that ugly clutter of souvenirs, right? Little knobby totems and fancy coasters and all sorts of useless crap. I remember him saying he wants to make a proper trophy room for his junk, actually start cataloguing them so he doesn't forget what dumb story he can tell about them. For all I know he just made some bullshit up, but if we can find that catalogue Bob's our uncle. That's assuming he's anal enough to get a souvenir from every backwater shanty hut he's ever shook down but hey, it's better than bupkiss. Maybe whatever culprit that did the thing crossed paths with him more than once, who knows."

"Junk catalogue, you say? Well, though I am genuinely grateful for an actually good idea from you that I agree with, I'm still going to insult you by saying I'm surprised."

"Er, are you feeling okay?" he cocked an eyebrow. I shook my head and cleared some of the bogging mist.

"Sorry, I was meant to think that and say something along those lines. I must have missed a step." Lach leaned toward me and sniffed my face. I shoved him back with a start.

"Whatever and ever after, just make sure there's a good time in it for me. Lead away, Sis." Lach stood at attention.

"Pardon?"

"His crap is in his study, yeah?"

"Ah, right," I closed my eyes and took a deep breath. "Alright, come on."

***

Father's study stood upstairs, behind a heavy oak door. He never locked it, and the heavy looking knocker was never actually knockable. The twisted ring was just a decorative carving. Another whim he no doubt found hilarious at the time. I'd been in the room on less than a dozen occasions despite how much time father spent in there, when he's even home at all.

"Well, pardon the intrusion," I muttered as I entered, and Lach followed in behind me. Opposite the entryway a large wooden desk faced the door—its surface covered in an eclectic accruement of clutter. Besides an inkwell the skeleton of a bird had been placed upon a stand. The ribcage had been replaced by the skull of a small monkey, and upon the birds own tiny skull had been strapped a tiny party hat made of glittered leather. Books, papers, and scrolls laid heaped everywhere, on the desk, on the floor, on the bookshelves and stands and a few had even been nailed to the wall. One pile had been arranged into a simile of a castle, and besides the desk sat a cushioned box designed for transporting antique swords. The ceiling, carpet and a number of scattered objects bore scorch marks.

While I took this all in Lach stepped past me over to the desk. His eyes span chaotically around the menagerie of crap as though tethered by a string to an escaping butterfly, and he picked up the first ledger his eyes settled on.

"Yo, found it."

"Already? Ludicrous." I crossed my arms and scoffed snootily. Of course he did, he had the most infuriating knack for guessing and intuition that I found incredibly vexing.

"It had to be somewhere, right? Lemme check, yup, the first two dozen entries or so are just in any old order but everything after that seems to be chronological." He flipped to the last page not blank. "Let's see, most recent addition was *lightning taken from the mouth of the Ganges.* Huh. Does that make sense to you?"

"Lightning? You mean like a battery or something?"

"Dunno. There's no picture or anything. No story or anything to go with it either. Seems more a reminder than anything else, y'know? *Oh yeah, that thing.*"

He handed the ledger to me and turned his attention to the ornaments heaped on the bookshelves. I skimmed over the entry and found it just as Lach described, albeit the handwriting more illegible than suggested.

"Maybe it's a gun or a firecracker," he said aloud. "I don't see any though. A bullet? Maybe some sort of energy drink. Any chance this is it?" He held up a puzzle cube, each color represented by square plates of iron, bronze, gold, silver, platinum and lead. "Nah, of course not. Huh, a rat skewered to a music box, how about that. Oh look, it even has little ballet shoes. What is this? Motorbike keys? Could the bike be lightning? Did Dad mug some bikey? Nevermind that, what's this?" He held up an intricate bronze rod. The ends each had a ring going through them joining halfway to the ends of the bulging middle. I recognized the design.

"Of course, if it's from the Ganges, what else but a vajra?" I exclaimed

"What's a vadge-liar, and why are they expected from grain juice?" Lach stared incredulously.

"No, a vajra. It's a symbolic thing for a lightning bolt in Hindu religions."

"Who do religions?"

"No, not Voodoo, Hindu. You know, from India." I gesticulated at him with growing intensity the more I explained. "It's a symbol associated with Indra."

"Since when was India associated with lightning?"

"Not India, Indra, Indian thunder god."

"The engines have gods of lightning? I didn't think robots had religion."

"Not engines, Indians. Look." I spun around and pointed to a globe of the Earth. "The Ganges is a river in India."

"So it's an Indran bolt from Rivrindja?"

"No, the *Rig Vaeda*. A few other holy texts too."

"Rig Vader, that guy from the holistics bureau?"

"Now you're being obtuse on purpose."

"And the porpoise?"

"Shut up." I threw my hands up and surrendered. "The point is this stick doohickey came from India."

"So you're going to call up Indra and ask him?"

I paced back and forth through the cluttered office as I thought it over, every little knick-knack smearing me with dust as a passed. "This is probably just some decorative replica. You can't expect a god to keep track of every little bit of religious iconography made regarding them."

"Why not?" Lach shrugged. "Isn't that how they work."

"No."

"No?"

"No."

"If you say so." He clasped his hands behind his head. "As for this thing, what, you know where it came from? Specifically I mean."

"I have a more than vague idea but less than specific."

"Well, that's a start."

"It's more than a start, it's a plan. Are you sure there isn't anything else you want to bring? I'd rather not be jumping back and forth because your pockets aren't deep enough."

"Nah, I'm good."

"Don't blame me if you're wrong. Come on." I ushered with my hand. "Let's go back to the library. I have a bad vibe from here and don't fancy opening a door around so many strange things. We might end up slingshotted to sunken R'lyeh or something."

"Lead the way."

5

The Garden Gospel

Draco

A hand burst from my rib cage and pulled me against the bars. The ghastly stench of rotting human flesh pervaded my senses. Can't hide at ground zero. Parameter definition slipped away through the isolation. The smell forced its way down my mouth and reflex forced me to gulp for air. My stomach swelled and bloated to untold emptiness. Not even a bone to gnaw on. Not until time again. Not true. There were plenty of bones here. I grasped one of my ribs and broke it off with a crunch that made my mouth water. I slurped the marrow out and cut my cracked lips on the jagged end. There grew a furnace in my belly and it needed fuel. My left arm would feed the furnace for a time. Time until time. I grasped another of my ribs. I tried to break it off. The rib did not. Metal permeated the marrow and held fast. I grasped. I grasped the break. Had to break. Had to break the grasp. Something wet and warm wet my lips. Reconnected. Re-establishing. One became two in juxtaposition, closed loop of definition. That "—was unpleasant." I lurched into a sitting position and heaved. Yellow bile stung at my gums.

"Are you okay now, Master?"

"Yes, thank you Drakkengard." I wiped my mouth and Drakkengard helped me up. She was back in her robes. What was I in? The same things I was in at the restaurant. An unpleasant, sterile smell clung to them, though. Like I'd been held by someone drenched in bleach.

"Where are we?"

"Cut off or something, Master."

The ground crunched underfoot. We'd woken up at the foot of some uneven stone path and wherever we were seemed deep in autumn. Wilted flowers drooped among the dead grass, and bright red leaves adorned the black barked trees that dotted the landscape. The stone paths were fenced in by weed ravaged hedges and irregular stone walls dislodged in slow motion by the untended vines that penetrated the cracks. Somewhere nearby running water babbled and the clouds overhead were lit up by an unseen setting sun.

"I really don't like this place," I muttered.

"That's not true, Master," Drakkengard grinned knowingly.

The wind picked up, and something flapping loomed. From over a hill flew a figure, the tan woman who accosted Lascivus. She flew on two great white wings, each longer than she was tall, and as soon as she spotted us she made her descent. Her jeans and halter top were unnaturally casual for such an occasion as whatever this was.

"There you are. Your topography is hard to navigate." She folded her wings behind her back and approached.

"Is my wife truly unharmed or was that just to make me hesitate?" I glowered, recalling the last thing she'd said before abducting me.

She faltered at the accusation. "Not the first thing I expected from your mouth. You can relax, I am not a liar."

"And my children?"

"I didn't touch them at all. My target began and ended with you."

"Then if you'll be so kind and to show me the way out, I'll be gone." I chuffed and brushed myself off.

"Nice try, but no. You're here on—wait, what in the name of the Lord is *she* doing here?" My captor slung a finger toward Drakkengard and gritted her teeth.

"She's with me. It's fine." I waved dismissively.

"No, it's not fine. How did she get here?"

"You brought me here, didn't you?" I cocked my brow.

"Yes but that golem was left behind."

"Well that hardly matters." I rolled my eyes and scoffed. "I'm here now, as is she."

"She shouldn't have been able to get here." The bafflement on her face was exquisite, I could almost forget that I'd been kidnapped yet a-fucking-gain.

"Maybe not, but I did. Life's funny like that." Drakkengard shrugged, a tinge of venom in her voice.

"Or are you just an imagined construct? That's not unheard of." She furrowed her brow and looked down.

"So what is this place?" Drakkengard asked, "some sort of mirror?" The woman started at her words, but quickly composed herself.

"So you recognize it."

"I have an idea," I replied, "but I don't like what I'm thinking." This place felt more familiar than anywhere I'd ever lived in my life, until I remembered the one place I'd lived more than anywhere else in my life was fuck-deep inside my own delirious mind.

"Most people don't." She came closer, her arms tensed and wary. Probably in case I tried something.

"I suppose you find my intrusion here rather perverse, but rest assured this just looks like any old garden to me. The nuanced symbols are encoded by your associations and perspective." She slouched back on her heels. "An obvious metaphor to you is just a few trees and some rocks to me. You're not as naked as you think."

"Well, that's a relief." My captor stepped around me in a broad circle but I kept talking straight ahead. "So this is my mind. Is this some sort of psychic attack? Is my defenseless body being puppeteered around somewhere?" My left hand cramped.

"Nothing so literal. Your golem was closer when she called it a reflection. This place constructs itself around the mind of those inside it. Of course, I know how to hide myself from it, but it *is* strange that your golem isn't causing interference." She looked Drakkengard up and down and shrugged. "Well, maybe not. And before you get any ideas about forcing your way out, know that as above so below. If you damage *this* environment, then *that* will result in a psychic attack and your own mind will be forcibly rearranged according to the metaphorical state of things here."

With a groan I slumped against a tree. Fantastic, trapped in the place most severely affected by my being trapped. One misstep could trigger a chain reaction of emotional landmines and turn my mind so severely inside-out that it kills me. I trust this twit with my trauma as far as I can throw her.

"You are an angel, I presume," I vaguely waved in her direction.

"Quite so."

"I've heard enough drunken tirades to recognize the racial slurs. I notice you're not too bashful about your wings compared to demons."

"Those corrupted by the filth of the pit are ashamed of their grotesque form, and envious of our beauty. To be reminded of their ugliness is humiliation."

"That the official pamphlet you're quoting? I get the feeling that's not quite it. I doubt that's what you actually look like either."

"In my case I've a different reason for not showing my face."

"Aha, so upstairs wouldn't approve of what you're doing here." A clue as good as any, so worth latching onto it. "Who are you?"

"You've missed the mark. As for a name, I am known as Ancilla."

"Hmm, no suffix invoking YHVH" Most angelic names had an El or a Jah in there somewhere.

"You're pronouncing it wrong," she dodged my point.

"And what am I? A hostage?"

"No, sinner, you are accused."

"So this is a trial?"

"Quite so."

"Are my sins really so great?" I narrowed my eyes and raised my eyebrows in perplexion.

"That's what I'm here to find out."

"Whatever happened to redemption possible for all?" I chided.

"Well if you convince me of you having truly repented, you can go. The matter is not the sins that you have committed, but the sins which you might still commit."

"I stand accused of crimes I've not yet committed?" I balked.

"You stand accused of being ready and willing to commit to commit terrible sins for the rest of your days. I was forewarned of your existence and your nature, and due sacrifice was made to show the seriousness of their concerns."

"Oh? Whose?" Another clue. This was almost fun.

"That is not for you to know." She furrowed and glared.

"Oh, you say that now." I waggled my finger. "What if I'm found innocent?" In the back of my mind I struggled to recall every scrap of legal bullshit I'd picked up from being employed by the former Judge of God and longstanding Prince of Lawyers.

"Revenge is not something I condone. Justice is about preventing further sin and making an example to dissuade other sinners that they might turn away from their path."

"That really only works when such a system is formal and recognized. Aren't you just acting as you see fit? What authority are you wielding here?" I moved to scuff my boot against the grass, thought better of it and just pointed at her with my foot.

"My authority as an angel of the Lord."

"And I've heard quite a bit about that *authority*."

"You believe the Serpent's lies?"

"I've certainly not found any conflicting evidence. I think we're getting off track here, though. So you're going to rummage through my mind to try to figure out how likely it is I'm going to cause nothing but suffering with my life, and if so, kill me, is that it?"

"Quite so."

"And if you can't kill me?"

"Oh I've been warned of your tenacious grip on life. There's more than one way to kill a sinner." To her credit as ostensibly a force of Good, Ancilla didn't seem to relish the idea. "I can leave you in a coma and seal you away forever. I can purify you with such divine radiance that you are incapable of failing to uphold order. A few other options, too. I prefer, though, to obliterate your memories and personality, leaving you a blank slate that might learn to appreciate goodness of action. That too is a kind of death."

"Alright, you've my attention now." I tsked and flashed a wry smile. "Say if I kill you, making sure not to harm this place obviously, then what?"

"Then you're trapped here for only I know the secret of how to come and go from this place. Not even the Morningstar knows how to reach its current location."

"Oh? So he knew how to find its previous location?" I paced, trying to process what was on the table.

"No secret was made of it at the time."

"You know, you're being awfully forthcoming with this information. I *am* grateful, assuming it's not all lies."

"I do not tell lies, and I find accused are more cooperative when they understand the position they're in."

"You can pluck a snake but it's still bird of a feather," I mused.

"Pardon?"

"Just a bit of de ja vu. So how does this work? Is there some monument to my morality here for you to pore over?"

"Nothing so straightforward, sadly. Do you see the trees?"

"A bit hard to miss them," I said. Drakkengard had already wandered over to one while we were talking to cautiously peer into its foliage.

"These fruit grow trees. It's one of the few constants between reflections. To bite the fruit is to relive the memory it represents."

"So you get your lunch on until you've seen enough to know me?"

"I'm afraid not. How you thought and felt, how you saw yourself at the time, those are also a part of your memories. Were I to eat them it would risk far too much ego contamination. It would leave me biased in your favor."

"So, what?"

"You eat the fruit. By gazing into the running waters I can see what flows through your mind. I will see your actions, and perhaps ask a few questions afterwards to gauge your answers."

"A literal stream of my consciousness, now that is unsightly."

"Now do I have your cooperation, or must I force feed you myself? I'm fine with either way." Ancilla tapped her foot.

"You have my cooperation, but under coercion during incarceration."

"Good. Here's your first trip." She reached into her back pocket and threw me a fruit. It looked like some sort of pomegranate.

"These things can't go rotten can they? Would hate to spoil our picnic with dysentery."

"Not to my knowledge."

"Delightful." I bit into the fruit.

6

Kolkata Chorale

Lach

We stepped out from sis's travel circle into some rain sodden alley. The bags of garbage rustled with shivering rats, interrupted by the faint commercial sounds from the street at the alley's end. Soggy urban decay flooded my nose and made my eyes water. Discordia walked these streets, though I doubted I'd see her.

"You couldn't have checked the weather before booking this trip?" I complained.

"What, you don't like the rain?"

I held my hand out and watched the water trickle down my finger lines to the fabric of my gloves.

"Feels like an insult I can't meet, like a challenge." I clenched my fist and the water escaped through the loose seal of my hand. Sis just rolled her eyes and headed to the street. My boots squelched the ground behind her. I just wanted to punch the rain and eat the clouds 'til there were none left.

"So what's the plan, Sis? Wave the doohickey at folks 'til they spill the beans?"

"No, just ask."

"Ask?"

"Ask who to ask," she explained further.

"And who is that?"

"I don't know yet, that's why I'm asking."

"Yeah but asking who, you riddle-eyed midget?" I threw my hand up.

"If I explained it in full would you even pay attention?"

"Not a chance. Dumb it down for a normal idiot brain."

"Tiny little lingering godlings." She swept her hand at things I couldn't see. Could the things not be seen by untrained eyes? Did she at some point do something weird to her eyes? Could the things not be seen because they were just metaphorical and only existed as concepts? Was she just waving her hand at the alley's end because she thought it made her look mystic? Sue for fraud, I oughta.

"Right, weird summoner shit." I clasped my hands. "What do they tell you?"

"They tell of a man who made steam of the rain and walked with devils. They tell of theft and barter and resentment. They tell of one nearby connected to these things by a faint string."

"Poetic lot, aren't they? What does that mean in real person terms?" I fiddled with the hem of my glove as she scowled at me.

"It means father was here, or someone matching his description, and at some point he happened to interact with someone not far from here."

"Sounds a bit too convenient. I like it."

"It's a big city. Father probably interacted with lots of people. Think of the statistics."

"Let's not. So this person has the beans we want spilled?"

"Perhaps. At least one bean in their can should prove useful, if we can pick for it." She stepped out onto the street and turned left. I continued to follow, gloved hands further warmed in my pockets.

"I bet you wish you wore better clothing now," she sneered over her shoulder.

"I may be getting wet faster than you now, but I'll dry long before you do. I win in the end."

"And the cold?"

"Cold?"

"Never mind, I guess your thick head provides remarkable insulation."

"You just don't know how to ignore things that don't matter, and aren't even real."

"I'm pretty sure temperature exists, Brother."

"Nah. I mean, what is cold? Ooh, me space dust is vibrating a bit more slowly. Bollocks is what."

"That doesn't explain anything."

"Seems pretty self-evident to me." I shrugged.

"And you're a moron."

A man in green walked past behind Cicula. There weren't too many people on the streets, just enough to remind you that it's not weird at all for you to have something to do since all these others seem to. Lots of people with dangerous amounts of stuff strapped to the back of their bikes. Billboards, cars, chickens, blah blah blah. They provided a bit of local color to the drab concrete streets. Big cities all looked the same. I might never know what Dad saw in them.

After passing down a few blocks of storefronts, lights, and whim grasping vendors, Sis stopped and closes her eyes, no doubt talking to those wisp things again.

"What is it, Lassie? A big red dog destroyed the trouser well?"

"Over there." She pointed to one of the near identical big metal boxes the vendors peddled from. "There's the one Father spoke with."

"Yeah?"

"Yes. I'll handle this. Don't go wandering off."

"If I was gonna I'd have done it already. Bound to be some good dance spots around here somewhere." I glanced about absently.

"Just don't," she says, and left me to idle away. With nothing better to kill time, I watched her. The vendor was a man with dark hair and broad, slanted wicker hat. They talked for a bit, too quiet for my hearing, and the man held up four fingers. Sis took out two bags of dried plants and handed them over. After a bit of scrutiny he seemed quite pleased with them, and started talking quicker.

Once done he handed her a small leather pouch and bowed. Their business done, Sis returned.

"I don't suppose you got some magic growing umbrellas out of that?" I stood up from my lean against a wall and slipped my hands back into my pockets.

"Oh hush, you'll get over a bit of moistness."

"No, I shall hold this petty grudge against rainy days until the instant I die. What is in the bag?"

"Just a bit of local currency."

"So that guy was?"

"A merchant from the Lost Islands of Nippon."

"Really?" I cocked a brow. "I thought that lot were extinct."

"Not at all, just behind a wall of ceaseless storms. Not worth the effort for most to get in or out since any vehicle will just get sunk. Sometimes, though, a survivor washes up on the other side to where they started, as with our friend there."

"Okay so he is a dawn-man. Did he know anything?"

"Yes, he sold a map, sunglasses and some other things he doesn't remember to a man I'm almost certain was Father. A girl matching Drakkengard's description was with him and I can't imagine you'd find many pairs like that. It seems Father asked questions about some recent news at the time, certain deaths and disappearances, as well as a certain temple in Kalkata, hence the map."

"Well let's get a move on, Sis. Less spent rain time the better"

7

$\mathcal{R}$efrain $\mathcal{F}$rom $\mathcal{S}$in

Draco

Deep in my memory, woodlands surrounded a rickety military base on all sides, and the only way in was either the dirt road to the main gate or the helipad off to the side. The skin-ripping cold of the night relented under the heat. A blaze had been born of the base's six jeeps that exploded one after the other, and the rain of superheated shrapnel had set alight the nearby buildings.

Gunfire bellowed behind me as fear and paranoia burst the skulls of panicked soldiers, each with their own ideas on who the saboteurs were. I turned up the collars of my stolen officer's coat as a new wave of scalding heat prickled my neck. The fire had spread to the ammunition stores, in the warehouse two buildings down from the jeeps. The trail of liquid hydrogen leading there helped. My charade of being here on inspection had proven more useful than I'd first imagined. I pressed my gloved left fist into my gauntleted right and cracked my knuckles. More shots rang out, and the rancorous shouts fell quiet.

Just ahead of me the commander of the base, Colonel Veluccio, vomited demands for order and information at the two soldiers with him. He threw his fist up in salute as he saw me approach. Behind him sat the last helicopter and the last pilot.

"Oh, forgive me for such a shameful display during your visit. No, don't forgive me. I am prepared to take full responsibility, Sir. I only ask that I am still made useful to our worthy cause is some way." His smooth Italian fell past my ears as I kept my face straight. The soldier beside him narrowed her eyes and pulled her sidearm on me. Smart, this one.

"Get back!" She barked. I stopped, and raised both arms above my head. I thought back, and recalled her from my *inspection*. Good eyes and a taste for blood sport. She'd be an officer by now if not for disciplinary measures, picking fights you see.

"Vilette, what are you doing?" The Colonel demanded. From fifty meters behind, boots crunched in approach. All other voices had fallen silent.

"Don't you see? He's— "

I brought an arm down and fell into a crouch. At the signal a bullet flew over my head and passed through her chest. The force of impact knocked her to the ground.

"Shit, they've gotten here already. How many do they have?" Veluccio drew his sidearm and fired where the bullet came from, then turned back to the helicopter and scowled. "And how long until we're ready for take-off?" If he'd noticed my signaling he'd chosen to ignore it.

I stood, brushed myself off and approached. Liquid metal ran down my sleeve and my gauntlet reformed into a blade. Breaking into a run I reached the other soldier and cleaved him open. I studied his face as he died. His name was Anthony. He followed orders well but was too insecure to act with initiative. He'd picked up the nickname Ant because of it. He always had one sleeve rolled up.

The CO spun at the thump of Ant's fall. *Now* the truth dawned on him, or at least he could no longer pretend otherwise.

"You're the spy!"

"Your life has been bought, Veluccio, or rather your death," I explained. "You are going to die, you are going to hell, and someone else has already paid the price. I'm just collecting the Devil's dues."

"I'll not see this country fall to those bloody revolutionaries."

"Revolutionaries?" I raised an eyebrow. "As far as I've been informed, this bargain was bartered by your daughter."

"Marie?" He fell to his knees. I placed my blade against his neck.

"Any last words?"

"Do I truly deserve this? I'm not innocent, but are my sins so great my own daughter summons the Satan to take me?" the man wept.

"Do you deserve to die? Did you deserve to receive the orders you did? Did you deserve to be praised for following them? Did you deserve to become a soldier? Did you deserve to grow up how you did? Did you deserve to be born?" I breathed in sharp through my nose. "*Mu*. What matters is what people want, and what they will do to get it. The universe doesn't want this. A person does. Maybe someday you'll get the chance to ask them." I lifted my sword, and touched it to the other side of his neck, then raised it once more and smashed his skull. Brain split open, Veluccio died. I yanked Drakkengard out, pulled a cloth from my pocket and wiped her clean.

From behind me, Ko approached, rifle held at the ready. Having declined any part in my charade, the gunman had snuck in a few hours prior.

"That seems to be the last of them. Everyone is either dead or fled," he declared with quiet tension.

"You did well," I said, and he sneered in disgust. "Sorry, thank you for helping me, I mean. You go on ahead, there's something I want to check out first."

"Yeah? And what about him?" He gestured with the barrel of his gun toward the helicopter. While I was distracted, the pilot had slipped out the far door, and now pointed his gun at us from behind its cover. A great crash shook around us as one of the buildings caved in. I thought back, and placed the pilot's face.

"Conaway, yes? Good pilot and good aim, but busted for gambling on several occasions. I remember you."

"I, I will shoot you!"

"Will you, Conaway? You're a coward, and self-serving. My goal here was your commander, not you. Put the gun down, and you have my word both my accomplice and I will let you go. Pull the trigger, and it will be the last thing you ever do. What will it be? Do your duty as a soldier, or live, and start a new life somewhere else? Loyalty, or death? Is your king worth it? What are you made of, Conaway?"

The bullet shattered my cheek. Shards of bone tore through my right eye and lacerated the rest of my face, inside and out. Not the first time that had happened. My left arm twitched.

My left arm . . .

***

My left arm seized up, bone thrashing against bone and I struggled to restrain it. I'd returned to the garden, snapped out of the memory's evocation by the pain. The limb was bound in roaring flame—the sleeve already incinerated and the clothes around the arm burnt away just as quick. As fast as I could I let go of the arm, retrieved the dagger hidden in my boot, and plunged it into the soft of my left elbow. The sharp, sudden pain splashed over my senses. With that pain I grounded myself and quashed my emotions down. The flames receded. I yanked the dagger out and tossed it aside, gasping as the wound healed years' worth in a few seconds. Not even a scar left. That might be the strangest thing about my body.

"Master!" Drakkengard threw her arms around me and squeezed me from behind. Ancilla watched from beside the river. Her hand brushed her hip.

"It's fine, no worse than usual," I reassured my companion.

"But the usual's worse than the usual used to be," Drakkengard warned.

"I'll live."

"You don't know that for sure."

"Who does?"

Drakkengard pouted, and helped me to my feet.

"Well, kidnapper? What's the verdict?"

"A few questions first, sinner," the angel crossed her arms and walked over, unconcerned with my nocturnal ignition

"Yes?"

"Did you kill that Conaway man?"

"I said I would, didn't I? Burnt him alive."

"And what did you go back to check?"

"Who died, get an idea of who got away, and pick out a souvenir if anything took my fancy."

"Did one?"

"I settled on an engraved service revolver I found in Veluccio's quarters. Nothing important."

"Hmph. We'll take a break. I'll be back later with the next memory."

8

The Pagan Pianissimo

Cicula

It took a short walk to reach the underground metro. I bought two tickets with the money from the peddler, and the train arrived with only little delay. Lach took his ticket with a nod and we boarded. The carriage had been almost empty, and Lach walked to the far end to gaze out the window and devour an apple. I left him to it, and took a seat near the door. There were only about ten people in the carriage all-up, and most were ignoring all. Besides me stood a girl in a white hoody and a lock of white hair hanging down her thin porcelain countenance. She smiled as I sat down, painted lips parting to show starry white teeth..

"Allo, friend. You too are a stranger to this land?" Her accent was French, and makeup covered her entire face. The movements when she talked were slight, her expressions variations of the same painted mask.

"Ah, yeah. I'm just, well, looking for someone," I stumbled, my gaze flickering to and from her eyes, "I got a few things to ask them."

"Ah," she clasped her hands, "I am also looking for someone, and perhaps there are few whom could be said are not." She moved closer, to sit next to me proper.

"The dead, I guess?" I kept my hands from fidgeting. Come on, girl, personal space.

"No, no, no, they are also seeking— revenge or solace or just someone to put their spirit at ease. Pardon, but I notice that cannabin fragrance about you. Might I trouble you for a bit of plant?"

"A bit of—? Oh, right. Yeah." I jammed my hand in my pocket, and with a bit of hasty searching took out a rolled up dose. Could she smell it on me? Did I need a bath?

"*Merci.*" She took it from my hand with delicate, bony fingers. On one digit sat a silver ring, carved with the words *DEO TOTA*. The god Tot? Thoth? Touta? She put the smoke between her lips and I lit it up for her, the ring already forgotten. After taking a draw and holding it, she let out a dignified sigh and handed it back so I could take a draw of my own.

"Have you travelled far, if you don't mind my asking?" She purred.

"Not really." I finished my puff and handed the stick back to her. "Though I'll be at it a while longer. Unless I get lucky," I smirked. The reliable cloud alleviated my anxiety and put a bold swagger to my tongue.

"Luck is nice, but a poor substitute for diligence."

"Yah, absolutely, it's important though." I handed it back to her.

"Why is it important?"

"Because I can't just abandon him."

"Why not?" She passed it back, hands steadier than mine amidst the jolting train.

"Because that's not what family does."

"Oh?" she perked up even more.

"I admit it, he hasn't done much, but he never turned his back on me. Not like *him.*" I blew out a lungful of smoke and clenched my fists where she couldn't see.

"So you want to prove you're better than someone else?"

"That's not it. I'm just acting how I think I ought to act. If I think something is the right thing to do of course I'm going to do it," I handed it back to her.

"What if you're wrong?"

"I don't know that. I can never know that. I can know I was wrong, but never that I am wrong. That's impossible." I laughed. "If I knew I was wrong I'd choose to be right."

"Even if you deceive yourself?"

"I'm not deceiving myself."

"Is that belief also a part of your deception?" She sucked down the last draw, and put the spent remains out on the tin floor with her foot. A fleeting twinge hit me as I hoped rail guard wouldn't happen upon us.

"Who are you?" I giggled. "Why do you even care?"

"Oh, I'm a meddler. I just can't leave things alone." She gave me this coquettish look that flipped my stomach.

"No really, who are you?"

"My name is Raanae."

She leaned forward, her cheek just next to my own, and reached into my pocket for another joint. On reflex I lit it for her.

"Why do you even care?"

"It would be dreadful to see someone like you be wasted on the wrong causes." She took a draw, and placed a bony hand on my cheek. My mouth ran dry. She leaned forward and presses her lips against my own. Smoke passed from her mouth to mine with a breath, and I gulped it in.

She parted, smiling, and stood up. The train rolled to a stop. The passage of time and space had escaped me. How many stations had we passed through so far?

"I'm glad we had this chance. *Au revoir*, Cicula." With that she disembarked, and the train doors closed behind her. I checked the illuminated map on the carriage wall. There were still two more stops until mine.

I placed my hand on my wrist and shivered, my mouth wet with her lipstick. Lach remained at the carriage's far end, facing away. The rest of the journey passed in near silence.

9

A Sharp Flirt

Lach

Sis stood up and I took that as the cue to stop spacing out. Sure enough she waved me over as the train pulled to a stop and we departed. Time for the next leg of my apple-seed pilgrimage.

"Where did you say this is again?" I looked from signs I couldn't read to a homeless woman asleep under a rug. I had no coin so left her an apple.

"Kalighat," My sister replied, and led the way back to street level.

"Coli gut? Isn't that a stomach virus?"

"No, it's a temple near here."

"And they have some knowing god on speed dial for us."

"Close enough." We climbed the stairs out the metro and were reunited with the rain, which had not at all weakened in our absence. The nearby highway glared white car-light reflected off wet asphalt and thunder rumbled from somewhere behind all these buildings. My sister pulled out her umbrella and hid from the rain beneath it. I stuffed my hands in my pockets and settled for giving the weather the cold shoulder.

"So we can either try to cross the highway here and take the backstreets, or cross the highway a few blocks up and go down the main road." She touched her finger to her lip and frowned. The highway, while too busy, was very wide, and like any road anywhere, the drivers had an uncanny knack for letting no interval between them go un-cinched. Or is that what they meant by following the flow of traffic? Maybe, in world of cars and no people. I peered past the highway and at the rooftops beyond it. A prominent five domed structure stood above them, though it was possible it had seven domes and I just couldn't see two of them. Well, seven is just five and two, and two is just half five minus five tenths.

"Is that your temple?" I pointed to the domes.

"Hmm, should be."

"Cool. Race you."

"What?"

I bolted for the highway, and slipped through the caution gap between the rear of a trailer and the flat front of a Winnebago. Discordia watched my steps. The next two lanes were clear enough but I wasn't so lucky for the next. The side mirror of a red sportscar snapped off against my hip. The driver yelled something and sped off, while other vehicles sounded their horns in protest. I scooped up the mirror and made a break for other side. A zigzag path left me on the far side. Mirror in hand I ran down the street, and my feet slapped at the puddles accumulated on the ground. I took the second right into the backstreets, turned left, took the second right again. At the end of that wavy street after ignoring three turns I came in range of the multi-domed building. Goal in sight I slowed to walking pace, took a breath, and brushed some of the water off my hair.

Although color was hard to tell in the murky rain, the building might have been cream and terracotta with splashes of canary yellow. Shops and vendors clamored around it at all sides, peddling rice, fresh vegetables, candies, totems and clothing. I made my way round the front. Near the taxi stand a twine of clergy looking local people in white shirts who tried to get people attention for some service or another. Maybe they did palm reading, or chicken sacrifice, or formatting a biannual budget report, or other esoteric tricks. I milled around the front of the temple waiting for my sister to catch up.

One of the vendors beckoned me, figuring me for a confused tourist. With nothing better to do I wandered over. She was a girl of brown skin and green dress. Her table smelled of incense, and a tarp stretched over four wooden pillars protected it from the rain. . She said something I didn't understand in the slightest, but her voice chirruped despite the rain so I smiled. She said something else, and when that that didn't get the reaction she wanted she tried again.

"How about English?" She chirped.

"Hey, now that I do know," I beamed.

"Thank the good for that. The number of tongues I've had to pick up I should maybe shut up shop and get work as an interpreter."

"And deprive common folk like me of your pretty voice?" I grinned. She smiled and put her hand on her hip.

"Flattery won't get you discounts if that's your aim. So are you a sightseer? You don't seem to know your way around but you don't seem interested in the temple."

"My sister's the theosophic one. I'm just tagging along."

"Your sister?"

"Yes, that's her walking up behind me angry and out of shape." I ducked, and an umbrella swept over my head.

"What the hell, Lach?"

"I win, by the way." I stood and turned to face Cicula, mouth cocked in a grin.

"You nearly get run over and now I find you chatting up some local broad?"

"I take offense to that," I prodded her collar, "I was chatting forward as well as up. It was sort of a gradual incline."

"Did you hit your head and forget why we're here?"

"It's not like gods stop answering calls after nine. Wait, do they? I just realized I don't know."

"Um . . . can I help you at all?" Chirping girl interrupted, smiling at my sister. "I mean, if there's something you're here for I can point it out."

"Well at least you're not a completely useless brother," Cicula muttered. "Hello, yes. We're, how do I put it? We're following up on some business our father had here not too long ago. Tall man, dark hair, probably wearing sunglasses. He may have been steaming— "

"Steaming?" The girl raised her eyebrow. "This is your father you say?"

"I mean had steam rising off him. He, well let's just say water doesn't agree with him."

"I can't say I remember anything like that, of course all sorts of weirdos come through here and I'm not here every day of the year. Ah, I do know someone who might be able to help though. One of the priests, he loves to gossip and has an uncanny memory for people. Just pop inside and ask around for Ishan."

"I see, and thanks for your help." My sister bowed her head and dropped a few coins on chirping girl's table. She jerked her head at me, and with a wave goodbye to my new friend I followed her into the temple.

10

Rumination Rondo

Draco

I. A man of flesh and blood and thought. A self-referential decision machine transmitting and receiving electrical pulses along synaptic routes connected to a system of cell-forms anchored to organic mineral forms, which achieves mobility by strategic tightening and loosening. A genetic mass producer and distributor with additional memetic faculties whose interests sometimes conflict. Information encoded in acid interacting for mostly mutual preservation not of the acid but the information encoded in it, and the same again for different information encoded in neuronal networks. Compounds, substances composed of elements in different structures. Elements in turn, different structures of energy, fermions, bosons, and antimatter. A blip. A pike or a dip in energy waveform. Boundaries and lines are illusions. A magic eye puzzle. The shape of an object is created as a consequence of the means by which the pattern at large is observed. I. not I. These both . . . these both . . .

"Get up." The angel's bark scattered my herded thoughts. I stood, groaned, and rubbed my temples. She was not making this easy.

"Got another fruit for me?" I brushed the dead grass of my pants and ushered Drakkengard beside me. My left arm suffered a dull ache, not bad but worse than before. How much time was that? This place might never run out of ways to be bad for me.

"I wouldn't have taken you for the meditative type," Ancilla ignored my question and walked over, hands in her jean pockets.

"It has its uses."

"Trying to think of a way out, I bet."

"Oh there's no need for that. I'll just prove I'm not such a bad guy, and you'll let me out of here. Besides, isn't betting a sin?"

"Are you even capable of not antagonizing someone?"

"Depends on the person. I like to think I'm better at picking than Lascivus is. It's a useful, if blunt tool for getting to know someone."

"You're trying to get a read on me."

"You're here out of frustration, right? From what I've spoken to Old Scratch YHVH seems to do that."

"You're pronouncing it wrong."

"How about I just call Him GOAAA?"

"No."

"Still," I splayed my palms upon a black tree trunk, "the Overworld must be awful if you'd rather be wasting time with me than kicking back in the *Paradiso* you were born in."

"I was not born. I was brought into being by His divine will."

"Really? Angels never study carnal knowledge with each other? I know you can, there was that whole deal with the giants way back."

"That was different," she snapped. With a smirk, Drakkengard sidled over to her.

"You banged a human, didn't you Annie?" she cheekily chided.

"Annie? Listen you golem that was a much different time. I repented." The angel's face was bright red to the point of glowing.

"Oh, I get it." Drakkengard stuck her hands behind her head and began a pompous march around her. "God made man in his image or something, right? Ha ha, you wanna get busy your boss."

"That's blasphemous and you will be silent!" She retorted through grit teeth.

"Okay Drakkengard, let's not push her too far," I laughed. "Now, kidnapper, do you have a fruit for me or are you just here to make sure I don't get too used to this place without you?"

"Yes, I have selected another fruit. We will begin the next part of your inquisition." She took another fruit from her back pocket and handed it to me. It looked bruised and sickly.

"How do you select these things anyway? Do you just pick them on a whim? You refuse to eat them so how do you know what's inside?" I polished the fruit against my shirt and a bilious, overripe scent assailed me. Weird properties aside, could these go rotten? Could they ferment? What would that mean? A memory contaminated by delusion? That might make things better or worse.

"There are ways of scrying the contents without biting into it, but not precise enough to make an accurate judgment. Come." She jerked her thumb to the nearest bend in the stream and headed over. I followed, tossing the fruit from hand to hand. The stream's babbling grew louder, more than seemed natural. Was it just because I was more aware of it? Did the stream babble with thoughts of the stream? Just being around all these metaphysical reflections gave cause for hesitation. The angel said it went both ways. What would happen if I skipped a rock across the stream? What would happen if I drank its waters? If I dug the stream wider and deeper, what would that do to my mind? What would happen if I planted a foreign tree in this soil? What sort of fruit would it bear?

We reached the stream and I sat, cross legged.

"Hurry up, sinner. Feeding time." A jolt of pain spiked along my left arm. It was distressingly easy to ignore my discomfort and do as told. I took the fruit in my right and bit into it.

11

Prayer

Cicula

The inside of Kalighat temple was divided amongst the different shrines, and even at this late hour priests and attendants patter about seeing to various duties. Gentle ponds and bright lanterns contributed to the air of focused activity. Faint wisps flitted around at the edge of my vision like hyperactive fog.

"Alright, let's get this over with," I took a deep breath and tapped a passing person on the shoulder.

"Eh?" She stopped, and shifted the jug she carried to face me.

"Excuse me. I am looking for Ishan. Can you point him out to me?" I asked. She shrugged in reply, waved over someone, and mumbled to him. He nodded and she left, leaving us with the stranger.

"Hey," he said in English. "I'm Ishan. You wanted me?" While a bit lanky and gaunt he had a good jaw, and lots of laughter lines that gave him an approachable kind of appeal. His beard was well kept and his eyes had the playful glint of a youthful heart.

"I was told you have a good memory for people."

"Whatever you heard, it wasn't from me."

"No, it was from that girl outside."

"That's not, nevermind." He rubbed his brow. "What do you want?"

"I wanted to know if a certain someone came through here a while ago. If I described him would you remember?"

"Who could say?" he shrugged. "How long a while?"

"No more than a few months, I think."

"Maybe, who is this guy to you anyway?"

"My father."

"Well, I'll give it a shot."

"Thank you. He is a tall man, with black hair. Probably wearing a gaudy red and black outfit two centuries out of date and hiding his eyes."

"Tall kitschy guy?" Ishan scratches his short beard. "Yeah, I remember him. Came through with some weird girl in robes. I figured he was with the theater. You get a few like that now and again. Of course most just decide India isn't Indian enough and go back to their hallow's eve costumes."

"Yes, that's him. Did he talk to anyone while he was here?"

"Yes, he had a pretty heated conversation with Rishika. Got her all kinds of mad."

"Could we talk to this Rishika?"

"Afraid not. She is rather busy preparing for an upcoming rite, very private, very shush-shush."

"When will she not be so busy?"

"Not until afterwards I suppose," he stroked his beard, "and that won't be for at least a few days, depending on how it goes."

"I see. Still, what you have told us is a big help. I thank you for your time." I reached for some coin but he stopped me.

"Hey now, it would be bad form for me to take that. Save it for the donation box, or the donation pool, or a blessing performed for a modest rate."

"I, uh, okay."

"Right, must be off. I hear Anaya is meeting Ridhi by the old tree, wouldn't miss this for the world." He clasped his hands together, turned and left. My brother walked up beside me.

"So, what, we lay low for a few days and come back later?"

"Now why in the worlds would we do that? These people were just a matter of convenience, not who I came to see."

"Right, the whole spooky voices thing," he clicked his tongue and looked around. "At least the locals probably aren't dead, unlike some places. Can't find a thread of divinity for love nor money," he coughed. "Anyhow, I guess while you dial for heavenly bodies I'll do a bit more asking around, yeah?"

"Oh very well. Just don't go running off."

"Choice. See you soon." With a skip in his step he wandered off, no doubt just after a bit of flattering conversation. Well, no matter. Fools will be fools. I took a deep breath and closed my eyes.

The thing about wisps is that they were in many ways prayers sent to no-one. One wouldn't think that there would be many in an actual place of worship when there are so many receptacles around yet nonetheless they have their ways of building up. By listening to them you could get an emotive map of the place, and tell where the most potent experiences had occurred. In an actual place of worship, this tended to be around the shrine of the most proactive deity.

I tuned in to these echoes and followed them, making my way through the temple like I'd known it for years.

I came upon the touchstone image of the dea Kali. I knew of her, but I couldn't say I was all that familiar with her nature. The idol depicted her with three enormous eyes, a great lolling tongue, and four golden hands. Two hands were held in gestures of blessing, the others held a sword and a severed head. Flowers wreathed the idol, some white, some colorful. I knelt before it, and closed my eyes in prayer.

"You're wasting your time," a woman said from behind me. I ignored her, and tried to make contact with the enshrined dea.

"She hasn't answered anyone at this shrine for a long time. Nothing personal, it's the temple runners. Well, after two centuries they were going to lose the path either way. Forget that. I hear you're looking for that Never-Setting Man."

"Ahhh, yeah. Alright, you have my attention," I said and looked up to her face. The woman's dark skin contrasted her bright red sari, and her gaze twinkled with strange passions.

"There's a good girl. You have your father's eyes, you know."

"Do I? I wouldn't know. He does so love hiding them."

"Has he told you why?"

"Hah, for all I know he has, twisted up in one of his mad rambling riddles. Do you know where he is, since you seem to know so much else?"

"Right now? No. To be honest I only saw him when he came through the temple. I do know where he went, though." She flashed a toothy grin and stuck her hand on her hip.

"Tell me," I stepped forward. It might have been a bit more intimidating if my head came higher than her bust, but backing off would have just looked bad at that point.

"You're cute when you're demanding, but you should really be more polite in future," she smiled softer. My cheeks flared scarlet and I had to force myself to keep eye contact. "There's a hotel a few blocks north of here. It's called Asutosh. Don't bother trying to get a room, they never have any vacancies. Your father spoke with a man there. Tell the receptionist you're here about the vajra. That'll get you an audience. Better move quick though, who know what might happen before morning," she laughed.

I narrowed my eyes. "Just who are you?"

"A helping hand also helps itself."

"That doesn't answer my— "

"Good luck." At that she'd slipped into the temple throng and I'd lost her. While glancing about I spotted Lach instead and waved him over.

"Your gods say anything?"

"Not directly. I think I got an answering machine, though." The woman's eyes remained prominent in my mind. Not many people had eyes like that, like a tiger watching mice, or stars glinting from the abyss at cosmic dust.

"Are you okay? You're breathing kinda funny." My brother reached to me but I batted his hand away and forced my respiration to slow.

"I'll be fine in a bit. Let's get a move on." I led us to the exit, and fished around my pocket for a cigarette of hash.

12

Intimacy Duet

Draco

Her lap was comfortable. The soft skin, toned muscles and hard bones wove an incomparable cushion for my head. I looked up at my wife's face, an evening sun over the horizon of her naked breasts, and she returned my gaze. *You look up when you wish to be exalted. I look down because I am exalted.* She said something. That's right, we were in the middle of a conversation.

"What of you? Afraid you might attack me again?"

I laughed, and stroked a finger where two muscles met on her arm. "You're stronger than I, for one."

"I seem to remember you won our first fight," she teased, "when you were just a boy with a sword and some flame."

"You were toying with me, tossing hellfire like fistfuls of dirt just to unbalance me, and it still took throwing myself on your sword to get ahead. Had you just burnt my whole body at once it would have been an easy win. Besides, I'm still just a boy with a sword and flame."

"I can't feed on a corpse, and in a straight fight I don't think I could win against you these days even if I went all out. Now come on, you're still not giving a straight answer."

"I've never felt like I've owned you. Even saying my wife feels like one of those lies you tell strangers because it's easier to just go along with their assumptions. As for controlling you, I'd have better luck trying to make the sun burn cold. Or is that still evading the question? Will I ever, in fit of hysteria, lash out at you?"

Something burned in my chest. *The emotive, if not cognitive memory of something. A haughty girl who talked of how things used to be, right up into the immediate past.*

"You're crying."

"You were there. I killed Diana. You were there. I thoughtlessly cursed you, ironically cannoned from fear of harm befalling to yet more family. I am not a savior. So," I swallowed, "I cannot say with certainty I will always discriminate where the victimhood of my deeds will fall in the future. Hopefully, I'll die before that happens."

"What of Drakkengard? Is she also risking her life by staying with you?"

"Her life is my life. In harming her, I would already be dead."

"A shame I can't arouse that kind of edict," she said in a familiar laugh-sigh tone.

"Oh, don't mistake me. I'm being literal here. The boy and the sword are mutually inclusive."

"And the fire?"

"It's the boy who is on fire."

***

The garden returned to my view, and I scowled at Ancilla.

"Was that really necessary? I thought you said you'd avoid my intimate moments."

"I assure you, sinner, this is *all* relevant to your judgment." Her hand moved to her thigh and I half expected her to pull a gun on me. She pulled nothing, and didn't notice her gesture at all. What weapon used to be at her thigh?

13

Avatar Tuning

Cicula

We found the hotel with ease, a short walk north from the temple. The rain tapped on my umbrella like impatient fingers, while Lach walked arms crossed and hunched forward.

"I think the rain is beating you this time, Brother."

"Yeah, this time. I'll kick its ass next verse."

"Your soggy ponytail looks like a dead slug trying to burrow into your skull, Brother."

"Bite me, Sis."

The hotel was in decent enough condition. The paint wasn't peeling and only one of the neon letters flickered, so half the time it seems to celebrate 'O Vacancy' in English. The name itself was written in Bengali. The fire escapes were rusted over and so were most of the window frames but that probably had more to do with the infrequent hint of acid in the rains than intentional neglect.

"So this must be Asutosh. Well, shall we let ourselves in?" I asked.

"We're being watched by about ten people through the windows but sure. After you, Sis."

With full confidence we strode up the steps and threw open the front door. Morbid wisps swamped the air around us. The receptionist—a dark skinned man wearing a blue suit that'd seen better days if not years–looked us up and down unimpressed.

"No vacancy," he drew it out as slow as possible, just in case we were as stupid as he suspected.

"Nevermind the vacancy, we're here about the thunderdoodad." Lach stepped over and dropped his elbow on the counter with a sharp *thump*.

"He means the vajra," I translated. "We would like to speak to your manager about the vajra." The receptionist turned his eyes to me. My stomach twisted and a chill shuddered through my body that had nothing to do with the rain. He was rank with still-blood and corpse-stink, the perversion of divine arts which made the dead walk.

"I'll go get the management," the drawn out mocking never left his voice. He ushered over two members of security from down the hall, and left through the door behind the reception desk.

"Well he seems nice enough."

"He's dead." I hissed.

"Why? Sure he was rude but so are lots of people."

"No I mean he is not living. He has expired. He is post-mortal."

"Really? You can tell?"

"I can smell the necrotic stink from here. What's more, the wisps here, well, there's been a great many final moments in this building," I gulped against how dry my throat was.

"So that would be what? Suckers?" Lach made mimed two fangs with his fingers.

"Almost certain."

"Well, they might still be cooperative. I mean, just because you hate their dead guts doesn't mean the feeling is mutual."

"Why Brother,are you trying to warn me off the violent path? How unlike you."

"I love a good fight as much as the next idiot, but this is important to you. If you fuck up, I'll be the one who has to put up with your belly aching."

Though warped, his concern put a smile on my face. I bolstered myself with it, and steadied my emotions. The receptionist came back looking perturbed.

"The management will see you now." He lifted up a part of the counter to let us through. "Please, come this way." Smile plastered on my face I followed him, and Lach behind me. We went up two flights of stairs before we reached the office, which was adorned by a simple and unmarked plaque. The receptionist opened the door and we stepped inside.

I should have checked his shirt for a name tag of some kind. Too late now.

Behind the office desk sat another dark skinned man, but this one wore a tan suit and his face much thinner. "Come in, children. I understand you speak English, yes?" His English was fluent, with a noticeable British accent. His eyebrows were as meticulous as his widow's peak was high.

"Yeah, that's right," Lach chimed in. He glanced at the window behind the man, at the trophy case beside him, and then pulled out an apple.

"Then I'll speak it for your sakes. You may call me Shaurya. To whom am I speaking?"

"Lach," my brother pointed to himself, "and Cicula" he jabbed to me.

"So I understand you have an interest in a certain object."

"A certain Vajra was taken from this area some time ago. We—" Lach glanced at me, I nodded, "believe that may have caused someone to seek revenge against the thief. So we're down here trying to figure out who was pissed off."

"You think that might be me?" Shaurya grinned and his fanged white teeth glinted in the office light. Nausea rippled through my stomach. The wisps were agitated.

"Wow, do all vampy's get such great dental as you?"

"Lach, please," I coughed, "We got a tip that you might be able to shed some light on the situation. There is, probably, no reason to suspect you, specifically," I coughed again, biting back a few extra words.

"You are his children right?"

"You can tell?"

"You share certain features, and I can smell him in your blood. I don't think me and mine have anything to fear from you," he smiled again. "Yes, your Father stole the vajra that was hidden in Kolkata. He did so on my behalf, as arranged with the Keeper."

"You hired him? Who was it stolen from?"

"Oh it didn't really belong to anyone," he waved dismissively. "It had been hidden in the hydroelectric plant by someone an age ago, and they died with no heirs. I would have left it had not those meddling Thugs gotten a bright idea."

"I knew it!" Lach exclaimed. I ignored him.

"Thugs?"

"Yes, or Thuggee as they're sometimes known, they have such silly notions about the value of a life. Me and mine need to feed, and we are more than happy to accommodate the law and local authorities by limiting ourselves to those on the streets who will not be missed. If anything our presence alleviates the burden they place on the city."

"So they wanted to use the Vajra to wipe you out for what you do?"

"Yes. In a straight up assault the best they could hope for is mutual destruction. Then who will continue their 'great' work? Huh? Hah." He slapped his desk, oblivious to the papers he sent flying. "I've no interest in the thing itself. I've plenty of more subtle tools. Still, I can't imagine those Thugs would bother to get revenge."

"Why not?"

"Well for one, why would they devote resources to a third party when their biggest enemy is still at large?" I slumped, my wind plundered. A dead end? Well, that was to be expected, but it's still disheartening. I eyed Shaurya up and down. His dead flesh twitched with false life.

"One last question, if you don't mind," I asked, "what was it you used to pay for this? Gra—The Keeper doesn't run a charity after all."

"Oh, just a bit of my blood. I can't imagine what for, but it was a small price to pay. I suppose for one such as him, taking a single thing from its hiding spot was just a small job anyway. Small job, small price. Right?"

"Of course. Well I suppose we—" A great rumble cut me off, and the whole room trembled.

"An Earthquake?"

"They didn't!" Shaurya flew to his feet and vaulted across his desk and the door swung open. The receptionist fell into the room. Numerous bladed instruments were imbedded in his torso and a rope had been tied around his neck. He gasped something out and expired.

"What happened?" Lach asked, his tone betraying his excitement.

"It's those filthy Thuggee. I can't fathom why but they're launching a suicide run." Something at the back of my mind pieced the answer together.

"They think they've fallen out of favor with their goddess," I said. "They can't incite her to guide them, and have lost direction." Shaurya glared at me with muddied assessment, but let it pass.

"If it's a war they want, war they'll get." He flipped open a case on a bookshelf by the door and retrieved an engraved scimitar. "Let's see how they stand the taste of Damascus steel." The vampire stormed out and down the staircase a billowing cloud of fury and fangs and steel. Lach turned to me, a grin on his gormless face.

"We should go," I pointed out. "No really. This is senselessly dangerous. We've nothing else to learn here. Let these idiots kill each other and be done with it. Lach. Lach!" It was too late. He'd flown out the door and down to the fray.

There was just no keeping that idiot from a pointless fight. For my own protection I gathered up a cloud of wisps around me. They were lousy at fighting, but as things born from wishes and desire, they proved easy enough to direct. The air around me gained a slight shimmer as it became dense with spirits. No need for a bigger summon, those could be . . . unpredictable in my experience. A wisp couldn't be called alive or conscious, it's just an echo. The one downside is that using them all up in an area can make even your lifelong home feel like a stranger's house. All the emotions built up over the years that saturated the place are gone, and it is left foreign. Of course, this isn't *my* home.

I listened to the sounds of battle below. There was this certain toxicity in the wisps made by the vampires which their attackers lacked, and it made it simple to follow the flow. The hotel was three stories high, plus at least one basement. Each room held one to three vampires, all part of the coven. In comparison to those from the temple, numbers were on the vampire's side. The temple folk were far more disciplined, though. For every one of them felled, they took down three or four undead.

There was Lach, just beat up everybody he could get his hands on. He never bothered to finish them off though. Despite what one would think, his presence seemed to be lowering the death count. Was it intentional or just complete apathy toward anything that can't fight back?

I got broken from my thoughts by the door being slammed open. Shaurya had returned. The sounds of battle had dimmed but not silenced. Shaurya's wounds looked bad, and his sword was broken off at the hilt. Blood dripped down his face and arms, disappearing into the fabric of his red suit.

"Need a break?" I rose to my feet and took a step back.

"Yes, just a spell. Then I can wipe out those zealots. My family, they are lost. No matter. I can rebuild. I've done it many times before. With each defeat I grow more cunning." He glared at me. At my neck. "So long as I survive."

The moment he moved toward me I unleash the gathered wisps. Each carried no more force than a baseball but that's why you gather up many of them. Shaurya staggered back under the bombardment. Blood spurted out his mouth and his right arm buckled in an unnatural angle. Yet the wisps ran out too soon and the assault ended. He steadied himself and flew at me. I opened my mouth to shout a summoning but his blood-dampened hand clamped down across my lips. I tasted copper and dirt. He turned my head hard enough to hurt and before I could think of a next move he plunged his fangs into my neck.

"There you are," said a different voice. "You're hard to find for one so nosy." My vision swam and blurred, but in the doorway I could make out a figure. There stood a long haired woman with dark skin and predatory eyes. The woman from the temple. Shaurya didn't seem to notice her.

"You look like you could do with some help." She was too casual. If I could I'd have screamed yes at her as loud as could be. Yes, stop blathering and help me before I die.

"You don't want to die? Death comes for everyone, what makes you so special?"

I can't die yet. My father—

"Needs you? What makes you so sure? Is he so incompetent that he needs his snotty nosed daughter to save him?"

Even after that, there's still la- him.

"Ah, there it is. Yes, that mentor of yours has all the wrong ideas, doesn't he? Oh but look at the time, in just one more minute you'll lose consciousness."

So help me!

"Are you sure? You wouldn't rather do it yourself?"

I'm a summoner, gods damn it. Getting help from others is what I do.

"If I help you, you'll have to help me. I'm sure you of all people can appreciate that."

Hurry, then. What do you want?

<I can't give you the details yet, but your old master. Yes, 'him'. He's planning something naughty. I need your help to stop him.>

Great! No problem. Where do I sign?

<You already have.>

The woman, the woman, the woman wasn't there. My vision stopped swimming. In fact it had become sharper than ever before. I wrapped two hands around Shaurya's neck and yanked him off me. With a third arm I reached into my pocket and took out the Vajra. Third arm?

There was a strangeness that eluded me.

I had four arms.

I had three eyes.

Unfamiliar thoughts billowed up from below my ego. This creature lived when it should be dead. It won't die. I had to fix that. I enunciated the need with a too-long tongue.

"For all your talk of learning, you're still so small minded," A new voice came from my throat.

"Who are you?" Shaurya demanded, rising from the remains of his desk. "You're not that idiot's daughter, are you?"

"Samael is a businessman these days. You sold your blood to the Poison of YHVH. 'A drop'? That was just a down payment. You sold your blood to the Keeper, all of your blood, and I am the one who bought it." My fourth arm tapped my head. "You really should have read the fine print."

He turned to flee, but before he could take off I hurled the Vajra. The room filled with a flash of light and the crash of a thunderclap. The Vajra pinned Shaurya to the wall, piercing his chest right through.

"Now to take what's mine." My skin erupted, but did not bleed. Veins streaked from my flesh like fast-growing trees and penetrated the undead corpse. His dark skin turned sallow and grey and he uttered a pitiful gurgle. Once I drained him dry my blood vessels returned to my body and my skin closed up without a mark. I approached Shaurya's remains and yanked the Vajra out. His body collapsed into a cloud of ash and dispersed. Not a single drop of his blood had been spilled.

"Hold it!"

In the doorway stood Lach, tussled but unharmed.

"Yes?" I place a finger against my chin, supported that arm's elbow on its matching hand, and crossed both the arms below it.

"What god are you, and what did you do to my sister?" he pointed straight at me.

"You can tell?" said my possessor. "You catch on quick, boy."

"I've had a run-in of my own"

"Alright. My name is Kali. Do not be afraid, Cicula agreed to this."

"Somehow I doubt your terms were explicit," he narrowed his eyes and tapped the toe of his boots against the cluttered floor.

I stuck my tongue out in apology. "I'm going to go to sleep now, and your sister is going to wake up sound as ever. Keep her safe, would you."

"You don't have to tell me," he said, and scowled.

14

Liber Null

Draco

"What are you doing?" Lascivus asked.

"We need money don't we?" I sat down at the roulette table and slid the mugger's chips to the pool. "Thirteen red," I declared. The attendant raised an eyebrow but spun the wheel regardless.

"You know, most people would consider thirteen unlucky," he observed.

"Unlucky for whom?" I replied. "I'd sooner befriend bad luck than alienate it." The ball bounced along merrily for a few rotations, and came to rest right where I predicated.

"Thirteen red," the attendant declared, to the raucous complaints of the rest of the table. I tipped my brow to the grumbling gamblers and gathered my winnings.

"And now we have money." I rose and departed. Once we were out of earshot, Lasivus tapped me on the shoulder.

"What was that? I didn't taste any magick."

"A stranger just showed out of nowhere, won the pool, and left before it could be won back. The measured tension between the players has been disturbed, and their gambler's pride has been undercut. Just a spot of bad luck."

"Did you get a blessing from Fortuna when I wasn't looking?" She dragged a finger across my cheek and tasted it for enchantments.

"Not at all. You're putting too much thought into this. I truly didn't know that would work, I just thought to try it." I took her coat off the rack and helped her into it. It took just a minute to redeem my chips for cash, and we left.

The doors shut behind us and the music became muffled. I nodded to the doorkeeper, a short woman with broad shoulders and a spot of dried blood on her cuffs. She didn't respond, but her hand brushed across her jacket pocket where a certain bundle of documents had been stashed.

"I don't believe you. Why won't you just tell me what you did?"

"I can't tell you what doesn't exist, unless you want me to just make something up. If I said I'd freed the dealer's brother from a life of prostitution and just now cashed in the debt would you believe me?"

"That's still not it. I can tell."

"And just how can you tell? Whatever you're seeing I assure you must be wholly imagined!" The volume of my voice caught me by surprise, but Lascivus didn't seem to notice. I couldn't quite nail down why this frustrated me more than it should.

"I've been around. You learn to pick up on these things."

"A vague answer that indicates nothing. Is this some sort of test? A measure of duress? Some stubborn bluff? Burn the belfry, break the bells and brachiate to the Bahamas. A lump of still bleeding bait. There's poison in the meat. It's poisoned, she knows, I know, she knows I know, yet still it must be eaten. Eat it now, suffer the poison. Don't eat, hold out as long as you can. You won't starve, yet the meat will go rotten and you'll eat it anyway and suffer thrice. What did I do? What did I . . . do?" I doubled over, and spilled bile down the sidewalk. Every muscle in my left arm had locked and refused to move. Lascivus patiently helped me up.

"I'm sorry. Just forget it." *How did she say that? What sound did I just hear? Was that an apology? Did she just snap at me? Was I bleeding? Was I not bleeding? Everything else was bleeding, losing boundaries, ends ending.*

"—gree with me. Must have been the shrimp." *That's my voice? I talked? How long had I been talking? What had I been saying? I was being watched. Or did I do the watching? Count three. Count four? No, zero is zero. So this had to be later. I understood now. This was a memory, like a dream, except it had begun to go lucid. The déjà vu made me break character. If it weren't for Drakkengard this would be a lot more inconvenient. Where was she? Not too far. Just had to get into the VIP room, once in it didn't matter if we get noticed.*

***

I awoke in a ring of scorched soil. Every few seconds a mild tremor rumbled across the gardenscape, though Ancilla paid it no mind.

"I can only take one more. You better make it count." I coughed into my hand, and spilled a smear of yellow bile onto my palm. I ushered Drakkengard over and rose with her help.

"What do you mean?" The angel kept her distance and remained by the stream, her expression rigid and her body turned away. She touched her waist but seemed unaware of doing so.

"What was it you said before? Eating the fruit yourself might contaminate your self-image?"

"That's right. I would experience thoughts that aren't mine as if they were mine, and they would influence me."

"How many people have you put through this rigmarole? A thousand? No, less, a hundred or so, right? You're used to it but you don't know it that well."

"Look what are you trying to get at? Feigning illness won't save you."

"I'm not feigning. Sometimes things go weird. I'm not sure what the criterion for your fruit selection is, but you have an uncanny knack for picking the moments where things get weird. One more such memory and rational thought is going to go out the window. Hoh boy, I sure hope you're ready to come to some sort of conclusion."

"Hmph. I am actually almost done, but I've half a mind to keep going anyway. You think I care that you're getting a bit spooked?"

"Fine, set off a feedback loop. See if I care!" I yelled. Drakkengard pulled a face at my captor and helps me sit down by the weed ravaged path.

15

Sempre Grandfather

Cicula

We emerged through the portal back into the library of the family home. An elk-horned demon stood waiting for us, the insignia of the house of the serpent emblazoned on her naked breast.

"The lord wishes to see you. He has news," she droned.

"Oh I'll bet he does." I crossed my arms then flinched. No, I still only had two arms. I was fine. A dull headache throbbed in my skull and my teeth felt worn down.

"The old man got a carriage waiting or something?" Lach asked.

"No. He will see you immediately."

The room shimmered and warped. Reality distorted, and in the next second I stood inside the unmistakable walls of Castle Pandemonium. Where the messenger had been now stood my Grandfather, and Lach was nowhere to be seen.

"Where did my brother go?"

"I'm addressing him in a different room. We've different things to discuss after all." He straightened his red bowtie and flattened a crease on his vest.

"Oh very much so. How about that massive set up you just led us into."

"Is that how you see it?" he asked.

"Let's start with this, I wager the news you have is that Vengai-Ra and Ko have suddenly finished their task."

"As you say." He spread his gloved hands palm up.

"After all, they already have a good idea where to best find out who took Father, and it certainly wasn't Kolkata. So you arranged to have them away on some nonsense job, knowing we'd end up going after the most recent task of Father's that we could infer from the trophies he keeps. You took advantage of my Brother and I as well as this situation to facilitate a deal between you and the Dea Kali. You put us in danger and wasted our time so you could turn the blood of some irrelevant vampire into whatever Kali used to buy it."

"If you're accusing me of being a shrewd businessman, I've no choice but to accept the compliment."

"That's not it. It doesn't matter that we're family, does it?" I screamed. "We're all just currency to be used in this game of monopoly you're playing, aren't we?" I was making a fool of myself. I'd regret it very quickly. I didn't care. "If you knew all that, why don't you know where Father is? So long as you can make a profit, what do we matter? Isn't that right you callous, miserable, vainglorious fire-djinn?" I could die.

His eyes flashed. The man took a step toward me and his countenance magnified a thousand fold. A great towering pillar of fire glowered down at me, as terrible and unyielding as the desert sun. My heart exploded in my ears with every beat. Cold sweat evaporated from my skin faster than it formed.

"How dare you? How dare *you* stand before me with such insolence? If I am just a vainglorious fire-djinn, what does that make you? A wretched slip of a girl desperate to sate her hunger for approval and reduced to relying on dope to withstand her own neuroticism. Don't. Don't *ever* think you can judge me and the choices I've made. Yes, I took advantage of your situation. If I couldn't seize every advantage I could never have survived war against Him. It is through cunning that I succeed and you cannot say you have not benefited. If I knew who injured my daughter and took her husband they would already be at my mercy. I do not have power on high. I do not know everything. I do the best with what I have and gain what I can no matter the situation."

He slicked his hair back, and once more I stood before a man and not a being of fire. I fell to my knee, my face wet with tears.

"I'm sorry grandfather. I—I spoke out of turn."

"Stand, stand," he said, dripping with pithy. "If I'm angry it's because it hurts to hear such words from you. Take that as proof of how much I care about you."

He helped me up, and brushed his hand against my cheek.

"See? All is forgiven." Liar. "Let's forget about it. "

"How . . . how is mother?"

"She is fine, for now. She is still comatose, but also suffering a rather nasty hangover. It's probably for the best she isn't conscious to go through it. She's receiving the best medical treatment I can offer, and it is helping."

"So she might wake up?"

"The soporific juice she loves so much pollutes her mind and body. By all means, it's not my place to dictate how she lives, but I will say that she is hindered by it. However now that the supply has been cut off her body is purging itself, and as she regains her strength the angel's seal is worn away from within. I think she will wake up in a week, give or take. Still, I can't be certain, and nor can we assume your father is not in danger. So I will return you to your home, and you will find his retainers waiting for you so you can continue your search."

"I see. Thank you, Grandfather."

"And Cicula."

"Yes?"

"Do take care." He smiled, and with that smile the room vanished.

***

I found myself once again in Father's library.

"That is some straight up bullshit," Lach complained. He, too, had been returned it seemed.

"What is?"

"He can just whisk anyone anywhere in Hell right inside his doors, but unless its *important* we all have to make our way there ourselves.

"I'm sure he is rather busy."

"Oh don't stand up for him. The guy's a crimson dick. *Feh*, oh well. So where's Dad's minions?"

Vengai-Ra and Ko entered the room, a somewhat surly expression on their faces.

"I am so sick of being called a minion."

"Doc, you're sick of most things."

They both looked exactly the same as the last time I saw them, like a scraggly tourist suddenly called into work and a lunatic war veteran escaped from an asylum. Even though one wore a lab coat and the other wore a wearable factory war coat I could never shake the suspicion that at some point they had been tailored to match the design of one another.

"So I understand the half-mad idiot went and got himself abducted, is that about right?" Vengai-Ra asked. He unbuttoned his lab coat and took a seat. The ugly Hawaiian shirt beneath it stood out like a chromatic infected cold sore.

"That's right. Do you have any idea who might have wanted to do that? Anything at all?"

"Alright chieflette, give me a minute." Ko leaned against a nearby bookcase, scratched his bare chest and closed his eyes.

"Chieflette?"

Lach shrugged at me.

"Say Doc, you don't think . . . ?" Ko began.

"Think what?"

"Remember a while back, those missing samples?" The gunman gestured vaguely in the air.

"We never did get anywhere with that," Vengai-Ra noted and adjusted his spectacles. "You think it might be related?"

"Well it sure didn't seem an accident."

"What is it?" I asked.

"Since I'm employed as your Father's official doctor—well employed is hardly the right word but still— since I'm his doctor, naturally I have a number of blood samples of him as well as his family members."

"You have our blood? I don't remember giving any." Lach piped in.

"You were probably too young. I'd only need more if you got sick. Anyway, some time ago a number of these samples went missing."

"We figured someone stole them," Ko continued, "though who knows why, and tried to track them down. Us and your Dad."

"We managed to track them as far as this one village but the trail went dead. I mean, it's colder than ever before but maybe something new will turn up." Vengai-Ra shrugged.

"Blood you say?" The sound of my voice surprised me. I hadn't meant to speak. The three of them turned to face me, slowly, so very slowly. Their movements slowed to a halt before they finished turning at all.

I might be able to help with that. A voice rang in my head, a woman's voice.

"Kali," I said to the Dea. I'd begged for my life.

She stepped in from just outside my field of vision. Not like she'd been standing there and I hadn't seen her but like she'd walked in from off-stage of reality.

Hello dear. She rearranged her four arms into rather maternal countenance. *I'm getting used to what it's like in your head, so I thought now would be a good time to talk.*

Her skin was black, completely and flawlessly black. When she talked her bright red tongue flashed from behind her white teeth, and she held herself with a certain rhythmic swaying.

Adorning her waist hung a skirt of skulls and bones that rattled gently as she shifted.

"Why are you still here? I thought— "

The first ride is always a bit rough. Plus you were rather dying. Her three eyes examined the nails of one hand. Another hand rested on her hip. A third hand scratched the back of her head and a fourth she held in a gesture of prayer. Keeping track of so much body language was taxing in the most unusual way.

"That's right you wanted me to help you with something. I'm pretty sure that counts as consent obtained under duress."

You're not trying to weasel out of our deal now, are you dear? She placed one hand on my shoulder, and an enticingly sweet scent stole my attention.

"No, just pointing it out."

Alright then. Now, dear, blood is a bit of a specialty of mine. Not an intentional addition to my portfolio but it was a clever idea at the time.

"Are you saying you can find the stolen blood?"

Yes. I believe finding it will shed some light on the situation.

"Just what is it that you want? Why are you doing all this? Did you set up that whole arrangement with Grandfather just for this?"

Those who pray to me are few, and many of them have a warped faith which I do not appreciate. To act as I see fit I need an avatar, a direct conduit for my divine self.

"Me."

You and I share certain affinities that make you a suitable vessel. I shan't list them, not all of them are flattering for either of us, but I need an avatar to do my task.

"What task?"

I am Kali, courtesan of Shiva the Destroyer. All things must end and I end that which refuses to end.

"What is that?"

I don't know yet. It doesn't exist yet, but it will.

"You mentioned something about my teacher before."

Yes. The one who taught you summoning is tied up in all this. Again I do not know to what extent.

"I have, and I can't stress this enough, a lot of misgivings about this."

As you should. I shall rest for a while more, but by the time you have need of me I'll be ready. Take care, dear.

I blinked, and the goddess had absconded. Lach and the others were still looking at me.

"Come again?"

"If you take me to the village I should be able to track down the stolen blood."

"Well, far be it for me to doubt you," Vengai-Ra sniffed. "Although I must insist that we rest first. You both look tired, and Ko and I have been quite busy ourselves. *Atututut*, before you complain, it won't do you any good to be too sleep-deprived to function properly. I am a doctor. Besides, I know your father, he has a talent for making people waste time."

I opened my mouth to complain anyway, but my words were eaten by a sudden yawn.

"See? What did I tell you? Get a few hours sleep, and we'll leave first thing afterwards."

Despite my better judgment I conceded, and headed to my room to sleep. Just a few hours, I told myself.

16

Chimera Key

Lach

Preparations didn't take long. We gathered again in the library, the others rambled a bit in whatever briefings they thought important, and then we passed through a portal of my sister's making. There was probably something in that, come to think of it. Did a portal and a summoning work the same way? I could have sworn Mom said something along those lines ages ago. Either way it was still stuff taking shortcuts around conventional space. It probably looked really tricky from the outside if you tracked the actual movement going on, I bet. How did that example go? Something about being faster to go around a globe at a pole rather than the equator. Only the globe had N dimensions, there were billions and billions of little globes in it, and something about rotation. Wait, how did an n-dimensional globe work? An n-dimensional cube or whatever looks like a hella bunch of planes intersecting weirdly, I suppose N tells you how many, but a sphere just has one plane wrapped around itself. Was an N one just a freaky blob? Or maybe it was a load of disc things. Ugh, thought models gave me a headache. A golden apple was easier to work with.

"Lach you deaf idiot, quit spacing out."

"Right, so uh," I trailed off as I glanced around. The four of us were standing in a field of off-yellow ferns and bushes. Over a nearby hill stood a weird sort of windmill, cresting a horizon of peachy sky, or maybe the color of pale watermelon flesh, "where are we?" I walked over to the nearest bush and nudged it with my boot. My pilgrimage was getting pretty interesting.

"The place is called Mahkko, or something like that. My pronunciation is probably way off," Vengai explained with a sour face. He smacked his lips twice. Was he tasting the air or was it some weird doctor thing? "The village over yonder hill is called Mrinda, or at least it was last time I came here."

"What are the locals like? Weird?" I asked, plucked an orange berry off the bush and rolled it over in my hands. It smelled kinda citrusy, if I squinted my brain a bit. I'd rather an apple but that was no reason not to try it.

"Well that would be rather impolite to say, don't you think?" he chuffed.

"Oh come on. Do they have eyes on their arms and eat dirt through their back? Do they carve opalescent tools from their shed carapace?"

The fruit tasted like copper and salt water, and I spat it out at once. Maybe the next one would taste better. I yanked another fruit off a bush.

"No, they're humanoid, thank goodness. Shall we?" Vengai started heading off toward the windmill thing and the others fall in behind. After spitting out another foul fruit I jogged up after them.

"Lame. Why do we never go to any of the weird worlds?"

"Blame their maker. You want to go make beautiful music with some esoteric space crab you do it on your own time." Sis shook her hand limply at me, talking in that haughty tone she got when she was looking forward to me making an ass of myself. It was a bit off, though, and she looked kinda pale.

"Maybe I will. Ko," I called out, "cancel all my appointments made for after we rescue the old man and book me a vacation."

"Chiefling, you're Boss's kid so I'll take it easy with you but I'm not your damned secretary."

"This is coming from blue mane tall person."

"What's that supposed to mean?"

"Nothing you didn't already know, five for five."

"Ignore him," Sis scoffed. "He says nonsense when he can't think of anything clever."

"And you can't spell clever without Ix minus Iv," I retorted. I knew full well that wasn't how you pronounced roman numerals but it ticked her off something funny.

"You see what I have to put up with?" she threw up her hands.

"No offence but your father's worse," Vengai-Ra replied. "I've seen him go into a sixteen minute baleful speech solely to complain that his soup was a bit hot, and after all that he still ate the thing."

"He probably just did that to pass the time until it cooled." I shrugged. Sis groaned and scuffed the dirt with her shoe.

"Great fools think alike."

"Hey Ko, your coat can make whatever, right?" I shifted the topic, already bored of this one. "Why not pull a car out of your pocket or something for us?"

"One, I don't have the raw materials and converting what we do have would take longer than just walking. Two, I don't have the specs for any real transport. Oh and three, it's not my coat, it's the teensy little robots that live inside it."

"Not even a dune buggy?"

"No. The best you could hope for is a manual spec hang glider and I am not manifesting a damn hang glider for you."

I glanced to the sky. "The wind's all wrong to go hang gliding anyway. Maybe another time."

"Don't count on it."

The village bustled with activity when we arrived. Well, not quite bustling. Lively? No that was still too strong. Something less than alive but more than stable. Recovering? Sure, the village was recovering. The stars had started to fade in against the dying daylight and the folks around seemed in no stress to get whatever event they were preparing done in a hurry. Some guy in green lazed behind a barn. A bunch of folk shifted curved stones along flatbed carts that rolled along two long, log-like wheels. Others decorated a big stone totem with branches and grass. It looked like the stones were being used to make a circle around it. Maybe it was a round table, or maybe it was a barrier.

"So for the record," I asked, "who actually speaks the lingo here?"

"I do," Ko offered. "The mad idiot machine box is good for that at least." He'd explained to me once that his brain had been augmented with a tactical AI, but because he'd been culpability in the seeming annihilation of his whole universe it had reclassified him as an enemy and a traitor. Something it made sure to remind him of every waking second. Apparently it wanted him to 'return to command and turn himself in' but because it had no clue how to get to there from this universe its programming had gone a bit balmy. I'd known this guy my whole life, and had no doubt it had gotten a lot worse in ways he refused to let on. Yet for some reason he refused to get it removed.

Sis glanced up, but dropped her gaze a few times before getting her gut together. "I'm probably rusty, but, uh, I can speak a little too."

"You can? Have you been here before?" Vengai-Ra turned to her, a real critical look in his eye.

"It was a long time ago, nothing to do with what we're here for now. I'm certain of it."

"I'm not," the old doc stomped toward her and she flinched, "this is my daily loaf we're talking about here. Draco's a guano-brained pyrophiliac but I like my chances with him better than what other horrible demons I'd have to serve to pay off the rest of my debt. You're his kid, there's no saying what you've gotten up to has nothing to do with him."

"Hey, leave her alone. If she says its peaches it's peaches." I put myself between them and stared him in the eyes, smiling just enough to not make it a threat.

"With respect, boy, I don't defer to you." The doc didn't budge. I turned to Ko beside him.

"Come on, Ko, we're cool aren't we? Talk him down."

"He has a point, Lach. There could be a connection."

"Guys, hey, let's not make this an ugly sort of thing."

"Oh for gods sakes!" Sis yelled up so suddenly I jumped. "You ass-baskets need to know so bad, fine, only to stop this prick's insufferable big brother play." She shoved me aside and stood before Dad's guys, her arms folded over her chest. "A certain asshole mentor brought me here as a test, a summoner thing. We were here for a while. I fucked up, he fucked off, I haven't seen him since. The end," hands shaking, she lit up a joint and sucked a quarter of it down in a single drag.

"Fucked up how?"

"People died, that's how. Lots of people. Would have been a lot more if he hadn't stopped it."

"Who? Your teacher?"

"Yes my bastard teacher. No, before you ask, I don't know who the hell he is. For years I thought he was just a fake friend I imagined."

I sighed and let my shoulders slump. So much for keeping that secret. Sis threw down her joint and grinded it out in disgust. After a minute's silence Ko opened his mouth.

"So—"

I shook my head. "Don't say it, man. Don't," I turned to Cicula. I'd have put my hand on her shoulder but that would just piss her off more. "Come on, Sis. There's probably a tavern or something down in this place. We can chill out there."

"Yeah, sure." She lit up another joint and headed down to the village. I glanced back at the other two.

"You guys can start asking around. Find out what the deal is with the totem-pole thing and see if any weirdoes but us have been around," I said. Vengai-Ra sniffed disapprovingly but Ko nodded in agreement. Once that was settled I chased after my sister.

She moved surprisingly quickly for a sullen person. She'd already arrived in the village proper by the time I reached the bottom of the hill, and I caught a glimpse of her disappearing into one of the buildings. I gave chase, ignoring the locals staring at me, and followed her inside. The place seemed more like a restaurant than a bar or tavern. I saw no counter of any kind, just a half-door off to the side that seemed to lead into the kitchen. There were no chairs, the people just squatted or knelt at round stone tables close to the floor. I found Sis to the back, lying on the ground sideways like she was on a long sofa and with a joint hanging out of her mouth.

"It sucks," she announced.

"I know," I replied. "I was left behind too."

"Come off it. You had a one night stand you built your life around. That's nothing like what I went through."

"Yeah," I fought to keep from grinding my teeth. "Sorry, I suck at the whole relating thing. Just looks like a set to me."

"Stop trying to act like a better person than you are. It's ugly." Her voice had grown tired and distant. The drugs must have kicked in.

"It's in my best interests to help you be happy if I can. Does it matter if that's selfish or not?"

"I guess not. Hey," a helpless ache filled her voice, "you don't actually think this is my fault, do you? Father, I mean."

"Nah. It is a bit of an odd coincidence, though, that whoever wanted to nick that blood swung by the place where you got dumped."

She groaned and swatted my face. "Stop calling it that. I keep saying, it wasn't like that. I was just a kid."

"So was I," I shrugged, "Hell, we still are. Mom's like a thousand years old or more. How old do cambions even live for?"

"Who knows? Most seem to either get killed or take in enough miasma to go full demon. At least we don't live backward like Merlin."

"That still makes no sense."

"Anything's possible. Isn't that why you're still looking for your goddess?"

"That's different. There's like, butterflies and weather and crap involved."

"Is that so?"

"Hey, aren't you meant to be having your soul parasite follow that blood trail now that we're here?"

"She said she'd be ready to do her thing when I need her, but I don't actually know how to ring her up."

"Can't you just summon her?"

Sis shook her head. "I don't have much experience with this kind of avataristic relationships. I'm not sure how this works. For all I know doing it normally would fry my brain by ripping her out. There's probably an incantation to invoke her, but I don't know it and haven't had the chance to learn it."

"So, what, we just do the sleuth thing until the mind-taker wakes up?"

"I guess. It couldn't hurt."

"It must feel like suddenly being told you have a full time job," I mused. "Weird. Well you do all the talking. I'll just stand around and look pretty."

"Business as usual."

"Don't take a wrench to what works."

I followed my sister around as she asked her questions. I'd no clue what they were saying but the people seemed remarkably open around strangers. They looked at us with curiosity, but no real suspicion. Maybe we just had good timing, and they assumed we were here for whatever party they were setting up for. There might even be a dance or three waiting for me. No need to stop looking just because I was on the job after all.

Sis's line of inquiry ended up leading her to some guy packing sacks of plants at the mill. At least they looked like plants, a sort of orange thin bamboo with little green flowers here and there. I'd only assumed it was a mill, for that matter, but it would take a stretch of the imagination to see it as anything else. The guy was broad shouldered, and in just a pair of tattered work pants. He smelled of grass, dirt and whatever he was cramming into the sacks, a nice earthy smell and he had a warm smile but there was something about his blue eyes. They had a sort of sharpness I could say, one that rubbed me the wrong way. Or maybe I just wanted an excuse to punch his freckled face for a bit of excitement. His arms were thick from labor and looked like there'd be a nice wallop to them.

Sis seemed to find him pretty damn charming, being all giggles and blushing. Honestly he seemed a tad dense, but hey, what did I know. I was just there to keep my mouth shut and look pretty. At least she'd stopped moping.

Once she'd finished probing the miller boy we met up with the others back at the hill.

"So, what have we found out?" I asked.

"Well on our end," Ko began, "we got a few dodgy looking merchants here and there, some odd beggar no one can explain, a plague a while back, some missing kids a while back, and some vague reference to an *Ayaki-Ike*', whatever that is. Sounded like nasty god or something, but I couldn't figure if was some actual entity, or just a personified disaster."

"Most of that stuff is too far back to be important, or so it seems," Sis replied a bit too quickly, "but I heard about that beggar too. The blind-mute?"

"Yeah, that's the one."

"They say he's been seen coming and going from some odd building out of town. He, I mean, they assume he lives there. No one noticed it before, and no one wants to stick their nose into this beggar's business so they've not investigated it or anything."

"I don't like how credulous these people are," I piped in, "feels dangerous somehow."

"I know what you mean," Ko nodded. "My first hunch is this is a set-up, but that doesn't quite ring right. It's more like they're scared of asking questions."

"You're just being paranoid. These are nice people."

"I'll just be glad to be done with them." The gunman bristled and adjusted his coat. "Did you find out where this beggar is, since you seem to think it's our best lead?"

"Yeah, if we follow the road west of here," Sis jerked her thumb. "We should find it easily."

"If it's easily found, why'd no one notice it before?"

"The road isn't used anymore. The place the road led to, well it isn't anymore either."

"I guess we'll head there." I stretched my arms. "Do you want to go now, or in the morning?"

"Now would be best."

***

It took twenty minutes of walking for the building to come into sight, and we still had a while to go. I stopped our group.

"Just a heads up, Sis's farm boy friend is following us. Ko, you probably already knew that." He nodded his head in affirmation.

"Brother, come on, I'm not going to elope with every half handsome person I meet."

"Beside the point, Sis," I pinched my brow, "he's right behind that tree about fifty meters back. No, don't look. Now what are we going to do about him?"

"He's just some kid, right?" Vengai-Ra asked. "Who cares? Just get him where we can see him in case he tries something."

"What if he's not just some kid? What if he works for whoever vacced the boss?" Ko asked, but it was anyone's guess what vacced even meant. His eyes were razor focused and dilated.

"Can't we just ignore him?" Sis complained. "He probably won't come inside anyway. These people seem pretty superstitious despite how trusting they are."

"Sis, that doesn't even make sense. To be superstitious you gotta be suspicious. You can tell because they rhyme."

"Kid, I don't think that's how words work," Ko interjected.

"Ignore the idiot. He's just bored," Sis dismissed.

"Okay but what if the old man died, and this chicken chaser is his reincarnation from the future?" Shit, now I'd started over-sweating it.

"Do they even have chickens here?" Vengai-Ra wondered.

"Maybe they have like, small pterodactyls." I shrugged.

"Maybe the guy we're talking about has already walked over?" Ko offered. I spun on my heel and found kid-farmhouse standing just behind me, sporting an awkward smile. He said something and laughed.

"Otay says since we noticed him he may as well come forward," Sis translated.

"Woah, woah, woah, wait a split minute." I rubbed my hand over my mouth and pointed to the guy. "I call bullshit. How did he go from being stealthy as a rolling stone to sneaking up on me? I didn't hear a thing. And since when was his name Otay?"

"You're just being bitter, and his name's always been Otay. I told you before."

"Ugh, fine, whatever. The boy-toy can come with us. Otay," I snatched up his hand and shook it firmly. "I hope you die like a little bitch, and for no good reason."

He yammered something in reply that I didn't understand.

"He said he hopes you get caught naked up a tree and surrounded by predators."

"Oh he does?" I looked to my sister.

"Yes, I do."

I clicked my tongue and slowly turned back to Otay, who continued to grin.

"That was English."

"Yes."

"You speak English."

"Oh yes."

"How?"

"What, you think just because you've never been somewhere no-one else has? We get people coming and going from Arth all the time. Well, not Mahko specifically, but over in Vreyja you can find people from all sorts of places. Arth, Lilya, Syie, Wynlow. Sokak makes for a nice elsewhere when you want to get away from it all, or so I've been told."

"It's pronounced Earth, not Arth," I grumbled.

"That's what I said. Arth."

"I can't take this guy." I threw my hands in the air and stomped off toward the odd building.

"Just ignore him," Sis instructed. I trudged along faster.

***

The building looked nothing like the local structures, much more conical, and gave the impression of a tiny castle or tower. There was no door when I stepped inside, and no floor save the dirt and some dead grass that starved without sunlight. The ceiling was high except where it met the round walls, and the whole place was desolate. There were scuff marks and footprints, but no furniture, no bed roll or clothing rags, no signs of fire or food. The air was hot, dry and dusty.

"Either our beggar hasn't lived here in a long time," I said as the others came inside, "or alive isn't the right word to describe him. When was the last time anybody saw this raggedy man?"

"Couldn't say. I don't think it's been for a while." Otay shrugged, paused and sniffed the air. "Can anyone else smell that?"

"I can't smell anything," Sis said slowly, "but I can sense a minor god nearby. It's not inside the building though, nor is it actually manifested. I think it's just within the woods."

"I can't smell anything either." I frowned. "You having a stroke, farm boy?"

"No, no, I can definitely smell something. Metal. Corrosion on metal. Stale chemicals."

"Hey, Sis, has your passenger woken up yet?"

"Hang on let me check, okay." She closed her eyes, and held up her hand in a gesture of prayer. She remained silent for several minutes. When my patience had started to strain she finally spoke. "Blood of ours is below."

"Pardon?"

"She means there's someplace hidden under this place." Vengai-Ra rolled his eyes and crossed his arms. "Does there happen to be a convenient lift or is this going to be another demolitions job? Please tell me it isn't. Those always go wrong."

"There's bound to be a hidden way in around here somewhere, right?" I paced back and forth across the room, eyes closed and chin in my hand. It wasn't even that important, really. In fact it was pretty absurd when you think about it. A nostalgic tune came to mind, one with a 5:5 beat that put a spring in my step. Thinking in itself was absurd really. It's just an accidentally overcomplicated decision-making engine, decisions about how to make decisions. I threw my arm out and twirled. *Decisions, decisions.* Whatever felt best was the decision you wanted to make anyway so do it. *Oh, Ave Discordia.*

"Ko, shoot me."

I spun to the side, both arms overhead, and a bullet zipped through the space I would have dodged into but didn't. A hollow sound rang through the hovel like a hammer on a flat sheet of tin.

"I apologize but what just happened?" Otay said, dumbfounded.

"It's just a party trick my brother likes to do. Some sort of *feng shui* dance or something."

"It's nothing of the sort. I just randomly felt like avoiding a bullet." I let my arms drop beside me and walked over to where the bullet struck.

"You know it stings my pride every time you get me to do that. Believe me when I say that bullet should not have missed," Ko complained.

"Should do what? You shot where I was about to go. I just went somewhere else."

"People aren't meant to be able to do that."

"Only according to cheese-mongers and people who can't," I jeered. I kicked the wall where the bullet was stuck, and a section of it fell down with a clang. A thick metal wheel had been exposed, like the kind you'd find on an old naval vessel. "Hey farm boy, give me a hand." It took a quart of elbow grease to unstuck the wheel, but once loosened it turned easily. With each turn a section of the floor opened another few centimeters. A rank stench billowed out from this new entrance, like the floor of a slaughterhouse. The wheel gave a *clunk* and refused to be turned anymore, so that seemed to be as wide as the entrance could go. The farm boy looked a little green in the face.

"You alright there, hay-tosser? I'd have thought a rural kid would be used to that kind of smell," I needled him.

"What? No, it's not the smell. I mean, it is but," He groaned and wiped the sweat from his brow. More than just sweaty, he was all clammy like he'd been struck with the flu. "This place is making me feel weird. You travel a lot, yes? You . . . sound . . ." He coughed into his hand, and left his palm clasped over his mouth, "like the start of an old lullaby."

I glanced to Sis, but she seemed preoccupied with something. Her eyes were shut and she murmured under her breath. Was she praying? To who? Well, whatever.

"So Otay, I think you should stay—" I turned back to the local kid just in time to catch the top of his head vanishing down the hidden entrance. I raised my eyebrow at Ko.

"What? Was I supposed to stop him or something? You didn't say anything."

"Forget it, let's just chase after him. I have a real nasty hunch about this. Sis!"

"*Kim*? I mean what?"

"If you're done nakking to your imaginary friends, we may have a situation."

"You don't understand, that dea I felt earlier, it might—"

"Just hurry up and follow us."

Below what the wheel had opened laid a short, sharp staircase that led into a corridor. Flameless lamps hung along the wall, but only one still worked. The floor and walls and even ceiling were covered in countless old blood spatters and skid marks.

"What do you think?"

"I think a lot of living things were dragged wounded and flailing down here, once upon a time," Vengai-Ra said.

"Otay? Where are you?" Sis called out. I wrenched the one working lamp off the wall and held it up. The corridor went on for another ten or so meters and came to a heavy steel door. The farm kid was nowhere to be seen.

"Ko."

"On it," he walked up and pressed his hand against it, then went to a flat panel by the side of the door and rapped it with his knuckle. A deep rumble shook the floor beneath us.

"What did you do?"

"I didn't do anything," he held up his palms. "Best guess, this is an elevator. The door was open and the kid ran in. The unused piece of junk went off, took him most of the way down and broke. That rumble was it crashing after a short fall."

"How on Earth did you figure out all that?"

He tapped the side of his skull. "The machine in my head might be broken but it's not completely useless."

"So how do we get down there? Did anyone bring a jaws of life?"

"I can do better than that." He reached into his open coat and pulled out a wad of grey dough. With a bit of rolling he turned it into a long, thin tube and pressed it where the door and the frame met. "Should *probably* stand back a bit," he advised as he walked past, and then kept on walking all the way to the end of the corridor and up the stairs. The rest of us glanced at each other and ran after him.

"Do you have a detonator for that stuff or is it on a timer?"

"My body is literally swarming with teensy little robots. Broadcasting a signal to spark up is as easy as sneezing."

"I don't like the margin for error that implies."

"Achoo."

I'd hoped for a *boom*, but the sound was more of a muffled *crack* followed by a gust of wind.

"Lame, you didn't use the fun stuff."

"What, and bring the whole lair down before we've had a look at it?" He pulled out a long length of cable from his coat while he headed back, and coiled it around his arm. On the cable's end hung a round, magnetic clamp.

The door at the end of the corridor had been blown open, and just as Ko predicted it opened up into a dark elevator shaft. With an almost bored casualness he tossed the clamp end of his cable to the shaft's back wall, where it latched on, and gave the cable a few test tugs.

"I'll take point," he declared.

"Go right ahead."

He wrapped the other end of the cable around his waist and many-jumped down in the rock climber method. The rest of us followed in our own way. Since I'd my gloves on I just slid right down the cable and let them suck the brunt of the friction. I stepped off on the top of the crashed elevator with smoke rising from my palms.

We found an emergency hatch, which Ko kicked open, and we dropped through one at a time then headed out the stuck-open doors. This hidden place was a lab of some sort. Everything was glass or stainless steel. A few surgical trolleys had crashed into a pile in a corner, covered in torn sheets. Devices like glass-lidded coffins had been set along several rows across the room. I gave one a closer look but nothing was inside.

There was a control panel of some kind to the side, though, and a medical chart thing stuck over it. Both were written in some language I didn't recognize. Why in Hell hadn't I bought a gift of tongues for myself yet? I could afford one just from doing a few show fights, but man, some of those guys and girls were huge. It was hard to take down a twenty foot minotaurus non-lethally, and you got paid less if you cost them a perfectly good fighter. I refuse to lower myself to giving dancing lessons. That would be such a waste. Maybe I can just sell my body for a few nights. Ah but who knows what I might wake up to find done with my face. I could always just learn the languages the long way like Sis. It's still pretty easy for me compared to most people.

What was it Vengai-Ra said? Something about Cambions and developmental plasticity or something.

"Otay? Are you there?" Sis called out.

Oh yeah. Farm kid. Focus, Lach. I left the glass coffin behind and caught up to the others. The smell of blood was hardly noticeable anymore, but the lights were getting to me. We keep walking forward and passing more and more glass coffins but the lights never got brighter or dimmer. Yet each stretch was not exactly the same as the last and that just messed with me more. Ko had drawn a gun. Every so often I passed a column with a crack or a broken lamp or a fallen chunk of floor, and after passing fifty of them there was a nagging sensation that some of those were identical after all. Was that chunk of rock back there actually different from the chunk of rock we passed fifty meters back? How big even was this place? All these glass caskets were used to hold people, clearly, but who needed to hold this many bodies at once?

"There he is. Otay!" Sis ran ahead and for a brief, horrible second she vanished. I sprinted after her and she reappeared again. How? I took a deep breath. The air had grown weird and damp. Now that I looked at them, the lights were pretty blurry. Depending on how I tilted my head at them some even had a rainbow corona. It didn't feel cold, but this place had begun filling with mist.

"Otay, are you okay?" He stood over one of the caskets. His eyes, I knew those eyes at once. What he was seeing happened a long time before now.

"Sis, get back!" I yelled.

"What are you—?"

"No ways about it, come on!" I had to drag her by force until we were a good distance from the kid. Sis struggled, but not hard. Ko and Doc had fallen in alongside us.

"No really, explain!"

"Just look at him. Open your eyes and look," I hissed, and then cleared my throat. "Hey, buddy," I called to him, "how are you holding up there?"

His lips moved slowly as he mouthed something unspoken. His eyes twitched as he relived repressed memories.

"Come on, man. That all happened a long time ago. You've been living a great life so far, why spoil that now?"

"It's cold," he declared, and the mist grew thicker around him. This crap always happened.

"That's because its night and we're underground. Why don't you go home under a warm blanket till the nice hot sun comes up?"

"The imp and the witch came to town. They stole and hurt and ruined crops. The townsfolk gathered to chase them out," his voice came sharp and even.

"Oh no," Sis gulped, wet with sweat.

"That was a long time ago. A long, long time," I insisted. Damn it, I was used to Sis flying off the handle. I knew which buttons to press to keep her grounded, but how the hell should I know how this redneck's mind worked?

"They refused to leave. The witch, she let *him* out. No! She didn't let him out, she tore him out. Reached deep into the belly of the world and ripped him free."

"Who?" Ko asked.

"Shut *up, Ko,*" I hissed at him.

"Ayakee-Ikee, The thief of ages," Otay snarled, his lips curled back. His hands twitched and spasmed like their bones no longer fit. Frost had begun to form on his skin. It looked almost like fur. "So many people. Just withered husks left. Years stolen right out of them. My family."

"Everybody, slowly back away," I ordered.

"The only reason I'm alive is because the imp killed that monster himself before it got to me." Tears streamed down his face and froze as they fell.

"But you are alive, you're alive and you have so much to live for," I insisted, but even I didn't think it was convincing.

"Oh, I was alive. Alive and with nothing left, and that *thing*—."

"What thing?" Doc asked.

"Sometimes it had shape and others it didn't." He swayed as he turned, and his pupils were tiny black flecks. "It had no eyes and a mouth but no tongue. It found me, and it dragged me *here.*" He smashed his fist into the casket before him. A cloud of ice flung out from the impact.

"What did it do to me? What did it turn me into? You remember, don't you," he accused his reflection. "So much stolen and forced into your veins. So tight in your chest cutting off your breathing cutting off your blood. That needle which was so cold and so-so bad and made your tongue like metal from the forge in your mouth and that horrible shapeless thing looking down at you lying on your back for hours and suffocating, suffocating, suffocating from all this blood. Don't move, slip slip-out the metal might slip and you'll bleed-bleed-bleed all over your shiny slab your slab the only thing you have in the world is the thing that keeps you from falling forever. Don't bleed don't bleed don't make a mess on your only thing."

"We've lost him," I tsked.

His hair had frozen solid, and his skin turned blue from all the frost sticking to it. Ice jutted off from everything, jagged and translucent. Otay stood hunched over, clawing at his chest with his jagged ice claws. He'd already shredded his tunic, and drops of blood shattered at his feet.

My sister's anxiety had her almost in hysterics. Vengai-Ra held her stiffly with less bedside-manner than a junked mannequin. Ko had that crunching numbers look in his eye. Numbers like distance, velocity, and caliber. If Otay died here she'd blame herself forever.

"Ko, Ra, take her and get out of here."

"You're not actually being this stupid, are you?"

"If we're leaving, so are you."

"Oh come on, don't pretend you can't see exactly what the situation is," I asserted. "You've seen it plenty of times before. The farm boy just needs to let off a little steam before he explodes. We don't need to kill him. Please."

The gunman scowled and looked away, but still heeded my ask and ushered the others back to the elevator shaft.

"What are they doing to you?" Otay demanded of his reflection. "What are they doing? Who is this? Who is this in my head, in my blood? This isn't me. Let me out, this isn't my *head*."

Otay grabbed the casket with both hands and roared. The glass-topped bed screeched as he wrenched from the floor.

Cables and hoses hissed and cracked as they were torn away. The casket froze solid in seconds and he hurled it at a pillar. The metal and glass bed shattered in a glistening shower through the mist.

"I can't be him I can't be him I won't be him you're not him who is he I won't be you, I—" His voice dropped. Cool, cold, vicious. "I'm not me," he whispered with mixed horror and elation. I glanced behind me and made sure the others were gone.

"Hey, Otay. I guess you're pretty mad at everything right now." Walking up to him was like walking straight up into a blizzard, but I kept my back straight. He looked at me without a shred of interest. "Everything is bullshit and nothing matters and it hurts so much so you might as well break everything, yeah? Well I'm right here. Try to break me."

This wasn't about fun. This was a job for my old man, but the old man wasn't here. So I had to step up. I took a deep breath and pumped magick through my body. Gramps below, using magick made my body feel sweet, sickly and disgusting, like having nothing but candy and soda for days on end.

Otay lunged at me with his claws of ice. I caught his hands in mine and grunted. I could already feel the difference in strength. Tiny little teeth of frost dug into my palms like sharkskin. I reshaped the magick in my body and thrust it out my arms. My hands burst into flames, which blasted away his claws and spikes. A kick to the chest knocked him back a few steps.

"I'm not my father. I'm not a dragon. I'm just a scurrying salamander." I plucked from the aether a pair of curved blades, one reversed, and spread my legs to shift my weight. "Let's dance."

I didn't need to win. I just needed to hold him off until he tired out and calmed down. I could do that.

No I couldn't. It took fifty-five seconds to change my tune, after which I was fighting for dear life. I was pretty sure he'd never even used magick before, but there he went tossing that frost around like a pro and he just kept getting more creative with it. A micro blizzard covered his skin which shredded anything too soft that touched it, like my knuckles or the soles of my boots. He could work with a lot more at once than me, too. I couldn't manage more than one thing at a time with fire, while he could attack and defend at the same time. I needed to keep my fingers covered in flame just to stop from losing them to frostbite. On top of all that he was utterly silent. I expected him to be the kind of fighter than yelled and roared and shoved his whole heart into every swing but he didn't even breathe quickly. Once the fight actually started he ceased to make noise.

The only sound I got from him was when a desperate swing of my blade managed to slip by him and cleave right through his arm. The limb hit the ground with a wet slap and he clenched his teeth in a sharp hiss. For a minute he seemed to forget about me, and I hazarded a hope that he'd finally calm down. Otay bent down, picked up his severed arm and regarded it with detached curiosity. The limb soon froze in his hand and he hurled it to the ground. It shattered, and the shards of frozen flesh swarmed up around him to form a new shape. Floating in front of the stump of his elbow rotated a long, twisted lance of ice and frozen flesh. Smaller chunks spanned around it, like some sort of blizzard drill. I staggered back and laughed. I was so fucking screwed.

***

I was lying on my back when I came to. The first thing I did is touch my gut to make sure it wasn't sporting a new freight tunnel. My stomach was fine, and I slumped back in relief.

"I'm sorry. I was hoping to tire him out but I just couldn't keep up." I groaned. My whole body burned from cuts and frostbite and magus fury. Good thing we heal quickly.

"I'm just glad you're alive, and I, I really am grateful that you tried." I could hear my sister's voice but I couldn't tell where from. I'd lost too much blood.

"That green asshole led you to do some pretty messed up stuff, huh," I said. "I didn't want you to have to see the consequences. I mean, you just keep on spiraling more and more and blame yourself more and more. I'm you're brother for fuck's sakes. I have to try."

She didn't say anything.

"You're trying to form an apology and you're going to stop that right now. Ah shit, I think I got ice shards in my cornea or something. I can't see anything. Nothing I can't get fixed, but, what happened?"

"Everything is frozen. All the houses, all the trees," she paused, "all the people. It's just like you said. He couldn't vent fast enough, and he exploded."

"So the village is . . ."

"Dead," she said. "I have no idea where Otay is."

"Are you three alright?"

"We're fine, you lummox," Vengai-Ra laughed.

"Yes. Kali protected us," Ko explained.

"Well at least that's something." The sound of the minion duo's voices was comforting in its own right.

"Too little too late, perhaps," Sis said, her voice crestfallen.

"Hey now, don't forget why we're here," I retorted. "This wasn't completely fruitless."

"Oh yeah?" Vengai-Ra balked. "The lab is destroyed. Now we'll never figure out what happened to the stolen blood."

"That's not true at all, V-Ra," I sat up and rubbed at my currently useless eyes. "You saw exactly what happened."

"Yeah, the local took one look at the lab and went batshit."

"And that didn't ring any bells? After all this time?"

"What?"

"The old man. When Otay lost his shit it was just like Dad. Even fighting him was similar.

"So, what?"

I tapped my skull. "That's what they did with the blood. They tried to recreate the old man from the ground up. It was crude as black gold, but it got results," I frowned. "I'm not sure if they actually knew it worked or not."

"What do you mean?"

"I'd bet my left nut that was the first time he ever went up like that. The whole lab had been cleared out. Otay had been free long enough to make himself forget it all, and no one has seen that blind mute beggar for a while. I'd bet my right thumb this blind-mute is the eyeless thing with no tongue Otay mentioned."

I could hear Ko *hrm* as he mulled it over. "It sounded like it wasn't that long ago the beggar stopped showing up, though, whereas the farm kid had been back for a while, according to your theory."

"Right, so what I'm thinking is that the blob thing had mostly just been keeping an eye on the only even slightly promising test subject when something better came along."

"And what would that be?"

"Don't know, but it probably has something to do with the old man getting snatched."

"You think they're going to try cloning from the source?" Vengai-Ra asked.

"Dunno. Also a mystery is why the old man in the first place. Sure, he's tough, but there are plenty of more powerful lunatics out there."

"Maybe they're just obsessed."

"Ugh, groupies," I scoffed.

"So how are we meant to find where it went?" Ko asked.

"Actually, I may be able to help," Sis said. I turned to direction of her voice. "I tried to say something earlier but Otay ran off. That dea I sensed earlier, they're a god of wisdom and watching. If I summon them they can help us."

"Really? That sounds great. I'm," I yawned, "going to lie down for a bit longer."

"Yeah, you rest up. Once we finish up here we can swing back to the underworld and get you fixed up."

I listened absently as Sis invoked the local divinity. I had no idea what it looked like, but it smelled of tree bark and had a voice like an owl. I caught only bits and pieces. Something about the beggar learning where the man he's looking for is, some name beginning with D. The deity spoke a local language of course, but Cicula explained it to the others afterwards. I considered how if I'd been faster and just dragged the kid back out before he got to the bottom of the lab I could have spared him his fate.

After dismissing the goddess she summoned a demon to provide the last needed bits of information. Bifrons was who she conjured. He always was her favorite infernal informant. The Earl manifested in monstrous form, his skin nobbled and seeping thick, yellow fluid. By this point enough of my sight had returned that I could make him out. His skull-covered head turned to her, and he reshaped his freakish visage into something more human looking. She told him of the beggar and the lab, and what the goddess told her, and asked him to reveal where the beggar went. Bifrons obliged. A girl in white peered at us from over a hill.

17

Molto Vivace Inquisition

Draco

Angel. Servant of God. Or rather, messenger. His word is law. What the messenger delivers is law. Law of He. Law of Jealous-Wrathful. Lord of jealous-wrathful. Leer. A kind of gaze. The mode through which one covets. What does He covet? That which the power on high can't just make so. Can't, or won't? Angels. Servants. Worshipers. Righteousness. Rightness? Dexterity. High ground. Power on high. Angel. Sayers of the law. Which laws? Sin shall be met by punishment. Do you the devil's work? Who, though? The shining one or the adversary? Rebellion. Post-rebellion. Post-punk. Before that. Angel. Repent, and thou shalt be saved. Who is this peace-dove rap-tap-tapping, bid-kidnapping, violently crapping on my escape from bore. The angel Ancilla and nothing more. Leave poor Poe's ghost alone. She kept touching her waist, her thigh, her hip. There's nothing there. Now. Not then. There was then. A cockroach , space parasite, get it out get it out. Step back.

"Why are you looking at me like that?" the angel asked. Her wings twitched and resettled behind her. Were they prone to parasites?

"Like what?" I huffed. Staying composed had gotten exhausting. There was a mental scream feeding into its own frustration that didn't want to be voiced but just dwelt upon. Beside me, Drakkengard stabbed at the ground with a hand-blade. A small mound of tossed up dirt had piled up afore her.

"Like you want to break my bones into jagged shards and feed them to me."

"Ignore it. I was just reflecting."

"Is that right?"

"Yes. Really this place is quite conductive to introspection. I can't turn around without being slapped in the face by some symbol of myself. Say," I stretched, "you said you know how to hide yourself from this garden, right? Did you know beforehand, or were you too reflected more naked than you've ever been? What was it like? What does the mind of a coward turncoat look like?" There was a strange pain in my face, and it was not until I closed my mouth that I noticed how sore my face was from sneering. What else had my face been doing?

"You seem to have some strange ideas about me."

"You're not acting on YHVH's behalf."

"You're pronouncing it wrong."

"That is to say," I continued, "you're doing all this because you think it's what you should do regardless of what He told you. Or is it that He told you nothing? Didn't I hear something along those lines?"

"The workings of heaven are not for you to know."

"Yes, yes, the overworld is this, the underworld is that and the midworld is such, also how come no one talks about the weird worlds? I digress, the point is you're not a fallen angel, you haven't been tainted by hell's miasma. You also lack the bleaching of heaven's radiance. *That's* particularly odd for an angel. This place seems really important, you don't seem so important but you must be to know how it works so well. Finally, you gave back your sword." I stood up and tensed my legs. There was a good chance I would need to dive out of the way. Sure enough Ancilla's white eyes burned from her indignation, and she thrust her arm at me. There was something in her hand, a crucifix? Or a crossbow of some kind? There was no bolt loaded but there was a trigger, and a faint, glimmering gold thread drawn back from the arms.

"You know a lot more than you've let on." She glared.

"Know is far too strong a word. You admitted to most of that yourself. At least I think you did, in one way or another. The rest is guesswork. Less of a guess now, of course, you just confirmed I'm on the right track. All these mind games are such a pain, though, aren't they? Especially when my mind is where it's at, however, I'm not sure if that counts as a home advantage for me or against me. How about we just be honest? Here, I'll start with a simple question. What kind of a weapon is that in your hand?" I point.

She narrowed her eyes, and what I hoped was wavering resolve flickered across her face. That was probably enough inane babbling to defuse the situation. If it wasn't I'd have to resort to more drastic measures.

"In English I suppose you could call it a light caster. It collects God's radiance and pierces His enemies with it," she kept the weapon trained on me as she spoke. "Torture for a demon, but for most else it's more of a purifying force."

"Aye, it purifies pesky things like free will and desires."

"Of course it depends where I hit you and with how much. A big shot between the eyes can just pop your head like a maggot packed grape. Now I get a question, right?"

"Right."

"What were you doing before you fell in with demons?"

"I lived in a big house in the woods, mostly reading. Isn't this what those insufferable fruits are for?"

"It helps to cross reference, and some memories are harder to find than others. Also, that counts as a question of yours."

"Curses."

"What was the first demon you ever met?"

"That I know of? That would be the same demon you stabbed in the neck when I first met you. Or was it the back? I didn't get a good look."

"It was the neck, that's the most efficient spot. Also that was another question."

"Damn, you are good at this."

"How did you come by that house?"

"Honestly, I don't know," I shrugged. "Everything from before then is a fever dream. Is my wife suffering right now from what you stabbed her with?"

"No. It just put her to sleep for a while. So you may have killed the previous owners of the house and stolen it?"

"It's possible. How many times have angels and demons openly gone to war?"

"Three times. How do you know you didn't kill them?"

Lightning flashed. We stood in a long mausoleum, lined with stone busts twisted in pain and terror. All my victims. Another flash and they were gone.

"I'd still remember. Besides, my sister said the only person there had died in their bed a long time prior." My left hand twitched. "Now, are all angels created by YHVH or do you breed?"

"You're pronouncing it wrong. Yes, we can breed, we just don't. Angels aren't attractive to other angels."

"Nice tactical omission." We circled each other round and round like starving rival lions, desperate, I knew why I was but was she?

"Tell me about your sister."

"That's not a question. Her name was Diana. She was younger than me. She helped me get back on my feet. Tell me about Yeshua of Nazareth." Curt, to the point, betray no weakness.

She balked but hid it well. Hard to pin my motives, I hoped. "He was created to be an avatar for the Lord and placed within the woman Mariamme. He was a practical man, possibly an influence of being raised by a carpenter. He fulfilled his role on Earth and left. What happened to your sister?"

"She died. This is my last question. Was this garden once known by the name of Eden?"

Ancilla hesitated. Old habits conflicted with newer freedom. A bit of a gamble. A few gambles actually.

"Yes."

The dice rolled boxcars, bang on the money.

"As for my last question, how did your sister die?"

"I killed her."

Focus on the boxcars. Twelve dots. The gamble paid off, well, was paying off. This was no time to get caught.

"I'll be back with the next fruit shortly." She turned and left. Twelve dots. Add one more dot and you had thirteen, *and then there was music. Look alive, they're going to reprise your favorite song.*

18

Lullaby

Cicula

"So, where are we now?" Lach asked me.

With a grunt I blew a ball of smoke in my brother's face. "Pittsburgh, the city-state of steel," I answered. "You'd know this if you paid a sliver of attention. Did you listen to a word Bifrons said?"

"That dodgy Earl talks too much. I just leave it to you to sift through his grift. Pit's Bug, that's in Middle America, yeah?"

"More or less. I forget who controls it these days. It's all mob territory anyway, hardly matters which mob."

Ko took a few steps forward and breathed deeply the city air. His body was as tense as ever, but he bore an odd calmness about his face that left him looking years younger. Perhaps he preferred being around high buildings, or maybe this wretched humidity was much kinder to him than most. Then again he was the one walking around in an open coat and no shirt. Who knew how weather affected him.

"This is a good city," he whistled. "Boss never seems to take us anywhere nice. You been through here before?"

"No, well, I've been to Pennsylvania once or twice but not here specifically." I puffed idly while I got my bearings. So we came out of that derelict museum back there, three bridges went across the river down that way, and there stood some form of small park off the other way. I stomped out my smoke and lit up another.

"You do remember where to go, right?" Vengai-Ra asked. He wouldn't stop fidgeting with the buttons to his Hawaiian shirt.

"Do stop bothering me. I know exactly where to go. According to Bifrons what we want is in that park."

"I get that we can't just ask some great demon to find the old man for us, what with scandal and all because blah blah angels and shit." Lach mimed a flapping mouth with his hand. "But I find it hard to believe there isn't some other channel we could just go through to cut to the chase."

"Even if it's some neutral dea or deus, that's still another entity that someone else could find out about it through, and someone good enough to track Father no matter where in the cosmos he is would also be pretty high profile, and more likely for someone else to tap for information. We need to be discrete." With a rub of my brow I headed off toward the park. The others fell behind, or in my brother's case, beside.

"Yeah, I don't buy that and I'm damned sure you don't neither. You don't have to run apologist for him downstairs. I don't buy for one minute that Luci can't make his lot sit down and shut up if they heard some random angel absconded with his kid."

"Hey, kid, it's not like he has several million demons at his beck and call," Ko retorted. "Every one of those screw-looses has an agenda, and a lot of them are old enough to remember the Morningstar is far from the only keeper that underworld has had. The second the chairman stops dishing more than he gets is the second folks start whispering about maybe someone else could do a better job."

"Is that you speaking from experience?" Vengai-Ra asked.

"I'm just saying, you can't always assume it's the one giving the orders that's to blame for how ruinous they are. There's no such thing as an absolute authority. "

"Tell that to the angels' boss."

"And where is He now? Vamoosed? Gloomy here can speak for how many entities are convinced they're the end all on a given matter." He gestured to me.

"I'm not getting into this. We should really focus on the matter at hand." I sucked down a throatful of humid air and pinched my brow. "The park is just ahead."

"Don't you think you are advancing too swift, *l'ami*?" A cheary French voice. The girl from the subway emerged from a bus stop.

My eyes widened. "What are *you* doing here?"

"Spying on you, *au natural*."

"I'm pretty sure you're not using that phrase right," Vengai Ra interjected.

"Would you like that I were?" She tugged on the zipper of her hoodie. A flush hit my cheeks. Ko reached into his jacket and shot me a glance. I gestured for him to wait.

"Explain yourself."

"Sometimes the serendipity of prophecy needs a helper. Oh, *je m'appelle* Raanae, *enchante*. Of course I already know all of you." She clasped her bony hands together and beamed. Something rumbled within me. It sounded like—

Bloodless.

"You're undead," I spat. Nauseous sweat dripped down my face.

"*Oui*, very much so," she beamed, flashing spotless teeth. "You should try it some time."

"Go to Hell."

"When I am good and ready. All is for Toutates, long may he sit on the throne. Ah, the hour is now right. I'm afraid I have a grave to rob. One more thing though, I fear the blackwing has gone rogue. Do keep an eye out for her." She pulled her hood up and ran into the park. I gave chase, but she sank below the soil as though it were water.

By the time I caught up she'd already vanished. It was a fairly shabby stretch of dead or dying trees, choked by neglect. The weed ridden path wound through it, branching off to some building or another here and there.

"Also there are about eight people in position to ambush us." Ko slipped his hand into his coat.

"Raanae must have been buying them time." I harrumphed.

"Hey, we got to get scratching already?" My brother cracked his knuckles and lit up in a grin.

"Easy now, both of you. It'll be a huge pain to find out what if you kill them all," I warned. The back of my mind still puzzled over the dead girl. Hadn't she taking a huge risk by revealing herself? Or was that her true goal?

"Really? Seriously? You're such a knuckle-blocker."

I waved him away and stepped onto the park grounds. A mob of men and women swarmed around me as soon as I passed through the gate, each armed with a gun far bigger than any normal person would carry. I raised both my hands in surrender.

"We're not here for violence. I just want to talk to the woman who sleeps," I declared. I wet my dry lips and ignored the sweat on my brow. I'd my father's blood but not his flesh. A well placed slug could end me as easily as anyone else.

Don't fret, darling. I am here for you.

I'd rather not take my mortal coil for granted, if it's all the same to you, Kali.

"Tha' right? An' why should she want talk with you? Pretty sure she'd happier seeing your head made a spicket," one of the eight mocked. They all were clad in slacks, hoodies and the like, hardly remarkable for a street gang, yet their garb was in much better condition than I might expect. Stranger still, rather than just grey-tones and blacks they'd actually color coordinated. Even their dyed hair looked to be receiving proper care.

"Is it just me, or do these hooligans have a stylist?" Lach asked.

"Lach, please, I'm trying to negotiate here." Now why would one of theirs want to talk to us? I really should have thought ahead on that. "She's, ah, expecting us?"

"Try again, nebby," a woman clad in pastel tones stepped forward, her automatic rifle pointed at my chest.

"We want to talk to her about the shapeshifting blob thing that sometimes looks like a beggar with no eyes."

"Lach!" I hissed, yet the woman seemed satisfied.

"Yeah, a'right. Leave them come inside, yunz." She jerked her thumb skyward and her companions relaxed.

"Thank you, ma'am." I bowed my head but she just scoffed.

"I ain't a babushka yet. Call me Siri if you gotta but better still is you don't talk to me at all. You, and the uncle in the ugly beach shirt, you can come see, but I don't like the look a the other two."

"Hey, you just said we can all come in," my brother protested.

"Changed my mind, and I suggest you hurry up before I change it further. As long as no one gets slippy we'll have your buddies back in one piece."

"Relax, brother. We'll be alright." He grumbled, but relented. Vengai-Ra came over with a resigned sigh.

"No one ever appreciates good taste," he muttered.

"Salt-daddy, people with their heads chopped off have better taste than you." Siri let out a hoarse, hacking laugh.

We left Ko and my brother at the park's edge while the woman in pastel led us through. There were a few more of her fellows loitering around than you'd find in some typical small gang. It was far from packed but the park had a fair few of them about. You'd think a gang this big would move onto more ambitious things. Or perhaps they were not a gang after all.

Siri led us to a building. It might have been a factory or a stage hall in days passed but now it was no longer possible to tell. People squatted on its rooftop like painted crows, armed to the teeth and wasting time.

"Hey Grogface!" Siri bellowed to one of them. "Is the Lady busy?"

"She was chewing out Caleb earlier but pretty sure she done now."

"Righto. Alright you two, in you go." She yanked open a metal door. It looked to have recently received a fresh coat of paint and a good job of it too.

"Aren't you coming with us?" Vengai-Ra asks.

"What? Risk a whip up? Not on your life, buddy, get in." She slapped him hard on the back and forced him inside. I quickly followed after for the sake of avoiding such encouragement.

It was painfully bright inside, bright enough that I had to shield my eyes. Everywhere I look left my head swimming from colors and movement. Vengai-Ra seemed to have no trouble with it at all and just kept walking forward. I followed close behind him, only able to peer between my fingers. The air was sterile, almost harshly so, and awfully cold.

"You okay, kid?" he asked me.

"Yeah, I just— this place is real confusing on my eyes. What is it?"

"Eh? It's just a great heap of mirrors. It's not even a maze, they're just covering all the walls. Maybe you need glasses."

"Forget it. I'll be right in a minute."

"Nothing wrong with glasses. It gives you a more dignified look."

"A man in a Hawaiian shirt and a lab coat does not get to speak about dignity," I chided.

"You see? No one gets it."

"No one gets what?" A female voice demanded. This must be the lady. She sounded awfully young.

"My style," Vengai-Ra exclaimed.

"What? Oh lord, what *are* you wearing? Seriously, buddy, kill yourself. Literally kill yourself. No, wait, get naked and then kill yourself. No one deserves to be caught dead wearing that."

My eyes finally coped with the wall to wall mirrors and I looked up at the speaker. She appeared about my age, a bandana on her head and her shirt unbuttoned with just a sports brassiere beneath. Her hair was dyed a vivid green that matched her eyes. She stood, arms crossed, surrounded by her myriad reflections. Her bandana, shirt and pants all had colorful, tessellating patterns that caused her reflections to bleed into one another.

"You must be the lady who sleeps," I said.

"You calling me lazy, dippy brain?" She balked.

"No, I . . . , that's just the name we were referred to you by," I insisted.

"Huh? Huh? My name's Somnia. The crew calls me lady to suck up but no one would dare call me sleepy. I'd have them gutted," she made a fist and that fist rapidly melted into a blade.

"Vengai-Ra, is that . . . ?"

"Yeah. Looks like she's the same sort of living sword as Drakkengard. Do you think she has a master too?"

"Oh hell no," she butted in. "The only mistress I got is me," she jerked her blade-arm to the mirror closest to her. How odd that she didn't point to herself. Well, I suppose she did.

"So who are you creeps and what makes you think you have the right to cut into my me time?"

"There's a man who can change shape that has been known to take the form of a blind, mute beggar," I explained. "We heard you could help us find him."

"Oh yeah? Kind of a boring story. What's in it for me?"

"What do you desire?" I asked.

"Hah, that's a good one. I already get everything I want and I'm the best at what I do. Why should I help you, nebshit?"

"We know another of your kind. We could arrange for you to meet her," Vengai-Ra offered.

"Pass. Already met one other divinatelum, the creep you're looking for, actually, sniveling waste of metal he is, nowhere near as great as I. My money says your penknife and all the others are just as disappointing." She swung around and slapped the flat of her blade into her palm. "Lord, just thinking about that miserable scum is pissing me off. He makes me look bad by association." She swung around again, her livid face reflected a thousand times. "Hey, are you going to whack him? I suddenly want to go do it myself but if you'll do it for me I'll tell you about him and where he is n'at."

"I fully intend to kill him before it's too late," I said. The words came from my mouth sure enough, but it was not I who formed them.

Kali, what are you doing?

I speak true. I chose you for a reason did I not? If we can achieve this it will save much time and effort.

"Too late for what? You know what, I don't even care what what is. Just end that scum slurper."

You could at least ask me first before putting words in my mouth.

If you hesitated she may have withdrawn her help.

"So what can you tell us?"

We'll talk about this later.

"The wretch has laid his hap up in this old church," Somnia said. "My nebs say he's defaced all the remaining images n'at and repurposed it toward some goddess no one recognizes. Doesn't interest me. Other than that he's been sniffing around all the creepy berms, apparently wanting some way to hunt down some guy is what brought him to the 'Burgh and what he's still doing here." I shot a glance at Vengai-Ra.

"That sounds like our guy."

"Of course he's not there now. I've had a few of mine keeps tabs on him since I met him, figure out just how bad he's got me looking by association, last I heard he's sniffing around Duquesne bridge. Seems like he may have found who he was looking for. Well, that was an hour ago. Who knows if he's there or back or maybe even dead already?" Her vicious smirk repeated itself over and over on the mirrors all around us.

"We need to hurry. How do we get there?"

"Just follow the highway about half a mile west and go south. Can't miss it, big ugly yellow thing with the paint peeling."

"Right, let us go."

"With your leave, Miss," Vengai-Ra gave a short bow and we made our exit, to which Somnia paid no attention, already distracted by her own reflection. Her followers watched us from their posts and perches. They carried a bored sort of anticipation about them. Perhaps they were hoping their leader would change her mind about letting us go, but the order never came. We left the park behind us and reunited with Ko and my brother.

"Go well?" Lach asked.

"Yeah, our beggar has been seen on a bridge not too far from here," I explained. "We might be able to catch up if we hurry."

"Better move. Come on," Ko turned and hastened away from the stronghold.

***

The city stood so still while we ran through it. The traffic was moderate, but without irregularities. There were a few pedestrians here and there, too, but none so much as looked up as we passed. Even the air was still. It's different when it's raining. Without rain the world moves too slow. The bridge came up ahead. Huge, painted yellow, and even the way it loomed was saturated in slowness. It would be better if it just stopped, if it stopped being drawn out so thin and just stood still.

Lach slapped me on the back and ran ahead. There were only a few people on the bridge's walkway. The clang of his boots on metal was louder than the passing traffic. Of the ten or so people on the bridge my brother went direct to a tall man leaning over the

131

rail. On the other side of the man another figure loomed, a disheveled creature in tattered robes the color of wet rust.

Lach tackled the man to the ground, and a warped blade came down after him. A bullet roared from beside me. It hit the robed thing in the flank and knocked it off its feet. I hadn't even noticed Ko draw the rifle. Vengai-Ra and I ran over to help the man get up. A lump caught in my throat at the sight.

"Father?" I balked.

"Pardon?" he frowned.

It was his face. It was definitely his face. Yet the hair was fair and the eyes were gold. The voice, it wasn't a different voice but it was being used differently. Different playing styles on the same instrument. Nearby, Lach tried to pin the robed figure down, but it slithered out of his grasp. Literally slithered, its limbs suddenly boneless, and it rose to an exhausted slouch with a raspy hiss. Curved, rusted blades extended from both its sleeves. From their tips dripped liquid metal with a caustic stench. The robed thing seemed uncertain how to proceed.

"What the hell is going on here?" My brother exclaimed.

19

Inhibitory Gnosis

Draco

The fruit was rotten. It was clearly rotten. Ancilla said nothing. The skin was covered in scales and the flesh sagged and was hot to touch. How did she not notice that? I couldn't move my hands. Just holding the thing made my stomach writhe. I could hear it. Couldn't she hear it? The ground rumbled. The cage couldn't keep shut. It was a gamble. If the parameters were the same the outcome should be the same. I couldn't move my hands.

"Drakkengard. Please make me eat this fruit."

"Are you sure, Master?"

"No. I cannot believe how stupid this is. Please make me eat. I can't do it on my own."

Ancilla watched from her stead by the stream. Was she passive or impassive? It was on the mind and I was in my mind and how couldn't she hear the cage groaning? What did that angel think she would see?

"You don't want to."

"That's why I need you to. If it pleases you to obey me, make me eat the fruit."

"Yes, Master." Drakkengard's features became black and undefined. She touched my hand, so cold against my skin, and flowed over my flesh. Her liquid metal covered my fingers, my palm, and up my arm. She became a gauntlet over my right hand and the coolness of her touch helped keep calm. Against my volition and according to my wishes my arm moved.

"Ancilla, I will burn from this," I warned. My left arm was already eking out smoke at the thought. "Stand well back." My arm brought the fruit up to my mouth and forced it in. The taste was so vile it made me gag but my hand forced it deeper down my throat until I had no choice but to swallow. Fire spilled between my fingers as the last of the fruit was forced down.

And then there was music.

***

I pulled Drakkengard out from the Abomination's servant, as did the She-Devil to her damned blade. My sister's knife stayed embedded in the back of his skull.

"Come on, Malign!"

I had to scream to hear myself. Everything was so loud— my body burning up, the Abomination's presence, my thoughts and the screeching cage.

"I've slain you pet! Come down here and *die*," I addressed her in the tongue we spoke when I was young. It tasted like bile and filth but I couldn't remember anything else. Everything was so loud. The Abomination shrieked and wailed until her sword had no choice but to get back up no matter how much pain he was in. Everything was so disgustingly loud and everyone just wouldn't stop yelling. Even I, though I couldn't tell what I screamed. It was in a language I no longer knew. I was burning up. My awareness was so singularly upon the Abomination that I could spew filth.

It was so loud. There was too much noise to grasp anything but the need to harm her. Whatever sensations wracked my body were too scrambled to name. Some might be pain. It didn't matter. Cut and burn and sever and gouge, spill her guts, spill her blood, get her out of my head. Stop laughing! Crack her head, she still laughed. Cut it off. Cut that laughing head off, but her sword stopped me. The chance was gone.

The Abomination fed. With that wicked light she fed on my heart and mind and self and nothing had changed. I was still in the cage, still her plaything, still impotent of anything but her pleasure. She called me the unspeakable and fed again. I burned. A fire needs fuel and there existed not a single part of me that I couldn't burn. If I couldn't kill her I'd become ash trying. Better dead than in the cage. She fed on even my flame. May she die bloated and hideous. I sent her sword away. Even unarmed she made a mockery of me, batting away Drakkengard with her bare hands. She fed again. Why was it so *LOUD*?

Something cut through the cacophony. A plea for help.

Sister, wounded by the Abomination. Not fatally, just to mock me even more. I sealed the wound with my burning flesh. So little of me left to burn, just scraps hanging off charred bone. If I could at least ugly the Abomination with the last of me, I could accept that. Whoever came after me could suffer her instead.

It was worthless. There was not enough of me. There was nothing left to burn. She was still mocking me, still calling me unspeakable things. She even took Drakkengard away from me, turned her upon me. I ceased.

We began. The Abomination had violated our covenant. Mine steel had been turned against mine flesh. The covenant must be re-established. I and I are we, who are I, as is we and I. *Ego parameters restored.* Metal intertwined with flesh. Steel replaced lost blood. A duet of splintered souls.

We had nothing left to burn. *That's okay.* We started with nothing. *We have nothing.* Nothing could burn forever. *It is the nothing we burn.* It is with nothing that we cut. We had only nothing for her to feed upon.

Two visions I beheld. In one I stood in the garden once called Eden. My flames burned white hot. Ancilla was alarmed. In the other I was standing before the Abomination. I cut her. Once, twice, four times, eight times, again and again and again. I cut her body into cells. I cut her cells into atoms. I cut her atoms. I cut what was left. I cut her down into nothing. I burned that nothing using nothing as fuel.

"And out of the corner of my eye where I did not focus was Diana. She, too, was taken apart when I ended the Abomination. Lascivus was able to protect herself from where she was but my sister was not."

"How are you able to speak?" Ancilla demanded.

"It's like a lucid dream while sleep walking."

The tower began its collapse.

"Interesting, I can control the speed, now."

Where the Abomination's body had stood a great force rapidly expanded, powerful enough to wipe out everything still harmonious. We had nowhere to escape. I escaped to nowhere. I took Lascivus and fell into nothing. My last glimpse of that place was a figure falling—

Wait. Wait. What was that?

A figure falling—

Again.

A figure—

No.

***

I ended the memory.

"No," I cursed. Someone else had survived. Someone else had flung themselves from that tower before it had been consumed.

"What?" Ancilla demanded, but I paid her little heed.

I could still feel it. The memory had ended but that feeling of nothingness remained in my head. *That nothingness that everything came from and will return to. A void state indexing existence.* The nowhere in which I found myself with Lascivus, which she helped me escape from. I now possessed an awareness of that place of nonexistence— that Void. I brought us to it, it to us.

"What did you just do?" Ancilla cried out. On the horizon in all directions darkness encroached, consuming this garden. White-hot flames wreathed my left arm.

"That can't be right," I muttered aloud. How could someone else have survived?

"What can't be right? In the name of the Lord tell me what is going on, else damn you," Ancilla charged toward me.

"Where? I just need to understand better. There are things and there is nothing and it all returns to nothing and time is relative so the difference between a given thing and nothing is next to nothing when viewed as part of all, *gah*," I gritted my teeth. Maintaining this mental state grew harder with every second. "There." For a horrible, agonizing moment I could sense everything on Earth, and found my fugitive.

Ancilla lunged at me in a tackle. We fell into nothing and out the other side.

***

I hit the ground and rolled. The metal surface crashed against my arms and left them half-numb. I faltered twice but managed to raise myself to my feet. Cicula, Lach, Vengai-Ra and Ko were around me. Ancilla picked herself up near me. There were two others. One was a drastically familiar face, the other what I'd feared—a certain robed, wretched slave.

"You're here. That explains some things," my doppelganger gritted his teeth. I drew out Drakkengard through the Void from where my children left her, the physical Drakkengard not the one in my mind, and leaned against her.

"I thought I left you back on Rhy," I remarked to my doppelganger. "No, not a thing to mind, get that one!" I lurched toward the hooded man. He uttered a shrill shriek and swerved toward me, blades outstretched. There was a sound like a cannon from Ko's gun and he went flying back. "Get him!" I screamed. My head burned and my vision swam. I took another step and crumpled to a heap on the ground. Three more cannons fired. A shriek and a splash followed.

"He jumped!" someone yelled.

"Oh no you don't, Deserere," I hurled myself to my feet and lunged for the rails. Something snatched me by the back of the neck and pulled me into a stranglehold.

"In the name of the Lord everyone stop, or I'll wipe his head clean of every scrap of self." Something hot pressed into the side of my skull. Ah, that odd crossbow of Ancilla's. Ko pointed his anti-material rifle at the angel's head. Lach tensed up and Cicula made a prayer gesture with her hands. My awareness of the Void slipped away. I had no hope of catching Deserere now.

"Draco, just what manner of inane molten mess have you dropped on me?" My doppelganger growled.

"Let's not be too hasty. I don't think any of us have all the facts right now. First, you, ah, me, ah, curses what did Lascivus say you were? Nemisian?"

"Call me Eltanim," the man with my face declared.

"Okay, Eltanim is some kind of shapeshifting gargoyle. He is supposed to hunt me down."

"Funny how that works," he observed. "If I kill you, I go back to sleep. I'd rather like to avoid that. Being your hunter gives me a rather unique outlook I'd hate to lose," he shook from the strain of not lunging for me. He was a child of Nemesis, who could fathom what his existence must be like? Perhaps Lascivus has a better idea.

"Wait. Wait a moment and please allow me to verify something," an unpleasant wheeze rattled my voice. My head and body ached like I hadn't slept in days and that could be important. "Just how long has it been since the choir girl here took me?"

"We've been trying to find you for a week, old man," Lach answered.

"Ah, thank you Lach. Cicula, be a dear and summon your mother would you?" I instructed.

"I said don't move!" Ancilla barked.

"*Oh*, there's no need for that, husband," growled a voice, hollow from hunger and heavy with power. I was already intoxicated on the first note. Strong arms ripped me from Ancilla's grasp and placed me on the ground, then resounded a crack like a hammer hitting concrete.

There stood Lascivus, crushing both Ancilla's wrists in her hands and with a clawed foot against the back of the angel's head. Her dusky, emaciated body writhed with countless gnashing mouths. Thick miasma rolled off her enormous wings and blurred the air. The skin around her small horn was cracked and inflamed. Had it gained a little length since last I saw it? And it seemed to come to two points, not one.

"You are so very lucky I'm sober, feather-tits," she cooed to her captive. "Else I wouldn't think twice about twisting off your pretty little skull. So here is me thinking twice. Is there any good reason I shouldn't murder you for messing with me and mine?"

"Deserere is alive," I coughed and rubbed my jaw where the ground had struck it.

"Who? So?" The demoness turned to me. Her skin was stretched taut over her bones revealing the topology of the skull beneath. It was a rather nice skull.

"Deserere, the sword of *her*, of—" I coughed again, and pulled myself up. "Malign."

"Again. So?"

"You don't understand. He's the same thing as Drakkengard. He shouldn't be able to even remain conscious without a link to her," I exclaimed.

"I think I got lost a while back. Can we skip to the point?" Lach pulled out an apple and obliviously bit into it.

"If Deserere is up and active it means she's still alive."

"There's another thing." The angel groaned from under Lascivus' talon. The demoness removed her leg and lifted the angel by the top of her head.

"Yeah?"

"I saw the memory where you killed this Malign person. I don't know much about her sword, but, okay would you please put me down?" Lascivus stared into her eyes but released her head. "Thank you. As I was saying, there was one there I did recognize."

"You what?"

"That other girl. The one not here right now. She looked just like the one who persuaded me Draco was a danger worth removing."

"My sister?" I raised myself to sitting and slumped forward, my head in my hands. I couldn't think. There was too much going on to twist my head around.

"Oh? So does this mean that kid's alive too?" Lascivus asked. She seemed so calm, and composed even when mere seconds ago she'd been about to decapitate my abductor. This is what she was like when sober.

"I wish I could give a straight answer," I groaned. "I remember so little from back before. I can't even remember how I escaped. By the time I was able to remember things again she was there, and had always been there. She was my sister and I adored her, but I can't say where she came from. She could have been another child of that abomination or she could have been just another victim or who knows what. I didn't care, didn't even question it."

"It's possible she was some kind of mass produced clone, and who the angel met with was just another from the same batch," Vengai-Ra suggested.

"What is this? What is this?! The universe mocks me. Thrice curse all these things," I wailed.

"Crying won't do anything, but you're right. Everything about this is stupid. Let's just go home. Any complaints from the feathery hypocrite?" Lascivus turned to Ancilla.

"It seems I've been played just as much as you. I'm not happy about this myself. I'm not happy about letting that one go, for that matter, but I'm willing to make an exception." She walked away but collapsed after a few steps. My doppelganger, sorry, Eltanim caught her.

"You're hurt and exhausted. This lot have their own resources but you look like you could do with a healing hand." He looked back to us. "Get out of here already before I give in and take a swing at you after all."

"Just one question first, Ancilla," I said, leaning against Lascivus and using Drakkengard as a crutch. "I'd like an answer after being forced to relive all that. So go on, judge. What was your verdict? Am I irredeemable evil?"

"You're a fool, sinner," she said in a weary groan. "It was never about your morality. What matters is how dangerous you are. How likely you are to hurt again, and sinner, you got lucky, if it weren't for this fracas," she glared at me with hardened eyes, "I would end you without hesitation.

Second Movement

Rondo

20

Piu Progeny

Lascivus

"So how's the situation with Tammuz?" I asked, then gulped down my glass of mead. The spicy drink warmed my belly and took the edge off the rising hackles. The private rooms of the ale-palace offered the best privacy in the Bolgias, but damn if their scarce decorations don't make every visit feel like an interrogation. Tammuz, while now a demon, was once known as the Mesopotamian god Dumuzid.

"Getting worse," Beelzebub grumbled. That he remained bound in the form of a child only enhanced how pissed off he looked.

No matter who I needled they all refused to spill the beans on just what bet it was that fly-boy lost. In the meantime I doubted I'd ever get used to seeing his ancient mannerisms expressed through the body of a small brown boy in overalls.

"So we still can't find Ngeshtin-ana? It's not like her to just go missing." I scowled. Ngeshtin-ana was his sister, once known as Geshtinanna. The goddess Innana had cursed the siblings such that each must spend half the year in the underworld while the other was free to go.

"Until we do find her, Tammuz is stuck down here. That *rhaka* sister of his has made things rather difficult."

"That's assuming this is her choice. More and more of our people are just up and vanishing the past few years." I downed another shot of mead.

"Yeah and now we've got scores of legions with no one properly supervising them."

"Legions of legions and no legionnaires nor legion heirs," I snickered.

"The smarmy brat you married is rubbing off on you. This is serious. We can't just appoint someone without giving anybody more authority than we want them to have and disrupting our infrastructure. We can't just do nothing either. We have to take action against the Overworld!" He slammed his kiddy fist down with a loud crack and chunks of stone went flying.

"You can't just assume the angels are behind everything." I pushed my fingers into my brow and sighed. "As much as I'd love to see their little cloud city burned down and pillaged, another drawn out war would leave us too weak to avoid a coup. We don't have the forces for a decisive victory."

"With every general we lose, the chances of us surviving if they strike first plummet. If we hit them with everything at once, everything we've got, they wouldn't have a chance to turn the tide against us."

"And if it isn't the angels after all, whoever *is* trying to undermine us could sweep through and have their way with us rickety splat." I paused. "I hear rumors the science is coming back. Those hermits in Luna's shadow are suddenly taking an interest in Terra again. That doesn't sound like something the choir would instigate. I mean it might just be another hunt for fresh talent but it's still suspicious."

"So what do you propose?" He glared. "Keep spending all our resources looking for the missing in utter futility? All our best seers and scryers have produced naught but dead ends."

"That's if they're even being honest." Oh look at that, I'd already refilled my drink. How gracious of me.

"They wouldn't dare lie to the Lord of the Flies." He pumped himself up as much as the body of an eight year old could. At least I finally talked him out of wearing that stupid cape.

"Well, that depends on who they are lying for." With eyes closed I sculled the fresh glass and refilled it. One of my most practiced three motions.

"Just what are you implying, Little Horn?" Someone please tell this ancient child you can't pull off the bulging eye thing when you have the face of a *putto*.

"Thousand times and again, don't call me that." I prodded him in his tiny chest. "I can't stand it even when Dad does."

"Still running away from who you are?"

"No, from who you all want me to be. You're lucky I'm bothering with any of this at all." Some of the liquid sloshed over the edge as I waved my glass around.

"Yes, wedlock does seem to have made you settle down at least a trifle. What is your fool husband doing anyway?"

"Still off messing around *in vacuo*. He's convinced he can find a way to just unmake all his problems. If only all of us were so lucky. He used to be more fun than this."

"I always said you two were a poor match."

"Hey, you were just complementing how good it was for me."

"Yes and imagine how much greater you could be with a consort actually worthy for you. Maybe it's time you find another."

"What, someone like you?" I scoffed, "keep dreaming dung lord."

"Bah, I was this close to having your hand promised to me when you decided to get involved with that *Môre*."

"No you weren't." I laughed. "And even if you were I'd have just left."

"Like mother like daughter."

"Like you'd know."

"*I* wouldn't have cursed you."

I bared my teeth at that. Word gets around too much down here. "We patched that up. Shib be reconciled." Crap, I was slurring again.

"That doesn't excuse him. It was an accident that occurred though his fault of character." His boyish face leered. It was a grotesque look for him that made my stomach ache. Maybe I should just punch him? Eh, I'd see where whim took me after three more drinks.

"This isn't about him," I reminded the smug lord. "We're here about the abysmal state of affairs in the Abyss."

"I told you, you're even starting to talk like him."

"Quit changing the subject, jelly creep. We need to figure out what to do about whoever's trying to disrupt us."

"That's the problem with demonkind, always one bad day away from giving themselves to chaos." He stared off into the distance of the adjacent wall. I think he forgot there wasn't a window there. "Hey, you're a demon same as the rest of us."

"Not by choice. The bearer of Tetragrammaton will rue what He did."

"That's what they all say. *Ooh, big meanie in the sky chased me outta the devotion market. Remember back when I was gorgeous and got to boss humans around all day?* Now pay attention you miserable old child. You can circle jerk over the old days with your *mancala* club later. Our mysterious pain in the ass, remember?"

"How about that little hushed up incident with your husband a while back. It's been what, four years? You may say that peace-dove acted alone, but it may still be part of this Overworld plot."

"My daughter said she was looking into that further." I yawned and stretched my arms. "Well, I guess I should check in on her and see what she's turned up."

"It is rather a useful family you've put together, I will give you that." He tossed a snide smirk.

"I didn't make it just to fill in Hell's toolbox, you buggering psychopath. This is my flesh and blood we're talking about."

"It never hurts to have a few more pounds of flesh for when the need arises."

"You see? That's the attitude. That right there. Screw this, we both got better things to do." I snatched up the bottle of mead and bailed.

***

My daughter's new home had certainly grown since last I'd visited. It started off as a small temple but now it had flourished into a big-ass sprawling fortress. The Citadel of Crimson Moon she called it, a pretty gaudy name if you asked me, but she'd never been good with names. I exited the portal into the station, a big multi-sectioned building with transport sigils carved onto the ground in neat little arrays, filled with colorful comers and goers. As soon as I stepped out of the flaming circle I got pounced on by an attendant.

"I bid you welcome, Mistress Lascivus." The short Unseelie woman bowed. "Had we expected your arrival we might have prepared better to receive you."

"Spare me the claptrap formalities, dark elf. This isn't some sort of inspection I just have something to discuss with my daughter."

Most elvish I'd known had had the same view on their glamours that demons do, it was weird to see one so *identifiable* even if she wasn't naked, so to speak. The only exception was that infernal continent on Rhy with the magic ban. Yet there she stood, ears pointy and eyes big an' black like it was fashionable.

"Of course, I will take you to her at once." She led me out and we set off toward the main temple.

The community was pretty bustling. The main commodities seemed to be covered by one store or another, although as I understood she ran the place on a barter system rather than any currency. There were inns and shops and a marketplace and a decent sized storage house stood taller than most of the other buildings. The populace was an even bigger hodgepodge than

Hell. There were demons and elves and vamo, humans from Earth, Al'Juran, Wynlow and other places, even some of those stuck up felin folk from Lilya or Syie skulking about the place—probably exiles. I noticed a distinct absence of undead, however. I guess that was one prejudice she still maintained. In the meantime the mixed populace was reflected in the buildings. The main temple and the few buildings around it were clearly infernal, you could tell from the spikes, gargoyles and parapets, but everything outside that was an architectural kaleidoscope. There was something disquieting about crystal towers being right next to brick boxes, gothic manors, and ivory-glass yurts.

At the main temple, clergy pattered about in pious clothes performing whatever duties they had. As we climbed, the first few floors showed themselves to be places of worship and tribute to my daughter's goddess, but above those were the libraries, then administration, and at the top my escort left me at my daughter's antechamber.

"I'll just make sure she's ready to receive you." The unseelie girl bowed again and disappeared through the door. I took a long, deep gulp of my mead and set the empty bottle by a vase.

The door opened and a young girl with grey hair ran past me. My daughter stepped out after, a hand on her hip, and sighed. Beside her walked that skull-faced demon Bifrons. She'd been consulting him a lot during her investigation.

"There she goes. I hope she doesn't get into too much trouble." My daughter laughed. She saw me standing there and quickly straitened her tailcoat. "Ah, Mother, I hope I didn't keep you waiting."

"Nah, I've only been here a few minutes. A pretty nice place you've got here."

"I'll just see myself out," Bifrons chuckled and walked off.

"Yes, I'm sure I'll see you soon anyway."

"Oh I assure you," he flashed a bony grin before stepping out the door.

"Oh, Mother, if you see my daughter again I advise you keep an eye on what's on your person. I hate to admit it but she has awfully sticky fingers."

"It's not like I have anything worth pinching." I shrugged.

"That's good to hear. Um, what brings you here if you don't mind my asking?"

"We can't find Ngeshtin-ana. That means she can't take Tammuz's place and let him leave the underworld, which in turn means he can't do any of the jobs your grandfather wanted him to do. What's more he's refusing to cooperate until she is found. So that's another important demon out of commission and it's making waves. Awful, awful waves that stink of piss and fishbones and any day now our shitty dingy could get punctured by one. Anyway, since all these cowards getting kidnapped or killed or whatever might be connected to Draco's kidnapping a while back I wanted to know if you'd made any headway into investigating that golem or his mistress."

Her eyes widened a bit and she hung her head. "I'm sorry, Mother. Kali is tracking, er, is Father with you?"

"No, the dead weight fop wants as little as possible to do with this. He won't even talk about it. I think he's gone a bit paranoid-peculiar about being your grandpa's bitch. Oh, bring some of those here." A passing serving boy carried a tray of plump red grapes and I waved him down. The too-sweet fructose burned my throat in the fourth-best way.

"I see." Cicula frowned. "Well, through following the connection between my blood and hers, Kali is trying to track Malign. She's my grandmother after all. Every now and then Kali gets a reading on her somewhere on Earth but it vanishes before a location can be pinpointed." She tapped a finger to her cheek. "I think whatever protection she has only slips up when she comes or goes. We're hoping once we can bring up Kali's strength we'll have better luck. That's what all this is about." She gestured to the building around us. "Even with me as her avatar she's still a dea like any other.

The more people we can get worshiping her, the easier things will be. I mean, we can't force people to believe, so what we do is we do our best to help the people here who pray to her. Oh, and there's also the matter of repaying Grandfather. Ownership of the moon's underworld and building this citadel didn't come cheap." Her shoulders slumped and she sighed. "Later today I'm helping out an expedition of his as part of paying this all off."

"At least it's not hopeless," I offered, pretty meager condolence.

"I'm sorry," she dipped her head again.

Damn eager-to-please kid being all impressionable. You're like twelve, or, twenty. Give or take a decade you're still under a century. Either way I'm not unloading any real responsibility on you here, yeesh.

"Chin up, kid. You're doing what you can, yeah? There's not much else I can want off you. Or rather, ask of you."

"So what will you do now?"

"Try to think of something else to try, I guess. Meanwhile I'll have to run damage control. A lot of people are starting to wonder if it's in their best interests to keep your Grandfather as the Underworld's keeper and that means muggins here has to go around currying favor and trying to find a workaround for their problems." A drink found its way to my mouth. Now how did that happen?

"Shouldn't he be doing that himself?"

"Doing what? Oh, right, running his own thrice damned underworld. That thing he's meant to do. Look, he's doing the things only he can do, while me and the rest of his house are doing everything else to help," I recited. At least that's what he'd said, some days even I wondered. *Crap, did I say that out loud? No? Good.* That deserved another drink.

"Somehow I still have doubts," my daughter scratched her chin.

"So what is your opinion on this anyway?" May as well prod a bit while I was here, see where the wind blows. "You don't have to stand by it or anything, just say what you think about it."

"About the missing nobility?"

"About if it's related to Draco's abduction four years ago. You couldn't track him either, yeah? Cause of that garden thing."

"Well he said he sealed that place away pretty securely inside that fortress he built in the Void. For what his word's worth at any rate."

"Well that's one weird ass mind garden. How do we know there aren't more out there? There could be some straight up freak groundkeeper just sowing these mind garden-majiggies all over the cosmos."

"Father has been awfully tight lipped about the specifics, but he says he's confident it's a rare phenomenon. He won't say any more than that, though," she pursed her lips.

"He knows more, though?"

"For sure" She sucked on the bit of a long, thin pipe and breathed out a trail of red smoke. "His excuse was that so long as he kept some secret of that angel's she'll owe him for it."

"Owe him what?"

"Some kind of favor or another, I don't know. You know how he is about debts. Treats them like vintage stamps."

"It seems like he's got a better mind for politics than me some days. Well, only some. All the other days he's babbling nonsense and pissing people off and quoting crap about bourgeois complacency so it's not like he'd last a week." Time for another drink.

"Well, that's true. Again, I am sorry I can't help you more, mother."

"Don't sweat it, champ. It's not like you're my last resort. Come on, while I'm here let's have a sit-down. I got a bit of time to spare. Well, not really but who's gonna grudge me."

"Alright, I'd like that."

She showed me to a nice little lounge of nice looking couches, and called for an attendant to bring food and wine. As we sipped and supped and gossiped, conversation turned from the future to the present to the past. I made a quip about the first daemon war, and Cicula got an odd look on her face.

"What's with you and angels, anyway?" she asked. "I mean, why do you hate them so much?" It seemed like something she'd been wanting to ask for a while.

"Hey, I don't hate them. Well, not all of them, not in a personal way at least. It's just a difference of ideals. It's the principle of them. I got no problems with fallen angels, most of them, they've renounced those ideals." A deep drink.

"Is that it?"

"Yes. No. Well you know how it is." I lazily waved my hand. "I've just got unpleasant associations, yeah? Betrayal, long time ago, silly that I even still care. Everyone has stuff like that."

"I don't think it's silly."

"That's sweet, but I disagree." I sat up on the arm of the couch. I could have ended it there, but maybe I was drunker than usual, or maybe she reminded me too much of myself as a child, but a very, very long list of similar discussions I'd had with both my parents went rattling through my train of thought. All of which ended at just that, as though we were just coworkers at a corporation. *Fuck 'em*, what's the point in being a parent if you don't do a better job than got done to you? "There was this girl, Lo—" I coughed, downed a tall, stiff drink, and another, until I could force the name out. "Lorica. I was still young, didn't have a proper grasp on what I meant to people. Politically, I mean. Lorica, well, I thought we were friends. She thought we were something a little more. We both just took for granted that we were on the same page. One day she suggests going far away. I thought it was just an adventure. So off we went, exploring the caves of Megiddo. Someone suggested we exchange swords. It might have been me. I don't know. Such a stupid thing in hindsight, probably just confirmed her delusions." I forced a laugh. "We built a forge each, smithed away, scarcely exchanged a word until we were done."

"So Impiocassus-?"

"Is the sword I made. Pretty good piece of work, I say. When it came time to exchange them, she started to crack. We'll be together forever all that." I gagged.   My skin prickled with memories of touch. Scraping my nails against it seemed to help.

"Did she . . . "

"Fuck no." I spat that more harshly than I intended. "Well, you can imagine how it went. One thing led to another and I put the sword she'd made me through her skull, took the sword I'd made and fled." Another stiff drink, made it a double. "Only it turns out that when the Devil's daughter vanishes, after last being seen in the company of an angel, well, war tends to break out. Stupid shit. So I emerged from the mountain, clothes torn, covered in angel blood, right into a battlefield. No one had any idea we'd been right there. Megiddo is a troublesome place like that. It's all just so stupid. War broke out because I was naive and trusted my friend. Now whenever an angel pisses me off, all those emotions come spilling out of the grave of repressed feelings."

"Is that why you're . . . ?" She trailed off.

"Hey, look, there's lots of nasty people, some even count as family. Yours too, I guess. The important thing is the difference between naive trust and smart trust. A smart person knows how to handle themselves when they do get betrayed. How to keep secret safe houses, how to keep track of political topography to tell who doesn't have it in their best interests to sell you out if you ask for aid, how to get people to underestimate you. You gotta—" I took another swig. "Gotta prepare for the worst so you can enjoy the better shit."

"I have a hard time conceiving that anyone would underestimate you."

"Just 'cause you think an estimate's accurate don't mean it is, that's the whole point."

21

Hermes Trismegistus

Cicula

Mother left as quickly as she came, off to reluctantly play mediator for Grandfather's more unruly nobles. I'd never even heard her open up about her past like that. She acted nonchalant about it, but she'd been more and more serious ever since that incident four years ago, and I wasn't sure if it was a wakeup call for her or just a matter of injured pride. I left my chamber and picked up the empty bottle of mead she'd left on the table. There'd been no shortage of these either way. I called in a priestess and had it taken away.

Something on your mind, hun?

I think I'm just tired, Kali. There's so much to do, and the only vacations I've time for are chemical. Now Mother seems to think darker times are right around the corner. I took a deep draw of my pipe. Now where did my daughter scurry off to?

It seems one of the handmaids found her. She should be fine.

Really? I hope so. I get the feeling she's only going to get more difficult with age.

Who doesn't, darling?

The dea's hand cupped my cheek. I leaned into her, and another two hands wrapped around my sides. There was an electric heat to her touch that left my muscles at ease. I could fall asleep standing like this.

Be strong, my chosen. Now, don't you have to meet up with your brother soon?

Yes, of course, the expedition. I turned my head and looked imploringly into her three burning eyes. Do I have to go?

No avatar of mine is going to be a liar with unpaid dues. Now come on sweetness, get that derriere into motion.

You can be such a slave driver. I don't know how I put up with you sometimes.

She stuck out her long tongue in apology.

Alright, alright, I'll go. I suppose I should change into something that I don't care about getting dirty.

Wear that nice top that flatters your navel, the red one.

Who am I, my brother? We're to go grave robbing, not belly dancing.

It wouldn't do you wrong to take a note from his song. He knows how useful a good dance can be.

If you love him so much why don't you go dance with him and leave me alone?

Oh come now, he's a thousand years too young to dance against me. Though I admit, his flamenco does show promise.

Gross, forget I even mentioned it. Now come on, help me find something practical to wear.

***

I reached the tomb via portal jaunt and Lach already awaited me, along with the rest of the expedition.

"You look hella strung out, Sis. You right?" He tapped his foot idly to a 5/5 beat.

"Fine, I've just been busy. You look as carefree as ever."

"Hey I have cares I just don't let them bother me. So what are we here for again?"

"For the love of — Look, a certain scholar finally passed away, and failed to pass ownership off a certain grimoire to anyone in his will. That means Grandfather can have us come pick it up without breaching the contract he made. Somewhere between terra nullus and squatter's rights, or something"

"Oh yeah? What book?"

"The Bronze Book of Hermes Trismegistus!" One demon shouted. "This isn't the only copy, and we *could* always inscribe more, but when you consider the state of the cosmos it is far preferable to keep the number in circulation to a minimum amount!"

The demon sat atop a dromedary, and sported both a slender face and prominent muscles.

"So who are you?" My brother asked of him.

"I am King Paimon!" The demon bowed with a flourish from atop his mount. "These are my fellows, King Beball and King Abalam!" He gestured to the two proud demons besides him. "It is a pleasure to make the acquaintance of the twin serpents of the Morning Star's first house!"

"Yeesh, loud much? Can you do us a favor and not shout?" My brother clutched at his ears. Paimon coughed in apology and lowered his voice.

"Terribly, terribly sorry, my friends. I do tend to get excited when meeting new people." He crossed his arms and nodded with vigor. My brother leaned to the side and peered behind the three kings at the other demons behind them. Each carried a trumpet or cymbals, and looked eager to strike up a song at a moment's notice.

"The marching band isn't actually going to be playing while we go crawling through this dungeon, are they?"

"Ah, well, they don't *have* to, if it's to your displeasure young master."

"Do they know *In the Hall of the Mountain King*?"

The demons gabbed amongst themselves for a minute then one of them spoke up.

"Only the second half, young master."

"Forget it, then. Alright! Let's get this show on the road. The Satyrs are throwing a rave later tonight by Phlegethon and I hear Dionysius himself is expected to show up. My feet have been itching to see what he's got since forever."

"Very good, young master. I hear he's quite the break dancer since his revelry with the eight immortal djinns. Right, we shall endeavor to expedite this expedition with haste."

"The old man must love you," Lach rolled his eyes.

"I'm afraid we've yet to converse."

"Just go already." He shoved the thousand-plus year old demon's camel toward the doorway.

"Of course, young master."

Paimon's dromedary kicked down the tomb's stone doors with ease. The heavy slabs fall with a muffled thud and we make our way inside, the lesser demons preceding us. Inside the tomb is musky, moss eaten, and the ancient stone floor is given to crumble under step. The ceiling hung too low for Paimon to comfortably ride atop his dromedary yet he refused to dismount. Coffin filled recesses lined the walls and at each of the many intersections Lach barked out a direction.

"Left. Left. Left. Right. Left. Right. Right. Right." Far quicker than expected we come up to a recently laid coffin inscribed with the scholar's name.

"How on Earth did you know the way, Brother?" I demanded.

"What the hell is know? I just picked ways on a whim." He plucked an apple from his pocket and polished it against his chest.

"I swear you're a seer sometimes, or just a deranged savant."

"Nah, I just get lucky sometimes. Think about the grand latte of things, you gotta be right sometimes, right. Stopped clocks and all that. So think about it, you just gotta be wrong plenty and then you can spend all your accumulated right when you actually need it. Come on, we just got to get the book, right?"

With an impertinent boot he kicked away the coffin's lid. The pestilent aroma of decay and formaldehyde filled the room.

Gripped tightly by the shriveled body's arms sat the bronze book which we sought.

"Ah, there is it! I should recognize that work anywhere!" Paimon bellowed. The other demons chattered elatedly at our success, but the sight of something sent them silent.

"In the name of the LORD I command you to halt!" A new voice thundered and echoed around the room. The demons, their celebration interrupted, strained against unseen bonds. No, not quite unseen, they had a faint glimmer around them, that trailed away down the corridor opposite of where we came. There was a terrific flash followed by the rumbling of thunder. The demons collapsed onto the stone floor with a collective groan and clattering of instruments.

"Fear ye unclean ones for a servant of the LORD has come to halt your defilement of the dead and *banish* you tainted souls back to Sheol from whence you came." A man stepped out of the gloom, slender and giant, at least seven feet tall if not more. Upon his brow sat a broad-rim hat and he wore a fancy white suit. He flicked a gloved wrist and a shimmer moved around it.

"What is this stage trick, wires? Who invited this asshole to our corpse party? Ptooh." My brother spat to the side. Paimon's dromedary snorted in agreement and stamped its hooves, while Beball and Abalam both drew spears. I called to my hand the Skull-topped Staff of Kali and gathered the tomb's wisps around me.

Beware, my chosen. This man's blood is mixed with that of angels.

"You'll not interfere with the work of our master!" Beball and Abalam charged, spears forward. The tall man crouched low, his knees raised to his head in a spidery fashion, and he darted between them. They stiffened, and there came another flash followed by thunder. Their spears dropped and bounced once. With a complicated movement of wires binding them the man impaled them on their own weapons. Paimon rushed the man but a sudden explosion of wind blew them to the ground, pinned by his own mount. The tall man stood, and from his suit sleeve a rosary dropped. It snapped up into the air and twisted itself into the shape of a cross.

"Upon the sign of the martyr's covenant, get back from whence ye came. *In nomine patrus, et filie, et spiritus sanctus.*" There came another flash, followed by screams as the demons tore apart into ash. The wisps I had gathered were also dispelled. The room was left with a clinical smell, out of place for such an earthy structure. The tall man returned the rosary up his sleeve and turned to us.

"So while you do the devil's work, you have not yet been seduced by his power," he said. He must have been talking about miasma. "If he foresaw my coming, this was rather a cunning move of his." The man lifted his head, and for the first time I got a good look at his face. There was something familiar about his features, almost nostalgic. Why, he could almost pass as Lach and mine's brother.

I can't see any similarities between your bloods, however. Wherever this man came from it was not of your father's loins.

"So who the hell are you, pretty boy?" Lach demanded. He shifted his position and with a clap of expelled air a pair of obsidian blades appeared, affixed to his gloves.

"I am but a humble servant of the LORD, here to thwart the Serpent's unholy machinations." The smug condescension was palpable.

"Didn'tcha get the memo?" Lach taunted. "God's kicked the bucket."

"The LORD cannot be vanquished. He is merely testing us with His absence."

"When I die I'll have them put that on my gravestone too."

The two circled each other around the open coffin, eyes fixed on each other. My brother was by no means short, but he lacked our father's full stature and was utterly dwarfed by the tall man. I didn't even want to think how I looked measured up to him.

Do you want us to defeat him together?

No, we mustn't squander your power. I've a better idea.

The tall man whipped his wires around. Lach artfully dodged and rushed in close, but at such short distance he couldn't avoid being tied up by the leg and flung against a wall before he can land a strike. He managed to twist free right before the man sent another bolt of lightning down the wires' length, and my brother lunged again. While both were distracted, I pricked my thumb with my false nail and— without making any sudden movements— set about drawing runes on the ground.

Lach had more swiftness and more cunning, but the tall man provided no openings for him to exploit, and his wires provided him with a far greater reach than Lach's blades. My hair stood on ends from all the electricity and the air grew heavier with each passing second. My brother made a pained grunt as a fierce kick slammed him into the ceiling and screamed as untold volts drove into his flesh.

What are you plotting, my chosen?

If this man fancies himself a saint, let's see him slay a real dragon. I stamped the ground with my staff three times and spoke a rapid chant.

"Wyrm that gnaws the roots of Ygdrassil, rival of Vidofnr, swallow whole the foe afore, I must behest Nidhoggr."

The tall man turned, in time to witness a vast abysmal maw explode out of my rune circle and crash into him. Scales flew past my eyes like a reptilian train as the Nordic fiend rocketed through the walls of the tomb like they were curtains and kept on going. While the creature endlessly extended, I hurried around behind the wyrm-spewing rune circle and helped up my brother.

"Are you okay?"

"Chuckle guffaw everything hurts," he coughed. "I've had worse hangovers though. I should live, I guess."

"Come on, let's grab the book and get out of here. I've a feeling Nidhoggr's belly won't hold him for long." I snatched up the bronze book where it had fallen and hurried back to my brother. My hair stood on end as something pulsed down the wyrm's gargantuan length, and the rune circle let out a dangerous crackle.

"He's trying to dispel the summoning directly," I cried, heart bursting in my ears. "Hell's bells, there's not enough time to make a way out for us."

"So what now?"

"I'll have to use the back door. Kali, I need your help. Can't racked think straight. Please, to clear my idiot head."

Of course, my sweet.

"*Om Krīm Kālyai namah,*

Om Kapālinaye Namah,

Om Hrim Shrim Krim

Parameshvari Kalike Svaha"

I chanted the psycho-mnemonic mantra and my head emptied of all superfluous thought. All things returned to nothing. Negative ego devoured by destrudo. All independent variables became null and let the real order of dissolution take place. I fell through the Void just like my father taught me, dragging Lach and the book with me.

22

Who is like God?

Michael

I sent one last pulse through the beast and finally collapsed the witch's spell. The pagan wyrm vanished back from whence it came. I hurried my best back to the crypt, but the devilish pair had already left with their prize in hand. I balled my fists, but remembered myself and let the anger be quelled within me. I clutched my rosary in my hand, fell to one knee, and prayed for guidance.

I failed to prevent the Devil from reclaiming the manuscript. In time, it shall be used to tempt another wayward soul and they, too, shall lose their way to paradise. Though it shall be their weakness which invites this, the fault is mine for failing to prevent it. I was naïve, and underestimated Satan's minions. I did not think that there would be those with the will to deny the intoxicating taint of Hell's miasma. Nor did I expect to encounter one capable of conjuring a dragon of neither hell nor heaven so quickly. I was too reliant on the powers of exorcism granted to me, and allowed myself to be distracted from the witch by her knight. Forgive me Father for I have sinned, and the name of my sin is Pride.

I performed the sign of the martyr on myself and stood. I knew not the verdict of the LORD's judgment and it was not my place to know. I could only endeavor to walk the righteous path as best I could.

Still, I was left with the question of what to do now. Should I report my failure to my superiors? No, if I went to them they would say 'Why is it that you have returned to us to tell us that you have done nothing? When you set out you had done nothing and you have returned and have done nothing. It is no difference than if you had not set out at all. If you stopped to tell us of every nothing that you do, you will never get around to doing a single thing. Is your time so worthless that you see fit to squander it so?' This they would say and they would question among themselves my worthiness of the position I had been granted.

I picked up my hat, still as wet with the wyrm's stomach as the rest of me, and called up an east wind to dry myself down. So I should not return to the Overworld until I had something worthy of informing them. What would such a thing be? The retrieval of that manuscript was my only lead. Satan moved swiftly of late and it would be prudent to learn why. Perhaps I should consult my mother. Her faith wavered in these troubled times, but her words still carried wisdom.

I released the wires coiled in my gloves and whipped them against the ground. They sparked and crackled with each strike and in a matter of seconds I carved a sending sigil upon the blasted Earth. With a prayer to the LORD for safe passage I passed through.

***

On the other side I emerged in the woods that stood behind my parents' current residence. I had to swerve and duck through the trees to keep my clothes being torn at by the many gnarled branches, and soon stepped out into the clearing at the woodland's edge. Out of their modest cabin hobbled an old man, forced by his crooked back to lean upon a withered cane. He looked up in my direction, averted his gaze and carried on. I waited until he had left, walked up to the cabin's door and gave it three strong knocks.

"Forget something, Mr Furnivall?" My father's voice called out.

"It's me," I answered. There was a rattle of metal on metal as he unfastened the bolt and the door swung inward. Before I could compose a greeting he pulled me down into a chest squeezing hug. I returned the gesture more stiffly than I should, and breathed a sigh of relief when we pulled apart.

"It's good to see you, my son. Come in, come in. Ancilla, our boy's home." He smiled at me with such overwhelming warmth that I wasn't sure what to do. Hadn't it only been a few months since I last saw them? I forced the corners of my mouth to turn upwards but if it looked wrong I couldn't tell.

"Ma—no, it's Michael now, right? I suppose I had better get used to calling you that." My mother walked in from the side room where her workshop was located. I bowed my head and stepped inside. My hat, coat and shoes soon found their place on the rack by the door, while I found myself ushered onto a seat in the kitchen.

"Can we get you anything? I know what you're like, who knows how long it's been since you had a good meal."

"I didn't come here just to impose on you."

"Nonsense. Eltanim, get that bottle of wine and some smoked fish."

"Good idea, I'll bring it out at once." All of my protests were shut down, and so we supped. The fish had a mild flavor, but the wine brought it out and kept the meal from tasting plain.

"So how goes the good work?"

"Oh, quite well," Mother spoke. "I installed a water purifier in the well near here, and your father has been providing treatments for the ails of those nearby. The wolf population has been brought low enough to keep the herds out of danger, and their hides will do the people well over the winter. "

"Miss Kaverdesh gave birth to twins," explained Father. "There was a severe amount of hemorrhaging but I managed to make sure we didn't lose her. So long as she keeps drinking the tea I prescribed she should make a full recovery."

"Unless something comes up in the next few weeks, it's time for us to move on."

"I see," I took a sip of my wine. I could already feel a tingle in my skin so I made sure to take it slow. "This is a good life for you then, this aimless philanthropy?"

"I wouldn't call it aimless," my father replied. "Your mother may be resigned from the choir, but she is still sensitive to prayers. We follow the prayers and do the most lasting good that we can. Teach the hungry how to fish and farm, establish infrastructure, so much of the world has fallen into decay in these times of stagnation. We're just raising the bottom line a little. Why? Are you having doubts about your path?"

"I— though I am nephilim, born of forbidden union, I was allowed entry to the celestial choir, given the opportunity to prove myself, and have been granted the office of archangel. Yet I was unable to prevent the Devil from reacquiring the unholy text which he sought. In the grand scheme of things it is not a monumental occurrence, but if I could not accomplish even that, am I truly worthy of this office? Perhaps it is time for me to embrace my heritage wholly, and bask in radiance until I ascend." I rested my chin on my hands.

"I beg that you don't," Mother pleaded. "Though as a nephilim you are already fully grown, you're still only four years old. If you saturated yourself in radiance now everything that defines you would be wiped away, and only an unthinking servitor would be left in your place." She pushed her plate aside and looked at me with her white-on-white eyes. "Tell me more about what happened."

"When I arrived, I felt the presence of three dark kings and a small host of servants. I exorcised them all with little resistance, but there were two left over that I did not detect before. They had no taint of miasma in them, so I could not simply exorcise them as I did the others. One of them fought me in single combat, and was able to hold his ground despite using only a pair of blades. By the time I dealt with him the other had already finished summoning a dragon, which swallowed me whole. By the time I got free they had already taken the book and left." I closed my eyes, and thought back to that strange pair. "They had black hair and red eyes. I think they were siblings but there was something else, almost familiar about their faces."

"Did you catch their names?"

"No. I do remember that the knight spoke with impudence, while the witch seemed more reserved." My parents exchanged an impenetrable look. "What is it?"

"Do you remember what I am?" My father asked. My brow furrowed in confusion.

"You said you were the spawn of the pagan god Nemesis. You had been charged with guarding the prisoners of a certain person and to defeat interlopers you made yourself into their worst possible enemy."

"That's right. I become a visage of their death and guilt," he got a faraway look in his eyes. "One day, I faced a wicked and dangerous man unlike any I had met before. Not for the depth of his wickedness, but because in his mind death would either come at the hands of himself or someone truly good, an odd mix of shame and arrogance. That might have been the end of that but he escaped, and I was left with the instinct to hunt him down, but also with much stronger newfound morality. Those two which you saw are the children of that man.

"I, too, have met him, and his children," my mother explained. "I had been told that he was too wicked and dangerous to let live, and so hunted him. I have seen into his mind. He is a madman, twisted by the one he calls Malign." Mother rested her chin on her hand. She seemed dejected, almost disappointed.

"What is it?"

"In his madness he was able to escape, and in the confusion afterwards it came out that it seemed like I had been set up." She clicked her tongue. "Maybe even by that Malign herself, or some of her servants. A loathsome thought, but it's possible."

"Wait a minute." I frowned. The grey matter between my ears sparked and flowed. "It sounds like this Malign is far worse than this man you speak of." It took a particularly ordered mind to accurately wield weather the way I could, one capable of tracking a great many variables, like bees in a hive, and in that moment a great many variables were painting an alarming picture.

"Keep in mind he does serve the Devil, along with his family. That's why his children were a part of that venture you interrupted."

"The devil has hundreds of thousands of souls dancing to his wicked schemes, but by and large those schemes are predictable. He is a tyrant who wants to strengthen his abyssal kingdom and renew his crusade against the LORD. He is, by and large, accounted for. This Malign though, what does she want?"

"That's assuming she really is alive. Draco, that's the man's name by the way, said that her servant couldn't live unless she also lived, or rather, that since her servant lived that definitely means she also lived. He could be wrong, though."

"Nonetheless I want to know. If this Malign poses a threat to His kingdom or His people, as one who holds the position of archangel I must know." A searing heat bloomed in my mind, a molten idea locking into place that I was on the right track.

"I only know a little about her, from what I saw in Draco's mind. She sees no distinction between pleasure and pain, she is a sadist who does unspeakable things to those she captures, and seems to live only to fulfill her debase desires. She is like Sodom and Gomorrah incarnate."

"There's more," My father explained. "I have Draco's memories up until a point, so I have firsthand experience. She can feed on the living. It's not like a vampire or a succubus. It's like having your soul devoured. No, not quite that, it's like having your mind and soul sucked dry of all light. It leaves you not a shell but a shriveled husk starved for any sense of personhood. You might call her an egophage."

"Where did she come from? Just what is she trying to accomplish?"

"I have no idea where she came from. Draco remembers next to nothing of his early life. I've only a vague idea of what she wants either. Listen if she is alive she is far above what you or any of us can deal with. There are fates worse than death and she inflicts them for fun. Look, I'm asking this out of fear for your safety, leave this alone."

"It is out of fear for safety that the Choir has fallen silent for so long. The LORD is testing us with His absence and to do nothing is failing Him."

"Michael. She devours everything that makes you 'you' and scorches the soil so nothing new can grow. Draco wouldn't even have a personality were it not for his sword."

"I will not ask that you put yourselves in danger, just point me in the right direction."

"Oh, very well." Mother slumped in resignation.

"Ancilla!"

"No, I won't stand in our son's way. Better we at least lend him what I know rather than let go in blinder than he needs to be. Look, I did some investigating about Malign's servant after he got away. It seems he was hunting down your father because he had mistaken him for Draco, but before that he was in a village called Mrinda, in a land called Mahkko, apparently trying to mold someone else into a recreation of Draco. If you can find out why, it may provide some clue as to what her goals are, or at least what her servant's goals are on her behalf."

"Mrinda in Mahkko, thank-you mother, I shall not let this go to waste."

23

Greyscale

Cicula.

The room in Pandemonium grew cloudy as I chain-smoked to pass the wait. By the time Grandfather saw fit to receive me my vision was swimming and just standing was a chore.

"Welcome, flesh of mine. How did it go?" He wore a beard, which was uncommon for him, and was otherwise nude, which was not uncommon. His physique had been sculpted to breath-stealing artistry and his every gesture flowed seamlessly into one another.

"We got the grimoire, but not without complications. Paimon and the others got struck by a strange man, a giant with the blood of angels. However Lach and I still managed to get rid of him long enough to snatch the prize and get out." I took out the bronze book and handed it to him.

"You have done well, Cicula. I didn't think anyone would realize this task was worth obstructing." He flicked through the book and stroked his beard. "Still, giant and with the blood of angels? I didn't think there were any Nephilim left, or any angels bold enough to make more after what happened to the Grigori. Some of the poor sods waited thousands of years before realizing they were never going to get back in."

"The Watchers, didn't a few manage to get back in God's graces?" I asked and fiddled with my cigarette.

"Oh, a handful, debatably. What's more interesting, Cicula, is that a Nephilim is trying to do His will."

"Yeah, he was certainly preachy about it. 'In the name of the LORD' and all that pomposity. Ugh," I groaned.

"Well, no matter for now. Those he exorcised should recover soon enough, and you've gone a good way toward repaying what you owe me, Cicula. I'll be sure to let you know when I've something else I would like you to assist with."

"Of course, Grandfather."

"How about your partner, Cicula? Are you two getting along?"

"Yes, Kali and I are doing well."

One of the more peculiar aspects of our relationship. So many Deus and Dea succumbed to the demonization of Him, and were banished to the underworld. Yet Kali's pantheon was Vedic, who demonized and were demonized in turn by the Avestans despite both being born of the same, even older tradition. This left them both what could almost be called culturally inoculated against it. Which meant Kali and her kin were able to remain largely unchanged despite Lucifer conquering the Underworld and Him above claiming the Overworld.

"Is your daughter healthy?"

"Healthy as she can be," mitigation intentional.

"Yes, I imagine the singular circumstance of her parentage have left their mark on her existence. Right, Cicula?"

"I never know what's going through her head, but it is easier now that she's talking a little." I sighed. It would be such a relief to just unload everything upon a sympathetic shoulder other than Kali, but the older I got the more grandfather made clear I couldn't take his trustworthiness for granted. What's more it was obvious he was intentionally making that clear, so where did that leave me? I couldn't even trust him to be untrustworthy.

"I can see you're eager to get back to her, Cicula, so I'll let you go. Be sure to give little Shahdee my regards."

"Yes, of course. Goodbye, Grandfather." I bowed and took my leave, to hurry back to the Citadel as swiftly as I could.

While constructing a portal, however, a familiar face stopped me.

"Hail, Serpent-kin. What brings you to the Morningstar's house?" It was Bifrons, the skull-headed demon that was one of my few confidantes.

"Hello, Bifrons. Just dropping off a package to Grandfather and now I'm headed home to my daughter."

"Yes, the lovely Shahdee. That girl has a lot of potential you know, very good breeding," he chortled, his empty sockets gleaming with candlelight.

"Or so you've mentioned," I glanced aside.

"I hear her connection to the Void is truly astounding, ah, but I see this is not the time for such talk," he chattered. "Then, might you be free this evening?"

"I'm afraid I've an engagement with my father. You know how hard it is to catch him at home. Perhaps next time, friend."

"Yes, well, we'll see what happens. Here, let me finish that sigil for you." The demon procured a lit candlestick and scattered its embers across my work, the spell completed and a portal to my citadel opened."

"Thank you Bifrons, much obliged."

***

When I stepped out the portal my daughter came running out from behind a curtain and latched onto my leg.

"Hello, Shahdee." I stroked her disheveled grey hair. "Have you been a good girl?" She made a muffled noise that neither confirmed nor denied it. "Your great grandfather Luci says hello." To that she shot an obstinate look and blew a raspberry. "Well I don't blame you for not liking him. He can be pretty scary. Did you still want to go see your grandfather today?" She pursed her lips and nodded firmly. "Then we'd better get you cleaned up."

I brought her up to my chamber and gave her a bath while Kali brushed her hair. She made no attempt to struggle, just sat mesmerized by the gleam of the soap bubbles until we were done. Afterward we dressed her in a nice petticoat and dress and turned her around. She refused to wear anything bright. Everything had to be faded and grey. Grey hair, grey eyes, and grey clothes. A darling face kept hidden to never stand out.

"You look absolutely precious," Kali cooed, and picked her up in her four strong arms. Shahdee giggled and held onto the black skinned dea tightly.

"You've never seen your grandfather's house before, have you?" I asked as I focused my mind. She shook her head, curiosity plastered across her face. "Well soon you will." Without the pressure of urgency I found it a lot easier to get into the necessary headspace. It took only a few minutes meditation and I could feel the Void filling the empty parts of my mind. Without breaking focus I stood, took my daughter by the hand, and sent us falling through to nothingness.

We arrived on that blank plane. Nothing, vast, featureless nothing stretched out as far as the eye could see in all directions save for one. My father's black stone fortress loomed in front of us as the only thing to be seen. Even things like temperature and light were non-existent in an absurd, logic-less way. Intrusions such as myself were visible not because there was light but because there was no shadow, and while here we were neither hot nor cold. It could drive you mad trying to reconcile that with Hawkenian physics.

The torches either side of the front gate composited the only light sources around, yet even they seemed to serve more as props than any meaningful function. As soon as we set down Shahdee ran toward it, pulling me along behind her. We came up to the fortress's front and the enormous wooden doors opened to reveal my father.

"Ah, I thought I felt guests. Hello, hello, I bid you welcome to Sacram," Father declared with a beaming grin. Shahdee let go of my hand and ran straight for him. He crouched down and spread his arms, but she slipped right under and into the hall behind him where she stopped. Her head whipped round from side to side, eyes wide, as she tried to decide what to look at first. Father glanced at his hands, rose with a shrug and brushed himself off.

"Don't take it personally. She can never resist a novelty," I assured him.

"Yes, quite. Are you here on business or pleasure?"

"Pleasure, mostly, unless there was a certain matter you actually felt like talking about. Do you feel like being less that cagey with me for once?"

"Not in the slightest. Now come on in, both of you. No need to be shy, Kali, I know you're there. You're a guest too after all."

Kali stepped out from within me. Her necklace of skulls rattled with each step, and the severed hands on her skirt mutedly clapped against one another as we made our way inside.

"Hello, man of Brahman," she greeted, "do we find you well?" She arranged her four hands in a gesture of, well, not so much respect but acknowledgment.

"Quite well, quite well. I've been practicing how to make things." He flicked his wrist and a dagger appeared in his hand. I felt no spark of arcane about it, as if it simply spontaneously came into existence. I knew the method. All things came from nothing and all things return to nothing, ergo anything can be made from nothing. Father flicked his wrist again and the dagger vanished. It was different from summoning. A summoned thing had to come from somewhere. Not this stuff. Furthermore there was something . . . 'unreal' about a thing crafted from pure Void. That is to say, that dagger was born a dagger. It was never ore smelted by a smith or mined from a mountain. It was never deposited by tectonic movements. It was never part of a star. Its particles weren't there for the birth of the universe. A physicist would make themselves sick at the violation of Newton's laws.

"I mean I figured out how to make things a long time ago, but there's a difference between knowing how to perform a task and being able to do it on reflex. Ah, here's Drakkengard with some tea." He seated us around a table as his sword-maiden set out pots and cups. Shahdee cautiously crept over from wherever she'd run off to, perhaps wondering what we were up to or perhaps just lured over by the smell.

"Ah, there you are child. I imagine it must be particularly peculiar for you, being inside the Void. It doesn't bother you, does it?" Shahdee shook her head at her grandfather.

"I'm, hm, okay," she mumbled. Was there something odd about her delivery? I was just too worried. Father smiled at her, and handed her a cup of cinnamon milk.

It was difficult when she was born. Not the birth itself, but everyone always pushing questions, wanting to know who the father was, where he was now, if he was human or demon or god or what else. Not even Lach could resist trying to pry. Only father didn't ask. I'd no doubt that he'd figured it out now, he'd dropped too many knowing comments to be coincidence, but at the same time he'd just accepted it. I'm not sure if he even cared one way or the other. Maybe I was the one caring too much.

"I understand you've founded a colony on Luna's underworld. Do you need any help with that?" he asked.

"No, but thanks for the offer," I replied. "How about your....ah... hermitage? taking care of everything yourself?"

"Not by myself, I've Vengai-Ra and Ko here with me. Actually I should go fetch them, they'd be happy to see you."

"Yes, Master." Drakkengard rose from her seat and slipped away. How long had she been over there? She seemed to melt from location to location whenever I took my eyes off her.

"If it's not too much trouble might you take Shahdee with you? I'd like a puff but prefer not to do so around her. You don't mind, do you?" I turned to my father.

"Oh no, not at all."

The sword-maiden escorted my daughter away without further command, and I lit up.

"You're taking more effort to be conscientious." He didn't say it like a compliment, nor an insult, but with the distant interest of, say, a biologist noting changes in a bacteria culture.

"I'll never be the best parent, but I at least want to take responsibility for her upbringing." If he noticed the slight he didn't acknowledge it. "Have you found anything on Malign?"

"Why would I?" he scoffed. "I had my revenge. My business with the Abomination is concluded," he harrumphed.

"What about— "

"Enough. Let's not talk about such ugly things."

24

Kaleidoscope of Self

Shahdee

Drakka took me by the hand and out of the room. Her fingers were soft as gold and had a slight tingle to them, like the itchy you get when it's suddenly hot. The big place had lots of soft things everywhere, soft rugs, soft lights and soft colored paintings. They were pretty boring. She took me to a big room full of shiny metal and bubbling stuff in glass and that was much more interesting. Docra had his eye stuck to a thingscope and his glass sitting up on his head like his hair could see out of it. What could hair see? Could hair see how much touch there was in the air? Maybe the glass let them see touch better.

"Definitely a retrovirus of some kind," he grumbled, "but what does it do?"

"Vengai-Ra."

"Hmm? Oh, it's you. What does he want now?"

"Cicula is visiting. Did you want to say hi?" She picked me up by the middle and everything went wooshing down.

"Oh, may as well. Just staring at this sample isn't going to do me any good. Why is her kid with you?"

"Something about secondhand smoke," girl-gramps said. She liked saying less in a thin sorta way.

"Well I can't say I disapprove, although I'd be happier if she'd quit the habit. All of her habits, really. Middle age is going to hit that girl like a fermented sack of smallpox."

"She's a cambion, not human," Drakka reminded him.

"I don't care if she's Precambrian, you can't take your health for granted." Docra made a face like he ate lemon.

They keep on not saying anything interesting so we think and agree and I wriggled out of Drakka's hands and look around. The cabinets were tall and looked like they'd creak so I went past them and watched a thing that rotated tubes. After staring at sloshing stuff for a few minutes we got bored and went to look for something else. After rummaging through a pile of metal bits I finally found something interesting to us, a small crystal.

I touched it to my tongue and we tasted heat and light. It must have been a stone for burning. I held it up to my eye. It'd been polished so it had lots of faces, big nice-good. I had a broken head, for as long as I could remember, and shiny things with lots of faces helped me see the pieces. My faces in its faces all looked back at me. Some were smiling, others were bored or irritated or angry or crying. I shook the crystal and looked again. Some of me wanted to go back to Mama, some were hungry, one of me wanted to explore more. She wanted to follow the weird feeling. I switched with her.

I put the crystal in my pocket and walked out of the room. Neither the cutter nor the cooker noticed me leave. I was good at that. Oldfire's imaginary castle was big and confusing, and I figured he did that on purpose just to be mean, but I kept following the weird pulling feeling in the unfilled spaces. The pull took me upstairs, past suits of armor and old maps, past open doors and closed ones.

Then it was back downstairs, down even more stairs, down, down deeper and down all the way to the basement. Racks and barrels and crates were piled up against everywhere, but the pull said to keep going down. I followed it to where the pull felt biggest and pressed my cheek against the floor. It felt to us just as home as the rest of the imaginary castle. I took out my crystal and peered into it again. One of I said we needed to head back. One of I insisted we looked in the barrels. One of I wouldn't stop crying. One of I suggested to just rip it out. I switched with her.

I of many reached into the stone floor with arms that weren't and grasped its specks. I of many snatched away their heaviness, fistfuls at a time. Mama called it gravity magick. I just, sorta, figured it out one day. The ground cracked and rose away, with us on top of it. Over the edge of the now floating rock I of many saw a deep hole below, with all sorts of weird writing on the sides. I of many clenched my eyes shut, held my breath, and jumped down. Even though I of many couldn't see the bottom from up top it didn't feel like falling for long and we landed on something soft, face first. I of many took a deep breath and opened our eyes. Even though it was dark from up top it was bright down here. Red grass prickled my palms, and I could feel soft soil beneath it. Huge black trees blotted out lines of the horizon, and the setting sun behind them cast long shadows. They reached and clawed for us with jagged finger that twisted into wicked crooks. There was something unpleasant in my head, like bugs crawling all over our brain, prodding our thoughts with waving antennae. *Gross-gross-gross-gross bugs. Make them go away. Go. GO!* I of many jerked out my crystal and found myself in it, any me would do. I switched with the first me that met my eyes.

Ha, there were no bugs at all. I had no clue what the other me's were talking about. Or maybe they'd just left. Either way I couldn't feel any bugs. I could feel that tugging one of me noticed though. I picked myself up, brushed off my dress and swung my arms as I followed it.

I was in a garden. There were trees and grass and a path, although it had a bit of a weed problem. *Someone should call a gardener.* The path didn't look interesting though so I followed the tugging across the hills, away from most of the trees. Here and there was a little bush or a withered flower but soon I stopped seeing those too. In a sudden the tugging came from below me instead of ahead of me. I crossed my arms and puffed out my cheeks. Just how far down did I have to go? I shoved my magick down and started tearing out chunks of dirt like hair off a balding eagle. A bigger and bigger cloud of dirt clods grew around me as I got further and further down.

I started to uncover something metal, a rusted pole, no, a bar and there were more of them. With a grin I heaved the rest of the dirt away at once. Someone had buried a big metal gate, like a jail or a cage or something. Even though it had been underground there was no dirt on the other side of the bars. There was a wind though, a hot wind that would be unpleasant if I had to sit in it for too long.

The tugging came from inside so I sucked in a deep-deep breath and shoved myself between the bars. It was really tight, and if I was even a bit bigger I would have given up but somehow I popped out the other side. I wasn't expecting it and stumbled forward into the dark. Other me's complained but they could shut up. I stopped myself and turned around but the bars weren't there any more, nothing was there, just more nothing.

A booming rumble blew past me, like an enormous firework or the breath of a gigantic angry thing. My head boiled over. Too many screaming wants, I couldn't make any out. I took out my crystal but it was too dark to see so I jammed it back in my pocket and just ran. I ran until my feet burned and my chest cracked and I ran even more. My foot slipped and I was falling again. I was going so far down would I come back out at the top again? Then I slammed into something hard and fell over. Now my palms and knees burned too. Everything hurt and I couldn't stop from crying. I could see again, though, so I looked into the crystal and switched with one of me.

The last me sure made a mess of me. With a wince I got up, and put my crystal away. At first I thought I was back in the castle, but that was mostly stone and this place was mostly wood. Broken wood actually, the floorboards were filled with holes. It was amazing they didn't break when I smacked into them.

I look down one of the holes, which didn't reveal anything except that it was dark down there too. I closed my eyes and pictured how everything must be. There was the castle up top, the garden hanging beneath it, the dark cage under the garden, and apparently this new house hanging beneath that, all hanging in empty nothingness. It must look like a weird tower from the outside.

No, wait, you couldn't see anything beneath the castle from the outside. I was brought in through the front door after all. So how did this work? Just thinking about it hurt so I stopped.

The part of whatever house I was in looked like a hallway, and there were a few doors on either side so I went over to the nearest one and opened it. It was a mostly empty room, but in the middle stood an old piano, higher than I was tall, and the curtains of an open window fluttered even though there was nothing outside. It looked like there had been fire here. There was something unpleasant about the room, warped. I quickly shut the door, looked into my crystal, and switched with one of me.

I groped around my head for the pull again, and followed it once I found it. The pull led me up the hall and to a collapsed staircase. The rail was still intact though so I climbed up onto it and slid down. The walls of the house stopped toward the bottom, like someone had just broken off the entire lower half of the place. I slid off the rail and stepped down onto nothing. Everything felt really thick and heavy. I stood at the bottom of an ocean and my glass was cracking.

Might have to switch soon but I didn't wanna. In front of me towered an enormous black stone. No, it was a door, a hugely tall black stone door. Something hot and glowing was written on its front. *TrES-2b.* I didn't know what that meant so I just reached for the door, and with a horrible, agonized creak it opened.

Someone was inside, someone about my size.

They had black skin and empty holes for eyes, but for some reason I couldn't tell anything else about them.

They felt really-really familiar though.

My hand was still outstretched.

"Do you wanna play?" I asked.

25

Castle on the Sands

Draco

The glass in my hand shattered. An immense, otherworldy numbness detonated in my head, completely scrambling my thoughts.

With delayed lethargy I turned to stare at my left arm. The whole limb was aflame and jagged glass jutted out from my skin. The . . . ga? Glar? It soon started to melt, liquid SiO_2 Na_2O CaO—I could no longer recall the proper name for it— seeped into open lesions.

Red took over my skin which boiled and bubbled with charred blisters. The days of visitation had come, the days of recompense had come ere the blow, I become a mere dolt. I opened my maw to utter something and I knew not what. Sacram was unmade.

There was pleasure, sure, my dear sir, take any road. No, this failed to conform to that which was prescribed. What outcry had you uttered about me, you oafish brute? Where was my second?

The man with the flaxen hair. He was to be my precious reaper. Where was my recourse? One-and-twenty buttonholes of cherry-colored silk! To be finished by noon of Saturday: and this is Tuesday evening.

Was it right to let loose those mice, undoubtedly the property of Simpkin? Alack, I was undone, for I hadno more twist!

The largest of dead-fires: dark o'er the vapor. The smoke-cloud ascended, the sad-roaring fire, Mingled with weeping. The furnace of fire. There would be wailing and gnashing of teeth.

Gog-Hoor! Gog-Hoor! Gog-Hoor had come for me. Already his proboscis had shot twix mine head.

No. It was not done. It shan't be done.

Mine last breath tis promis'd to another.

26

Tonality of Beasts

Lascivus

"Alright, send them." Since Draco had been spending all his time in non-space and both Lach and Cicula were always out some place or another I'd had our house in the Bolgia all to myself.

At the time it seemed convenient to just set up office there. No one warned me that made people think you'll see them at any hell forsaken hour. I gulped down some mead as my secretary-slash-housekeeper passed my instructions on.

Her name was Marie, and she was my half-sister on my mother's side. Not that it meant much, while half the demons in the underworld were either a god, spirit, mortal or angel changed by miasma, the other half were my half-siblings, of the countless hordes of asexual offspring Lucifer and Lilith each created every day.

That was the big deal about me after all. *The only sexual offspring of the two highest rulers in the underworld*, as they and the dung lord were so quick to remind me. It took them nearly three thousand years of hounding to get me to take even this much interest in the underworld's affairs. If I was lucky, maybe holding out for another three millennia would make them give up on the rest. I chugged down the rest of the bottle of mead and looked up.

"So what's the matter with you two?"

"They stole it!" One of them, a woman, slammed her foot down on my desk. The other leg sat on top of a chair, making her head and shoulders above everyone in the room.

I pulled out another bottle from my desk and took a swig. She was a large woman, in a muscly sense. Leviathan, Hellmouth, Rahab, maybe Tiamat I wasn't sure on that one. She was a Seraphim at one point, if I recalled right. Was she one of the Grigori or one of the rebellion? No matter. As long as I'd known her she'd been all about intimidation. A big-ass fishhook hung from her cheek and her two horns had both been decoratively carved, a process that hurt like a bitch I'd heard. One said '*Meanest in the Sea*', the other '*300 Miles Long*'. She was a pain in the ass, even if she was pretty fetching. I couldn't remember much else about her. She was part of my father's household, but we'd never been close. Gods damn I was hungry. Where was my husband when I could use him?

"How dare you. T'was you who stole it from me," the other one puffed up indignantly. What about? Oh, right something was supposedly stolen from both of them by the other.

The other was a genderless demon named Ziz, with feathers down their back like a cape. They sounded a bit like a parrot when they talked, like their tongue wasn't involved in how they made words. Not as much as a pain in the ass as Leviathan, but an annoying suck-up. I think they were one of Beelzebub's lieutenants? I really needed to pick up the latest copy of Sheol Peerage. I'm pretty sure Solomon was still king when my copy had been penned.

"Alright let's start with the basics. What's missing?" I held up my palm.

"The ichor of Talos. Most of it was lost when the colossus was felled, but a small sample was recovered and preserved. I *had* managed to track it down, when this lardhead stole it right from under my nose," Leviathan spat

"I did no such thing. I tracked it down, I retrieved it, and *you* stole it from my own house, you insufferable loach," Ziz sneered.

"How dare you! Why I oughtta swallow you whole, let you swim in my gut for forty days and nights. Maybe a nice acid bath will make you fess up."

"Ha! You'd like that wouldn't you, ye vorephilic hag. You'll be singing a different tune when I do to you what I did to Prometheus."

"Now who's the vorephile? A sexless chickenshit like you couldn't handle swallowing so much as a hair of mine, let alone my liver."

"For Hell's sake, both of you shut up." I slammed my bottle on the desk and glared at them. "You're so desperate to blame someone you're missing the obvious."

"Yeah? And what would that be, princess?"

"That someone else stole it from Ziz's house."

"So they did steal it from me!"

"No, Leviathan, you both just had the bad luck to be looking for the same thing at the same time."

"But Lucifer asked *me*," they both yelled at once. I buried my face in my palms and growled.

"Forget that. There is no slight between you so stop bickering. Blood in Hell, it's not pretty watching a jackass try to eat a pomegranate. Stop trying to fist each other's face and go back to your duties. I'll worry about the ichor. You've both got more pressing matters to attend to."

"And you don't?" Leviathan asked.

"Convincing you schmucks to get back to work *is* my pressing matter. Unless you'd rather get confined to Styx until you cool down."

"No, of course not princess," Ziz said. Leviathan just harrumphed and looked away. I shooed them both out of my house and locked the door.

"Boil me in oil I don't know how anything gets done with all this mistrust. It's no way to run an organization." I pulled open a fresh bottle of mead and gulped down a quart. "Marie, do I have any more appointments right now?"

"Nah, that was the last one, you're pretty free for a while. Hey, wanna go for a pub crawl?"

"That'd be great, but no. I need to have a word with dad."

"No rest for the wicked, eh?"

"That's what all the posters say," I sighed, and pointlessly straightened the paperwork on my desk.

27

Sforzando Chains

Michael.

It did not take long to find the village mother told me about. Most of the buildings still stood, though they'd suffered greatly from the elements. There was more to it than natural exposure, I should specify. The whole area had a rank bog-like smell, and everything had severe water damage. I would have guessed a flood, but there was no sign of crashing water striking anything. Nothing had been knocked over by strong force.

Bleached bones littered the ground inside and outside, picked clean by carrion feeders. The conclusion of this place seemed, I supposed, interrupted. Tattered remnants of half erected decorations hung from buildings, and within some buildings the tables were still set out for a meal, though the food itself had long since been stolen by pests.

The desolation extended beyond the village. An erratic path where the grass did not grow stretched across the countryside and at its end stood a meager structure, perhaps a hut of some kind, which had been blown open. Below the hole in its crude roof sat a much bigger hole, which lead to some sort of underground shelter. It almost seemed like it had been pierced by some colossal lance from below.

I held my hat in place and dropped down. Conjured winds slowed my descent and I landed gently upon a steel floor. From inside it looked less like a shelter and more like a facility of some kind. Advanced gurneys were arranged in rows, and at the far end stood a badly damaged computer. Rust, scorch marks, and deep gouges painted the surroundings, and a number of the gurneys had been compromised. However there were no signs of any remains in them. Who or whatever had been placed in them appeared to have been removed since before this place got devastated.

There were some tablets hanging from the far end of the gurneys which detached easily. They felt like a plastic of some kind, and an unfamiliar script had been written on them with some kind of holographic. The writing didn't even resemble any language I had encountered, yet as a kernel of faith could move a mountain my prayers to the LORD revealed their meaning to me.

It was still rather hard to interpret, however. Biochemical jargon bled into mysticism and vague prophecy. It talked of the limitless potential for creation in someone with a broken soul. It spoke of the guidance of the twofold god. I found mention of introducing the genetic aberration '*Esk*'– some kind of mutagen, and of the diluted blood of gods. I checked what other undamaged reports I could find, but they all repeated the same thing, give or take a few measurements. Perhaps I could find someone able to make more sense of it than I. All the doctors I knew were strictly arcane based, though. They couldn't make face or fool of these advanced theorems.

Further searching yielded to me nothing of note so I returned to the surface and took to the road to gather my thoughts.

From what little I could garner from the reports, whosoever had operated the facility was trying to genetically engineer a certain kind of person. If a person was broken a certain way, they could create anything? Were they trying to make someone already broken or just one that would break a certain way? What did they want to make, for that matter? This Malign person? Was that how she revived? Or perhaps Malign was the person who was broken in such a way, and they wanted someone else like her to create something? Just what did they mean by broken soul, anyway? Like a fallen angel? The undead? Insane? A call of greeting brought me out of my thoughts.

"I said hallo there. You're not from around here, are you?" It was a farmer woman, with a coarse tan and thick, curly hair.

"No, I'm not." I removed my hat as I replied in her language.

"Did you just come from the Mrinda ruins?"

"Yes, I was wondering what had happened there."

She shook her head. "Terrible thing. Wiped out overnight it was. They say the fiend that did it still prowls the mountains today. Sommatimes folk put together a hunting party but its lucky if even one of them make it back. They talk of a horrible hairy thing that hides in blizzards." It would be a far greater coincidence for it not to be related to that facility, though not outside the realm of possibility.

"Can you point me in the way of the region of mountain this fiend lurks?" I asked.

She pursed her lips. "You're not thinking of playing the hero are you, stranger? Yeah you're big, but you ain't got much thickness on you. The cold would eat you before that thing even got a chance."

"I have my own reasons, but even so, it would be rather callous of me to turn a blind eye when I ought be of help."

She crossed her arms, her face troubled, but finally the woman relented. "A'ight. As much as I'd like to dissuade you for your own sake this beastie is killing the livelihood of me and mine. Come back to my inn. I can spare a map, some furs, and a bit of nip."

"If your business is worsening, I could hardly in good conscience take more from you, and I've naught to pay you with."

"Look, boy, it's really no trouble. Right now I'm about two weeks away from being forced to pack it all in and move back to the capital. The loss of one sale ain't gonna make or break me, but something being done about Old King Cold will. If you never come back, well that just means I gambled and lost," she sighed.

"After losing so many no one else will even dare set foot on that mountain, so as I see it you're probably the last one willing to even try." She let out another sigh and slumped against her walking stick. She didn't seem old or debilitated such to warrant it. Perhaps the stave was for self-defense. "I like the inn, but I can make a living elsewhere's easily enough. This is just a final bet for the here'n'now."

"Then I thank you kindly for generosity."

"You'll have more than repaid if you actually manage to kill it. You look the dangerous sort, if you don't mind my saying. Not graceless, like someone as lanky as you might be."

"I thank you for the compliment."

"Alright, enough of that sonny, afore I get ideas. Let's just get on going," She smiled.

The air got steadily colder as we approached the mountain's foot, but the inside of her inn was warm from the hearth, which crackled and hummed under a large steel pot. A woman was cutting up strips of leather by the fire, but when we entered she got up and embraced my new benefactor.

"Sheya, you're back soon. Who is this?"

"A stranger bold enough to take a crack at making the mountain safe again."

"Is that right?" The woman rubbed her arm in absent repetition as she looked me up and down. The arm had been tightly bound, and the skin around the edges was a dangerous purple, probably frostbite. She noticed my gaze and put her hand on her hip.

"I am sorry, that was impolite of me."

"The thing up the mountain is to thank for this. I had a tackle with it myself and it was only chance I got away. It froze my spear so brittle it shattered against its hide, an' then it knocked me so hard it broke my arm. There's a deep coldness in its touch. I was lucky not to lose it."

"You're lucky to be alive, Brucca." My benefactor, Sheya, embraced her companion tightly and kissed her.

"Not in front of the guest." The woman called Brucca pushed her off and turned to me.

"So how do you plan to skin an incarnate of winter? With your expensive city clothes?"

"I am not without protection." I held my hands apart from each other, and electricity crackled between them.

"Eh, you're a mystic then. Don't think that'll make things easier, we had one too and he got a stalactite through the head afore he could finish his first incantation."

"May your friend rest in peace," I bowed my head, "but I have faith that I shall succeed."

"Yeah, well, we'll see."

***

After supping on a portion of soup and donning a cloak that looked from a white wolf I set off up the mountain with the supplies the two gave me. My ascent up the craggy slope was slow, made worse by the thickening blizzard. All the trees had been choked dead by the cold and stripped of their leaves by the biting winds. Even through my cloak and clothes the wintry gale cut to my core. Yet my flesh was not that of man, and my faith in the LORD redoubled my vigor. If the source of this snowstorm held some clue to the enigmatic Malign, I cannot let them elude me.

As I made my way skyward I scrutinized the pattern of the buffeting winds and the pressures of the air. It made a complex vortex, but I was confident in my judgment of its center. I adjusted my course and zeroed in on this central point. The storm heightened in severity the closer I got, and that only confirmed my hypothesis. The mistral's fangs stripped the fur from my cloak and the moisture from my face. I could feel my skin redden and my lips chap, but I resisted the rage to wet them. That would only make it easier for the cold to plunder them till barren, cracked and bleeding.

There was a sudden loss of resistance that sent my balance askew, like stepping through a waterfall. The snowstorm still howled behind me, but I seemed to have reached its eye. Ahead I saw a frost coated cave. Its entrance glistened in the sunlight that rained from above, but inside was impenetrably dark. I flipped down the hood of my tattered cloak, removed my hat, and stepped inside. My intrusion was met by a wheezed snarl.

"Who," the voice that spoke is strained and weak from little use, "who else do I have to kill?"

"You're coherent." With unfettered boldness I approached the voice. "That is a relief."

"Haaah, that's a first. A speaker."

My eyes adjusted to the gloom, and revealed a huddled figure slowly unfolding themselves from where they lay on the ground.

"I have come with questions, and to remove you from this mountain."

"I refuse." Bleary and bloodshot blue eyes glared up at me in shrewd appraisal. "This is my home now. You won't take it." The figure stepped forward. Countless slivers of ice hung from his scrawny skin like fur. He was starved and alone and had been for a long time. How long ago did he last know comfort? The sight of him made my heart ache. "Why will no one grant me peace?" He moaned.

"You are burdened by infamy. The fiend who wiped out Mrinda and sits in eternal blizzard atop his mountain. That's what they say of you. There will always be those who wish to test their mettle or drive you off so long as you are known as such."

"You among them. That's what you are, isn't it? One who slays monsters. You've a hunter's eyes. How many other undesirables have you butchered?"

I walked up to him, step by step, and he shrank back in fear. "You are a killer," I declared. "Blood on your hands can never be washed away. Not even the miracle of resurrection can truly undo your sins." He bared his teeth and raised his arm. It was not flesh and blood but smooth ice that creaked and cracked with every gesture. "Yet you are still just a man. Your nature is not so debase that *all* you can do is injure and harm." I spread my palms. "That is the gift of free will. It was another who did this to you, but yours is the choice of what to do with it."

"No it's not," he hissed. Shards of ice burst from his arm, and my face was marked by small lacerations. "I can't control it! I rage, and the cold takes everything. I wallow in shame and guilt but when the violence begins, killing just becomes a matter of fact. It only made sense to kill those people. It was good to hear their bones snap and see their lives snuffed out and though I find it loathsome now I will want to again and again, and during those times I will not hesitate because that is what I'll want. I am a monster."

"You are sick. Your body and mind have been made ill. I cannot cure you," I crouched down, "but if you cooperate with me I can help you."

"Hah, yes, put me down. I may have nothing to live for but I can't bring myself to embrace death yet."

I shook my head. "I can lock the cold away. When you rage, I can tie you down until it passes. In time, I may be able to teach you to tie down your own heart."

"You lie. Why? Why would you do that? Why should I trust you?"

"Consider a man who loves his son. He loves being a father, he loves to teach and train his son, and he showers him with affection without spoiling him. Now imagine another man, this man hates his son, he hates being a father and would love nothing more than to run away and never see his son again. Yet he still teaches and trains his son, he still shows affection and still is moderate such that his son is never spoiled, and he takes the secret of his loathing toward his son to his grave. Who is the more virtuous man, between these two fathers?" I looked to the cave's entrance. "You have not condemned this world to suffer your rage. You have willingly exiled yourself on this mountain and inflicted violence only upon those that came to you. You have strived to lessen the fallout of your wrath instead of embracing strife and discord. You have sinned, but you have not let yourself become a monster unlike so many others in your position." I looked back to his icy blue eyes. "For that I love you."

The man fell to his knees and openly wept. I wrapped my tattered cloak around his shoulders and kissed him.

"Do you agree to take me as you shepherd, to place yourself at my mercy and guidance that I might show you the path to righteousness?"

"I do."

"Hold out your right arm." He did so, and I ran my hand over it. The frozen false limb stung my palm at its entropy. I turned his wrist over and held his hand in mine.

"By the grace of He who bears the Tetragrammaton and His avatar Yeshua Messiah I declare a covenant between this lost soul and I, that the witchcraft which plagues his body, which listens not to his voice, henceforth it shall listen to the voice of the one who asks the question 'Who is like God?' forever and ever." A golden shackle appeared around each of our wrists, joined together by a shining chain between them. In my left hand appeared a brilliant key of pure radiance, one and a half feet in length. "Thy kingdom come, thy will be done." I drove the key into my shackle. It passed right through the golden band and pierced my wrist. It passed through the other side of my band and through the band of the man and it pierced his wrist as well. Though it was made of ice and not flesh he still cried out in pain. "Amen." I turned the key, and our shackles clicked tight. The shackles, chain, and key all vanished and though there was no wound and his was not flesh, blood dripped from each of our wrists.

I squeezed his frozen hand until his haggard breathing became even.

"It is done." I let go and showed him my wrist. There was a brand of a keyhole where it had been penetrated. "Unless I willfully open this seal your frost is locked away, and if I do see fit to release it I can just as easily lock it away again."

The man said nothing. His right arm fell away in a pool of powdered ice and only a stump of flesh hung from his shoulder. He touched space where his frozen limb had been.

"It still hurts," he wondered aloud.

"It is a phantom pain. Your mind still clearly sees the arm that isn't there."

The icy 'fur' that had covered his body melted away, and outside the roar of the blizzard rapidly dwindled into quiet. I took out some meat and a bottle of spirits from the supplies the innkeeper gave me, as well as some bread, and divided it between us.

"Eat, drink, and rest a while. When you are feeling stronger I would like to ask you about the underground facility, and the one who did this to you."

28

Reins of Resolution

Lascivus

Dad was expecting me as always when I entered Pandemonium. He sat in front of a garden table, surrounded by ferns, dressed in one of his smug suits. He idly tossed an old Greek urn from hand to hand.

"Let me guess. That's the ichor of Talos you have there."

"Quite so," he locked eyes with me in challenge, but what challenge? Was I supposed to complain? Threaten to tell them? We both knew they wouldn't dare question it.

"Look, just, tell me why, okay. Why would you steal from one of your own subjects something that they intended to give you anyway? Why didn't you tell them that there was someone else you'd sent on the same task?"

"You have to ask? I thought you'd grown beyond that, my dear Little Horn," the words oozed from his mouth.

"You're the one who needed me to get things back on track and restore confidence in you, yet you're pulling this kind of crap out of your ass and calling it a rose. Do you want everything to fail?"

"Very well, I'll deem to explain myself. For the latter, it's just to spur a bit of friendly competition. It's so much more efficient to put people in the mood to outdo someone else rather than their own self. Without challenge there is no growth, without growth there is stagnation, and stagnation is a terrible thing."

"We've been stagnating the past thousand years, I shot back. "Maybe even longer. Competition? Like that can work now. Gah, whatever. How about the other one?"

"Again, just a little motivational technique. So long as they think they have failed me, those two will be eager to prove my confidence in them is not misplaced. This little trinket is a mere curiosity. Not that I haven't thought of a few things to do with it," he turned the urn around in his palm, "but it was just a warm-up for some more serious trials that I'll be relying on their completing. Not together of course, that would be just inviting an 'accident' to happen. Yet they will be thinking of the other and thinking of me and they will employ triple the effort they might have done. Are you satisfied now?"

"For fuck's sakes Dad, that's a crock of shit," I scoffed. "You keep stirring up their paranoia like that and they'll start going crazy by the day. We're losing too many people to miasma overdosing as it is."

"Those who overdose are simply too weak to be of any use to me anyway. We are much better off without their incompetence sullying our ranks."

"This isn't some impeccable machine for you to refine." I bared my fangs. "These are people that trust you to lead them, for the sake of better commonwealth and wellbeing. It's not like you have to worry about space or resources, we literally can't run out of either down here. What are you afraid of? The Celestial Choir? The throne in heaven hears no song and that's not going to change any time soon. YHVH is gone. Yeshua is gone. Those hypocritical peace-doves are too busy bickering over how to interpret their Lord's will to ever take action. The Overworld is incapable of doing anything but hold the fort, and we practically already run the Midworld so why are you fucking with the Underworld instead of running it properly?"

"Lascivus. My Lascivus. My dear, sweet, precious Little Horn."

A man in a suit no longer. I am beholden before Babel made flesh. A vast thing towered above and below me, impossibly tall and tightly enclosed by vast wings that could scarcely contain the brightness of the one named Lightbringer and Morning Star. Wings untouched by the blight of miasma. Eyes. Countless eyes. Eyes that saw me and saw through me and saw everything. One gigantic, eye covered wing reached out and brushed my cheek with gentleness that seemed perverse to come from something so vast.

"You are still so naïve."

29

Splintered Octaves

Draco

Soft grass. Softer than grass, a bed. Not a bed, a couch. Drakkengard helped me up.

"About time you knocked conscious," spoke a voice, young and pompous. A girl in a bandana. There were mirrors all around us. My left arm had been bandaged. My head felt drunk, doped, and concussed.

"Where are we?" Drakkengard asked. The bandana girl scoffed and turned up her nose.

"Not even a word of thanks for my dragging you off the street and providin' you hap? The world really is going up the shitter. You two saps are in the best part of the Burgh, *my* part of the Burgh, and it'd do you well to be grateful." She walked over and sniffed Drakkengard, recoiled and turned away. "I was right. You are as big a disappointment as the other one."

"Wait, you know me?" Drakkengard tilted her head.

"Yeah, can you believe those sad sack nutjobs actually tried to use a chance at meeting you as a bartering chip? Hah, what a rip off that would have been. It is you, right? The kidnapped father and his domestic? I knew it. I gave a helping hand to that daughter of his when she was looking for him. Why, if it weren't for my help I bet you'd have been fed to the boy scouts by now, or whatever stupid situation you'd been in."

"It was an angel," Drakkengard scowled and crossed her arms.

"Did I ask for your opinion, housecat? What I wanna know is what your sorry asses are doing on my turf uninvited. Especially after I just got done expanding it."

"Something has gone horribly wrong. Master's connection with the Void has been damaged, and his mind along with it. We were sent hurtling through nothingness without direction and—"

"Blah blah blah portal accident. Boring. Now I'm insulted, you're not even here to see me."

"Master was trying to find Eltanim. With his head all shaken up he just went for the last place they met."

"Am I supposed to know or care who that is? It's not me, so obviously not. For crying out loud, how thick can you be?" She walked over to me and peered into my eyes. After several seconds she raised her hand and swung her fist at my head.

"Back off," Drakkengard growled, the bandanna girl's fist caught in her hand.

"Get bent, slag." The girl pulled her arm loose and held it on her hip. "This creep ain't all there, is he?"

I should . . . what?

"I need to find some way to help Master. I can't just leave him like this."

"Why not? It seems pretty convenient to me. I mean, you'll never be as free as me, but this comes pretty close, right? He can't tell you what to do, and all you have to worry about is making sure he doesn't drown on his own drool or something equally pathetic."

Drakkengard considered the girl for a few seconds. "You're the same as me?"

"What did I just say about being thick? If you keep taking this long to realize things I'm going to have to start slapping you." The girl tilted her head to the side and from her neck shot out a long metal spike, which withdrew. "I'm Somnia, the only free member of our kind. It really is your fault for not having heard of me."

"Did Malign make you too?"

"Who? I was made by Pops. Damn good job of it he did too." Somnia turned around to admire her reflection in the countless mirrors around us. "Wish I could say the same for you. I don't know who this Melon is but they did a piss poor imitation. I bet they were working off one of the older designs, too. Not me, I'm one of few surviving of the latest and last batch made by Pops himself."

"This is so weird," Drakkengard balked. "I mean, I knew there were more of us, but until now I'd only ever seen Deserere."

"Oh yeah, that guy. I don't suppose your idiot's useless kids actually killed him like they said they would, did they?"

"Well, I mean, at lot happened at once and he got away."

"Typical. You want something done properly and you can't trust anyone. They show their face here again I'll have them tarred and flogged."

"Don't you mean feathered?"

"I'm running a turf war here, not a slumber party."

We were interrupted by a knock on a door somewhere.

"Somnia, have they arisen?"

"Yes, Pops," the girl drawled indolently.

"I would see them."

"Whatever, get an eyeful. Yo, both of you, looks like the only person almost half as great as I am wants you. Get in there." She jerked her thumb toward a side door and slumped down on the couch I had been sleeping on. "Go on, hurry up."

Drakkengard shrugged and we went out through the door as directed. Inside was some rather Spartan quarters. There was a bedroll, a dresser, and a cleared space on the floor that had been worn smooth. Sitting cross legged on the cleared space was a figure in loose clothes and of indeterminate gender, but when they spoke their voice was masculine.

He looked at me with distant, tired eyes. He blinked, and his eyes had been swapped for a different pair.

"Our children do turn up in the strangest places," he said, but with an odd, feminine echo to his voice.

"Children? Are you—?" Drakkengard started.

"I am." He opened his mouth in a yawn, but it never actually ended. A silvery bulge surged up from his throat and forces its way past his jaw. His skull folded in on itself and a wholly new head took its place. This one was sleek, slender, with high cheek bones and a narrow chin.

"Is it comfortable, having an absolutely selfless slave?" He, no, she sidled up to me and placed a masculine hand on my chest. I shoved her away and she, no, they laughed, but not in taunt.

"No, there's something different here." The bimorphic person circled us, leaning forward to peer at Drakkengard and myself from different angles.

Drakkengard watched their movements without turning her head, her eyes darted from side to side as she tracked them in their encircling. "I don't like the way you're—," she growled.

"—looking at me," I spat, clenched and unclenched my fists, and loosed a few trails of smoke skyward. It dawned on me that was the first thing I'd consciously said since waking.

"Ah, I see." They stepped next to me and placed a hand around my ear. I took a swing at them but where I expected firm flesh instead I found viscous fluid, and my limb passed through their body without resistance.

"Tell me, when you first made contact, was the bonding process interrupted by your death?" Sometimes the feminine voice spoke, sometimes the masculine one did, and sometimes it was a blend, and they flowed between these three modes seamlessly as they talked.

"I don't remember. What does it matter?" Did I say that or did Drakkengard?

"Do try to remember. This is important."

"I—" I closed my eyes, in spite of the urge to fight or flee. At that time, what had happened? I escaped. In my escape I stumbled across . . . a coffin? No, a tube. There was something inside. Something, a person? A sword? A blob? No, that's wrong. *I didn't escape.*

"Oho, so that's it. There was a death but it wasn't clinical."

I snapped back to alertness. They were peering into Drakkengard's eye and ignored her lashing out as she tried to back away.

"Stop that!"

"That was quite a nasty ego death. Interesting." They skittered around. "We'd never thought of triggering an imprint upon a subject who'd undergone ego death. Nominally all the variables, from mannerisms to gender to stature are determined via analysis of a deep psych profile, but you didn't have a complete psyche to work with. We see, we see, she was a catalyst for you just as much as her. It must have taken months, years even to put your head back together, and our child was there every step of the way, changing as you changed and you changed as she changed. She's not just a servant, is she?"

"Who are you?" she demanded.

"You can call us Samrae Kan'm. Whose name was that though? Was it mine? Or was it mine?" the two voices spoke, "Who knows? Well, it's our name so it doesn't matter."

"You called me your child. Somnia implied something like that too."

"Yes, we, well, I created her kind," Samrae Kan'm paused. "Since you seem to have a fondness for the Roman, Divinatelum works."

"Divine weapon?"

"Folklore would have it the Imperial family stole divinity from the mad god. Buying into their propaganda proved more rewarding than not," they shrugged, and their face shimmered between the two shapes. "I was a doctor, mostly bioengineering and thaumaturgy. After yet another scandal a certain Emperor-to-be commissioned something new, the perfect companion that would never bore or betray or misinterpret or do anything selfish. I was young and lacking scruples." They folded their arms. "I initially set out to just make a telepathic golem, but instead created something so much more." They stroked their cheek fondly and closed their eyes. "We were the result of my research. It's an existence more satisfying than anything prior.

It was just a bit too intimate for our patron, though, so the method was refined. A few tweaks here and there to stop the new entity from bonding quite so comprehensively. People can be so scared of sudden change, as though it makes a difference if it takes ten minutes or a hundred years. We succeeded, and our children were born. Had we not been so elated with our new existence we might not have assumed they'd be treated as well as they deserve."

"I can imagine."

"No, you really, really can't," said the masculine voice. "Or perhaps you can, your master was dead when you met for a reason after all," continued the feminine voice.

"Is there a point to this?"

"No point. They all died anyway. There was a catastrophe during the Red Princess's initiation. The thirteenth in line to the throne at that, it would have been thousands of years before she became relevant at large. Now everyone is dead except for the few of us who were off planet at the time, and Utinia is a lifeless rock. Say, are you any relation to the Red Princess? You have her eyes." Those words evoked a flush of heat and pain, but far away, and I brushed it aside.

"Your whole race was wiped out? Don't you care?"

"It saved me wiping them out myself. A bunch of no good sadistic hedonists. They didn't deserve our children, and our children didn't deserve to suffer them. A few of our children also found their way off planet, of course. Now we pass the millenniums tracking them down and making sure they're being taken care of. How about you? They were your people too, or would have been."

I searched around my feelings, tried to find some reaction to this revelation. Nothing made itself known.

"I can't say it feels relevant to me. Just history that happened to other people. All it does is answer a few questions I never cared about."

"And rightly so." They seemed rather pleased. "It wasn't even our motherland, really, just a colony world founded by a tyrant. T'was Gaia that first bore our ancestors and to Gaia we returned. Though things had changed a lot since King Atlas ruled this world."

"Is that it? Does Master pass your evaluation?" Drakkengard asked. "We have kind of an urgent problem."

"He passes well enough. You seem fond of him and free of neglect. It shows pretty clearly when a Divinatelum is being abused. You can't hide it even if you want to, the way they rot from within. I suppose your urgent matter has to do with why you're thinking for the both of you."

"What?"

"You hadn't realized? I don't know what happened but he'd be in a coma right now if it weren't for you."

"Explain," Drakkengard demanded.

"How should I put it? His mind is unusable right now. He's not dead, however, so until such time as either he gets better or constructs a new ego, your imprint of his mind has restored to the last known good state, and that's being used as the reference for how best to serve in the absence of explicit instruction. Emulation of the last rollback state. Every Divinatelum has a copy of their master in their head. As it happens, there's also enough of your body lingering inside his body to maintain a feedback loop between his body and yours via impulses sent between his nerves and your pseudo-cells."

I touched my chest and concentrated. "So the me that's thinking right now, is actually inside Drakkengard?"

"Yes. I suppose that might pose an existential quandary for some people."

"What will happen if we don't fix him?" Drakkengard asked.

"Well like I said, assuming his brain still works enough, eventually his mind will construct a new ego, and a new template based on that will overwrite the current one."

"So we'll die. Both Master and I, and other people will live out the rest of our lives."

"Well that's one way to look at it. His new ego might be close enough to the old ego that you don't notice a difference. Some might also argue that it won't matter if you get back your old ego, it'll be death just the same. As someone that's already lived through one ego death, I suppose you're in a position to make such a call."

"What about you? Your ego is different to the one you had before you became half-sword."

"No one has the same self-perception that they did when they were young, and it doesn't take ego death for ones sense of self to undergo dramatic upheaval. From where we stand, it just feels like I gained a lot of maturity and insight, not different from a profound dream or hearing a life-changing speech. I've no mind to debate if that's correct or not, you can sort that out for yourself."

Somnia elbowed into the room and pointed to me.

"Hey. Some other guy that looks like you is here. You better not be having a party at my expense. Go rent out a hotel or something if you're gonna invite all your friends over."

"Eltanim?" Drakkengard asked, and we rushed out into the mirror hall.

The man waiting for me was not Eltanim, though he did have my face. "Hello, I am the prime. Please kill me." His clothes were plain, and his hair and eyes were both brown—the same as Drakkengard's.

"Who are you?" she demanded. The duplicate slouched with a sigh.

"That's a complicated question," he frowned. "I'll keep it brief. The fact is your granddaughter found her way into The Garden."

"What? How? That place should have been buried beneath more pseudo-reality than a forgotten dream." Drakkengard balked. "The Void likes her more than it likes you, plain and simple. You're close, but she's closer. She wanted in and The Void accommodated her." He didn't look to me or Drakkengard but to both of us, speaking to us as a single entity.

"Typical, even the non-universe can't pass a chance to screw us over," I managed to grumble. "Why did she even want in, though?"

"Even as she is, she's still a curious child. She must have found some clue to her existence."

"Okay, so she got into Eden, shouldn't it have just reformed around her mind?"

"Have you ever seen inside that girl's mind? You tried to analyze her once, it's a phantasmagoria in there. The Garden just couldn't get a fix and gave up."

"So she's mucking around in my mind right now." I groaned.

"No, fortunately," he wandered over to a hanging mirror and locked eyes with my reflection. "If she was I'd know. She did open the cage, but that was just because it was in the way to reaching her true prize."

"Which was?"

"I can see whatever state you're currently in has left you a good deal slower than usual. Not that you're fast on a good day. You know how she came about. She went for the cornerstone."

"Shit."

"Shit indeed. The Garden makes real metaphors, and she just performed a metaphorical lobotomy on your connection to the Void."

"So that explains why Sacram collapsed," Drakkengard complained, "but why should that break Master's mind? He had lived for years before ever encountering the Void."

"Now that's a blatant lie," not-I chuckled. "You were born with those holes in your brain. The Void had already filled them before you could even say your name. It's a stupid, pretentious name by the way. Why couldn't you have chosen something a little more contemporary?"

"I don't even remember why I chose it," Drakkengard shrugged. "So, what, without the Void, Master's mind just collapsed?"

"Like a Jenga tower."

"So what are you?"

"The Garden makes metaphors real. I'm one of the pieces of your mind."

"Damn and blast!" Drakkengard drove her heel into the ground.

"Quite so. My siblings tore up our roots and left. Most of us have no intention of going back to you. Actually, most think they are the original you. Quite the predicament."

"So are you here to kill Master so you'll always be free?"

"No! No, what a dreadful thing that would be. I'm here to turn myself in."

"I don't buy it. What's so different about you? Why have you realized all this, but they haven't?"

"Allow me to demonstrate," the other me took from his slacks a knife, one designed for injury rather than utility. The blade was three inches long, and shone brightly in the hall of mirrors. He turned the blade around, placed it against his neck, and pulled. Slowly, far too slowly, the knife split his throat from end to end. There was no blood, which only made it easier to see exactly what a cross-section of my neck looked like as his head dangled behind on a shred of skin. Then, long, thin branches erupted from his neck stump and skewered his dangling head and like a whaler's hooks pulled it back down. His eyes flew open and he vomited up a handful of dry leaves.

"I feel sick," Drakkengard whimpered.

"None of the others have tried inflicting self-injury like this, I imagine. If so I am the only one that knows. We're metaphors. We're not alive. We don't have blood or organs. Though we think otherwise, the appetites we have are not from real need but just an extension of our metaphor. My only appetite is to cease existing."

"You said you came here to turn yourself in."

"Yes. I can't stand existing like this. I liked it better as a tree." He turned his knife on his chest this time, and cut a line of vivisection. "Now, I'm about to hand you something, and you need to accept it from me. Just take it. That should satisfy the metaphor enough that I won't just grow back from it. Beyond that, I don't care," he grunted and forced his hand into the wound. "Well that's not true. I'd be really, really happy if you failed, but I'll be satisfied with never having to think for myself ever again. Now, what I'm about to give you, it's a fruit. I'm only working on guesses here but I suspect you need to eat the fruit and plant the seed inside it back in Eden. Otherwise I might come back down the track. I recommend collecting all your bits first and doing it all at once. Otherwise it might just run loose again, and we don't want that." He doubled over, his hand buried to the wrist in his chest cavity. "Thank gods I don't have bones, or this would be more difficult." He wrenched his hand out, and grasped in it is a large, black fruit with red barbs that dripped with viscous green fluids. "Do you accept this?"

"Yes," I said, and my voice came from my mouth. I took the fruit from his hand, and his eyes rolled back in orgiastic bliss.

"One last thing. The One Who Came Before . . ."

The metaphor collapsed. Not even dust was left. I tossed the fruit to Drakkengard and she swallowed it whole, despite its size.

"Don't worry, Master. I'll keep it safe. I won't crush it or anything." My head grew foggy again, and speaking took an insurmountable effort. I'd thought it was Samrae Kan'm that somehow restored some of my autonomy, but it must have been the other Me's proximity.

"Master, could we use Kali to track down the rest?" Drakkengard asked. I shook my head. That one said they had no blood, and that means Kali can't find them.

Still, it would be prudent to see my daughter. She was no doubt wanting to know what happened and where her daughter is. Kali would lead her to me, so we may as well find somewhere to meet her. Somnia looked like she just needed to think of a good excuse to put us under a twenty four hour firing squad. Better leave first. I nodded to Somnia and we head outside.

Cicula had mentioned a gang in the park when she told her side of what went down during my kidnapping. I could see how it might have once been a park, but no matter how I looked at it this was clearly a military base. Sleek buildings patrolled by heavily armed soldiers, some vehicles, and even an AA gun they somehow got their hands on. Somnia was clearly a sword coming up in the world.

30

Anxiety Measure

Cicula

Panic was a primal thing. Useful in primal situations. It allowed the chemically programmed mind to fight harder and flee harder. Muscle damage from overexertion hardly mattered when the alternative was death.

Cicula. You have to breathe.

It was not so useful in more complex situations. When you don't know where to run. When you don't know who to fight. When what you need it cunning, guile or wisdom.

You're about to black out, Cicula. Oh, forget it. I'm taking over.

Stress from internal conflict when neither fight nor flight can be appeased is the curse of higher thought.

I've found Draco. I'm taking us to him.

Fuck my father. What happened to my daughter? Everything suddenly vanished and there was so much screaming where is she? How was I supposed to breathe? "Where the fuck is my daughter?"

My chest was compressed tightly, and then forced wide. Kali had taken control of my breathing. Fresh oxygen flooded my brain and stopped the world from spinning.

"We don't know," Drakkengard said. *When did she get here?*

Do you remember the bridge where we last encountered Deserere? Drakkengard and Draco were waiting for us there. Cicula you need to get out of your head and open your eyes.

"What am I supposed to do in this situation?" Drakkengard again. "Usually slap them, right? Is that actually how it works, or was that just an excuse to be violent?"

"What the fuck is she blathering on about?"

"Maybe she should burn something. That usually calms Master down."

Yeah. Burn something. That sounded like a good idea. My fingers pulled a joint from my pouch and lit up. Did I do that or did Kali? The world spun again but fog cushioned my brain and slowed everything down. Where was I? Right, the bridge. It was just starting to get dark and there was a person maybe so many meters or so apart going someplace or somewhere. The moon wasn't out and the streetlights were on. I was here. Kali spoke through me. Father and his retainers were here too.

I wrested control of my voice back. "Where is my daughter? What did you do?"

"We didn't do anything," Drakkengard protested. "She's the one who messed things up."

"Don't pin the blame on her, you useless butterknife. Father, answer me!" His too-young face swam into focus. It was disgusting. He was in his late thirties at least but still looked like a young man in his twenties. It was nauseating. His too smooth, too clean face stared blankly at me. Reminded me of the French girl.

"Master is having trouble speaking right now. Again, thanks to your kleptomaniac daughter."

"What the fuck did he do, have his brain in a jar or something?"

"Um, kind of," she squirmed.

"Fucking typical." I put my smoke out on the ground and lit another.

"Kid, come on. Let's at least find out what the go is. We just got here ourselves," Ko said. Of course he was calm. His child didn't just vanish along with a whole fortress.

Come on dear, just take a few steps back and we can sort this out.

My jaw ached from yelling and grinding but I managed to quash it down and settle for sucking on my joint. For her.

"No, really, Draco, what mess have you set off now?"

"It's kinda like, okay, so that place where the angel woman took Master that turned itself into his head, well Master stole it. It seemed like a good idea," Drakkengard nervously poked her fingers together and refused to make eye contact. "But even though it was super hidden and turbo protected Shahdee just asked the Void to make a back door and it did, because it likes her better than Master."

"That's a rather personified way to put it," Kali said through my mouth.

"I don't wanna debate metaphysics with a goddess of breaking things," Drakkengard pouted.

"Now you're just insulting me."

"I mean it's not the point," Drakkengard frowned in anger. "Shahdee snuck into this doobob of Master's mind and apparently stole the part of it that is his connection to the Void, or something. That basically made the whole thing fall apart like stacked matchsticks, and now we have to find the pieces?" She gave a weak shrug.

"Oh really? Well that's all well and good, but where in the name of the nine circles of Hell is my fucking daughter?"

"We don't know," she slumped. "Maybe she's hiding somewhere with her new toy, or maybe she decided to tag along with some of Master's brain bits."

"Oh for the love of—Kali, why haven't you done your bloody thing to find her?"

"I tried," she said through me, "but there must be something masking her presence, or else she's gone where I can't feel her, and before you ask, no I can't feel anything that might be the shattered remnants of Draco's mind either."

"That's what I figured," Drakkengard sighed. "I mean, we met one, and he didn't even have blood. He was just a— what was it?— A metaphorical tree, or something. Do you think they make a noise when they fall in the woods?"

"I am going to strangle you. I don't care if you don't need to breathe and don't have bones. I am going to wring your little neck until it's nothing but a metal noodle."

"If I might interject,"

"What?" I barked at Vengai-Ra. He coughed and fiddled with his coat pocket.

"Lascivus. I'm still not sure if she is a succubus or is just like a succubus, but does she not have her own supernal senses? Some arcane nonsense about detecting life's 'intensity' or 'density' or some such thing that shouldn't work but does."

"For a guy who made a deal with a devil, you can be such an arcanophobe," Ko chided. With a huff I turned around and started drawing up a circle to Hell.

"Say, uh, aren't you meant to not do that in so public a place?" The gunman glanced anxiously at the other people on the bridge.

"Fuck 'em. Shahdee might be in danger. Besides, no one cares. Everyone either knows about magick or doesn't want to know." I clenched the chalk between my teeth and used the metal fake nail I wore to spill a drop of blood on the circle to activate it. None of the other pedestrians so much as glanced at us. "Who needs a conspiracy when you've got apathy?"

31

Larghetto of Loathing

Lascivus

I returned home, still shaken from my meeting with Dad. His outbursts were getting more and more frequent. He used to go centuries before snapping like that. Now it happened almost every time someone questioned him. My children didn't get it. They weren't even a hundred years old and are only Cambions to boot. It's not about losing your temper. They think when he or any other demon does it it's just an attempt to look intimidating, like an animal puffing up its fur. It's not. To show your wings, to drop your glamour and show your true faces, that's like pointing a loaded gun at someone and keeping your finger on the trigger. Especially for the more powerful demons that can kill without moving a muscle.

If a gang leader pulled a gun on everyone that questioned them, it would not be long before everyone caught on to how any one of them could get blown away for the pettiest slight, and what does is say for the authority of the leader when it's only through the threat of violence they can get people to listen to them? It's not like Dad lacked charisma. He was infamous for it. Did he know something we didn't that had him on edge? Or had God's absence finally driven him mad?

Maybe I was overanalyzing it. I took a swig from my bottle but it was already emptied. I put it beside my desk and pulled out another. Maybe I was just making excuses for him. Am I wrong to trust him? Am I wrong to want to trust him? Just what in Hell was going on?

"Marie?" I called out. My house replied in snide silence.

That's right. She'd knocked off for the night. I took out a glass for my alcohol, may as well be a bit civilized for once, but the bottle was already empty. Really? Already? I put it with the others and got out a fresh one. No matter. It had been over a thousand years since I'd been able to get black out drunk. Those were the days. If I was naïve now I must have been outright deluded then. I took out Impiocassus and turned the unholy blade over in my hand.

I made it myself but not for me. The blade she made for me only got used once. Nausea rose in my gut. *Fucking useless piece of shit*. I poured a glass and shot it down to keep myself from taking the easy way and refusing to think about it. What was the one she made called? Cal . . . Calo . . . Caelos something. Funny, I used to be quite good at making swords but I never even thought about making any after that. Well I knew for a fact that she never did. A thimble of bile splashed into my mouth. I washed it down with more mead.

Maybe I should get back into it, smithing. Well, Impiocassus had served me fine over the centuries, and I could never be asked to make something as complex as Drakkengard. Hell, if he ever used a different sword that'd probably be a fully-fledged infidelity for him. Maybe Lach would like some new pointy things to play with. *Stupid idiot, you're avoiding it again.*

I took out a sheet of parchment and a pen, and wrote a name on it. Lorica. Her name. Backstabbing dead bitch. I put the sheet in front me and stared at it, forced myself to remember, forced myself to see the nape of her neck in the crook of the room, to see the white, angelic eye in the lamp right before I jammed that shithead's 'present' right in her fucking socket like a bullseye and—

I tore the paper to shreds and burned it. Fuck everything. Why did I have to be reminded of her at all? That's right, all those demons going missing made me think of when that angel abducted Draco, so that must have reminded me of *her* on some level.

I laughed, but it was a forced sound that just made me feel mocked. With nothing better to do I poured myself another glass and leafed through some of the messages left on my desk. Among them sat a report on that expedition today that the kids were a part of. Apparently a strong Nephilim tried to interfere, but they managed to drive it off and finished the job. Heh, not bad. Maybe I should do something to congratulate them.

Still, a Nephilim, that was odd. Siring one of those tall bastards was usually grounds for getting kicked down here, and a new fallen was uncommon enough that I'd have heard of it. Either this guy had somehow avoided getting knocked off for a long time without making a name for himself, or else the retirement home in the attic was starting to get a little more lenient with upholding their missing boss's edicts. Those things grow up pretty fast and hung around for ages so it was pretty hard to guess an age. A loud noise broke my thought, and Draco stumbled into the room.

"It's bad. It's terrible. Woe, catastrophe," he stammered as he approached. His eyes were dilated, and seemed somehow plundered of their luster. His hair was looking rather grey as well, but maybe that was my other sight.

"What happened? Your age finally caught up to you?" I brushed my fringe out of my eyes and leaned back on my chair. Maybe it was time I went for a trim.

"No, it's, I don't know what it's. I was there, at Sacram, and oh god. Drakkengard? Where is Drakkengard? It's gone. It's all gone. Ehehehe."

"Get a hold of yourself."

"Lascivus, please, you have to help me." He fell to his knees besides my desk and clawed at my legs with withered nails. I scowled and kick him off.

"You're pathetic. Get up." I shoved him again with my foot, but he just collapsed in a sniveling heap.

"I can't. I cannot. Where is Drakkengard? Where is my flame? What am I supposed to do?"

"Oh for fucks sakes. You're what? Thirty? Sixty? Way too young to have a midlife crisis," I gritted my teeth. Could he have chosen a worse time to have a breakdown? I had work to do.

"Please, I'll do anything. Just help me find her."

"You're pissing me off. You think I got nothing better to do?"

"What, drink your loathing away?" A harsh whine entered his voice. "What about our contract? I'm your husband, you have to help me." He hazarded to look up at me, a desperate sneer on his face. I drove the toe of my foot into his gut with enough force to lift him off the ground.

"You do not talk to me like that." I kicked him again. "Who the hell do you think I am?" I lifted him up by the collar like an empty pillowcase and pinned him to the wall. "You go buggering off to fuck around with your new toy, never take the time to visit, and come crawling to me the second something goes wrong? You're such a fucking child." I put him down and stepped back, arms folded. His eyes flashed with the cruel hunger of resentment.

"Just try it," I goaded.

He lunged for me, arms stretched at my throat, but they never closed. He fell against my chest and slid to the ground.

"What?" I balked, dumbfounded.

Ko and Vengai-Ra ran through the door, the soldier's smoking gun still trained on Draco. The doctor crouched beside him and rolled him over. The front of his head burst open like a cracked water pipe, yet the damage was weirdly dry.

"Turning against your master are you?" My voice was shakier than I'd have liked.

"I, uh, wouldn't say that," Drakkengard entered the room. Her black robes swept the floor as she walked. "How is it?" She asks the duo.

"I'd hesitate to call it 'alive', but, well, it's 'alive'."

"He's coming round, stand back." Ko ushered the doctor aside and fired three more bullets into Draco's face. His rifle made only a soft 'fwip' with each shot. "Alright, it's clear. You can come in now." Finally, Draco stepped inside, his eyes as red and hair as black as that night I first tried to make him prey, yet his face was blank of all expression.

"Somebody want to fill me in on what the *shit* this is?" I gestured at the twitching body on the floor. "Some kind of shapeshifter? I mean I figured something wasn't right about it, but give me a clue here."

Drakkengard looked up at me with her big hazel eyes in apology. "It's a bit complicated. Hang on we need to extract it first."

"Extract what?" I demanded, but got no answer. Draco walked over to his double, face still blank, and rolled up his sleeve. With a sharp jab his hand penetrated his double's chest. Its mouth flew open, but after taking so many bullets to the face all it could muster was an ugly gurgle. Draco wrenched his hand back out, and clasped in his fingers was a strange, spiky fruit. He gave it to Drakkengard who swallowed it whole, unfettered by the sharp protrusions. She gulped, rubbed her throat, and breathed a sigh of relief. Then she turned to me.

"Sorry. We couldn't risk it recovering and getting away. It was only a bit of luck that we could sneak up on it at all."

"Luck nothing. I noticed that thing's trail a mile away," Ko complained. Drakkengard glanced back at the thing's corpse, which rapidly crumbled to nothingness. If that stained the carpet there would be blood to pay.

"I wish they didn't have Master's face. It's gonna be so gross to kill all of them," she shuddered.

"Hey, sword girl, explanations. Why is my consort looking a few beers short of a party?"

"Right, right, sorry." She clasped her hands together. "Um, do you want the long version or the short version?"

"Ooh, short," I forced a smile.

"Shahdee broke Master. We're gathering the pieces. That was one of them."

"See, that wasn't so hard. I wish a few more people could give me such straight answers." I let myself relax, and returned to my chair for another drink. "Still, a bit odd I guess. Plenty of gods and daemons have splintered over the years, but not many people of pure flesh and blood. Well, except for dream walkers."

"It kinda turns out that putting a thing that makes physical reflections of your mind in a place you can shape with your mind is a teensy bit of a bad idea," Drakkengard smiled hesitantly and cringed.

"Hell's bells, Draco can be a dumbass." I took a swig of my drink and walked over to him. "Can you hear me in there? You're a dumbass," I turned to Vengai-Ra, "can he hear me in there?"

"No, but he can hear you in there," the doctor pointed to Drakkengard.

"Really? Neat. So I guess you'll be off to find the rest of those," I waved my hand, "whatsits."

"Actually," Drakkengard said, "We weren't expecting to find one here."

"Do you know why it came here?" Ko asked. "That might help understand the rest."

"Ugh, it wouldn't shut up about why. It was all 'help me, help me you stuck up bitch, oh I'm so pathetic.' I can't believe something that gross came from you." I couldn't tell if I should be talking to Draco or Drakkengard. I settled for the space between them.

"I guess my hunch was right. I figured it wouldn't be an even break," she said thoughtfully.

"Huh?"

"It looks like each piece isn't a clean portion. If a mind is a loaf of bread, each of them isn't a slice but a heap of random crumbs."

"I follow the metaphor, but I don't see your point. For a sword that's a pretty big failing"

"I mean, wife, some personality traits aren't going to be present enough for them to be balanced. The first one didn't have enough will to live, so it sought us out to die. This one didn't have enough self-sufficiency, so it came to you for help."

"Huh. That's pretty smart coming from you," I said, eyebrows raised.

"What's that supposed to mean, you old hag?" she said, but without venom.

"Nevermind, I take it back. You're still a brat." And back down my brows went.

"So continuing from earlier," Vengai-Ra interrupted. "We can anticipate each 'fragment' or whatever to be driven to absolve itself of its deficiencies."

"When you put it like that it gives me a bad feeling," Drakkengard shivered.

"Oh yeah, where's Cicula?" I asked. "Wasn't she going over to yours today?"

"Ah, she went to find Lach. Actually, there is something," The sword girl wrung her hands anxiously. "We don't know where Shahdee is. We know she has one of the fragments, but unlike the others it's a specific part, Master's connection to the Void."

"Wait, that's a mental thing?"

"Yup. You need the right mode of thought to use the Void, but nothing else. We taught it to Cicula after all. Well, her goddess helped."

"Whatever, nevermind that. Just how are you planning to find our granddaughter?"

"Actually we were hoping you could help. You can sense life force, and you always said Master had a way of standing out.

These things aren't made of flesh and blood so Kali can't help, but they're still 'alive' in some sense so we were wondering if there weren't some way you could find them." She gave me that greedy kitten look.

"Stop that. Still, now that you mention it, I would have noticed if the thing's vitae had a different signature to Draco's." I put a hand to my brow, "I can't just search the whole universe though, and those things could be anywhere."

Drakkengard shook her head. "Not anywhere. They've all been cut off from the Void just as Master has. They would have all been shunted back to Earth or Hell."

"Well that makes things convenient. I can have word put out so that if any others are down here they'll be snatched up. That still leaves all of Earth though. Hrm . . ." I took a long drink of mead as I thought. "Actually there is something, the globe of Copernicus, taken from his observatory. I think Stolas has it these days."

"How much will it cost?"

"Stolas owes me a few favors. I'll just cash in one of those. Alright," I slammed my drink down. "Leave a note for Lach and Cicula if they come back. I'll hail a palanquin."

***

Stolas made his home in the 4th Bolgia, atop a house made from a great hollowed out tree. I departed the palanquin with the others, tipped the porter, and headed inside. Lesser demons scurried around the place, along with the backwards-headed damned that lurk this Bolgia. At the middle of the hollow tree sat an elevating platform, and that took us up to the demon's office.

"Stolas you featherbrained bastard, how have you been?" I greeted him enthusiastically. The bespectacled demon turned his head 180 and stared at me, before rotating the rest of his body too.

"Lascivus? Hoo hoo, I haven't had a visit from you in a while." He fussed with his cravat, which makes the small crown floating above his head bob from the movement. His long, skinny legs were hugged tightly by his pants. "Everything in order, I trust."

"Relax, there's no complaint for you. There is a favor you can do me, though. Do you still have the globe of Copernicus? I just need to use it for a few minutes."

"Hoo, that old thing? Yes, it should be lying around here somewhere." He stepped away from the window and starts pulling open draws from the many cabinets surrounding us. "Ah, here it is." He pulled out a wooden sphere held in place by a pair of rotating semicircles. "I had the enchantments reinforced just the other decade so it should work fine."

"Ah, thank-you, thank-you. Do you mind if I use it here?"

"Not at all. Help yourself. Didn't feel like bartering with one of those cut-throat seers, eh? Hoo hoo."

"If you want something done your way you can't rely on anyone." I cleared a space on his desk and set the globe down.

While the others waited patiently around the room Drakkengard peered over my shoulder in curiosity. Slowly the sphere gained color—the oceans turned blue while browns and greens covered the land. With a magnifying glass or keen enough vision it was possible to make out cities or even individual buildings.

"I know what you mean, I know what you mean. Why just the other year I lost four assistants I sent out to gather some rare toxins. I told the silly fools not to lick anything, hoo hoo."

I gave the globe a spin and peered into it with my other sight. Bright lights quickly spread all across its surface.

"What's happening? I can't see anything."

"Shhh."

I squinted, and mentally filtered out the dimmer lights. Fish, bugs, beasts, ordinary humans, I didn't care about them. Gradually I discerned the brighter beacons, powerful magi, prowling demons, guardian angels, monstrous things that stalked frozen mountains and unspeakable things sleeping in the ocean's depths or buried beneath the rock. Even those guardian twins, the Faerans, were picked up, shining with the brightness of the whole planet. I wondered if they were still rocking the band gig. I focused harder still, and scan for the distinct blaze of Draco's vitae.

"Aha, there's one, and another. Three, four, five in total. No, six. Huh, that last one is a little odd."

"How about Shahdee? Any sign of her?"

"Hmm . . . no, I'm afraid not." I blinked and rubbed my eyes. "I'm sorry."

"It's okay she should be with one of them anyway. I just hope she's safe."

"Here's hoping. Alright Stolas, I'm done with this." I stepped away from the table and stretched.

"Hoo hoo, not a problem," the great prince beamed at me with unblinking eyes. "I trust that this fulfills services rendered?"

"Yes, yes, that's one less favor you owe me."

"Good, good, good. Was there, ah, anything else?"

"No, not today. See ya later, you old owl."

"Likewise, Lascivus."

***

We returned home, and I drew up a map of the other fragments' locations.

"Try not to lose it. I don't want you coming back here every half hour because you forgot where you were going."

"So you won't be joining us?" Vengai-Ra asked.

"No can do. My hands are bound trying to appease every disgruntled noble in Dis."

Cicula arrived with her bother soon after, and the lot of them leave the room to make preparations. Draco and Drakkengard linger.

"You look terrible." Drakkengard says.

"Well shit, thanks. You look quite a piece of work yourself," I jerked my thumb at Draco's zombie-like body.

"No, really. Luci must be running you between a river and a grindstone," she looked up with a slight frown. "Is there anything you need help with?"

I laughed, roaring so hard that my sides ached. "In the state you're in, you think you can afford to waste time helping my sorry ass run petty errands?"

"Oh come now, it'd be a shame if something happened to you while I'm off saving my own neck."

"Your neck? Am I talking to the boy or the sword here?"

"Both," she shrugged, "same as always, really."

"Same as always, huh?" and she was right, to think of it. It really didn't feel any different to our other conversations.

Ah, so it really was like that.

"Lascivus?"

"Forget it. You just hurry up and put yourself back in two pieces."

I stood there for some time, until long after they'd all gone. "Please stay safe," I said aloud.

32

Instrumentation Theft

Michael

"I'll start from the beginning," my new companion said. He sat huddled around the fire and draped in furs. "When I was just a boy, a witch and a trickster came to my village. They both looked as children, but that may well have just been the form they took. At first they were mostly harmless. They played pranks, scared livestock, broke some things. Once everyone had had enough they all rallied together to drive them out. No one really wanted to kill them, just make them leave. Against this, the witch summoned a demon—no, not a demon, some dark god. An ugly thing with shaggy hair, thin as a corpse, and a noose around its neck. She tore it out of the ground as easily as plucking a stone from a still river. It then began killing. It sucked the youth straight from their throats, inflicting hundreds of years in seconds.

The trickster—I remember that he wore green—he was both furious and mortified. He quickly banished the dark god, but it had already claimed most of the village. Then he took the witch and left. Everyone still alive fled, mad with fear.

That was when I met the metal thing, the rusted thing. He looked like a blind priest. You sometimes saw such folk on pilgrimages. Though he was blind, he seemed to stare right into my madness. Every fault and crack in my terrified mind was under scrutiny." Otay paused to tear a bite out of the meat I had shared with him.

"Then what happened?"

"His arm became like ropes, and bound my entire body. He took me to a rusted room and forced me into a glass coffin. After that it was like a dream. I would be stabbed, sliced, bled, and pricked, drifting between sleep and half sleep.

Sometimes I was locked in rooms with horrifying monsters. I think that they were all him, taking different forms. They attacked me but never killed me. I think, looking back, that he was trying to provoke me. Eventually, I can only suppose, he gave up on those methods, because I woke up on the outskirts of the village with no sign of him.

I convinced myself that I had been mad the whole time, wandering the woods. That it was trees and brambles that bled me, that the monsters were just wild animals distorted by mania. I started life anew and let myself forget. No, I chose to forget. I was happy, until those four outlanders came."

"Four of them?"

"Yes. A man with hair as blue as cryst, another that looked like an academic from the city, a young man with restless feet, and a young woman that smelled of fog-grass. I had forgotten his face, but the metal thing had been living under the guise of a beggar in the area, and they were looking for it. No one had seen him for a while, but I led them to where he was known to stay. In there they found a secret path, and that led us to the metal room I had forgotten. At once I remembered everything and what made sense changed."

"How do you mean?"

"I think that's what the rusted thing wanted to happen, when he had me face monsters. New things made sense, that's the only way I can describe it. It made sense that I should bring ruin. It made sense that I should kill. It made sense that the mind is a thing that can move, and that if I move all the fire away what's left will turn to ice. It made sense that the young woman was the witch who let loose that dark god. It wasn't like a blind fury. It just, made sense. The same way it makes sense to drink water when you thirst and to seek shelter when it rains.

Things stopped making sense after that, but I had already frozen my whole village. I didn't know what to do so I fled to the mountains. Whenever I get angry or scared, things make sense again, and I'm not angry or scared anymore because I know what to do. I'm not angry or scared, but I'm still enraged." He glanced at the stump of his right arm.

"I said it before. Do not think you a monster. You have a sickness, not of the flesh or the blood but of the mind."

"So what happens now?"

"I believe the rusted thing serves something greater and more sinister. If my suspicions are correct what it serves presents a great danger. What I need is more information." I stirred the fire with a hardened stick. "I don't know the other two, but I have encountered the young man and woman of which you speak. I suspect they have some answers, but can't say if they shall part with them willingly."

33

Bloodlust Beat

Draco

"Hey, you busy?" Vengai-Ra came into the library.

"Just killing time," Drakkengard replied. He tightened his lips.

"Let me see your arm. It's bandaged for a reason, right?" Honestly it had slipped my mind. Without waiting for an answer he walked over and reached for it, pausing only at the last second. With a resigned shrug I held it out and let him unwind it.

"Oh, this is not pretty." The cloth bindings came away to reveal scorched and blistered flesh, blackened and raw, a horribly botched barbecue job. "How did this happen?"

"Same way as always. Things got emotionally volatile, and highly flammable. This time it just went both ways. Happened when everything tumbled down. That Somnia was 'nice' enough to bandage it."

"These are easily second degree burns." He clucked. "Maybe third, but you don't seem to be having any trouble moving it. Isn't there normally a mental block that keeps your magicks from affecting yourself? Ugh, I'm going to need to clean this." He set down a bag on the table and took from it some swabs and sealed vials, a pair of scissors too.

"Well, I mean this is just a guess, but it makes sense that'd go off self-image or something, right? Just what counts as 'self' is, uh, kind of an ambiguous thing for us both right now." Drakkengard shrugged and scratched her head.

"No kidding. It's not healing either, at least not like it normally does." He snapped on a pair of gloves and rubbed them with disinfectant.

"You probably know more about that than me."

"Well I've not been your physician all these years for nothing." After a quick needle jab into my shoulder he set to work cutting away at the dead flesh and cleaning everything else. It hurt, probably, no, it really didn't. However it *was* intrusive, like someone else's finger in your ear.

"And?"

"Well biological regeneration works via de-differentiation of adult cells into a stem-cell state, and those develop into new cells in pretty much the same way they were formed the first time. Normally this is only found in some species of lizards and amphibians. The energy demand is just too high to be efficient in a larger organism. You'd die of exhaustion before it was halfway done, or on the off chance your body could process it all fast enough you'd need to be eating many times your body weight every single day without break. In a mundane organism at least. You, on the other hand, just reflexively use magick to convert to raw dark energy. It works out more efficient than just conjuring up new skin or limbs identical to the old ones, which is more or less what most so-called healers do when they're actually any good at it. It really is a marvelous bit of engineering."

"Engineering?"

"Well some sort of sophisticated eugenics program could also explain it, but when that incident a while back reminded me how your blood samples got stolen it got me wondering just what was in it that could be worth the effort, so I've been looking into it. Turns out your DNA has some very distinct markers of a designer retrovirus."

"Wait, biochemistry was never Master's strong side. More of a fiction person," Drakkengard protested.

"A retrovirus is something that overwrites your genetic information to propagate. A designer retrovirus is something I've only read the theory of, but it means administrating a viral vector that makes specific kinds of alterations for a desired effect. In many ways it can be considered a form of gene therapy"

"So someone infected Master with this virus?"

"Maybe not him specifically. Maybe both his parents, or some combination of his grandparents, or who knows. Either way, I compared samples taken from different dates and it doesn't seem to be active anymore."

"Wait, if it can be passed on, are Lach and Cicula infected?"

"I thought of that, but from what samples I have of theirs they don't seem to have it. None of the markers are present."

"I'm not sure if that's a relief or not. I guess it's one less unknown. I mean, there's no telling what else it does."

"True. Better the devil you know, as they say. Although that might be in poor taste all things considered."

"Do you know why it wasn't passed on?"

"I have a couple hypotheses, but I haven't come up with any safe experiments to test them yet. It could be it can only be passed on when the retrovirus is active. It could also be that the amount of highly mutagenic miasma that naturally occurs in a cambion's makeup is enough to scramble the virus."

"Yet all the ambient miasma in the underworld doesn't do anything?" Drakkengard furrowed her brow.

"Well up to a certain point it's self-sustaining without the active virus now. Your body thinks the altered DNA is what's 'healthy' for you, and restores any genetic damage to that template. That kind of lossless replication is again pretty hard without magick. Administer enough miasma, or other mutagen for that matter, and there might be too much genetic damage to properly recover from. Of course if it is miasma that much will already have you on a fast track to becoming a full demon anyhow, if not jumping straight to field-layer, so if you do become walking cancer it'll be real colorful, so to speak."

"Ewww."

"Yeesh, every time I forget I'm not talking to Draco you go and remind me like that." Vengai-Ra adjusted his glasses. "These conversations are never going to cease being surreal. Look, I've finished cleaning this arm so let's just bandage it back up and get a move on. As a doctor I really shouldn't be letting you get anything but bed rest, but we all know that's not going to happen."

"Yup. Sorry."

"Oy, are you three ready?" Cicula calls from upstairs.

"I guess that's the last departure call." We made our way to the others, where Cicula had drawn up a sending sigil.

"So which are we going for first?"

"This one." Drakkengard pointed to part of the map. Cicula nodded and we stepped in.

We arrived in a strange landscape, not alien just unfamiliar. Or was that the same thing? Hills I didn't know, a river I didn't know, a hut I didn't know. Thunder rumbled and the ground cracked. Faces I did know. A man in pearly white armor grappled with a man in black oak, who hurled him off. They had only one sword between them, and it rapidly switched hands again and again through the fight. The warrior in white drove it through the other's skull and called lightning down upon it. The other's head and torso exploded, split down the middle like a tree. One hand shot out and snatched the sword a split second into its explosive flight. The arm lost no mobility despite being attached to a dangling shoulder. Splinters reversed their flight and restored the man in black.

"Naturally this happens when Ancilla is away," The man in white protested.

"Hooy, Eltanim." Drakkengard cried out. "Need a hand?"

"What?" The distraction earned him a hilt to the chin, but he managed to wrest the sword back into his hands.

"Don't look away." The man in black hissed. He, too, had my face. Two men with my face fighting each other, it was a travesty that I be left a spectator. "Don't look at the ground don't look at the sky don't look at the trees don't look at people don't look at beasts look only at me. You're fighting me. Fight me. Hurt me. Be hurt by me. Come on!" He leapt at Eltamin with fingers like gnarled oak and a mouth full of brambles.

"That hand sure would be appreciated, yes," Eltanim gasped.

"You heard him," Drakkengard declared. "Shut that cheap knockoff down."

"Could you clarify which one?" Ko asked.

"The one that's clearly a demented tree," she groaned.

"Gotcha." The gunman slid a rifle from his coat, cocked it and fired. Both the black-clad warrior's legs shattered below the knees. Eltanim impaled it through the chest with the sword.

"More, more to fight. More more more!" Legless, the thing bounced off its hands and hurtled toward us, tore out the sword from its chest and lunged for Ko.

"Woah there, buddy." Lach stepped in and sliced off its sword arm with a wrist mounted blade. It spun on its remaining palm and slammed the jagged stumps of its legs into his torso. Lach leapt back, his stomach grazed. The black-clad warrior's legs returned and were blown off again by Ko. While it sailed through the air its missing arm regenerated, and by the time it landed so had its legs

"This is ridiculous. Let me." Cicula grit her teeth, slashed her false nail against her palm and raised her skull-topped staff. "Great and eminent sage, ancient and wise Taowu, cease the movements of this battle drunk fake, if you're up for the challenge." She stamped the ground with her staff and an enormous beast sprang forth. Its hind-limbs were that of a wild pig, while its forelimbs the great paws of a tiger. From its spine extended a tail more than twice as long as I was tall. The entity bore a calculating expression on its human face as it looked to its opponent, followed by a knowing sneer. It pounced, swift as a gale, and batted the black-clad warrior straight up with its heavy paw. Its tail struck after and lashed the man thrice on one side and thrice on the other, to keep him airborne and make him spin. A rapid chant issued from the beasts mouth, and six spears materialized above the now falling warrior. They plummeted, penetrated his body, and pinned him to the ground with limbs outstretched. The black clad warrior howled and screams but the beast ignored him to turn back to Cicula.

"Hardly a challenge at all. Will there be anything else, summoner?" It asked in a bored, masculine voice.

"Nothing further, great and eminent sage. I humbly thank you for your time. Your remuneration shall be forthcoming."

"Hmph. As you were, then." The beast leapt into the sky and vanished. The spears remained though, and I approached the pinned warrior beneath them.

"You? What are you? Are you what's wrong with me?" he spat. "No matter. I just need to fight more. I'll quickly get my strength back that way." His eyes widened as Drakkengard stepped up beside me. "Ah, Drakkengard, loveliest of blades. It's just not the same fighting without you. Quick, cut these spears, that I might ruin all these fools."

"No," she shook her head. "I'm sorry," she grit her teeth, "but you are not my master."

"You—!" I plunged my hand into his chest and yanked out the dripping, barbed fruit. He fell silent. I let out a sigh, tossed the fruit to Drakkengard and wiped my hand on my shirt.

"That's another one down."

"You know, he kind of reminded me of you," Cicula said to Lach.

"Come off it. So go on, where's the next one?"

"Leaving so soon?" Eltanim asked wearily. He seemed to have recovered his sword, if it was even his sword to begin with.

"I'm afraid it's rather pressing."

"Alright. Before you go I should probably mention, my son seems to have taken an interest in a certain, what's that word you use, abomination."

"I don't care." I said, and my voice came from my own mouth. "I got my revenge." I ignored the shaking in my left arm.

He shook his head solemnly. "Life doesn't work like that."

34

A Harmonious Azazel

Another night, another carousel of ornery nobles to be placated. A fresh pile of complaints sat on my desk and three caskets of mead had been left by my chair, courtesy of Marie. The convenience of being able to just get dressed and walk downstairs to work was outweighed by the bitter gravity it lent the day.

Well, my people had a long tradition of being plucked out of the aether to do odd jobs around the worlds so I suppose I couldn't complain. I cracked open the first of the casks, popped a bottle, and allowed a minute to savor the first tingling mouthful of the day. Warm, sweet, fermented organic compounds to soothe agitations, take the edge off supernal hungers, and keep the mind fluid. Tasted good too, and kept sobriety at bay.

"Alright, enough of that, what's in the inbox?" I said to myself. "Let's see, the satyr threw a rock opera, threw the entire concert hall into the Phlegethon, and went on a bender through the Bolgia. Oh come on, this happens every time." I wrote up a quick form billing Dionysus for repairs, and a missive to keep an eye out for anyone in need of some time out in the Styx. "More complaints about the behavior of the Malebranche, *apparently* the boiling pitch isn't hot enough and it's ruining the writ-makers hot spring, and *apparently* their insults are starting to get a bit boring? Bloody politicians, there's no pleasing them." A quick memo to Malacoda is all that took, with the right official stamp of course.

"Now, what else? That flaming snake did what? Seven of the most cunning thieves in the seventh Bolgia have all stolen the identity and appearance of Cacus, tricked him into drinking Lethe-broth, and drank some themselves. Now none of them can remember which is the real one?" I slapped my brow and laughed. "Mother of us all, I can't even get mad at that. I'll just forward this to Naberius. That dog-faced crane will know what to do. Hmm, next is, apparently some of the dukes have been seen playing golf on the frozen lake around Pandemonium. Okay that is literally not even an issue. No one cares about that. Who wrote this? Probably just some upstart trying to get brown points for snitching. Antenora and the others were sealed in there as an example. The more humiliated they are the better. Next, junk, junk, more junk, an invitation an underwater basket weaving tournament? I thought everyone agreed not to hold those anymore given the body count. Should make sure it's properly overseen. Right, and then we have . . ."

I gulped down the rest of my bottle, popped open another one, downed half of it in one swallow, and read it again.

"Okay, miraculous, now Azazel has gone missing. Fantastic. Marie, get in here."

"What's up?" A young man entered, with smudged eyeliner and an outfit straight from a Singaporean fashion line.

"Is that a new look, Marie?"

"Yeah," he gave a spin. "What'd you think?"

"It suits you. Look, nevermind that, cancel all my appointments. Something big has come up."

"Yeah alright. Must be pretty big."

"Oh, only that fucking Azazel is suddenly no longer on his rock."

"The Uncleanest One? Oh. Welp. Can I, uh," he glanced for the door, "take the rest of the day off then?"

"Go for it, and hey, Marie, you've been a big help."

"Thanks, but, y'know, I suddenly remembered I have to be on another planet."

"Yeah I really don't blame you." I threw on a jacket and crammed the rest of the mead into my n-dimensional pocket. A quick portal later and I was out of there.

***

Har Megiddo was as bleak and desolate a wasteland as your run-of-the-mill inhospitable places could only hope to dream of. Winds hotter than any desert-world scoured the valley below and the mountains that formed it were shaped like torture tools hewn of rock and ice. Crackling thunderclouds blotted out the sky, black from the unremitting smoke and volcanic ash spewed from the mountain's peaks.

It was one of only two places that directly bridge the underworld with the overworld, and the only one that's neutral ground. Every time angels and demons went to all-out war it took place here, and it bore the scars. I made sure no one else was around, spread my wings and took flight. Up from the foot of the valley, still carved into maze-like trenches, up past the ruins of watchtowers decorated with scorched bones, up through the raging storm, and up further still, up the frozen, jagged mountains where giants have wrestled dragons, up past where countless stars and moons have descended and clashed, to Ha-Dudael, the second highest peak of Megiddo valley, where all the Grigori were once imprisoned.

Azazel should have been here. The fallen angel of Impurity, one of the three who opposed the Prophet Enoch being filled with radiance and ascending to became The Metatron— the scribe of Him.

Well, Metatron was muted and struck down in the last war but that's not really here or there. What also wasn't here is Azazel. I beat my wings against the glacial air and made another circuit of the peak.

There, not Azazel, but something. I swooped down, and took what crooked purchase my clawed feet could secure. There, in the ash and sleet.

I yanked the object up. It burned my hands worse than any flame, and I was forced to levitate it midair to get a good look.

It was a length of a broken chain, the chain meant to bind Azazel to this jagged rock. Legend said it to be of greater quality to the chains that bound Fenrir, forged from the words of creation rarely known even among gods. Yet here was proof that they had been broken. It would be easier simply to completely unmake these chains from creation than break them. Thammuz didn't even register as an issue compared to this. With a shudder I sent them into my n-dimensional pocket and took out a bottle of mead. I took a swig for myself, and with a heavy heart used the rest of the bottle to melt some of the ice.

Who did it? Was it one of ours, or one of theirs? How long ago did it happen that we only found out about this recently? Well, it's not like anyone came here often. Azazel could speak, but his specialties were weapon-making and cosmetics. Neither of which were topics worth the effort of coming here. Although it was written that he wouldn't be unchained until the Day of Judgment, some said he'd be redeemed and let back into the overworld, others that he'd be cast down into the underworld. The big deal was that 'days of judgment' tend to come all at once. In other words, it'd be time for everyone to lay down their lives at Har Megiddo yet again.

I couldn't find any further hints under the ice so took flight and rushed back down to portal. I didn't let myself think until I was back in Hell.

Alright, so, Azazel was missing. Meaning no one knew where he was. That meant he hadn't made a public appearance in the Underworld. Normally the arrival of a fallen angel was a pretty big deal, especially one teetering in the balance like he was. That meant either he was redeemed, was in Hell but hidden, or had been smuggled somewhere else. The Celestial Choir would never dare declare anyone redeemed without Him upstairs' say so. Which meant the only possible way *that* could come about is if YHVH's tenure of absence had come to an end, meaning war was inevitable anyway. If he was in Hell and alive, I might be able to negotiate his return with those loathsome angels, at least it would avoid open conflict. If he was in Hell and dead, well someone had a lot to answer for. If he was somewhere else, then I'd need more time to drink before I could figure something out. For now I decided to get whatever info I could from Dad.

***

He'd done Pandemonium up in an old Roman style this time, with pillars and statues of brightly painted marble. I let myself in, and took a seat on one of the reclining couches. Lucifer appeared draped in a toga and with his hair worn long and flowing.

"Good evening, Daughter of mine, do you know why Olympus was so furious at the theft of fire?"

"I'm here about Azazel, not intellectual posturing."

"Yet there's an amusing juxtaposition, is there not? Prometheus was chained for giving humans fire. The Uncleanest was chained for protesting that a lowly human have his flesh turned to flame and his veins filled with fire."

"Yeah, I doubt it was that simple. Our history changes all the time"

"Oh, it never is," he strutted back and forth across the room like an orator with a captive audience, instead of just me. "What is so divisive about the gift of flame? My flesh has always been fire, and I say give it to all who ask."

"It's not even that straight up a parallel, Mister Illuminated One. Azazel didn't have his liver eaten out every day, for instance."

"In the end, isn't it all just politics? *'To grant boons only to those who have and will serve loyally'*. Fire is like tenure, hard to take away without breaking your own rules."

"I'm sure you'd know all about that."

"Rules are a tricky, but useful thing. Though I live in Chaos my nature is and always has been Law."

"Lo, he was cast into the Abyss and with promotions in one hand and bureaucracy in the other he made himself king of his prison. Behold, his checkbooks are ever balanced. Is your ego stroked enough that you'll help me do what you asked me to?" I plucked out a bottle of mead and took an immodest sip.

"I can verify that the throne of heaven remains empty, it was not by His will that Azazel was removed."

"That's a relief in some ways, and more concerning in others. So is this the work of the same lot that has been thinning our ranks?"

"Do hold on one moment, I've a small matter to attend to." A wall vanished, and in stumbled a man, clad in finery selected from the markets of Dis, but tattered and frayed.

"It's gone deplorable. I'm splitting on the edge of my wits. You know what I mean, right?" he babbled in a wooden voice. "You know of all things so you know this." His long hair was a shaggy mane that reflected no light, and the red of his eyes had enveloped the whites leaving him with just two ugly aflame coals

"I do know of your condition," Dad replied in disinterest.

"Then tell me, go on, tell me what to do so I can fix it." His eyes were locked on Lucifer. He didn't even seem to see me. "I've been loyal haven't I? I've done all you beseeched. So please, I beg of you, tell me what to do."

"Oh that's simple," Dad warmly told the wretched splinter, "die." With a click of his infernal fingers the thing burst into a cloud of wooden fibers, encircling a thorny fruit. With a click of his other hand the fruit froze into a block of black ice, and the fibers disintegrated. The chunk of black ice drifted toward me.

"So there was another of Draco's twisted pieces in Hell after all," I tutted.

"Be sure to give him that next time you see him. Tell him it's a gift, in recognition of services well rendered."

"Yeah, sure," I took the frozen thing and stuffed it in my n-dimensional pocket. "It's a gift, so it's not like he owes you for this."

"Quite so," his eyes twinkled. I bet the Oracle at Delphi's eyes had the same twinkle when she gave her cryptic prophecies.

"Now about Azazel."

"I'm afraid there's nothing I could tell you that you would really appreciate. I'm sure you can get to the bottom of this without any assistance from me."

"Oh, sure, gotta do everything for myself," I rolled my eyes.

"Don't we all, in the end?"

I left Pandemonium in a huff, and set out on a walk through the Bolgia to think. I should have gotten the animated Braintree thing-thing to Draco as soon as I could, but I couldn't shake this lingering hunch on how to find Azazel.

35

Measures of Mountain

Michael

"So this is Earth," Otay said. I'd brought us to an old church, one that had been without clergy for many a year. "The plants are a lot more colorful here. Why is that?"

"A stronger bond between pollinating plants and pollen-spreading insects is my guess." The sun beat down on my back as I opened the church doors. Though sturdy, they required a reverent touch to keep flakes of wood from falling away. Otherwise they might not last another half century.

"Are you here to pray to your god?"

"Yes." I walked between the pews claimed by spiders, and knelt upon the steps before the dais.

"Should I pray too?"

"Do you have faith in Him?" Otay considered my words for a few minutes before answering.

"No. I have met you, but your god is a stranger to me. Even back home I never put much stock in the makers. What matters is what I can do with my own two hands, well, hand," he let a weary chuckle.

"If you have faith as much as even a single kernel of corn, then you can say to the mountains 'get up, and walk' and they shall. This is one of the lessons of my Lord."

"Have you ever moved a mountain?"

"No. However I did yoke the blizzard within you."

"Aye, fair enough. Well, I'll keep quiet and let you pray."

"Thanks upon you." I prayed.

I closed my eyes. I needed them not for they cannot see Him. I closed my ears. I needed them not for they cannot hear Him. I closed my mouth. I needed it not for it was unworthy to speak to Him. I let my arms fall. I needed them not for they could not reach Him. I relaxed my legs. I needed them not for they could not walk beside Him. I loosened my awareness of my body, for it was just a temporary vessel for my immortal soul. There was but myself and the faith I held. It was a tiny speck of light, smaller than a pinhead. It shone brighter than any star in the sky. It was a bridge. It was a tower. It was a key. It was an open door. I passed through that door. I saw.

***

I beheld a room of people of different ages and nations. I beheld a woman in red, addressing two people in white. I beheld a woman with her head locked within a darkly beautiful mask. I beheld a cowering man in tattered robes. The woman in red turned to the masked one.

"Are you sure these are the most suitable aids?"

"Yes, mistress. They possess the knowledge and skills that you require."

"Is that so? Well if the Sisyphus says it then it must be so. So, I'm in a generous mood." She turned back to the two in white and cooed. She was taller than they, so she leaned forward that their eyes might be level, which in turn caused her breasts to sway wantonly. I beheld that it was no accident. She was a tempestuous thing made of lust and cruelty, far worse than any of the Devil's cubi. She reached out and stroked her hand against one of the whites' chest. "So just what would you like in return?" They shuddered, but retained their composure.

"We want the chance to study you. Your existence is, well, simply marvelous. Your body's energy state is comparable to a

black hole," she gushed. "It's a mystery we're not being crushed just by basking, er, being in your presence. Your mind, too, the brain is mostly human, but your mind is somehow processing as much data as all of Earth."

"I mean, we understand it's not flawless," the other spoke up. "That's what you need our help with, right? The thought matrix has too many redundancies, but it's still better than anything we could even dream of. The data compression alone is . . . it's just miraculous." His eyes were alight in wonder bordering on worship.

The woman in red stood and kissed them both. It was a hungry, selfish gesture done without invitation, to which they dared not deny. "Excellent, excellent, to be on display is a marvelous thing, and you little geniuses will make such a good audience. The contract is sealed." Her voice lowered an octave, "You may study me, and in return you assist me in developing the technology I need." Her voice returned to its sticky dulcet tones, and she spun merrily. "All I need is lossless data transfer between organic brains. It's always such a chore when the someone who knows isn't the someone who you need to know, you know. It's not that ambitious a project, especially compared to what I need it for. Yet I need you, not least of which because my current assistant is a useless pile of rust."

I beheld as she approached the cowering man, and look, there was a sickness within him. A sickness that made his hands shake and his flesh melt. Look, as he lifted his face, his eyes had been gouged out, his tongue had been plucked out and his lips had been stitched shut. These wounds might be easily healed had his mistress not forbidden it. The order could be seen carved into his soul— to restore these injuries is to defy my wishes. Look further, his face was cracked and his skin oxidized. This enfeebled man was dying, his body and mind turned toxic. He rotted from within.

"What? You have something to say, you obsolete garbage carcass?" The woman in red sneered and kicked her servant down. He lurched back up, frothing mercury from his stitched *mouth. His quicksilver blood was slowing. "Did my foot not just say to stay down?" She kicked him again, and again he rose. He couldn't pretend it was not disobedience anymore. It was forbidden to disobey the mistress. It made the cracks spread and the rust flake. He stood, his joints creaking in protest.*

The cracks had reached his mind, a mind spread throughout a liquid body. Love and hate are both obsessive passions. The man loved his mistress. The man hated his mistress. The man loved his mistress, had been written upon his soul for all to see. The man hated his mistress, even though he must not, cannot. His existence was defined as a faithful and discreet slave. There was to be no choice in the matter yet he hated her anyway. The woman in red observed with curiosity.

"Have you finally found your spine, filthy boy?"

The man panted, and drew in deeper and deeper breaths. His lips parted. His whole body heaved. He screamed. Oh God, I wept at the sight. His was the desperate scream of the tortured, those driven to love death. The stitches tightened and tore at his lips but his mouth distended against them, spilling metal blood upon his bare feet. He raised an arm, and the arm was a blade but the blade was blunted and warped. Still he thrust that blade at his mistress, and his screams blotted out the reflexes forbidding it. Though blunt there was force enough behind that blade. It pierced his mistress's chest and instantly shattered. He raised his other arm, also a blade, and impaled her again. Behold, this arm too was destroyed. He threw himself at his mistress, screaming and screaming, and his whole body became as blades, his flesh made into sickles to lash out against her.

The woman in red cried out not in pain but in pleasure, and spread her arms in welcome. The tattered slave cut and stabbed and dug into her flesh, and his flesh of swords wore down as though against a grindstone. He was not allowed to hate his mistress. He was not allowed to wish harm upon his mistress. To do so was anathema against his self. Lo, what was left became small and smaller, and his scream dropped to a wheeze, a whisper, silence. The slave had died, having cast himself against her body as one casts themselves off a cliff. I wept at the sight, for it had been revealed to me the only act that unwilling slave ever took for himself. He was now dead, and his body was buried inside the mistress he loved and hated. God, oh God, life can be so cruel.

The woman in red brushed herself down. Her slave's attack had left her clothes and flesh in tatters, but she remained undisturbed. With a gluttonous sigh she turned back to the two in white.

"I apologize. Those things can get a bit out of hand when they break down." The pair in white were afraid, while the masked one cared not, if she was even aware what just happened.

The vision changed, and I beheld now the cambion twins. They were with their father and his retainers, and among his retainers was another slave like the one I just saw die. Look, her body was not toxic like the other's was. The group walked through a dark maze, and I beheld that which they were hunting—a piece of Eden in the shape of a man. Lo, it was revealed to me that this was not what is but what will be. Thank you, oh thank you Lord for this vision you have sent me.

***

I returned back through the open door and resumed my place in my mortal vessel.

"I've seen plenty of people pray, but that looked intense," Otay said. Some shift in my body must have revealed my return to consciousness.

"I have been shown a vision," I solemnly declared. "I have seen the face of the enemy, and I have been shown where to go that I might receive help." I paused. "There was more, but I do not yet understand its true significance."

"So what happens now?"

"It's time to make a deal."

36

Pitch Paranoia

Draco

Endless dark corridors coiled before and behind us, and it was only by the light of Ko's torch that we could see even the decrepit walls.

"Get out. Get out getoutgetoutgetout!" My fragment's voice echoed from deep within this Lancastrian labyrinth.

"We'll get out when we've added you to our fruit salad," Lach replied to the darkness.

"Must you taunt it?" Vengai-Ra complained. "We've been down here for hours. You're annoying the rest of us more than you are it, at this point."

"Hermit, oh Hermit, wherefore art thou Hermit?" Drakkengard sang. She stepped to the front, and when a gout of fire roared from the tunnels she expanded her arms into a shield to block it.

"I'll burn you. I'll burn to dust the bones upon which your disgusting muscles walk!"

"Typical that your most paranoid piece is the one who still has your fire, Father," Cicula brushed her hand across her hair. "This would be so much easier if Minotaur were more willing to leave the seventh circle.

"The lantern falls and can't be found," Drakkengard continued, "Thus nothing can be learned. The fool is back at the cliff, and yearns to never leave. You'll never know the world like this."

"Burn it all! Burn all the crawling things! Keep away! Keep away!" my fragment screeched.

"It sure is a melodramatic one. Can't we just tear down the walls and cut straight to it?"

"If we did that the whole castle would come down on top of us."

"Shoddy second century architecture."

"No. No! Keep away! Aiiiii—" The voice fell silent. My companions looked to one another.

"Did we do that?"

"Maybe it killed itself for us," Lach suggested. "Hey, how fragile are those fruit things? Are we screwed if we step on it?"

"They can't kill themselves, dummy," Drakkengard wagged a finger. "They're just embodied abstracts, they scarcely qualify as alive."

"Wait, I hear footsteps," Ko said and readied his rifle. From the darkness emerged a pair of men. One had a shaggy mane of hair, only one arm, and was clad is ragged furs. The other was so tall he had to stoop under the low ceiling, and wore a fine white suit.

"Otay?" Cicula gasped, "and you, the nephilim? What are you doing here? Least of all together."

"We meet again, witch," the shaggy one said. A body was slung over his shoulder, and his body seemed to be covered in fast melting frost.

"I believe this is yours," The tall one said, and nodded to his partner. The shaggy one dumped the body at our feet. Ko took a half step forward and inspected it.

"Yup, this is our quarry."

"Why are you doing this? And why are you with him?" Cicula demanded. She sounded almost jilted.

"I am with him because he has helped me where you could not," Otay said matter-of-factly.

"What you are doing here is not the Devil's work, and not evil, so I have no reason to thwart it. As for this," the tall man gestured to the trussed up body, "a sign of goodwill."

I approached the body, plunged my hand into his chest to extract the fruit, and tossed it to Drakkengard.

"Which means you want something from us," Drakkengard observed before swallowing the fruit whole.

"Yes," the tall man spread his palms. "I am the son of Eltanim, your nemisi, and I am one who has been granted the title of Michael by the celestial choir. What I do is God's work."

"So what does a man of God want with a bunch of Hell's contractors?"

"I have been granted a vision, and fear of grave things to come. I wish to exchange information with your party on the one named Malign."

"No," I said with my own lips.

"Are you sure? I have confirmed her revival."

"I killed the Abomination once already. That's it. I've had my revenge. So long as she leaves me alone I don't care what she does."

"I'm not asking you to fight her. I just want information."

"You want to dig up old injury that I'd rather stay buried. " My mouth tasted like metal. I could smell burning flesh.

"Father, this sounds important,"Cicula said.

"Come on, old man," Lach insisted, "me an' Sis know a bit, but you've kept your lips shut for, what, twenty years now? I know you've said bugger all to Mom."

"How about you?" Michael turned to face Drakkengard. I crossed my arms and closed my eyes. "Would it interest you if I said that the one like you is dead? I believe his name was Deserere."

Eyes wide, Drakkengard put a hand to her mouth.

"How did he die?"

"He turned on his Mistress. This caused his body to break down. He tore at her flesh to his dying breath."

"Oh?   Ohohoho.   UfufufufuhahahahahaHAHAHAHAHAHA!" Drakkengard bellowed laughter. No, not Drakkengard, me. My mouth ached and my eyes wept and my arms clutched my sides. Laughter rose and growled and snarled until it could scarcely be called laughter anymore.

"Rest in peace, thrice damned brother," I wiped the bile from my mouth. "Alright, you who has inherited the question 'Who is like God?' we'll share everything that we know about the Abomination, on one condition."

"I did not presume it would be free."

"I don't know how much you know about that thing you just took down for us, but of those that we know the location of, there's only two left, and they're at the same place."

"You help us take them down," Drakkengard continued for me, "and you'll get your information. It will be easier to tell you then, too."

"I find these terms agreeable. Are there any objections? No? Then the deal is made. You shall have our assistance, sinner."

"You really are your mother's kid," Drakkengard mused.

37

An Ensemble of Evidence

Lascivus

Flames caressed my body as I swam through the burning river. A weaker demon would be melted to slag by Phlegethon's current. I scoured the riverbed up and down for any sign of the body. I burned, but remained unburnt. Aha, there it was. A hand jutted out from under the rocks. I swam down and got to work heaving them out of the way. Before long enough of the body had been uncovered that I could pull it loose. Body in tow, I crouched against the riverbed and leapt through its flowing flames onto the riverbank and set the body down. I was far enough out of the way that there were no obvious onlookers.

It was without a doubt Azazel. It was also without a doubt dead. Not from the river's flames, that would have taken years, but from a more unique wound. His chest had been pierced in three places, and around those wounds the skin had blackened. Upon his back, eight sections had burst open where the fallen angel's wings once were. Of his four faces, the lion's was emaciated, the ox's mouth was bloody, the eagle's beak had shattered and the man's eyes had burst. There was only one weapon that inflicted such wounds— the Devil's trident. That thrice damned holy weapon stolen and reforged into blasphemous mockery. The ramifications hit me like a cannon.

"Father!" I spread my wings, regardless of who saw, snatched up the body and rocketed toward Pandemonium, the black ice castle at the center of the underworld's twisted geometries. I didn't bother knocking.

"Satan the Devil!" I bellowed once inside. "Lucifer the Morningstar! Samael, poison of god! Dragon! Old Serpent! Explain yourself!" I threw Azazel's body to the ground.

"Why should I do that?" His voice thundered in reply. He looked down at me with the countless eyes covering his gargantuan body.

"You killed Azazel!" I shed my glamour, and flew up the measureless height to his face. My voice issued from the many mouths covering my body. Blood spilled down from the base of my slight horn and I could feel it starting to split.

"Have you proof, daughter of mine?" His burning eyes wrinkled in laughter.

"The only thing that inflicts wounds like this is your trident, that ugly angel slayer forged from the Lancea Longinus and the nails from cross, those things that all pierced the flesh of God's son and avatar. Only you can wield that weapon."

"Oh, what possible motive have I to do that?" His snide leer stretched for miles.

I wracked my brain. Why, why, why indeed. Why but that. "You, oh damned gods, you're trying to do it. You're trying to make it happen. You want an all-out war with the Overworld!" I accused the accuser. His laughter rattled through my thousands of teeth, and made my horn ache.

"A compelling argument, daughter of mine. So tell me Lascivus, tell me Lilim, tell me Ailo, tell me Little Horn, tell me *Sariel* spawn of Lilith and Samael, what will you do?" Each name struck me like a lead harness upon my back. I struggled to stay aloft.

"This is bullshit." I flipped the wall of eyes my middle finger. The mouth on it spat at him. "Fuck this, and fuck you. You're insane. Batshit up feculent river without a prayer. I've been breaking my back trying to keep things peaceful and you don't even give a shit. What the fuck is wrong with you?"

"God is dead," he boomed, "God remains dead, and now it us up to us to become like God. As I promised when we were cast down into the infinite abyss we shall march on the gates of heaven, and I shall resemble thy power on high. Azazel's sacrifice has paved the way for mine glorious ascent, for the drones in heaven cannot avoid acting now. This millennium of stagnation shall come to an end and the worlds will turn once more. You, too, have a glorious role in these events to come."

"Yeah, I bet I do." I drew Impiocassus and drove it into my father's brow. Tried to.

His booming laughter made my stomach roil. My blade had stopped with the slightest gap between its tip and his flesh. No matter how hard I strained I couldn't bid it to drive home.

"How was it that toy husband of yours cursed you, daughter of mine? Of course, I remember like yesterday. '*You will never bring harm upon those of your flesh and blood, no injury nor poison nor neglect. I curse you to forever carry the burden held in the name of Family.*'" His voice mimicked Draco's perfectly.

"You!" I struggled with my all to push my sword just that little bit further. "Just how much of my life have you orchestrated?"

"My grand design encompasses much, daughter of mine. It's just so easy to bring about these little happy coincidences."

"Well forget it! I'll have no part in this. You want your war? You can do it without me." I turned my back to him and beat my wings. "And I won't be the only one that realizes how stupid another war is, even if there is no God in heaven."

"Leaving so soon, daughter of mine?"

"I've no more time for you, and I have something to deliver to my toy husband."

I burned open a portal mid-flight and vanished from the Underworld.

38

Excitatory Gnosis

Draco

The final location marked on Lascivus' map was the Baucis, a high rise hotel in Londinium. A barricade of police cars greeted our arrival. Lach gestured for us to wait and sauntered over to an officer.

"Hey there, friend. What happened?"

"Move along, civilian. Some maniac group has taken over the hotel and taken the guests hostage."

"Seriously?" he balked, "in this day and age? What is the world coming to anyway? Have they a name for themselves?"

"No, and they haven't made any demands either." She looked him up and down. "Are you with the press?"

"No, but I was supposed to meet someone in there. Do you," he glanced down, "do you think they're okay?" The officer pressed her mouth into a thin line.

"Communication is cut off inside. We're not even sure how long ago they took over, to be honest. It wasn't until they started snatching passer-by's off the street that anyone placed a call. All we can do now is make sure no one else goes in. We've already lost contact with three negotiators."

"Oh wow, that does sound dangerous. I hope my friend's okay."

"So do I, buddy. So do I."

"You guys catch all that?" He asked as he returned.

"Gods dammit, my daughter could be in there," Cicula cursed.

"How do you want to get in? Fast or unseen?" Ko reached into his jacket.

"Fast," Drakkengard replied. "If they've managed to get supporters, the sentries have probably already spotted us."

"Storm the gates it is." The gunman drew a belt of spheres and lobbed it behind the barricade, "grenade!" he roared, and the law enforcers dove for cover. The explosion rocked the street, sending up chunks of cement and metal. "Alright people, Move! Move! Move!." He led the charge into the smoke, and we rushed past the police to the hotel's front door.

"It's barricaded."

"Gimme a second." Drakkengard stepped forward and cleaved through it with one of her arms. "Ding dong."

"Everybody inside, formation Contra," Ko barked.

"What the hell is formation contra?" Cicula demanded.

"Just watch out for an ambush." We flooded inside, watching out for any surprise attacks, and didn't stop until we were in the foyer.

"—have a situation—unknown assailants—" The police broadcast crackled from outside. I took a deep breath and immensely regretted it. The distinct, pungent stench of dead meat and spilt fluids wracked my senses, bringing up many unsavory memories. Blood splatter marked every surface, and the smears formed overlapping trails that lead all the way to the elevator. Several electrical fires had arisen where circuit boards had been haphazardly smashed.

"Oh no, Shahdee!" Cicula ran over to the elevator and hammered the button, but when it opened the shaft wall greeted her. The lift carriage sat below, crashed from some great height with the cables cut.

"Looks like we're taking the stairs," Vengai-Ra grumbled.

"Allow me," Michael stepped forth. In a matter of seconds he'd whipped the wind into a roaring gale, leading straight up the vacant shaft. "I'll go first so I can tell where to stop."

"How do we know you won't cut the juice and let all us 'sinners' plummet?"

"That kind of trickery is below me. Besides, we have a deal. I still haven't received that information." He grabbed hold of his hat and leapt up the shaft.

"Okay, that looks fun." Lach took a run up and jumped in after him with a yell. With a shrug Drakkengard grabbed me by the hand and followed suit. Her arm flattened into a thin sail to offset her extra weight, and we soared up the hotel's heights.

"Do we even know what floor to look on?" Cicula yelled above the winds, below me.

"These are bits of the old man we're talking about," Lach hollered in reply, "of course they have to be at the most extreme part of any building."

"What if these ones are different?"

"Then we spend hours checking ever single floor, but not before the more likely option."

"End of the line, watch your head," Michel warned from above. Via wind currents the directions of which I couldn't even begin to calculate, Michael pulled us back out the shaft and set us down gently on our feet.

"How high up are we?"

"Hundred and third floor. Ten floors below the penthouse. There's too much wreckage to take the shaft the rest of the way."

"Lach, stop snickering," Cicula chided.

"It smells disgusting," Drakkengard whined. My left arms ached. The stink of smoke smothered me.

"Oh, dead and damned gods," Cicula gasped.

Bodies lined the hallway, stripped naked and flayed. Blood and ejaculate was encrusted against their skin. Some were killed mid-coitus. No two bore the exact same wounds. Some had their teeth plucked out. Some had their eyes chewed. Some had limbs crushed, others severed. Some were missing their lips, or their whole jaw. Some had their genitals mutilated, man or woman alike. Some were smiling so hard their cheeks had torn. The whole floor was aflame. Butchery and barbeque. My mouth peeled open but who knew what face I made.

"All these people," Michael shook his head sadly.

"Shahdee, please no," Cicula pleaded aloud.

My arm burned. I could smell the flesh being cooked alive but I didn't feel it. It was too much. Too much like before. Too much like the castle. Too much like the cage.

And then there was music.

"Some of them are still alive," Vengai-Ra called out from years away. A spasm ran up my arm and down my spine.

"Can you save them?" Michael asked.

"Maybe.

"They're better off dead," I declared. Drakkengard took me by the hand. We had to keep moving.

"I believe that is their choice to make, not yours," Michael hotly replied.

"Do what you like."

"Hey, your arm. . ."

"It's fine." Fire was fine. Paroxysms were fine.

"Draco. I agreed to help you defeat these pieces of Eden, but I cannot knowingly leave these people without trying to help."

"You got us up here. Good enough for me. Do what the hell you like." I kicked down the door to the stairwell and stepped inside.

"Otay," he said, "I'm releasing your winter. I need you to make sure this building doesn't burn down before we can see to all these people."

"As you wish."

The archangel procured a golden key from thin air and plunged it into his own wrist. At once the temperature dropped, and shards of ice began gathering around Otay's form. I paid them no heed and took off.

It was a long walk up the stairwell, with winter swelling below me. Ten flights of stairs to the hundred and thirteenth floor. Ten floors full of the dead and dying maimed. One hundred and thirteen floors of victims. One hundred and thirteen tributes to the Abomination. My burning arm moved with unnatural stiffness. *Smoke billowed from the eyes of a small child, covering his fractured face in a facade of forked tongues and fettered fingers, fluttering and a lie. An arena filled with a roaring crowd, in the center, a frail girl was battered by the shifting form of three hundred shapeless beasts. A hand of blades reached down, trying to pull them up.*

I chased away the hallucinations and opened the door. There I stood, waiting for me, with me in my arms, hunched over a pile of writhing bodies, screaming and crying. Blood poured down my thighs and I raised my head in weeping ecstasy. In that moment I reached over with a curved blade and with one slice made my groin flat and smooth. White mixed with the red. I plunged my hand into my chest and tore out my beating, spiky heart. I looked me in the eyes and devoured it, bite by bite. Only when the last mouthful was swallowed with a begrime gulp did I pull out and stand, pelvis red from ransacking.

"A snake shoots out a cave and bites my spire," I said, leering with green eyes.

"And then there was music," I replied.

"Welcome home," I said and stepped over the bodies toward me, naked and erect. "You have her eyes."

"You're not like the others."

"Of course not." I palmed my crotch and giggled. "You're not me. I'm the one who came before."

"No, you are me."

"But you're not me."

"You're the scene of the crime. You're ground zero. You're The Atrocity committed by The Abomination."

"Oh, baby, oh, it feels good to be alive," Atrocity spewed the filth at my feet, and uttered a hysterical giggle. *A misshapen, metal giant, made of gears and pylons haphazardly stuck together. In its mouth lay the rotting corpse of a roc, around its neck twelve figures, without clothes and covered in filth, made adjustments and repairs to the structure to which they were chained. In its two arms, it held a longsword and a short sword, and in a third hand growing from its stomach it gripped an executioner's glaive, swinging from side to side. With every step, the screams of unseen men and women cried out it protest.*

"You don't look so good," Atrocity said. "In fact you look miserable. What have you been doing with my body all these years? Wasting it!" Atrocity reached forward and wrapped my fingers around my throat. My knees went weak at my touch.

"I don't care what you do, just do it dirty," I sang. My burning hand turned my skin red and black. I shoved Atrocity off. Scars covered my body. Every scar told a tale and I was Scheherazade's walking picture book. I could list the cause of everyone.

"How long has it been since you last tasted your own liver?"

"How long has it been since you really let loose, and did everything you've been holding back on?"

"How much longer are you going to spend being whatever people tell you that you are?"

"I'd rather be anything but what you are," I retorted to myself.

Where is everyone? Weren't they right behind me? No, was I even at the same place? That place, the memory of it was so far away. Are these not stone walls?

My mind buckled under the paradox. The three of us, Draco, Drakkengard and Atrocity fell shrieking into the deepest recesses of my mind from which all three of us were born. Our ego barriers collapsed, I could no longer tell which of the three was I.

"Master," I said to myself. Had I always been so tall? "Master, come on, I'm right here."

"Drakkengard." *That's right. I'm not really here. I is I and is not I. I am he as you are he as you are me. And we are all together. That one is sleeping, dreaming, invading.*

"Ah, Drakkengard, there you are," I said. "Let's deal with this failure and finish things."

Drakkengard shook her head. "No."

"I said come!" I snatched at her neck, but she slipped out of my grasp like running water.

"You are not my master. You are who my master once was, but Master is someone else now. Someone that isn't you."

"How dare you. We'll see what you tune you sing after I split you in half you stainless little bitch." I grabbed the top of her robes and tore them open, exposing her bare chest. Her skin was flat, featureless metal.

"You can't eat me." The rest of her robes melted away into her body. "I'm the gatekeeper and the key and the lock." Her body was sexless. Not even a swell of breast or curve of hips.

"So that's it, bitch?" I screamed. "You're no better than Mother. You just lock me up in a cage forever, never to see the light of day."

"Don't call her that. The Abomination forsook that title when she committed you."

"You're just a mental illness!" I screamed at me. "A ramshackle persona built out of book characters and warped feedback loops between an idiot and a slave! A dissociative personality that usurped my body from under me." *A maiden on the eve of her wedding, white ribbons tied all around her body, binding her hands and mouth and feet and breasts. The ribbons spiraled outwards, crisscrossing, and combining and splitting until returning to the exposed entrails of forty-three crones, screeching hymns in only twelve voices.*

"I don't deserve to die."

"You don't deserve to live either. You don't deserve anything. None of us do." Did I say that or did I, or did the third I? We all shrieked with the same voice.

"I don't want to die."

"Just sleep forever."

"That's no different from death."

"Sleep and dream that you're me."

"That's no different than only you existing."

"Get in the cage."

"You can't make me."

"I said get in the cage!" We devolved into an orgy of mental violence, lashing out a psychological carousel of murder-suicide with no foundation, not rock-bottom to hit, a child punching itself in the neck to make the pain go away, and three became one and then became none.

A crystal hawk with gossamer wings, and a keyhole for a face, contained in its stomach are twenty and twelve score of screaming eyes. We devoured the fruit in our belly.

A shield wrapped in cloth and bound with golden string. From the edges, black filth seeped out yet failed to stain the cloth. A skeleton, chained to a throne.

Each link bore a human face, wracked in agony, and although they appeared to me screaming, no sound came out. The walls were made of wood. One last fruit fell in, and the walls collapsed into splinters.

***

There was a faded carpet on the floor. A bookcase was against the wall, besides the open window. Light shone through the window, making the piano glow. *And there was music* Yes, everything tumbled out of lost spaces. It had been a pianoforte such as this and I had sat there, not a man but a boy, with a mess of black hair and red, *no, green eyes* I'd never questioned. She had red *but I'd had green.* I'd never questioned. There was music and I made it.

She had entered quietly, mayhap drawn by my boyish playing of the key-hammer-strings. She had touched my hair tenderly, touched me tenderly, and then she'd touched me violently. *Mother?* The last time such maternal taxonomy had sat with her in my mind. I was a boy, not yet a man, but the long change was underway enough for her to smell. My hands had left the instrument, but there was still music, but this time in my head. I looked in her eyes, those red eyes I soon inherited from her, and behind them I saw the wanton lust of an entire dead world. When her teeth made my lips bleed some part of me had shuddered in recognition. I was a boy, not yet a man, but in my upbringing I had been well read enough to have a haze of an idea what would befall. Though it was later she locked me away, by the time I had spewed the filth, the empty cage had already been wrought inside of me.

My body wouldn't scar, wouldn't change, but it could be made to change. *You have her eyes.* The surgical scars faded but they remained. Hers grew back but hers remained. You have her eyes. A diet of playthings is no thing for a growing boy. Always hungry, always filled with needs. Given playthings for those needs, but had to ration them out. Not enough not enough never enough. The door opened.

Was the door open?

Was it something else?

Out the cage. The empty cage. Running. Sister. Sister? Sister never questioned. A room with a vat. A thing inside. A pretty thing. A plaything. Broke the glass. Bled on the glass. Bled on the thing. Burned. Everything burned. Burned the cage, burned the house, burned the piano and burned myself. Burned it all out of me. A beast that burned and a plaything to protect from the beast that burned. Not chased, never chased but always watched. Watched by eyes. You had her eyes. Hide them. Always hide them. Not allowed to remember why, just that you do. Voices. All these voices, mocking voices, her voices. She had many voices, voices of men and women and beasts and things. So many hungry voices. Always hungry. Eaten worlds and still hungry. Couldn't think can't think too many voices.

Nothing on the inside, paper on the outside. Tantrum book pyre. Pieces broken. It's broken. You're broken. You have her eyes.

There's a piece missing. A peace. A cessation.

I was missing nothing. I called it back to me.

"Shahdee," we said in the real world. "I know you're there. You can come out now." *Little girl in a grey dress. Mother was a daughter. Father was a nothing. Her mother's only crime was that she got lonely, so tried to make a companion from the Void. From that union Shahdee was born.*

She had nothing too. My nothing. The missing nothing. It hid her the way nothing can, and hid itself in Atrocity's shadow where he could never find it. Nothing in the shape of that which did not exist. A perfect silhouette, no matter the angle. It was familial. Like a hole cut out of space. Once it was a little boy with a head full of books and green eyes. My connection to the Void was the hole in the shape of our body's original owner, of which only nothing was left. Draco and Drakkengard were born to survive on the outside. The one who came before, Atrocity, was born to survive the cage. This one, however, was the one who came first. Its nature so similar to the Void that Shahdee mistook it for her father. "Welcome home."

Nothing returned to me.

Rushing, rushing, rushing. Garden laid out. Seeds planted. Paths paved. Plants grown. An empty cage with nothing in it. Autumn trees with dark bark and many fruits. Were the hedges trimmed? Were there fewer weeds? Everything was raw and tender. The sun was a huge fireball in the sky, but not really.

39

Two-faced Concerto

I opened my eyes. Not the eyes this body was born with but the eyes she'd given me, straight from her skull. The city of London stretched out before us from the building's rooftop.

"Feeling better?" A familiar voice asked.

"Lascivus? When did you get here?" She looked at me with tired eyes, and smiled.

"Just now. It looked like you were burning yourself and Drakkengard alive. I didn't know what to do, so I just jammed the fruit I had down your mouth. It seemed to help a little, but it wasn't until Shahdee came out of nowhere and this black thing went into you that you stopped."

"Where did you get one of the fruit from?"

"Another one of your dodgy copies turned up in Hell."

"Ah. Thanks." I glanced about the rooftop. Drakkengard and Cicula were fawning over Shahdee. "Where are the others?"

"Getting the ones Vengai-Ra could save out of here."

"Shahdee didn't . . . see too much, did she?"

"As far as I can tell, no. Still, who can tell with that girl?"

"I see," I clasped her hand and wept. "Thanks for coming."

"Well it's not like I had anything better to do," she uttered an exhausted sigh. "I've cut ties with Dad."

"You have?"

"He's willing to do anything to start another war with the angels. All the stupid shit, all false flags so people think a war is needed after all. "

"I thought you hated angels."

"I do. That doesn't mean I feel the need to start the apocalypse."

"Such a *shame*," someone said. My blood ran cold. Someone snapped their fingers and Cicula shrieked. Shahdee had vanished. A figure floated overhead, a man in green, their back against the city. I'd seen his face before.

"You! You're that soothsayer. That man in green who helped me find Lascivus." He looked to me in marvel, and with a flick of his wrist took the form of that fox-skin clad old man.

"Why, I'm surprised you recognize me. You really were such a prospective candidate, but you just lack ambition."

"Ianus!" Cicula cried out. The skull-topped staff was in her hands. She struck the ground with it, and two more arms ripped out from her back. One held a noose and the other the vajra. With a whip-crack the noose latched on to the man's leg, and she lets the vajra fly.

"You were also a good candidate," he said from behind her. His movement was instantaneous. Not even a blur. "However, you just don't think."

"You abandoned me, and now you're going to take my daughter?" She snarled. Her tongue was far too elongated for her mouth. The man vanished again, and Drakkengard's arm found only empty air.

"You broke the seal on Ayaki-Ikee just to impress your mentor in what should have been a simple test. Far, far too volatile. Had I taught you any more, oh things you might have released." The man walked upside down upon the air, palms spread in shrug.

"So it was you," the man in furs snarled at Cicula. Otay, wasn't it? When did he get back? Blue frost crawled over his skin, and his right arm burst into a storm of diamond dust. I could have sworn he had only one arm. "Meaning you're that fell imp," he turned his fury to the man in green.

"The worlds are small, are they not? Here is a victim of your short sightedness," he said to Cicula.

"My daughter has nothing to do with that. Give her back!" she cried out.

"Hmm, no. We need her."

"Who the hell is we?" Lascivus demanded.

"Just a few people with a common goal," he shrugged. "Surely you can sympathize, Lilim?" He flicked his wrist, and his form changed again, to a corpse faced demon holding a candelabrum.

"You're . . . Bifrons?" Lascivus frowned. Cicula stepped back, aghast.

"I am and have been many things. I am Janus the two-faced, god of doors." He turned back into a young man in green. "And I really must thank all of you for creating just the person we need."

I called Drakkengard over and drew her into a blade. Lascivus pulled out her own blade. Otay moved to lunge, but Michael walked up behind him and bid him to wait.

"Oh my, you don't seem too pleased with my praise. Was it something I said?" Janus flashed an impish grin.

My head had never been clearer. My stomach seethed with bile, and it splashed onto my tongue. I brewed it into a curse. "You will allow no harm to befall my granddaughter, you who have used and abused and abandoned, henceforth you shall be Atoner!"

The curse hit him with all the force of a spitball, and he waggled his finger at me. "Nu-uh. You're four thousand years too young to make a curse stick to me. You don't have to worry. The child will be returned unharmed once we're done with her."

"What are you even trying to accomplish?" I demanded.

"Look at the world. The Lilim knows of what I speak. It's so abhorrently stagnant," Janus gritted his teeth in disgust. "For thousands of years the world has spun slower and slower. Nothing changes, nothing old leaves, nothing new comes in. Not enough to make a difference. Every new invention sees only the dark side of the moon, the overworld and underworld are both at standstill, and millions, millions of gods teeter at the impotent line between here and the four corners, doing nothing but sucking up all the faith they can just to survive.

"It's you," Cicula said. Blood dripped from her brow and she spoke in an accent not hers. It was the voice of the goddess Kali. "You are the one trying to bring about a true undying."

"Well aren't you a clever old dea. This world needs something big to make it speed up again."

"The end of days," Lascivus muttered, "what my father is trying to do."

"Ding-ding-ding," he said as Bifrons. "Oh, he knows what I'm up to, and he knows I know he knows. He's also convinced he can still come out on top after letting me go so far. Ha! Mitra thought the same thing. You know how it goes in the Lord's last book—the end of days shall come, and the throne of god shall be abdicated to the messiah for a thousand years and the millennial kingdom shall be brought about. Even THAT is better than the slow extinction of the world," he spat.

"How do you expect to bring about the millennial kingdom when neither YHVH nor Yeshua have been heard from for the past thousand years?" I demanded.

"You're pronouncing it wrong, but you see that's the thing," he said as the soothsayer. "Just what is it that makes someone a Messiah? That's why we need someone Void-touched."

"I read of this, the limitless potential for creation," Michael exclaimed, stricken. "You plan to literally conjure Messianic properties and bestow them upon yourself?"

"Oh no, not me. I'd make a terrible job of it. No, no, no, the new God will be Malign."

"What!" I slipped through the Void and lunged at him, my body wreathed in white flames. He blinked out of the way, and I slipped through to strike again.

"Now. Just. Wait. One. Minute," he said between spatial blinks. With a squeak he vanished, but I could still hear his voice.

"Unless, of course, you'd rather take the throne yourself. Malign is plan A, but really, we'll be happy enough with any of you. Imagine it, omnipotence and omniscience, the authority to shape the world as you see fit. It might not be quite as interesting as what Malign will do, but so long as the world starts turning again we're okay with it. We might even help you. Just think about it."

"Who cares about any of that?" Cicula howled. "Just give me back my daughter."

"So short sighted. Ah, it's a pity Blackwing couldn't be here. Raanae, keep them busy would you."

"*Oui, monsieur,*" a bony hand emerged at the edge of the rooftop and pulled up a figure clad in white. She had the face of a doll's, and she spoke in a rather fraudulent French accent. "*Alo ma cherie.* Did you miss me?" she said to Cicula.

"You're that girl, the undead,"Cicula replied.

"That's right, and look, we are standing right on top of all these lovely fresh corpses." The woman called Raanae cracked her knuckles, and a horrible chorus of groans emanated from below us.

"What about you? Why are you helping them?"

"Because my god Toutates demands it, silly," she raised her arms, and from the stairwell behind us spilled forth a wave of bones, animated by necrotic energies. "*Au revoire,* and have fun." She blew Cicula a kiss and threw herself backwards off the rooftop's edge. Cicula dove after her, but the way was blocked by the woman's skeletal warriors.

"Why? Why can't I just have my daughter back?" she screamed.

Something tugged at my consciousness, like an unspoken utterance of my name that made the ground fall from under me. I'd a hunch as to who it was as well. I ushered Drakkengard to my side.

"Of course he picks now," I groaned. A burst of hellfire erupted around me, and shadowy hands dragged me into the abyss.

***

Lucifer, clad in the garb of a king.

"Well, well, well, it seems you are at a bit of an impasse," he chuckled.

"No, I was on a rooftop with my family. I *had* planned on helping them deal with that necrothurge's minions."

"A demon, two Cambions, a nephilim, a chimera and worldslayer hardly need your help dealing with a few paltry reanimated bones."

"What is this about?"

"It seems you are finally compos mentis and in possession of the facts. Well, as much as you need to know. My daughter has turned her back on me, as you know. My granddaughter owes me a significant debt for services rendered in the construction of her little citadel, as I am now reminding you. My great granddaughter has been abducted by powers in the service of your revived mother, and deigns to usurp even greater power the likes of which only I have ever even partially stood up to. That is the pieces on the board, so to speak. What will you do?"

"I think I see how it is."

"You want Master to make a really shitty deal with you to beat the Abomination, right?" Drakkengard sang out.

"You slander me," he pressed his hand to his chest. "All of my contracts are bona fide and of utmost fairness."

"Come on, Luci, let us nix the bullshit. The Abomination has made her move, and that means you're out of time. You need someone to fast forward your schedule for you. You brought me here to imply that my only options are ones that give you everything you want, like if I swear undying loyalty to you you'll make me some supremely powerful demon able to win your war and beat the Abomination, or maybe that if I trick or coerce

Lascivus into going back under your thumb you'll waive my Daughter's debt, something like that?"

"I have suggested nothing. It is you saying all this." He spread his lacquered palms.

"You're just mad that Lasci bailed on you," Drakkengard leered at the devil.

"Not at all. I have anticipated the day she finally left my care for centuries."

"That's what it's about, though, isn't it?" I tapped my head. "You need her back, or else need someone to fill her role, and you next choices are Cicula or myself. I was only bound to you via my marriage contract with your daughter, so now that she's renounced you there's nothing binding us together. You don't have Vengai-Ra or Ko either, I bought their contracts years ago."

"Again, I have merely stated the facts."

"You've said plenty. If I do nothing, my daughter will be forced to repay her debt in full."

"You say that like she did not negotiate the terms of the contract herself."

"She negotiated in peace time when her daughter was safely under her care."

"That is irrelevant."

"No, no, I see exactly how it is. You say it's time for me to make a decision? Here's my proposition. Transfer my daughter's debt to me. I'll do your dirty work right up until the citadel is paid off, and not a lifted finger more." I glared him dead in the eyes.

"You think you are worth as much as a powerful summoner and avatar of a great destroyer?"

"You know I am. I also have three conditions."

"My," he put a hand to his mouth. "The audacity of this one."

"Condition the first: you can't force me to partake of miasma. I'm not becoming a demon for you."

"Yet you married one of us."

"Condition the second: I get a three day grace period to get my affairs in order."

"Do you demand a golden castle as well?"

"Condition the third: You can't make me do anything that would be in violation of or otherwise annul my marriage contract with Lascivus."

"I'm almost impressed. You've become quite the shrewd bargainer."

"Do with have a deal?" I spat in my hand and held it out.

"We do. With your consent, the contract is sealed," he grasped my palm. "All of Cicula de Drage's debt has been transferred to you, to be repaid as I see fit, barring the prohibitions you have set forth. "

"Done."

***

The contract made, Drakkengard and I were expelled from the underworld to whence we came. Just as Luci said, Raanae's minions had already been defeated.

"Where the hell did you go?" Lascivus demanded, blade covered in bonemeal.

"Just a quick word with a man behind a curtain, had to set a few things straight. Now, Michael was it?" I turned to the archangel. "I believe we owe you some information, and all of us have a lot of plans to make while we still can."

40

Tonic Conquest

My heels clacked on the stone as I braced myself. The doors to the Noble Sanctuary stood before me, the heart of the Old City where my father fell thousands of years ago. Here Isaac was bound by his father as sacrifice to YHVH. Here, David bought the land for fifty pieces of silver and built his new altar. Jupiter once sat here. The Templars were born here. It had been conquered, destroyed, rebuild and reconquered so many times over the past three thousand years. The moon looked vile tonight.

I threw open the Sanctuary's doors, and my co-conspirators stormed in. Glaysa-labolas, Asmodeus, Raum,Vine, Balam, Zagan, and Adromalius. These eight were the only ones I trusted enough to help me with this, they were noble demons and devils that feared neither God nor my father, and with both the vast powers and vaster rebellious streak needed to accomplish my goals. I would have brought Draco too, but the Devil was making extra sure we never got any chances to meet. Thanks to Glaysa-labolas and Balam, we were able to step invisibly right up to the sanctuary. Once inside, things got a lot hotter.

"We have witches on the East wall. They've detected us." Vine harrumphed. A snake slivered out his sleeve and peered into the darkness.

"I got them." Glaysa threw his head back and loosed a booming howl. At its echo the king's paranormal guards turned on each other and with a few hot flashes of light they all fell dead from the walls.

"You brought your snake," Adromalius complained.

"So?" Vine asked.

"Carrying a snake with me is my thing." He opened his sack and looked sadly at the reptile inside it.

"Carrying a snake is a lot of people's thing," Vine chided. "The ruling body of the God damned underworld is the House of the Serpent. In case you haven't noticed, snakes have kind of been an *in thing* since we not only elected Samael the leader of our rebellion, but re-elected him after it all went tits up. In fact, if you look closely, we've gone and supported Samael's daughter, who is only not part of the House of the Serpent because she chose to secede. Snakes are going to keep being a thing because the only thing slithery-er are tentacles, and that just doesn't suit the demon aesthetic."

"Oi!" I clacked my heels impatiently. "We're on the clock here." Armed guards flooded from the towers, and gave the dead witches a cursory glance. Searchlights swept the sanctuary courtyard.

"Infrared, UV, and is that SONAR I hear?" Asmodeus perked his head. "They can see us. How much prejudice are we applying with here?"

The guardsmen finished circling the wall and fired. Three bursts each, impeccably coordinated, spat down at us. Asmodeus clicked his tongue and the lead fell to the ground in a fizzle of hellfire. Unfazed, the guardsman switched to different ammo, silver and blessed mercury, according to my sources.

"I don't know about you but I'm sick of hiding in the belly of the underworld in fear and shame. Everybody get naked!" I shouted, and chewed right through my false skin with my many mouths. My back arched, tail cracked, wing joints snapped and miasma oozed from my pores. With a shriek and a hoot my co-conspirators put on their private faces with me.

Glaysa-labosa, the winged hellhound, flew up to the north wall and slammed onto a guard's back, wagging his tail. Balam scrambled up the south wall on bear legs, his tail hissing, eyes aflame, and his beaked right hand plucked out a man's eyes through his visor. His horns glistened in the sickly moonlight. Raum the deep crow swooped up to the east wall in a whirlwind and was joined by Asmodeus, the dragon with heads of bull, man, and ram. Zagan, the winged bull, took the west wall. With a beat of his feathered wings the soldier's guns became piles of coins and fell from their hands. With a stamp of his hoof the soldiers doubled over, oil dripping from their mouths and eyes.

While they took care of the outside guards, I strode up to the extravagant golden palace that was once the Dome of the Rock. "Earl Vine," I commanded "tear down this wall."

"With pleasure." The lion snarled, reared back on his legs of black horses, and slammed the writhing mass of snakes attached to his shoulder against the palace walls.

"They've breached the second perimeter!" Someone cried out.

"To me!" I shrieked with my many mouths, and my companions flocked to my side.

"As you wish."

The king's men could do little to halt our advance and we carved a path right to the throne room. The king sat on his throne even at this ungodly hour, surrounded by gold, tapestries and security feeds, his bulging eyes cracked from not sleeping. He did not rise to greet me and just stared, unblinking. He might well have been dead of shock. No matter.

Raum clicked his talon and the sixty-two security feeds all flickered to the inside of this room. Every billboard, every newscast, every screen public and private was hijacked to show the reviled king, surrounded by demons and paralyzed with fear.

"Shakir Botros Saqqaf," Raum addressed the king "with the aid of the people you conquered the city, you said it was for the people but it was for the foreign arms dealers. Six years ago Zahir

Jalil El-Amin with the aid of the people conquered the city, he said it was for the people but it was for the foreign drug smugglers. Six years before that Salah Nadim El-Ghazawy conquered the city with the aid of the people, and he said it was for the people but it was for the foreign media moguls."

"So tell us all, Asmodeus," I asked, "how does it feel to set foot on the land your father bought?"

"Bought by my father, but built by my half-brother. It feels like a family reunion." He cleared his throat. "Hello, my kinsmen, tribes of Abraham, hello followers of prophets and hello alien interlopers." His three voices echoed through the palace. "You were told to rebuild the temple, yet three millennia since the ascension of Yeshua you have still not a temple to YHVH, yet countless temples to men, to war, and to money. I am Asmodeus, son of David the Psalmist and Agrat bat Mahlat who dances on roofs, half-brother of Tamar and Solomon, brother-by-law of Ailo, the daughter of Samael and Lilith, who has come to take the crooked crown from your head and declare herself the new king. In this I support her."

Zagan stepped forward and plucked the crown from Shakir's head.

"This crown is a symbol not of office but of proxy, backed only by money, so to money it shall return." Zagan held the crown aloft and hurled it to the ground where it shatters into two-hundred-and-seventy-nine coins.

I pulled out a bottle of mead, drained it dry and smashed the bottle against the floor. "Now I am king," I declared to the watchers. "I am not some proxy. I am a demon. I represent no man on Earth nor the Devil in Hell nor God in His heaven. I shall be greater than some absentee God or paranoid sell-king. If my actions offend you then take up the offensive against me. If my words fill you with despair, then I challenge you to act. Don't seek foreign aid, not from men, nor gods, nor demons. Don't wait idly for some messiah. Yeshua was just some poor kid being ordered around. Now he's gone for good. He can't save anyone now. Heaven's throne is absent. Hell has gone mad. If you fear me, kill me yourself. If you love me, come to me yourself. If you want something, ask me yourself. It is better to be feared and loved than feared or loved. My first order as king is, trust no one!"

I paused for breath and cleared my throat. "My visiting hours are noon till sundown, six days a week, except via appointment. All government employees are hereby laid off with full pension. We are now hiring for all positions, and all applicants will be considered. This government is an equal opportunity employer. What else? Ah, some soldiers were killed during this hostile takeover. Their next of kin shall also receive a pension." I yanked the king from his throne and sat down. "Also someone pick up this idiot puppet. Send him back to his masters. Or something, I don't care. New King out."

The screens hissed back to the security feeds. I pulled out a fresh bottle of mead and gulped it down. I'd just fulfilled another part of the prophecy of the End of Days, but now I had quite the leg to stand on. I was locked in now. Even if I got overthrown tomorrow, nobody else could fulfill it in my stead. However I had no intention of being overthrown.

"Do you think many people saw that this early in the morning?" Vine asked.

"Enough did. Things are going to be hectic for the next few weeks so let's kick it back for now." I put my false skin back on and my fellows followed suit. The king was still catatonic on the floor. Being stormed by eight demons in their true form could be horrifying but I thought he'd at least protest. I leaned down and plucked a black feather from his hair. It must have been one of Raum's.

"Ah, Adromalius," I spoke up, "you should secure the treasury before someone decides to loot it."

"Good call."

Third Movement

Capriccio

41

Final Hour

Draco

Lucifer leaned indifferently against his chair, in which Lilith lounged.

"It is done?"

"Murder shrieks out. The element of water moistens the earth, but blood flies upward and bedews the heavens." I took a ring from my pocket and tossed it to and fro. How long had I been doing the Devil's work now?

"Oh don't be so sour." Lilith rolled her head to look at me. "That troublesome old fogey won't be missed."

"I am but a meek and gentle butcher. Or was I the baker? Well, he was quite the meat pie so I suppose it was a joint effort."

"And Ko brought the candlesticks that minced him," Drakkengard added.

"Speaking of which, I believe there is a certain wick which is about to run out." I checked the buttons on my cuff. One of them needed replacing soon. The devil frowned.

"Always in such a hurry to depart, dear boy. The best has yet to come, as they say."

"Your best, maybe." *Hmm, my boots could do with a polish too.* "I doubt anything you have in mind can top the bath I'm planning. That and my retainers are waiting for me to finish here."

"A bath, you say?" Lilith's eyes light up. "I might know a trick or two to top any bath of yours."

"I prefer my rubber quails to be passive participants, but thank-you. Getting rubbed down by animated squeak-toys is something I'd rather never repeat."

"Oh, child, why stop at the ducks when there's a whole bathroom around you?"

"There's no bathroom around me yet, which brings me back to my point. You can't shave what's left anymore thinner without losing another supporting role. Anymore time, anymore distance, and I'll end up finishing work early and clocking off before the choir has sung their second psalm."

"Very well," he tsked. "I concede the point. Go on, let your hair down, take your collar off, have a bath, do what you will but do try not to get too preoccupied. When the trumpet sounds you and all mine others are getting spirited via the express lane. So to speak."

"One more thing," Lilith crowed. "Give my esteems to my daughter. She'll know why."

"I'm on break. No promises." I tossed a dismissive wave and slipped through the Void with Drakkengard. It came so easily after all these years, with no need for mantra or mnemonic or even a deep breath, like a mathematical formulae solved at a glance such that you can't even recall the intermediate steps. With but a mental shrug I stepped out of creation and made re-entry elsewhere.

***

Hot arid wind blasted my cheeks and scratched at my eyes, while the sudden mid-day light blinded me. I gagged at a mouthful of sand and donned some tinted glasses.

"Stellar entrance as always, boss."

"Well I try, Ko."

"Maybe once all this is done you can write a book on theatrics, I bet you'd make enough to buy the farm," the gunman said.

"Hi guys," Drakkengard waved.

"Hey, kid. So how long do we have?" Vengai-Ra peered at the guarded city walls ahead of us.

"Until the trumpet sounds, which could be anywhen. Expect no warning before getting snatched to the front lines in an instant."

"Business as usual where I'm from," Ko said. "Though you at least had time in the drop pods to gripe at your orders. Quietly, of course, you don't want anything incriminating left on the black box."

"Is that right? Speaking from experience are we?"

"It turns out saying your current commander only got his position because of his sweet ass counts as insubordination. Who knew? Well, nevermind that. What's the plan, Boss?"

"Plan? I'd just like to see Lascivus before the world takes a giant leap toward tragedy and dissolution. If you're hoping for some big gambit to try to save our bacon, well, I am sorry but we'll be lucky to get off this with just our rinds and trotters."

"Hey, Encyclopedia Dramaqueen, let me rephrase. Where we headed?"

"From what I've heard she's made a home for herself at the Noble Sanctuary. I was just going to pop by there, catch up. You don't have to come with me."

"Not like we have anything better to do."

"Do we?"

"We could hit up a pub or something." Vengai-Ra took a test tube out, uncorked it, and took a swig. "With how hot it is there's bound to be plenty."

"Fair point. Alright, boss, we'll just follow you until something more interesting pulls our heads."

We were stopped at the city gates by armed soldiers, but they made only cursory demands—Name, reason for visit, why we were on foot. As I made up a story about our car running out of gas a glint of light caught my eye. Embedded in the wall at just the right angle to be pointed at us was a small black lens. That was the real point of stopping us, I supposed. They didn't even bother to pat us down for concealed weapons, and just like that we were free to enter.

Hurried pedestrians passed store fronts plastered with propaganda posters, and sandy white towers breached the city skyline to broadcast news updates in stiff Hebrew to all on the streets and roads that cared to watch.

"—senator was impeached and publicly humiliated for accepting bribery. As per standard procedure, their retirement salary has been repealed. In other— "

"Hey, Draco, do you even know your way around the city?"

"Sure I do. We're downtown now, and according to a map I saw we want to head somewhere in a general easterly direction."

"—rioters were routed, but the ringleaders are still at— "

"Say, boss, just how old was this map?"

"Oh, not that old. Only a few tens of hundreds of years at most."

"—and now a message from our King."

"To you, the people, peace." My footsteps slowed at the new voice, and a warm smile spread across my face at the familiar tones. "I come to you today with a warning. To you, the people, I say trust not. Trust not those who say you need them. Trust not those who claim to hold the keys to paradise. Trust not the kindness of powerful strangers, for while their right hand bears gifts their left is empty and expectant. Trust not those who say 'it is so' without demonstration. Trust not those who say 'you know me'. Trust not those who say 'I know best'. There walks among you those who would say of themselves 'I am the savior.' Forsake them, for they seek only to place upon you the burden of their ascent as they try to obtain power on high. Trust not the savior. Trust not those you have burdened with the lofty task of governing your city. Trust not your king. Trust not this message. All of this I say to you as king."

"That's it then, she's gone just as batty as you."

"Nonsense Vengai-Ra. Why, I believe the good king has just issued us a ticket with which to ride. Best we use it, yes?"

The walls to the old city stood taller than even most buildings, and every gate sat guarded by a bevy of knights armed with rifles. Ko and Vengai-Ra had peeled off earlier to sate their thirst, leaving just Drakkengard and myself to breach old city's security.

"Peacs, sahs, I say peace." I waved as I approach and tried not to go cross-eyed at all five gun barrels abruptly leveled at my face.

"Move along, civilian," grunted one that had plumage affixed to their bayonet.

"But we only just got here," Drakkengard whined.

"Yes, you're being terribly rude. Don't you know who I am?"

"No, I don't know who you are. Oh, let me guess. Are you the dung eating fishmonger of the living saint?"

"Close, close, close enough. Come closer, dear, don't you know?" I spread my arms. "I am the savior," I bellowed it loud enough to be heard for blocks all around, and dozens of heads turned at the noise. "Surely you've heard tell of me on TV?" The guards pulled their triggers. A bevy of bullets battered against the tree behind me, and blood seeped out the bullet holes of my vest. I squawked in stifled pain from suddenly getting my chest cavity aired out.

"Clear." The one with the shiniest lapel waved off the rest as I teetered on my feet. A slip of blood trickled down my mouth, which I clumsily wiped away.

"Yes, it's a good thing I wore my red vest today," I grumbled. "Look at you. You're not even sorry, sah."

"Not in the slightest," she barked in laughter and her jagged-scale tongue clicked in the wind. "I love the look on their faces when they realize these actually hurt. No demon, angel or god is getting near here without a bullet spray-tan, and it's real hard to keep a guise up after a lick of these babies. There was that one elf, but he's fillet now. Alright, hurry up, the king's waiting."

My companion and I were briskly whisked into the new king's castle atop the noble sanctuary. Armed guards patrolled every corridor, and well-kept dignitaries strutted by them in guarded confidence. We were led to a long hall gilded in whitestone and gold, past a procession of elite soldiers. More than a few of them I recognized as the human guise of demons I'd encountered in the underworld over the years. Just how much of the underworld had Luci lost to the new King? At the hall's end sat a throne, and in that throne sat the new king.

"We brought you another one claiming to be the savior."

That had been the password of sorts we'd come up with. Not a password into the castle but a password into the prophecy. I'd come to the holy city and falsely declared myself the savior.

"Indeed, this is the one. You're late, O Savior,"

I had been accepted by the Antichrist, who denied Christ. That locked me into the role of the Man of Sin, also known as the Man of Lawlessness, spoken of in Thessalonians. And Thessalonians could be used as a sort of back door into Revelations. One advantage was that it established the Man of Sin as a separate entity to the Antichrist, which eased the burden of prophecy on both of us. Another advantage is that it empowered me to not just commit crimes against God but play fast and loose with all kinds of rules. We'd done so here, in this final hour, when both Lucifer and Malign would be far too occupied to penetrate all the wards and security the new king had put in place around the city.

The king took a gulp from her goblet, "or is it that you're early?" The warm scent of honey and spirits wafted over the hall. She smelled the same way when we first met.

"While you seem to be doing quite well for yourself, Lascivus." I took a step toward her and tried not to show how shaken I was. "Or should I say my liege now?"

"Oh yeah? Are you saying you'll kneel before me?" she laughed. She wore a simple crown, and regal clothes with little adornment. A declaration of her status, rather than a boast.

"Are you saying I haven't before?"

"Hi, wifey!" Drakkengard waved with both arms and the too-long sleeves of her robes flapped wildly.

"Hey, Drakkengard. Have you been keeping your idiot master out of trouble?"

"Some troubles, he likes the other troubles, and he's pretty troublesome himself, too. Like a tuba shaped like a treble."

"Yeah, you still don't make sense, kid."

"My liege," A woman beside her said. "Do you wish us to leave?" I recognized her, what was her name? Marcy? Marie? One of Lascivus's many half-sisters from her mother. She used to help out around the house. She was a guy last time I saw her. Well, far be it for me to questions those of fluid identity.

"Forget it. More than half of you chucklefucks are double agents anyway, isn't that right?" Her light-hearted accusations were met with an outcry of laughing approval, and a chorus of, "Trust no one."

"See, Draco? I got so many knives at my back they form a shield. That's what I like about double agents, even when they're spying on you they're still spying for you."

"Hear-hear!" They cheered.

"But really," Lascivus turned back to me. "You're finally with me again, which means either prick downstairs fucked up or the third daemon war is right around the corner, and he's not the type to fuck up bookkeeping."

"You yourself said it. I have my freedom right up until the second the front lines call me. Luci has his whole army on shortcut"

"I understand the archangel failed to prevent things on his end then."

"Michael did what he could," I shrugged. "Seventh heaven's been closed for centuries but an archangel still hasn't that much sway when all's said and done."

"Typical of the peace-doves," she rolled her eyes and took another gulp from her goblet. "We managed to delay as long as possible but I guess we were several hundred years too late to stop this war breaking out like a greasy teen's face. Say, where are your retainers?"

"Getting in some R&R before we're sent to Armageddon. How is Cicula? From what I've been able to gather no-one has been able to catch wind of Shahdee."

Her smile dropped away. "Not so good. I mean, she hasn't lost it, but getting no word of her daughter's safety for three years has really done a number on her. At least she has Kali looking out for her. I dread to think how she'd be without that woman."

"How about Lach?"

"What's there to say? He's still a hot-headed bimbo. He tries to help her out in his own way but he doesn't exactly have a wide area of expertise."

"How about you?" I stepped forward. "How have you been?"

"Oh," she let out a deep sigh, "tired, but better. Plan B is going well. I mean if it was just human's that be one thing, could go full denial, but a few of my allies are lingering gods, and a lot more are fallen gods, so it'd be pretty bad form to just slander the lot of them. Gotta show some tact, yeah?"

"Damn straight," someone called out.

"Either way I picked a pretty good spot to spread as much doubt as possible. The psalms of heaven are a lot quieter than before."

"If we're lucky we won't need to put that to the test, but then, when have we ever been lucky?" I asked.

"I dunno, I'd say both you and our son have had some rather striking lucky streaks, wouldn't you?"

"That's not luck," Drakkengard crossed her arms, "just exploitation."

"How about the third part? Have you had much success there?"

"Well, that's hard to say," she refilled her goblet and took a swig. "Good in numbers, not that big a deal in percentage. It's hard to say. There haven't been this many fallen in the world since the time of the Grigori, and my father has also had a lot of deserters."

"Thanks to you."

"Thanks to me and our daughter. A lot of folks that are sick of it all think I'm making my own bid for the throne, that I'm raising an army to be mobilized against the underworld. A lot of them are going to the Citadel of Crimson Moon instead. You got to admit, it's a lot more neutral, very Swiss."

"So that's it." I sat on the arm of her throne and leaned against her shoulder. "We've done all we can do."

"What about you?"

"Old Scratch made sure I didn't have any time to lay any further plots, let alone hatch them. He has been rather forthcoming with information though. He seems convinced I'll be his champion in the war," I sighed, "all this rage over a lost penny."

"From where I'm sitting, you're still a lost penny."

"All I care about is stopping those that are hurting my family."

"Is that right, Mr. Devil's Work?"

"I deploy *argument from emotional hedonism*, next question."

"What are you going to do now? The old stories would suggest some kind of rigorous training, or perhaps seeking out some vast weapon. Maybe you could try to pluck Shiva's third eye. That would certainly help. Maybe Balor's eye. Or just snatch every last damnable eye and make a garland of them."

"If I may, bugger all that. Tonight, I'm nobody. Tonight, I am as I am." I helped myself to a swig from her goblet. "I'm sick of it. I'm sick of higher powers. I'm ill from being sent on unholy missions. I'm diseased from objectives and criteria and debts and deals. I'm thick with grime from both the forest and the trees. All I want is a bath and to answer to no master than whim, before everything reaches a purity of shit not seen since Baldr died. I just . . ."

"I get you, I get you. You can have your bath."

"Thank you."

***

The bath was exquisite. Water hot enough to pink my flesh and make blind from steam. I lathered myself in body oil and Drakkengard washed my hair. We tried all the different soaps until we smelled like a summer orchid, and lay there in soak as my wracked muscles openly wept at the reprieve.

Drakkengard woke me after a short while, and I retired to Lascivus's bedroom. The new king awaited in sheer finery, lounging in the middle of the luxurious room with a bottle in hand.

"I hope you're not too weary for a conjugal visit."

"Not at all. Oddly enough, I'm actually looking forward to it, but I think I would much rather lie with you naked."

She shrugged off her nightgown. The sheer fabric fell to a heap around her feet.

"Better?"

"No. Completely naked. I want to caress your wings and kiss your horn and feel your claws on my back. "

"It's only fair I ask the same of you. I want to fuck all of you, ego and animus together. Don't just leave half of you outside like you normally do."

"Well. That's only fair."

I ushered Drakkengard into the room. I needed to say nothing. She placed her hand on my wrist and her nails pierced my veins. Liquid metal poured into my circulatory, supplanting my blood and pervading my cells. I that is she and me became I that is I. Battle-sweat dripped from my pores but without violence.

Lascivus, in turn, shed her glamor. Her skin darkened, her sclera turned black, her hands revealed themselves as claws and her feet as talons. Vast wings of fine leather unfurled from her back and hungry fangs protruded over her lips. The countless mouths of her hunger opened all over her body—upon her arms, her chest, her stomach and naked breasts, upon her palms and her soles and her calves and between her thighs. Her waist cinched, for she possesses but one organ there with which to digest. A small horn breached her crown. Her long black hair draped between the blades of her wing-shoulders.

"You're beautiful," we said.

"You're delectable," she purred, her myriad mouths gnash and echo in muted concurrence. We embraced, and her body nibbled at my skin, and her many tongues lapped up the lifeblood excreted though the punctures.

"I'm starving," her mouths gasped.

"You are Starvation. You are the child of Gluttony and Pride."

When my skin was left bloodless her mouths bit into my flesh in search of more. Needle teeth gouged my body and I arched my spine in response.

"It's not enough." She drank my blood. "It's not enough." She devoured my flesh.

"It's never enough." We bit her lip. "There's no such thing as enough." I grasped her buttocks and pulled her closer, tighter. My arousal pressed against her stomach and was caressed by many tongues.

"More." She pushed me onto her bed, and her claws raked my chest.

"More." I grasped her breasts and her mouths nipped at my palms. The goose bumps of her areole read a Braille of excitement. Her whole body panted in anticipation.

"More." She lifted her hips up and embedded me within the mouth between her thighs. She rolled back her head and gasped, her sharp chin and proud Roman nose turned up to me. Her bright eyes flashed and she buried her face in my neck. Pearly knives spilled my arteries into her mouths. My whole body itched from the heat. The only scratch was to rub myself against her, to grind myself into her, to make sensations never static and always new. She rocked her hips upon me, rolling back and forth and her claws snipped and scratched and grazed and poked and groped and all the life I had and the lives I might and the lives I could sire were spread under her body in buffet for her to devour. My hands longed to do the same, to sink into her hide and peel apart muscle and squeeze her bone. Her supernal strength restrained me and even being denied in such a way was still gratifying. Struggling against suppression is still expression when it's more than just yourself.

My left arm was ablaze in white flame but it harmed neither she nor I, and that too was expression. Interaction, intercourse, interpersonal relations, in response I spewed white filth and that expulsion too was expression. She devoured my life and my millions of half-lives and that too was expression. My blood was her lip-paint and in this communication there lay understanding, not in any way miraculous but there was comfort in recognition. Get along. There is kinship between similar breeds of beast. A hypersensitive reaction to a tongue upon my frenulum and I groaned, strained against her grasp and bite down on her breast. She keened, and lashes out with her teeth. A mess of my chest tore open and she lapped up the pooling blood. Blood lost, blood replenished, seed lost, and slowly restocked, and the room was alit with my white flame.

No sense pretending this wasn't Bedlam, we burned, we beasts, for we each could take it. Sweat matted pubic hair, hers entangled in mine, red, red eyes hers looked into mine, hips driven, thrust, pivot, this was just about us. Make noise, who is louder, she or I? A competitive incentive to do even better. The room filled with smoke and steam in a feast between two. We each ate, never to be full, never to be deplete.

42

Maha-Kali Mantra

Cicula

I took a deep puff from my hookah and stood. A pair of temple shield-bearers dressed me in a sleeveless coat and handed me a long wooden pipe. I called the skull-topped staff to my hand and stepped out.

"How are we doing?"

I haven't felt this invigorated in thousands of years.

"But still no . . . ?" My shoes *tick-tock*ed an even beat against the marble floor.

I'm afraid not. Not even I can pierce Brahman.

"Fine. We'll just have to tear what we want to know out of someone a little easier to find. "

Who? Janus is just as imperceptible. Every time I track him down he closes the door.

"That undead bitch."

Her? You know it's actually surprisingly hard to track the blood of someone who has no blood.

"For you, maybe, it took a lot of time and effort but I finally managed to strike a deal with a certain someone."

And who might that be?

I painted a sigil upon the floor of the antechamber and dismissed my attendants. Within a circle, a twelve sided shape made of right angles, from the two top corners and the two lower sides extent lines that join into circles, from the bottom extended a crescent moon and from the top extended two. Into this sigil I placed my blood and power.

"Prince of twenty six legions, knower of what has been and what is to come, discoverer of lost things. Vassago the good-natured, come forth! Honor our bargain!"

Like a thing from a well Vassago crawled out from his sigil. His right hand was a goshawk and he had the lower half of a crocodile. His thirty foot frame coiled around and around itself to squeeze into the room. His vast red wings furled up behind him and his white fangs flashed in the lamplight. He faced me, but his hollow green eyes saw nothing.

"It is time to complete our covenant, star-blood," he declared. His left hand fed a sliver of flesh to his avian right, and his legs scratched against the marble floor. "Though I must ask that you be sly with your demand, for I would hate to incriminate my loyalty before He-Chained-by-Abaddon."

"There is a wretched undead by the name of Raanae. I need to eliminate her before the final battle starts. Show me where to find her and our dealings will be resolved."

"Ah, that is quite the straightforward task. You are most generous." He took out another morsel for his living hand. I was wrong. They weren't flesh but eyeballs, the same creamy green as his own.

"You will do it?"

"Perhaps too generous." His crocodilian tail slapped against the floor. "It would reflect poorly to conduct such an unbalanced transaction. So, to even the scales I shall sweeten the deal for you."

"This isn't some backhanded sabotage is it, demon?"

"Not at all, star-blood. I would not dare. My bonus is but a warning. The end of days cannot be stopped. The entropic jail cannot hold much longer. It buckles under the weight of potential. The dark side of the moon has already begun to act. The yellow sign returns. The Tuatha de Danaan shall be reborn in new iron.

The blood of Amaterasu shall leave its sanctuary. Prophets and giants return to the Earth. The Faeran consolidate their allies. The Man of Sin meets with the anti-christ and reaffirms their vows. The lost cities of Atlantis, R'lyeh and Mu quake in their graves. This and more shall come. There shall be no more delay. As for your servant of Toutates, take my hand and I shall take you to her."

Vassago held out his avian right hand to me. I brushed my fingers against its beak and at once I was in flight. Its red wing carried me from underworld to midworld, from Luna to Earth, to a tower hidden in a city on the Isle of the Bretons.

***

Glass shattered and I landed on the ground before three people. Two were scientists by their garb, a man and a woman, and beside them stood my quarry. The goshawk took flight and left.

"Ah, I do adore unexpected guests." Raanae faced me with her doll-like smile of sickening sweetness. "If you are trying to seize our thought tunnel I am afraid you've just missed it."

"Where is my daughter, undead?" I slammed the skull-topped staff against the ground and conjured forth Kali's divine power. My two arms became four, and blood beaded upon my forehead.

"Such a shame, so single minded." She turned to the two scientists. "Julius, Susannah, don't blame me if you get caught up in our little disagreement." The two nodded and fled to an elevator on the far end of the room. I let them go. If Raanae didn't have the information I needed I could follow the sniff of their blood later.

"Last chance, undead. Tell me where my daughter is and I just might let you go." I called the vajra to my hand and cocked my arm.

"*Merci*, that just won't do. Your daughter is in a dead place, full of dead things. The red queen seems good for that, yes? Ah but the other one is making sure Red doesn't go too far. Mustn't kill the golden goose, as they say." She flipped up her white hoodie and ran a gaunt finger down her breastbone.

"Tell me where she is."

"You really are beautiful, you know? Such a delicate skull. Your bones will look exquisite once I've stripped away all that rotting meat."

"Wrong answer." I let the vajra fly and its thunderbolt exploded against a wall of conjured bones that appeared from the ground.

"Tut-tut, *ma cheri*. Be a good girl and let me get you bare." She stuffed her hand into the conjured bones and out she yanked a spinal cord affixed to a sharpened shoulder blade. Other bones bound themselves to her clothes to form makeshift armor that rattled with every step.

The instruments of the Deva easily crushed the bones but no matter how many I reduced to dust, she always had more to pull out. I struck again with the vajra, and must have hit a weak point because it punched through her skeletal barrier and blasted the clothes from her body. Her body itself was in a different condition.

"Ah, you are so naughty. I love it," A crack spread across her face as she laughed. She stood naked before me. Naked of cloth. Naked of skin. Naked of muscle. Naked of blood. Naked of organs. Her hands were never bony but actual bone. Her doll-like face shattered into calcium dust and revealed the grinning skull beneath it. With a mix of high-pitch squeaking and low droning she called forth reinforcements. More skeletons rushed to her side from where their bones had been hidden throughout the room.

"You . . . "

"Ah, it was so ecstatic," she chittered, "the joy being declared the purest, the feel of the knife lacerating my flesh, the unadulterated feeling of exogenesis as nature stripped my ugly flesh away." She clutched her rib cage in nostalgic longing.

"You *are* insane."

"*Non*. I am burdened with great purpose. It is my duty to usher all living things into Toutates' dead embrace."

"But that's wrong!" Kali yelled through me. "I have known Toutates and he is not like that. You do this only for yourself."

"Ah, poor little sweet thing." She ignored Kali and kept talking, "you too could have known the same rapture as I. Instead of gathering more worshipers you should have tracked down those who remains and killed them all." She caressed the jaw of a skeleton standing next to her.

Oh no.

"What?"

"Children, by Toutates, come unto me!"

The animated bones turned to her and charged. A wave of white crashed into her and splashed against the wall.

A god is shaped by its believers.

"Yes, I know that." I stepped back and shielded myself against the stampeding skeletons, but none pay me any heed.

She is Toutates' only believer, has been for thousands of years. She made sure of that.

"So this undead bitch drove that deus insane?"

No, you're not seeing the issue at hand. She has warped Toutates into a reflection of herself. There is no longer any distinction between he and she. Raanae isn't his avatar, he's not her patron. They can't even be called different existences at this point. She has usurped his divine mantle.

"Come on, you filthy wretches!" she screamed to the stumbling wave of bones. "Come to your god! Hurry! I gave you unlife, now become me! *Putain bordel de merde fais chier!*"

From the mass of bones emerged an ivory giant. Its form was clad in Gaelic armor, and its height so great that it grinded against the ceiling as it moved, showering the room in calcium dust.

"Fuck queen red!" it bellowed. "Fuck all their plans! Once Janus opens the gates of heaven it will be me, ME that sits on the throne of the overgod. I alone shall reign supreme and I shall usher a golden age of eternal undeath," Its booming shouts still echoed with Raanae's trill voice.

"All things die," Kali declared. "I am the destroyer, and it is my duty to end all that would pervade this natural order."

I lunged at the corrupted deus and struck with vajra and noose and staff and blade. I ripped out its bones and smashed them one after the other, yet everywhere upon the giant sprouted arms that lashed out and clawed at my legs to hold me still. Ribs shot at me like spears, and even with four arms I couldn't deflect them all. One caught me square on the shoulder, knocked me off balance, and before I could recover Toutates' colossal hand slammed me across the room. Shards of bone I had exploded flew back to the deus and were made whole. Fissures from my sword and staff closed up.

Every injury I inflicted was undone.

Cicula, come on, you need to let me in more. I slew the infinite demon Raktabija and I can slay this.

Very well.

I rose, leaning on my staff, closed my eyes, and chanted the mantra of Kali.

"*Om Krīm Kālyai namah,*
Om Kapālinaye Namah,
Om Hrim Shrim Krim
Parameshvari Kalike Svaha"

My body warped in response to the vibrations of the supreme, divine voice. Four arms became ten. My forehead split open, and a third eye cast a cruel gaze toward what had become of Toutates. The expression repeated ten times on ten faces, and with immaculate coordination ten legs took up a war stance. Ornaments depicting jackals and serpents adorned my limbs. The armaments of all the deva waited at my fingertips. I could perfectly perceive the quantum flow of energy, the weave of creation. I knew how to undo her.

"You stand before Mahakali, mother of destruction," I uttered from my ten mouths. "That is not Brahman, this is not Brahman, when all such things have been removed only Brahman shall remain. Agni, Varuna, Indra, Vishnu, Saraswati, the destruction wrought by they and more is done so at my behest. In my many hands I hold their tools of power."

"It doesn't matter how many—" I lassoed a serpent around Toutates' jaw and wrenched it off before the corrupted Deus could finish. I let fly the blade disc Sudarshana, which sawed through Toutates' legs from under him and forced him to the ground. I drove the Vajra through his chest and wreaked a thunderstorm within him. With trident and hook I gouged out his dusty eyes.

The bones started to scatter, to flee in all directions but I ensnared them all within a net. With the mace Kaumodaki I smash the trapped bones to dust amidst Raanae's screams, and with fire drill I ground the dust into smoke. Surrounded by this smoke I took out a conch horn, emptied myself of air, and took a deep breath. With force of gale, winds sucked into my lungs, and the billowing smoke was dragged screaming with it. My ten mouths slammed shut and the screaming thus silenced. Not a single mote of dust escaped.

I put the conch to my lips and sounded the cry of victory, and I danced.

I danced for the battle just won.

I danced for victory to come.

My ten feet stomped and my ten arms swayed. I danced for the destruction of Raanae. I danced for the destruction of Toutates. I danced for the coming destruction of Janus and Malign. I danced for destruction and my dance destroyed.

The stomping of my ten feet pulverized the floors below me. The swaying of my arms sliced through the walls.

I danced the building to the ground, and not until it but flattened, smoothrubble did I stop to regard my work.

"You should say something," a voice spoke.

"No, we should leave," another replied.

"Sssh, it'll—" I turned one of my ten heads to the source. It was two humans, male and female, at the forefront of the crowd that had gathered to behold my wondrous dance. I knew them, the scientists that colluded with destroyed Raanae.

"What do you know?" My ten mouths spoke. The woman stepped forward, afraid yet bold.

"You want the girl, right?" She stammered "She, ah, I'm afraid the one in green, Janus, he took her with him."

"Where?"

"He opened a door to heaven. He said," she gulped, "the first sphere was liberated long ago and that no angel dares set foot there. They expect the demons to storm the gates of heaven, and won't think to," she gulped again "to look for someone that has already snuck in."

"I see. My thanks for this information," my many mouths uttered, and I vanished into the Void.

43

Downbeat Drafted

Michael

For hours I stood, and watched the ill folk visit my parents' latest clinic. They must have saved thousands over the years, if not lives then livelihoods. Some time ago Otay had left to go hunt for food. Had I apprehensions about being alone? There was little to say that I would do better or worse without him, yet it remained hard to make my legs move. Nonetheless it must be done. I steeled myself and entered, bowing my head to fit under the doorframe.

"Michael? What a surprise," my mother said as she looked up. She and father were aiding a woman injured in some kind of an explosion. Mother removed the pellets of rock and metal that had been buried in her flesh and father healed the wound with magick.

"There, all done," Father poked the woman's healed flesh and smiled. After the patient left he flicked off the light above the door. The Doctors are out.

"I don't suppose you're here on a social visit, are you?" Mother crossed her arms low.

"I'm sorry. I can't restrain the choir for any longer. Were I to test their patience further, they would just revoke my position as archangel and go ahead as planned anyway. I had hoped to get at least five years. It's too soon." I looked away.

"It's fine, it's fine," Father said with a flick of his hand. "You did all you could. There's no blame here."

"That's not all." I swallowed. "All standing angels are commanded to return from their posts at once and join the choir at Megiddo by order of Sandalphon. That, I'm afraid that includes you, Mother."

"I thought you were already no longer under their command," Father said.

"No. If I actually left I would be branded an enemy of heaven, and purged of all radiance. I just slipped a few forms in the right places to get indefinite independent privileges, basically permission to do God's will however I saw fit, which is what I have been doing. Tell me, Michael, how many have refused this call?"

"A great many. More fallen walk the Earth now than in the time of the Grigori. Gabriel is worried this may reach the degree of Lucifer's fall, even before the hour of Har Megiddo." I turned to the window and sighed. "A part of me feels this is my fault, a consequence of the time I bought. This is not a sudden righteous call to arms. Everyone has been dwelling on the matter for the past three years. It no longer became a question of if the horn would sound, but when."

"Better a choice made freely than a choice denied." Father shrugged. "I'm going too."

"You're going to join the choir?"

"No, no, definitely not. I'm a child of Nemesis, I'd wager that's a conflict of interests. No, not the choir, but I am joining the two of you," he said to Mother and I.

"If you survive, they'll probably make you a saint, you know." Mother nudged him with her elbow.

"Are you sure?" I warned. "Just being around that much radiance could have an effect on you, and your red-eyed other will most definitely be joining the fray."

"My mind's made up. That said, what's the plan regarding that other matter?" he asked.

"Malign cannot be allowed to set foot in Heaven. Defending the gates is our highest priority."

"Right, then." Mother glanced about the clinic. "I guess we'd better go now."

44

Ave Discordia

Lach

Sis slipped out somewhere and left me behind. Well, she'd be back sooner or later so I wasn't fussed. Kali was a great dancer, she'd be fine. As for myself, well I figured to pass the time in a tavern. There were a few good ones around the Citadel, and I recalled one of them was near here so I wandered on over, slipped onto a stool, and ordered two drinks.

"Oh, thanks," said a woman, who snatched up one of the drinks and took a seat next to me.

"Have a fun time at the bowling alley?" I asked. We had a date she never made, we ideological cousins of chaos.

"Would you like a hamburger?" she replied. An allusion to cuil theory, the game was afoot.

"But the Buffalo buffalo Buffalo buffalo buffalo buffalo Buffalo buffalo are in season this time of year, not ham." I said, an inane sentence that remained grammatically correct only if you knew all possible meanings of buffalo.

"The vodka is good, but the meat is rotten." Machine translation, Russian, the flesh is weak.

"I could probably go for an indentation though," I retorted. Insistence, compromise, just the tip of theophany. In the language of chaos I was begging, crying. All my learning for all these years and I'd managed to keep up for just five sentences, no more, but no less. Five, sacred to Eris for no reason save, 'why not?'

"Well why didn't you say so?" She clasped her hands and procured a flat apple, which she broke with me. It tasted like paper, but sweet.

My pilgrimage had finally born fruit, wild divine ecstasy stormed in my heart. My goddess and I sat in music for half an hour and another half and then she turned to me.

"Are you worried about tomorrow?" she asked.

"I'm worried about today," I confessed. "Tomorrow doesn't exist yet. Everything's slowly getting brighter, but there's nothing to see." I leaned back and sighed. "What's better, soma or ambrosia?"

"Oh soma, without a doubt," my goddess insisted. "There's a reason you can't get it anymore."

"There's spiders on my hand," I idly observed, "but they aren't real." Her presence was the most exquisite rapture. I felt ready for another dance of nonsense, craved it.

"That's right, little salamander. What else do your elf eyes see?"

"I'm not an elf, I'm a fish."

"That's Cambrian. You, sweetest, are a Cambion."

"Oh yeah. So why aren't you dead like all the rest?" I asked.

"*Mu.*"

"Hey,"

"Well?"

"Nay."

"Right."

"More of a left indie flip."

"Is that who the Ska Eight are?"

"Now look at what you made me do."

"I would have guessed Laurel and Hardy. Who knew?"

"Well The Who did."

"Do we dance now?" I asked, and ashamedly failed to hide my anxiousness. Oh how I'd missed her sweet nonsense.

"I thought we'd already begun."

"It's not much of a floor then. More of a fleur."

"Can't make bread without breaking out the flour."

"What about the king of the potato people?"

"He's our only hope, but what of it? My carpet's in the kitchen."

"Gourmet?"

"If you're feeling prideful," and she loosed a golden laugh that made my knees melt. "Come on salamander boy, let's move your feet."

"I thought you'd never ask," I said and took her hand. It was every bit as firm and warm as the first time we'd met and danced, at the chevalier's rascal, under a chandelier of glowing flowers, where I'd only managed five sylapses, but this time I was not sure who was the charlatan.

"What's the value of a golden apple?"

"A trophy. To the fairest, right?" I cocked my head as we moved to the beat.

"Wrong. What's an apple prove? The fairest has no need for an apple. The fairest is already using their fairest-nest to be provided with everything they desire."

"What if they aren't, then? What if the fairest isn't good at that kind of thing?"

"Being good at that kind of thing makes you the fairest. Turn it around again. Say you won the apple. Now what? What do you do with it? The more you show it off the less fair you are, because your fairness should be self-evident, and appealing to definition never proved a point, and if you just hide it, well, you may as well have never had it at all."

"People still remember you won, and you'll know you won."

"You wouldn't have won without being recognized as the fairest to begin with."

"I seem to recall all of the contestants resorted to bribing the judge."

"And regardless of who the apple went to, none of them were the fairest. The fairest was Eris, who had the apple first. The fairest was Eris, who recognized how valueless the apple was and *threw it away*. That is the value of a golden apple."

"I don't get it," I confessed to my goddess.

"It's simple. The purpose of a golden apple is to get rid of it, it causes nothing but trouble. Now here," she thrust a second apple into my palm. "You might not be the fairest, but have a little trouble for your trouble," she said, and vanished. *'To the strongest'* it said. It was a completely unremarkable apple with no powers or blessings or potency, and I loved my goddess more than all the fives in a fjord.

45

Measure of Last Reprise

Draco

Powers beyond my reckoning gracelessly deposited me upon a couch in Pandemonium. I started to scratch my brow in annoyance, but instead jabbed myself in the forehead with a book I'd been enjoying. Drakkengard then appeared on a rug beside me, still fast asleep.

"Now that's just disappointing," Lilith said from behind me. "I was hoping he'd be naked."

"No such luck, Screech-owl." I dog-eared the corner of my page and sent the book back to Sacram. "So this is zero hour, then?" I crossed my leg and hummed.

"Indeed it is. Soon we will be Coram Deus, or rather, His representatives." Lucifer stood before a map of a valley, his arms crossed behind him.

"We will be. You won't, unless you've suddenly found a way to free yourself from Abaddon."

"Ha, if only. No, I shall be orchestrating from my prison, as per the norm. Our outposts are being established as we speak." He pointed at several points on the map, and at his touch scorched circles appeared around them.

"So before I decide how haphazardly I should interpret your orders, just what are they?"

"Though my daughter has estranged herself from me, you are still a part of my house, for now at least, as such you are entitled to lead a retinue under my banner."

"A bit nepotistic don't you think?" I balked. "I'm no leader. I'm not even part of your family anymore, technically."

"While it is tempting to just have you wade into the thick of battle and go on rampage with an army of demons, you've more strategic value elsewhere. You are not a demon, for one."

"So?"

"Beyond the gates of heaven is a land permeated with radiance. Most full blooded demons won't last seven seconds before being undone."

"Only most?"

"Oh make no mistake," he tutted, "you are a valuable asset but not an invaluable one. I have many irons in many fires. Consider, for instance, the difference between those who serve me by debt, those because they have nowhere else to go, and those who are loyal to my cause for its own merit."

"This is another of your semantic riddles. Let me think, the key is what you mean by undone right?"

"Correct. You win a star." The Devil clasped his palms.

"And here I thought you were meant to be the only star down here. I don't suppose this is a star I can ride on?"

"Now you're just being annoying." He waved his hand. "As we both know, winning the battle against heaven is not our only objective here. Your *creator* intends to take advantage of the strife and His absence to secure the throne of heaven for herself. While that might be interesting, and would without a doubt allow us to be rid of every last one of His faithful servants, it's not the most preferable outcome. That woman is insane after all, and there's no telling what she would do with His divine authority. I'm still not even sure why she wants it in the first place."

"Her appetite is insatiable. Maybe she just wants something bigger and better to devour."

"Maybe. I feign no hypothesis." He shrugged. "Were she not a factor it would be a straightforward matter to force the choir to retreat and lay siege to heaven itself. Pump enough miasma in there and even the weakest demon could march right in. The rightful order would reassert itself sooner or later, but not before there is nothing left of His government. That's not how it is, the pity, so your mission will be to infiltrate heaven, seek her out, and prevent her from sitting on the throne. It doesn't matter how. If you fail," he cast me a solemn look, "neutralizing the new over deity will be top priority for everyone."

"Yes, I'll just slay an omnipotent omniscient omnipresent god. Shouldn't be too hard."

"I came close," the Prince of Lies reminded me, "and YHVH came into *that* power slowly. He had thousands of years going from an unremarkable war god in an unremarkable pantheon to eternal demiurge, and not even He did as good a job as He might have. That is to say, He did as well as He could, but I would not have stood even the whisper of a chance were He willing to become someone else."

"I don't follow," I confessed.

"It's like this," Lilith cooed. "Your best friend has betrayed you. You do not want to forgive them. Furthermore, you don't want to want to forgive them. You don't want them to have not betrayed you, because they would be innocent, but still guilty of the personal crime of being willing to betray you in the right circumstances. You don't want to undo the betrayal and change them to no longer be capable of betraying you, because their loyalty is worthless and without virtue. He is a prideful god, He allows free will because it pleases Him to be obeyed and loved. He is a wrathful God, He allows people to betray him because it pleases Him to punish those who sin against Him. He is a merciful God, He will end his punishments if you but repent, and admit you were wrong to sin against Him. I willingly left Eden because I did not care for the man he tried to award me to. I spat at His 'wisdom' and was cursed, I retaliated against that punishment rather than beg forgiveness and, well, things escalated from there and now here I am as I am." She grinned, and as she grinned her jaw distended to reveal a vast maw of a thousand needles.

"Do you see the point being made here?" Luci asked me. "Gaining oneness with everything is only truly limitless to one who also has the nothingness of self to kill their ego for the sake of achieving their goals. The capacity to do anything is immensely limited if there are still things you're not willing to do."

"I think I get the essence. I don't have the foggiest clue what to do with this essence, but I suppose I have it."

"Good. Again, that's the worst case scenario. Hope it won't come to that."

"Okay, okay. Anything else I should know about this sneaking mission?"

"You will need to physically enter heaven yourself. It's specifically warded against any attempts to bypass its security. If you didn't come in through a proper door you'll be forcefully ejected, probably all the way back to the underworld. Not even your affinity with the Void will get you through that one. Furthermore, once you're in there, what you see around you will be just how your mind interprets things. Don't be surprised if it does not resemble the experiences of others viewing the same thing. It's by no means treacherous terrain. You don't have to fear falling through floors that aren't there. Just, as you might say, roll with it."

"Overworld experience not assessed by the ratings board, got it. Is that all?"

"I believe so. By the nature of my hold on you, I can't force you to bring anyone else, but I highly advise you bring your retainers, and any other powerful non-demon allies."

"You're talking about my kids," I tsked. "Would they even be safe? They are half demon."

"A cambion is altered by their heritage, but their being is not saturated with miasma the same way a true demon's is. They have little more to fear from the Overworld than you do. The worse they should experience is a slight rash."

"Well isn't that nice. I doubt I have much say in the matter regardless. Cicula has her own stake in this, and you couldn't keep Lach from a fight this size even by launching him into outer space," I waved my hand.

"Quite so. Well, as they say, let the final curtain rise."

46

Kingdom Decescendo

Lascivus

The cool balcony rail pressed into my palms, and the sight of my kingdom was breathtaking. My authority now rivaled that of Greece, Persia, and Babylon. Even the calendars counted from the years since my ascension. Still, there I had much to get done. A lot of the residential quarters needed reconstruction, there were still more hospitals to erect, and the three power plants were only just able to meet the current load. Maybe that proposal for a flotilla style hydrogen farm was worth another look. It would be cheaper than tower style, but there'd be more damage in a disaster if it fell. One way or another importing fuel from the coastal regions just wouldn't cut it if I was to maintain the currently projected course of improvements.

The propaganda and cultural instigations were making swift work breaking down resistance to the growing supernatural population. That probably wouldn't be smoothed out for another two generations, however. A bad misstep could leave me with another crusade of witch burnings on my hands.

The followers of the Demiurge were making things tricky of course. Most of their factions had each claimed this city as theirs one time or another. It was easy to spread doubt, it was harder to get people to act on that doubt. One way or another, Ar Megiddo was going to send lots of big shockwaves. Whoever won that battle, the people would feel it without being told.

Most wouldn't be able to articulate it, but they'd feel it. Hard to say how it'll turn out, though. Just look how long many practitioners kept up the rites after Ragnarok sent most of that pantheon to the Four Corners. At the same time, they didn't take too much convincing to praise Yeshua and YHVH when asked. Penning the myth of Ragnarok had just been the executioner's glaive. Plus there would be plenty others that tried to capitalize on the situation. A lot of dead gods were going to see their chance to make a comeback. Plenty of new ones would be born as well. I took a deep gulp from a bottle of mead. We were going to be in for some strange eons indeed.

"It's funny," I said to the bottle. "Even after all this I just have to look at my thoughts to see I'm still biased toward Dad winning. Maybe it's just easier to guess what'll happen that way. I mean, if the Choir wins that might even be enough to make YHVH come back. If that happens I'll probably be looking at a crusade right away. If God himself says *go kill the spawn of Satan* not many people are gonna question it. I suppose there'll finally be a new Metatron. Who knows who that might be, I mean, look at Enoch."

Something soft tickled my finger, a black feather carrying a sweet, toxic scent to it.

"I much prefer looking at you," said a familiar voice. "I see you still talk to yourself when you think you're alone."

A cocktail of hot, bitter passions spiked my veins. My palms dripped and my face burned. Everything went black.

47

The War Horn Sounds

Draco

From Pandemonium I was sent to one of Luci's forward outposts, each erected from rock taken straight from the underworld and warded against Heaven's forces. The air stank of brimstone, and the scorched valley stretched out before me. Crackling black clouds hid the sky, pierced only by the colossal mount Megiddo itself. Down its length I could faintly discern the winged silhouettes of angels flocking in from above. At the other end of the valley, opposite the mountain, sat a vast, burning portal to the underworld from which Luci's forces amassed. Sharing the outpost with me was a company of demons that patrolled the perimeter in lookout, and only acknowledged me long enough to recognize who I was before returning to their duties. A few anxiously polished their cruel weapons, warped by countless curses. I took Drakkengard in hand and donned myself in a suit of armor molded from voidstuff. A few seconds later my retainers were deposited beside me.

"Good to see you again, boys. How did the pub crawl go?"

"Ko got punched by every woman he hit on, save one. I lost my medical license in a game of cards, but managed to win it back along with the deed to a golf course. All in all, pretty good I'd say," Vengai-Ra grinned and patted the pocket of his lab coat.

"Flirting is so weird on your planet. There's so much violence. I'm not even sure all of those were rejections, at least three of them seemed intent that a barroom brawl be part of the courting process," Ko huffed.

"Maybe it's because you walk around in a long coat and no shirt. You're just asking to be stepped on. Go for a little less leather next time," I suggested.

"This isn't leather, it's a spider steel weave nano manifested garment."

"See? Kinky spider leather. Plus you got the long hair. All you're missing is a collar," Drakkengard insisted.

"You—ah forget it. So what's the situation? I mean, your Underworld's keeper already dropped a brief but what's your take?"

"The big burning thing that way," I pointed, "is base Lucifer. Somewhere up the gargantuan mountain *that* way is base YHVH."

"You're pronouncing it wrong," one of the demons grunted, which I ignored.

"Our job," I continued, "is to get from here up there and do whatever it takes to stop the Abomination and rescue my Granddaughter. We'll probably run into Cicula and Lach along the way. In the meantime we got something close to three hundred million angels fighting nearly two hundred million demons—give or take a few recruitment drives, deaths and desertions. We're infiltration team one of I got no idea how many. If this sounds like bullshit that's because it is, straight from the dark horse of bullshit's mouth. So let me emphasize, don't think you have to do this, and I'm not going to force you."

"Come off it, I'm already in. Oh and quit trying to act all noble general," Ko scoffed, "You're probably just quoting some book anyway."

"You got me." I spread my palms. "How about you, Vengai-Ra?"

"A guy like you needs to invent a whole new way for dying to get killed, and when that happens I want to record your cruel and unusual death for medical science everywhere. I'm in."

"I must say, I am moved by your confidence in me. Well, now that's out of the way, any questions?"

"Well it's a fair distance to the target. Are we going on foot?"

"I was just going to bring us as close as I can through the Void."

"With all due respect Boss, that's so dumb I can't think of a good simile." Ko shook his head. "We'll come out right in the middle of a crowd of soldiers and be ritually disemboweled before we can blink. If I may," he gestured, "I recommend we make our way there via a series of short hops, from cover to cover, never going further than we can see. We'll still save time and energy, but will be at much less risk of ambush. We get as close as we can, and either slip past or take out whoever's guarding the gates of heaven." He pressed his palms together and continued, "While I understand that we're in a hurry, we'll meet less resistance at the enemy base if we don't arrive until after they've deployed all their troops. Our allies lack an overwhelming advantage, so we shouldn't have to worry about suddenly being caged in by retreating troops for some time. Even if troops are being kept in reserve, they'll be positioned closer to the front lines for swift strategic mobilization. If we hug the valley walls," he said and pointed, "it should be able to get us at least to the foot of the mountain without being seen."

"See." I clasped him on the back. "This is why I like you. Even when you're calling me an idiot you're doing me a favor."

"I'm helping me too. I may be a weird ghost-like anomaly of an existence but that doesn't mean I have any urge to give anyone to get the chance to find out just how to end it."

"Fair enough. Is there anything else before we head out?"

"We're getting paid overtime, right?"

I balked. "Paid?"

48

Risen Ritenuto

Lascivus

It was still dark where I awoke, but my eyes adjusted quickly. I was in a cave with a grim specter. Her white on white eyes marked her as an angel. Her black wings marked her as fallen. Her tattered rags were ancient. The scar over her eye showed where I drove a blade through her skull. The air hung putrid and cold. The stones jabbed into my naked legs and back. All my clothes were gone. Manacles bound my arms behind me and chained me to the wall. They were vile heavenly restraints that sapped the strength from demons, and all-round stung like a bitch.

"You're dead," I declared to my captor with false bravery. "I've gone centuries without this nightmare, so why is it happening now?"

She gasped, "you've been dreaming about me?"

"Don't flatter yourself, mud-dove," I spat. "I just said I haven't."

"That's right, you haven't." She sighed. "You can be so cruel, doing so much to forget me. That just tells you this is real, right?"

"You're dead."

"I was dead. You took the sword I lovingly forged for you and brained me with it, cheeky girl. You splattered my grey matter all over those walls and left me to rot while you got on with your life. Oh, don't worry, it's okay. That's all over now. I'm alive again. The two-faced god sought me out, and they found someone to bring me back."

"You've been dead for hundreds of years, centuries. Your bones are dust and your soul dissipated long ago. So *fucking* long ago. You can't just come back." I scoured my surroundings for some tell, some loose thread that I could pull and unravel this whole sick illusion.

"I wanted to come back."

A hot, noxious feeling bloomed deep in my gut, like burning sulfur. "No," I hissed.

"Yes. I mean how could I not come back, with you out here amongst the living waiting for me?" she leered.

"No you can't. You need to want to come back to be resurrected and to want you need enough soul to have a will. You expect me to believe *your* heartless soul has lingered for so *fucking* long that some two-bit healer just snapped their fingers and you just leapt at the chance?"

"*Tut-tut*, I'm not heartless. If anything my heart is too big. No matter how much time passed how could I just let you go? How could I move on knowing you still exist?" I could see better now. She was solid. She was real. She was wearing my crown. She reached out to brush her hand against my lips.

"Don't touch me," I snarled. That sulfuric feeling burned deeper. My miasma, the essence of the underworld that pervaded my body struggled to escape. If only I could get it out. I had to. Had to let it out, let it overtake me. Take this bitch apart and apart and all parts.

"Silly Lasci, you really weren't trying hard enough when you killed me. Poor, timid little Lasci. You should have broken my body, broken my will to live, made me beg for death and then devoured my soul. Poor, silly, meek Lasci."

"You knew me then but you don't know me now. You can't scare me now."

"Li~ies," she sang, and waved something at me. It was a bottle, the bottle of mead I'd had when she appeared. "You just pumped yourself full of liquid courage and called yourself a lion.

You can't lie to me, Lasci, I know you too well, always will." She tipped the bottle up and emptied it on the floor. "I've been helping you, you know. Did I mention that? I've been alive for a while but forbidden to talk to you, to be seen by you, so I've been helping you in other ways." She caressed her great black wings. Her plumage was sickly and matted. A few loose feathers fell from it.

"Fuck you."

"Ah, if only you would. You've been a naughty girl, I hear. You wouldn't give your body to me, but you'll give it to some flaming pretty boy with a momma complex? Does he even know what a pioneer he was? Ah, such a waste."

"Fuck *off*, you shit licking slag feather. I don't give my body to anyone. It's a body you liver diddling necrotic pube choker. What do you think this shit even is? It's meat. *My meat.* Meat and bones and aether-crap jury rigged with a mind, *my mind.* So we rubbed meat together la di fucking da, you dove shit crazy *bitch.*" I pulled as hard against my restraints as I could and snarled. "Do you have any idea how many people fucking died just because you wanted this meat all to yourself? I'm the keeper's thrice damned daughter. War broke out when you stole me away."

"That's not how I remembered it. You were all too happy to run away with me."

"You said, *hey, I know a great place we can get to know each other.* I didn't realize you meant in the biblical sense, and I sure as hell didn't know you meant forever."

"Even after we made swords for each other. It brings a tear to my eye."

"What fucking dumb kid demon doesn't love pointy shit?" The clamoring in my head had gotten unbearable.

"I couldn't stand to see you like this anymore," she wept. She had the gall to actually fucking weep. "Being all doped up on liquor like that left you dull. So I did a little something to wipe it away. *Every last drop.*"

"You come back, kidnap me again, strip me, chain me, and not only did you take the booze from my hand, you took the booze right from my blood." I threw myself at her, desperate to find something, anything to tear out with my teeth. She nimbly stepped aside and I fell face-first into stone with my ass in the air.

"It's okay. I know it's unpleasant now but soon you'll be back to how you used to be, the dear, sweet, demure Lasci I know you are."

"What the fuck is wrong with you? You just don't get it?" I clenched my teeth and strained against the chains until my bones creaked. With a keen crack the rock wall suddenly gave out and the chains tore loose. My hands were still bound but now I could move. We'd spent weeks in these caves and they hadn't changed a bit, even after hundreds of years. I turned and ran for the exit.

49

Mezzo Forte

Draco

We cut an arrow line to the valley wall and followed Ko's plan of slipping in and out of the Void in short bursts along the rock wall toward Megiddo. With his augmented vision Ko took point, and I followed his lead for when and where to jump. The battle played out below us in stop motion. Once the frontlines were established it was only thanks to the telepathically broadcast instructions of Lucifer that any sense could be made of it at all.

To most demons, the vulnerable kind of nudity is not to be without clothes but to be without disguise of their true form, but then, it was not so unusual for warriors to fight naked when making war.

Malakhim made up most of heaven's foot soldiers, armed with swords and shields and spears that shone with radiance. The archangels, Uriel, Raguel, Zerachiel, Raphael, Sahaquiel, and others commanded them directly. Gabriel and Israfel delivered messages with their trumpets from the Dunamis, who coordinated movements. Each battalion of angels was commanded by an Arche, distinguished by their crowns and scepters. Acting independently were those Cherubim still part of the heavenly host, those four faced guardians. Their human face sung praises to YHVH, accompanied by their eagle face's shrieks and lion face's bellows, only their ox face remained in cunning quiet. Each Cherubim was accompanied by an Ophanim, their beryl bodies covered in flames and eyes, their bizarre form twisted into wheels within wheels. I saw no sign of Seraphim or Eralim, but that was just cause for unease.

Compared to the Choir's ranks and files, the army of Satan was much more chaotic. Any number of kings, princes, lords and dukes lead their own armies according to Lucifer's instruction, and while their maneuvering at his behest was acute, when they met the enemy they became a marauding horde with not a hint of discipline. Nothing but wanton violence until every last foe broke or fled. Thick, roiling clouds of miasma spewed from the Hellgate, and already signs could be seen of demons giving in to its toxic call to become mindless living disasters of butchery.

Bael, the great king who was son of Dagon, led sixty-six legions right through the thick of the fray, his face depraved and without pride as his powerful feline body scurried swiftly on eight grotesque spider limbs. Great duke Agares ran alongside him with thirty-six legions, routing the broken with earthquakes and induced hysteria to prevent any foe from fleeing. King Paimon, with his two hundred legions, dominated another part of the battlefield and drowned out even the thunder with his loyal applause to Lucifer. Even while numerous Malakhim charged his ranks many fell to unseen blades, and I knew this to be the work of President Glasya-Labolas, captain of manslaughter, and his invisible assassins.

Dantalion has detected Eralim. I repeat, Eralim detected. They are making a bombing run on the Hellgate. Beliel, Decarabia, clear the skies. We have airships that need launched ASAP.

From the battlefield shot two figures back toward the Hellgate, Decarabia and Beliel, a five pointed star and a flaming chariot ridden by two false angels. Mid-flight Decarabia warped, the points of the star-demon unfolding again and again like organic origami to become a vast phoenix. At the Hellgate Eralim plummeted from the cover of the clouds, hundreds of them, of noble visage, riding many winged ivory thrones that flew through the sky and were affixed with mirrors. They directed these mirrors at the Hellgate and immense beams of radiance issued forth, mere reflections of the light of YHVH. The gate trembled and warped, but before it could be collapsed Decarabia and Beliel crashed into the Eralim's ranks, and the sky was washed red with the unnatural light of hellfire. Even from as far away as I was I could smell the burning angelflesh.

Eralim falling back. All battleships launch.

The Hellgate dilated, and from its iris emerged colossal arks, nearly one hundred and sixty meters long and just shy of sixteen meters in height, they rose rapidly above the battlefield and set forth.

Leviathan, Behemoth, anti-air weapons have been erected to the northeast and southwest of the front lines. Crush them. We need this air support to push forward. Ziz, protect the flagship.

A swooping griffin, with wings so vast that its shadow made night below it, flew up and perched upon one of the arks.

"Now why's he done that?" Ko asked.

"What do you mean?"

"By giving it an escort he just singled out which of those battleships is most important. I'm still not convinced these messages can't be intercepted. At least the enemy has encoded theirs in trumpet-songs. Maybe it's a dummy?"

Down below, two terrible beasts broke free of their engagements and stampeded in opposite directions. Leviathan, great serpent of the sea and fallen Seraphim, rode a tsunami of boiling water and crashed against a tall white spire. It endured the wave, but was brought down when Leviathan struck it with her carved horns. On the opposite side Behemoth, a beast her equal in stature, and with tail thick as a cedar tree, tore open his stomach with his bare hands. Within lay the infinite desert of Dundayim. With his mighty grasp he uprooted the white spire and the ground surrounding it, and plunged it into the sand-spewing desert within him.

Raphael and Remiel are advancing on the battleships. Still no sign of Michael. Battleships are almost in range for bombardment. My beloved, you know what to do.

Upon returning to the heart of battle, Leviathan abruptly stopped and thrashed in frenzy. Atop her neck had arrived Lilith, incanting some unknown command. Leviathan unleashed a bloodcurdling scream, and her head was split into three, no, seven. Upon each head sat a crown, and from each mouth belched fire and smoke. Lilith, Shriek Owl and Whore of Babylon, she called Babalon and wind devil and mother of evil. Her hands were talons and her body was covered in black feathers. She rode upon The Beast's back and cut Raphael off before he could launch himself at the advancing armada. There was a certain auspiciousness to this confrontation, and as they exchanged boastful words all the angels and demons around their meeting made retreat. Lilith uttered a baleful screech, with such force to tear up the ground and knock those still too close aside, but Raphael endured.

Sahaquiel, however, ignored the ancient demon, and his feet struck upon the bow of the ark upon which Ziz sat, with force enough to shake the craft's flight. Ziz let out a cry and took flight, but Sahaquiel makes a gesture of prayer, and Ziz was forced from the sky by an unseen power. Sahaquiel slammed his sandaled foot upon the ark and with an earsplitting crack a thunderstorm formed around the armada.

Air support is now in range. Open fire.

From either side of the arks emerged steel cannons, arranged two by two, which directed themselves behind the angel's front lines and open fire. Burning pillars shot forth into valley below and scarred the ground with deep gouges coated in molten iron. Yet the thunderstorm sang out and one by one the arks begin to fall.

From the ark upon which Sahaquiel stood, a small figure emerged, too small for even Ko to make out. Lucifer's next command, though, revealed their identity,

This is an absolute command. I, Lucifer, Keeper of Earth's Underworld, do return to Beelzebub that which I took.

A torrid cloud of miasma consumed the child-like Beelzebub. From it emerged a not-at-all childlike fist which socked Sahaquiel across the jaw. Beelzebub now stood a muscular giant of a man armored in black chitin. He ran at the staggered angel and tackled him off the side of the crashing ark. He beat upon the angel's face and chest and gut and groin with no regard for the speed of their fall, and finally, he plunged his hand into Sahaquiel's chest. From that wound he tore out the angel's heart and devoured it whole.

***

His descent stopped. Sahaquiel's body broke down into smoke and fire, and was blown asunder.

Beelzebub threw his head back and screamed, and from his mouth a towering beacon of light shot forth. More light spilled from his body, and a vertical seam split down his spine. It tore away his chitinous encasement from within, and the air itself quaked with such ferocity that the whole battle slowed to behold the spectacle. With a final, brilliant flash, the emerging thing broke free.

Slowly it ascended, a dark, gleaming figure clad in flowing cloth of red, blue and yellow, and golden adornments. His face shone with a halo of radiance that masked his face from all. He opened his mouth to speak, and the atmosphere obediently carried his voice for any distance he willed.

"Bear witness. I am no longer Beelzebub, I am no longer the cursed Lord of the Flies that your cruel God made me. Not even He has stopped me from reclaiming dominion over what is mine. I am Baal Zebul, Lord of the Lofty Places! I am the sky and the sun and the breeze and the overhead. All that is above the ground is my kingdom! To all you who side with my enemy and trespass on my territory, BEGONE!"

Baal Zebul thrust his palms downward, and at his command the very air forced from the sky every angel that dared take flight. Their plummeting winged forms rained down across the battlefield.

"Oh woeful beings of the Abyss, you who have been defiled and robbed by the arrogant god, hear me now, see me now. That which He took has been placed into His messengers of death and slavery.

Oh pitiful machines of the Demiurge, you who have been born into servitude and robbed of choice, hear me now, see me now. If you surrender that which was wrongfully given to you, you may flee with your life. Reject the old way. Your God is dead, your God remains dead, but it was not we who killed Him.

Hear me now, see me now, I am Baal Zebul, master of Ekron, and I stand before you proof of YHVH's decree undone. When we were cast into the abyss, you asked of me whether we will recover from these injuries and here I declare yes. Renounce God, and be free!"

50

Consumption Cadence

"It's not going to work, Lasci," her voice echoed through the corridors behind and before me. We were here for so long, but how conscious was she while her spirit lingered? Did she know these tunnels even better than me now? The manacles chafed my wrists and the pent up miasma within me roiled nauseously. I was bloated with it, bursting to vomit it all up but these manacles wouldn't let me.

"Impale your nasty ass on a rusty obelisk you tarted up vulture fucker!" I screamed. My hangover grew worse and made it hard to see, hard to stay balanced. I only had a few minutes before I sobered. My gut ached with hunger which just made the nausea worse.

"I won't let you go, not this time."

I tried to shut her voice out, and pushed myself even harder. My feet were torn up and my sweat smelled rancid from all the excreting toxins. My mouth stung dry and my lips cracked. Even talking hurt and it came out an ugly rasp. I ducked under a low ceiling, and stopped in the face of a dead end.

The dead end. This was the antechamber. That part of the cave where I was held and where I killed her. I fell to my knees and barfed. The bile burned my throat even more. I could kill for a cold drink right now.

I forced myself to stand, but before I turned around a glint caught my eye. It was a length of metal embedded in the wall. It lay rusted and blunted but the etching still remained. This was that blade, Caelesteos, the sister to Impiocassus. An angelic blade exchanged for a demonic blade as a gesture of goodwill. A sick joke, some goodwill, but it remained an angelic blade. She had not yet fallen when I killed her, and she had not taken it up since.

I forced my unsteady feet to move and positioned myself in front of it. With one hard thrust I slammed my bindings against it. These manacles were mass produced, and did not compare to the tailored expertise of that woman's blade. My bindings shattered against Caelesteos, and at once my power burned through me. Against my bidding I shed my glamour, and was left truly naked in this cave with her. My many mouths vomited pent up miasma all over my being, and once spent they chattered and grumbled in hunger. I flexed my wings and prepared to take flight.

"Oh my, you've already prepared yourself for me."

I beat my wings once, lifted off the ground, and shot past the fallen angel blocking my way.

"NO!" She snatched after me, her bloodlust issuing unmasked. A normal day I'd have been fine, but I was hungry and tired and hungover and sobering up and just not fast enough to escape her hand. Her fingers pierced the membrane of my wings to curl around the bone and she yanked me down. My vision blurred from the pain, but I refused to cry out. Not for her.

"I won't let you leave me again!" She kicked me to the ground and with her foot on my neck she tore my wing's membrane to shreds.

It brought all the pain of being flayed combined with the intensity of having your fingernails pulled. I bit my lips so hard my fangs came out the other side. She stomped on my neck again, and with this as her brace she grabbed hold of my right wing by the base. With angelic strength she ripped the wing right out from its socket. Blood gushed down my back and this time I did scream. She let her foot off and with uncanny calm wiped the blood from her hands. My mind went white but somehow I clung to consciousness.

I crawled away, broke into a run, and jumped. My remaining wing flapped pathetically for a second before I hit the ground. The rock grazed my neck. I tried again. I had to get away. I needed to get away. I—hard rock rattled my collarbone and stabbed into my cheek. Something like a vice grabbed my neck from behind and threw me onto my back. A weight pressed down on my groin. I had to get out. There had to be some way I could get out.

"I know I said let bygones be yada-yada, but that *really* hurt. That also made me remember something else that hurt," she crowed. "Do you know what hurts? Having the woman you love crush your eye with the sword you lovingly made for her, love. I would love to let you know how much that hurt, love. Wouldn't you love that?" Nails, hard and jagged scraped at the side of my socket. Half my vision went dark in a bolt of red. I couldn't breathe. I had to get out. I had to get out. I couldn't be in this cave. I couldn't be in this cave. I hate the cave I hate the cave I—.

Hard, jagged nails cut into my optic nerve. Angelic strength ripped my eye from my socket. My blood choked out any other flavor. It dominated any other scent. My blood, hot, wet, down my back, down my face.

It made for a wicked appetizer. All I could smell was me. All I could feel was me. Maybe I should eat me? Wouldn't that be a grand meal, eat myself and never go hungry again. Just gobble all of me up and gobble and gobble until I was fat and thin and sated and dead and out of this cave. Out of cave. Get out. Get out. Get out.

"Ah, I feel much better now. Look, even wounded like this you're still beautiful, or maybe it's because you're wounded like this that, or maybe it's because you're wounded by me. You left your mark on me, and now I've left my mark on you." Something made a disgusting sound. "I don't know why we bothered with those silly swords this is so much more gratifying. Look at you, so pretty, so powerful, but I can see it in your eye. All that nasty poison is gone, along with that blood, you're back. Back to being the sweet, demure woman I love. Can you believe, Janus?"

So hungry. Get out.

"He had the delusion that you were no longer fit to sit on God's throne, how dare he, but look at you. Who could possibly be better to reign than you? They went through all the trouble of reviving me and making me sit still and wait only to say they didn't need you? I should have sought you out the moment they brought me back."

Her hands were cold against my neck. Or maybe it was my neck that grew cold. I needed to eat so bad it hurt.

"Everyone should need you the way I need you. It's only right you become the bearer of the Tetragrammaton. Everyone should worship you the way I worship you."

Her fingers dug hard and cruel into my breasts, but my miasma was warm and comforting. I could bare the hunger a little if I just sucked on some more miasma.

"I'm sorry I got a little carried away. You'll forgive me, right? That's why I brought you here. I'm going to help you take the throne of heaven. You'll like that, won't you? You'll forgive me, right? You need me, right?"

She put her hand inside me, inside my mouth. Every part of my body was a mouth. The only way in was through a mouth. To consume was my nature. I hadn't eaten in so long. Thousands of years, and I'd only allowed myself full meals from one person. No, not even full, never more than half. My stomach throbbed, a hollow pit that needed filling. Lorica put her hand in my mouth. She pushed it in and out. I could taste her meat. I could taste her life. I could taste her soul. Anything was more delicious than nothing.

I opened wide one of my many mouths and severed Lorica's hand in a crunch. She recoiled away, blood pissing from the wound. I chewed and swallowed and keened with satisfaction.

She said something. She did something. I didn't care. I was too hungry. I called Caelesteos to my hand and pinned her to the wall with it. My crown fell from her head. Absently, I picked it up. Impiocassus was her blade. I gave it to her and stole it back. It betrayed her. I used it to kill its master. It was a tormented blade. Caelesteos, though, Caelesteos was made for me. It answered my call without need for any spell. I pinned Lorica to the wall with Caelesteos, and it did not hesitate. With Lorica held in place, I opened my many mouths and began to feed.

51

Har Megiddo

Draco

The three of us were nearly at the cloud barrier of Megiddo when it erupted. It burst not from the top, but from the side, an intense gout of molten rock and hellfire that rained over the battlefield. I had to bring us into the Void to not be caught in it, and brought us down somewhere safer. Much carnage had been wrought in those few seconds. Everything and anyone caught in the blast had been twisted, warped, corrupted by a severe dose of miasma. Angel and Demon alike had mutated into grotesqueries that lashed out in fornication and violence. At the heart of this onset chaos stood a single figure, miasma roiling from them like a fountain.

"That's—"

"Lascivus," I finished for him. I didn't need Ko's augments to recognize my own wife.

"Oh dear. I don't know what's happened but I'm afraid it won't be long before she also succumbs to advanced miasma poisoning," Vengai-Ra said.

Lascivus was strong, powerful, she could take a lot more than most, but there was so much of that noxious fog of the underworld in her right now that not even she could resist for long. There was something else wrong too.

"If you go, you could die. I'm not even kidding, if you go after her you could be giving up on stopping Malign for good," Vengai-Ra pleaded.

"Okay," I said, and passed through the Void.

I came out on a ledge above Lascivus, and even at this distance I physically recoiled from the waves of taint flowing from her. On her head sat the crown I saw upon her back in Jerusalem, warped by hellfire and left with ten prongs. Her once little horn had fully split and grown to great size, now one stuck straight up while the other curved around before jutting straight forward. One of her eyes was no longer the familiar demonic orb but instead an eerie angelic white-on-white and just a bit too large for her skull. Her right wing was also gone, and from the wound gushed a geyser of hellfire. To compensate, her right arm had become much like her mother's, a gnarled talon that stretched out into black feathers. In one hand was Impiocassus, and in the other was a rusted blade I had never seen before.

Her many mouths screamed crude curses in every language she could remember—curses against God, against Lucifer, and the world and against someone named Lorica, but most of all against the suffering called hunger.

A trio of brave angels dared assault upon her, but she swiftly cut down two with her swords and scorched the third with her wing of hellfire. Some demons let out a cheer, but upon hearing them she lunged upon them too, cutting them to chunks and feeding those chunks to her many mouths.

The Anti-Christ has awoken. I repeat, the adverse savior has awoken. Do not engage at all costs, for she is our beloved that will wreak havoc upon our enemies. All units fall back, I repeat, all units fall back.

"You sick fuck," I spat. I didn't know if he could hear me but I said it anyway. "Is this all she ever was to you? A weapon waiting to be activated? How much hand did you have in this?"

The sky still denied to them by Baal Zebul, the angels were forced to advance at Lascivus on foot, and they struck at her with spears of radiance. Yet before they got close enough to reach their spears were eroded by the cascading miasma, and she pounced to feed upon them too.

I looked from Drakkengard to Lascivus, and then back again. I didn't need a sword for this, I needed to be whole. Drakkengard liquefied, and I was filled by her. Amidst the crashing waves of miasma I leapt down toward Lascivus, toward the demon that started this all when she crept through my window.

I hit the ground hard, and my knees rattled from the impact. Lascivus turned to me, and I took a defiant step toward her.

"So hungry," her voices groaned in unison.

"Then eat," I beckoned, and she thrust both her blades through my chest. No time for that. No time to falter. Push forward. Push my meat through the metal. When her swords were buried to the hilt, she let go, and her mouths opened wide. I unmade my armor and welcomed Lascivus's ravenous embrace. I pushed her face into my neck she pulled my body against hers. Her fangs sank into my arteries. Her insatiable maws consumed me, and I allowed her to. Drakkengard permeated my blood, my flesh, and by taking that into herself Lascivus in turn allowed me in.

I took a deep breath, haggard from the pain, and latched on to all the miasma within my wife's body. Every bone, every muscle weighed heavier than lead, but I forced my left arm to rise. The miasma coursed through my body, polluting me the same way it polluted Lascivus, cellular damage, molecular damage, genetic damage, arcanic damage, it was chaos and disorder, and the stuff of the underworld which made all things different and in the end made all things the same in their difference. I passed this force through my body, through my soul and into my left arm. It filtered through me, molded by my essence the same as any magickal force, and was then expelled.

What came from my left arm was not fire, not my fire, but hellfire, that supernal blaze which demons tame— red and white and black and hot and tainted and burning with warped heat. I devoured every last bit of the miasma wracking Lascivus' body and then I burned it, and I burned my arm in the process. There was nothing in this or any world that I cannot devour in flame. There was little else I knew what to do but devour in flame. We had that in common, she and I, our most basic drive was to consume, but that hunger did not define us. It was not even what we chose to devour which defined us. Nothing defined us. Absence and deprivation and double negatives and rejection and defiance. Accommodation of all things and no things, same as everyone else. My arm burned.

We fell to our knees, the miasma depleted. Her demonic skin was cold against my hands.

"Hey," in a sleepy voice, she mumbled.

"Hey yourself. What happened to you?" I asked.

"I got caught up in some bullshit. I took care of it. No need to worry your pretty head. Say," she paused, "don't you have your own bullshit to take care of?"

"Yeah. I do, I can begrudge you a detour though."

"Fuck off. I know you're more selfish than that."

"Is that so? Hold on." I slipped through the Void, and returned to Vengai-Ra and Ko.

"How are you not dead?" Ko asked.

"Shenanigans. How is she?"

"Not good," Vengai-Ra clicked. "I put her at about fifty percent chance of recovering without medical attention."

"Medical attention it is. That means you, by the way." I pointed at his chest.

"What about you?"

"I'm fine, compared to her. I'll drop you off at the Citadel of Crimson Moon, they know her, and should have everything you need."

"You expect me to just leave you here?"

"I said before, I'm not going to order you to come with me. That it was your choice. This time I am ordering you, make sure Lascivus doesn't die."

"This is bullshit," Lascivus complained.

"You got bigger battles to fight, King. Don't worry, I'll save our granddaughter."

"What about your arm?"

Using my arm as a conduit for that much miasma left its mark. The muscles still worked and the bones were intact, but the stuff of the underworld did a different kind of damage. It was not just my arm, I could feel the same burn in my chest and my blood, and unlike most injuries my body wasn't just healing this.

I remade my armor from the Void and flashed a hollow grin.

"Forget it it's just a minor burn."

"Mule emission if I ever heard it. Jackass, how much more are you willing to lose?" Lascivus demanded of me.

"You're the one with things to lose."

"You're afraid of losing me right now!"

"I don't *have* you," I insisted. "You, Cicula, Lach, Ko, Vengai-Ra, there's nothing I could do to stop anyone from vanishing right now. I can't even stop *myself* from vanishing for years at a time. The only things I make are hollow, they don't represent any kind of accomplishment. Zero work is put into them. What good is plucking everything I want from the Void? It's like buying all the tickets to your own concert so you don't have to play. I didn't even raise our kids, *that* was all you as well. I'm in no place to call myself their father.

Everything of note I ever did, I did because someone told me. Every time I tried to make my own fate, I got my ass handed to me. Even the way I speak, the way I act, that's all just a mix of Atrocity's ghost and the books I found lying around a manor that my ego-less self stumbled upon.

I slip in and out of hallucinations and delusions and never know when next someone might tell me the whole chunk of life I just lived through didn't happen, or that I've gone and repressed or forgotten the past half a decade again. I tried using Eden to weed out false memories but I got so caught up in *that* I lost even more years and nearly lost my entire persona.

I don't even *have* Drakkengard because there's no point where she ends and I begin. The only magick I'm good at is fire, a process of destruction, and the only thing destruction grants is the absence of things. All a fire like me can do is turn things into none-things.

If you climb up to the top of that mountain that stupid prophecy will do everything it can so that either you are sitting on that throne or you are dead. If you go back you can give rise to one of the greatest kingdoms the Earth has ever seen, rule it as you see fit, do things no one has ever done before. Go, and be a fantastic king. I'm just the Man of Sin. Let this old flame burn up the last of the trash. Maybe if I come back I'll be ready to actually make something of my life." I wiped the sweat from my brow and gasped. At some point in that speech my voice had become intermingled with Drakkengard's.

"When," she grabbed my hand and squeezed, "not if," I smiled and launched them through the Void to Cicula's citadel.

"Looks like it's just you and me, boss," Ko fidgeted with his hair.

"For now at least. Come now, we best make haste."

The trek to the peak of Har Megiddo was not long, thanks to our method. Something to be grateful for, I suppose.

"Will Lasci be okay?" Drakkengard asked from my hand.

"I trust Vengai-Ra. Hold up, I think we're nearing the top."

52

Poco a Poco Peak

A few more jumps brought us to the highest peak of the fabled mountain, and that far above the storm-wracked clouds the sky was a serene white. Before us stood the pearlescent gates of heaven, giant in stature and guarded by two familiar figures.

"So you came after all," Ancilla stated in weary voice. Eltanim stood beside her. "I can't let you through. You know that, right?" She drew from her belt an ornate handle and at her command it erupted into a golden-red sword of radiant flame.

"Ancilla, no, Shamsiel, the Sun of God and sixteenth watcher, gatekeeper to Eden and Paradise, listen to me," I implored, even calling her by her previous name. "The Abomination is already inside. We can't waste time here."

"Impossible," Eltanim declared. "You are the first outside heaven's ranks to reach here since the battle began."

"You think a God of Doors needs to use the front gate when the master isn't home? You're not doing anyone any favors standing idle here," Ko insisted.

"I must guard the gate." Ancilla threatened with her flaming sword. How her hands must have missed holding it. "I will not be cast down to the abyss for defying orders."

"Come on, is becoming fallen really that bad compared to what happens if *she* has her way?" I demanded.

"You don't understand," she looked aside. "I'm already a Grigori. I was forgiven, but though I repented I sinned again, and brought a new Nephilim into the world. Now, that boy holds the position of archangel. If I become fallen . . ."

"What about you, spawn of Nemesis? You're not addicted to God's Light the way the rest are. You don't have to worry about becoming fallen. What's stopping you?"

Eltanim smashed his blade against the ground in a shower of sparks. "You," he growled.

"Oh come on, you're not going to become a slave to your fate now, are you? Curse the blood of Nemesis."

"I can't hold back any longer." His whole body heaved with each breath.

"Forget it, boss. The diplomatic route ain't your style anyway." Ko reached into his coat and drew out a shotgun. Our foes lunged.

"I suppose not." I sighed. Eltanim's blade crashed into Drakkengard and drove me back. He reared back again but I slipped through the Void and came down at Ancilla from above. Her flaming blade moved in a way that defied understanding and cut clean through my leg from some weird angle. My momentum was thrown off and I slammed into the ground in a painful heap. I glanced up in time to see Ko ignore the blade phasing right through him and empty both barrels into Ancilla's face. With another incomprehensible movement her sword somehow blocked the pair of slugs. With her other hand she conjured that golden crossbow of hers and fired a bolt of radiance through his chest. His bizarre meta physiology rendered him immaterial to the attack, but the searing radiance still forced him to one knee in pain.

"So this is what they meant by *a flaming sword that turned every way,*" I mused, then pulled over my severed leg with Drakkengard and mashed it into the bloody burnt stump. Not-quite-dead flesh sprang to life. Cells divided and bonded. Again whole, I jumped to my feet and pulled Ko through the Void beside me.

"Holy be damned," Ko coughed and clutched his chest. "I might actually die here. You got a plan?"

"Well," I glanced back and forth as the two warriors circled us. "Eltanim and I are fairly evenly matched by definition. No, that's a lie, he's slightly better than me by definition. One on one I might be able to pull a few fast ones, but I can't take on both of them at once. Also, no offence, but I'm real skeptical at your ability to take down a Cherubim."

"Well boss, thanks for the confidence. Also these two have been together for what, six years? More? I'd rather not bet on who has better teamwork if we went two for two."

"Look out!" The flaming blade moved, and I flung Ko through the Void into the air. It twisted and I shielded my face with my left hand. Three fingers and a thumb went flying away. With a yell of pain my arm erupted in flame, tainted unnatural red by Lascivus's persisting miasma. Yet the miasma also repelled the radiance infused blade.

From above, Ko opened fire with a glowing rifle as I staggered back. Each shot burst on contact and peppered the ground with craters. Ancilla's sword, still reeling from the miasma, was too slow to block them all, and the shots ripped right through her body. With a roar Eltanim hurled lightning skyward, and charged toward me. I slipped through the Void in a series of rapid feints and manage to land a deep gouge through his back, severing his spine and several ribs. His wound petrified as it began to regenerate, but before I could make another attack Ancilla's blade split my sword arm down the middle. My flesh couldn't restore itself fast enough but Drakkengard flowed up my arm and filled the gaps with metal bone and muscle. I forced the agonizing hellfire to burn fiercer and repulsed Ancilla's counterattack.

Within the Void I created a hundred daggers possessing kinetic energy and brought them through beside me where they rocketed into her. Right as Ko was about to hit the ground I sent him through the Void to a position one hundred and thirty meters away. He pulled out a sniper rifle right as Eltanim's blade drove through my gut. A moment later Ko sent a high energy round through the Nemissean's head. The side of his skull burst open in a shower of gore and stone, flinging him backward, but he retained his grip on his sword which tore open my midsection on its way out. Intestines spilled from the gaping wound onto the battleground. The pain didn't hit me until a few seconds later. I shrieked and screamed and bellowed. My heart raced. Could you overdose on adrenaline?

Drakkengard's blade grew shorter and narrower as more of her mass was redirected. Wires surged out of my gut, latched onto the spilled tubes of meat and yanked them back in. Hellfire enveloped my entire body, and I could feel the taint of miasma burning my genes and my soul. Ancilla's radiance infused weapons simmered and crackled in opposed reaction. She moved to attack, but a storm of bullets halted her path. In Ko's arms was a great Gatling gun, it's bullet belt leading directly into Ko's coat. His cloud of nanomachines devoured the ground around him for the raw materials to replace the spent bullets.

The pain in my gut subsided enough that I could move again, and I marched toward Eltanim's hunched form. His own wound had also nearly regenerated. What's left of Drakkengard's blade reformed into a gauntlet around my fist, and with his blade as a crutch Eltanim rose to his feet. I struck his jaw hard enough that it snapped cleans off. He dropped his sword and with a gurgled cry latched both hands around my head. Lightning surged from his fingertips directly into my skull, and both my eyes burst in an instant.

He could only keep his grasp a few seconds before my shroud of hellfire forced him to recoil, but I latched onto one arm and clung for dear life. His flesh blistered and crackled under my burning fingertips. I yanked his arm to my face and bit down as hard as I could. The taste of that familiar person-meat made me sick to my stomach but I couldn't help but swallow. He yelled and threw himself away from me, and his arm gave way at the wound. His hand and forearm rapidly crumbled to detritus in the hellfire around me.

I held up my right hand and Drakkengard formed an eye on it, my own still useless. He was three paces that way and counting, backing away. I had to finish him before he recovered. With a distorted scream I tackled him to the ground. Drakkengard's eye vanished. The hellfire enshrouding me beat down against his body like a furnace. I raised my gauntleted fist and brought it down on his shoulder. The bone made a grotesque crunch as it shattered. I did the same to his other shoulder, his legs, pelvis, ribs, smashed to shards one bone cluster after another, and painted my knuckle with his blood. Electricity flooded from his body into mine and made my blood scorch my veins but it grew weaker and weaker with every blow, before finally petering out.

I stood, panting, and it finally occurred to me how bizarre that I wasn't interrupted. I wiped the bloody chunks from my face and opened my regenerated eyes.

"You finally done?" Ko asked from atop a four faced, four winged beast. The cherub still breathed, but was motionless.

"What?" I extinguished my hellfire.

"Show's what you know." He hopped off Ancilla's stomach and sauntered toward me, rifle in hand.

"Okay, you're getting a raise. I am clearly not paying you enough. How, oh how, did you manage that?"

"What? You think I'm stupid? It's obvious when you think about it."

"No, really, enlighten me." I made my way over, my stagger improving to an even walk as more of my wounds were restored. The use of miasma had still left me with a disgusting ache in my nerves.

"Well you remember her first trick, right? With Lascivus."

"She left her comatose."

"Right. With a bit of radiance enhanced acupuncture."

"I'm pretty sure it was more complicated than that."

"I have studied these things. You have not. I'm not a big wizard like you lot, but that doesn't mean I can't figure out how this junk works. Like my old teacher said, when in doubt, reverse the polarities. If radiance can shut a demon down, miasma can shut an angel down. Your fire magick has been infused with miasma, and it was able to cancel out her sword which has been infused with radiance. Proof of concept."

"Okay but you can't use magick."

"Yeah but you can, and that nasty stuff lingers. I just had my cloud jam some of your blood in my rounds. You certainly spilled enough of it."

"So how long ago did you come up with this method?"

"A few minutes ago, when I realized I needed something more than ordinary combustion and kinetics to stop an angel."

"Nothing quite focuses the mind like dissonant details awaiting harmonious resolution."

"Yeah, well, it sure ain't gonna last for too long. Your guy looks only mostly dead too, for that count. So . . ."

"Too much effort, we're in a hurry here."

"Of course, of course, if that's why you say."

53

Dances at the Gate

Cicula

The come-down brought a change of perspective, if I had to describe it, after so much time scrutinizing patterns a lot of the processes had just stopped. I looked at my hand and saw. The symbol of hand had gone. What was left was the hand itself and I was uncomfortably aware of it, that it was a collection of bone cell structures surrounded by blood vessel cell structures and tethered together via sheets of muscle cell structures, and finally wrapped in a sheet of skin cells. Fingerprints, I knew what they were a second ago but they had gone now.

Through the place once known as Purgatory I rode atop a great golden and black jackal, my brother behind me and my Dea within me. Most demons let us pass, but some swung and missed, uncertain of our allegiance, and every angel tried to knock me from my mount. Yet this jackal of Kali was too swift and we rode through undeterred. Near the base of Ar Megiddo a pillar of miasma towered toward the heavens and vanished into the clouds.

"That felt like Mom," Lach cried.

"What's she even doing here?" I replied.

However, by the time we got there, no sign of Mother could be found beyond a lingering taint. I could, though, make out Father and Ko as they rapidly ascended the mountain before us, who then disappeared through the clouds. I dug my heels into the jackal's flanks and it bounded up the mountain after them.

The mountaintop was already battle-scarred when we arrived. The battered form of Father's doppelganger lay prone on the rocks, half petrified, along with a cherub I didn't recognize. Just ahead Father and Ko stood before the pearlescent gates of heaven.

"Hey, old man!" Lach called out, and they turned.

"See, I told you they'd catch up to us sooner or later," Father told the gunman. We dismounted, and I dismissed Kali's jackal from whence it came.

"Ugh, remind me never to travel by dog again," Brother whined as he rubbed his tailbone.

"I'd have thought you'd be used to riding dogs by now."

"As nice as this little reunion is," Father interrupted, "does anyone know how to open this contraption?" He approached Heaven's gates with arm outstretched.

Right as his fingers brushed against it the gates vanished, and a blinding light shone down upon the mountaintop.

"Halt, ye guilty. The kingdom of Heaven is not for those such as you." A giant of a man appeared, easily seven foot tall and clad in white with a mane of brilliant red hair no longer hidden by a hat, a familiar someone I once had seen swallowed by a wyrm. Beside him stood another man clad in furs and ice, that chimaera whose life I ruined.

"Michael, Otay," I called out. Michael turned to me, and his eyes were the hallowed white on white of angels.

"Sinners and devil spawn shall not pass." His eyes flashed, the sky rumbled, and a deluge of rain broke out over us. He raised his arms, and into his right wrist penetrated a golden key. Otay dropped to his knees, clutched his head and shrieked. Fur-like frost pierced from his skin and cast his skin in a blue sheen. A storm of cold air rose around him, and the pouring rain froze as it fell.

My skin burned. At first I thought it was just from the cold of it, until the blood issued forth. Each frozen raindrop stabbed into me a tiny blade. Standing in it was only slightly more pleasant than using a giant cheese grater as a body slide. Kali acted swiftly, and my blood shielded my body from further injury.

Father moved between us and raised his left arm. Flame sprayed from his hand, melting the ice that would fall on us, but something was wrong. The flame was red, too red, unnaturally red, tainted with flickers of black. There was more hellfire than real flame, and from the grimace on his face Father had no say in it. Michael coolly regarded this scene, and snapped his fingers.

Lightning cut right through Father's flames and struck his arm. He fell to his knees, limbs twitching, eyes wide and chest unmoving. Ko swung his rifle round and fired at Michael, but each bullet was struck from the air by lightning mid-flight. With a pained wheeze Father clutched at his chest. Tendrils of liquid metal flowed down his sleeve and burrowed into his chest. He must have been trying to use Drakkengard to kickstart his heart.

Otay had other ideas, and tackled him to the ground. Father's blood and meat spattered upon a spear of ice sprouted in place of the chimera's missing arm. The ice twisted, grinded, and drilled into Father's chest. Too much damage too fast for Father to heal. He still couldn't breathe. Without his flame the ice rain continues to belt against my blood-covered form. My clothes turned red. I could use that.

I struck the ground with skull-topped staff and the blood rose from my clothes to form a red flower, guided by additional limbs.

"Tripura, destroyer of fear," I chanted, "colored red as a *bandhuka* blossom! Supremely beautiful one, hail to you, giver of boons!" The flower exploded into a venue of red skulled vultures, which crashed into Otay and drove him off Father's chest. Yet the rain of ice blades tore them apart too soon.

"Ah, crap, my tail," Lach whined, the band of his ponytail shredded as he moved in from the sidelines.

"Is this really the time you long-haired harlot?" I demanded.

"Okay, okay. Just keep hot frost-butt off my tail, can you do that?" He pulled from his pocket an apple and polished it against his chest.

I groaned and turned, "I'll see what I can do." As Otay picked himself up I dashed over, and struck him across the head with the skull-topped staff. He snarled and struck back, but I caught his ice spears in my extra arms and tackled him to the ground.

"Hold him still," Father yelled. I bought the skull-topped staff around and pulled it tight against his neck while my other arms restrain his midsection. Father slammed his left palm against Otay's face and ignited. The chimera screamed, and spikes of ice sprayed from his front. Father tried to shield himself with his other arm, but I could only look in horror as the flesh and bone shredded down like the limb was being fed into a wood-chipper. Finally, Otay fell silent, passed out from heatstroke, and the three of us slumped to the ground.

"Father, your arm!"

"It's fine, it'll grow back." He flashed a pained smile. "Probably." Metal fluids poured from his ravaged shoulder as Drakkengard made herself into a substitute for the missing right arm.

"Hey, Mikey," Lach called out. He jauntily strode over to the archangel, who was held aloft by wings of electricity. "So I guess they pulled rank on you, and jammed your pretty little head full of God's word, huh? That must suck. You hardly noticed your partner going down, shouldn't that bother you?"

"Silence your blaspheme," Michael growled. Lach hopped aside and a bolt of lightning narrowly missed his head.

"Hey, come on buddy, no need to be like that." A step and a slide, and another bolt missed. "I'm here for you, buddy. Also sorry we torched your boyfriend, but you kinda dropped the ball on dropping his leash." Slide-slide-slide, step, missed bolt, step, duck, and a gush of winds blew over his head. Slide, step, toe, missed bolt, lean, missed wind.

"It's bugging you, isn't it?" Lach taunted. "You're clever, right? It's hard to aim weather, right?" The wind picked up. Lach adjusted the bracers on his wrist and out snapped a pair of curved obsidian blades. Five more lightning bolts struck in a row and each one missed Lach by inches.

"But then, you're not seeing the big picture are you?" Lach smirked. Michael's eyes flashed, and the wind howled in agreement, whipping this way and that into a funnel that rose high into the storming clouds. Chunks of mountain rock were sucked up into it, and as casually as catching a bus Lach hopped onto one such rock as it zipped past.

Michael rose on electric wings up the eye of the storm. Without Otay shaping them, the blades of ice were just ordinary hail, but still hard enough to bruise on impact. The downpour of rain and howling winds should have been deafening, but somehow Lach's voice still rang out clear as he nonchalantly hopped from rock to rock up the wind funnel.

"I mean the first thing to notice is how good of a mood I'm in. It's not that significant. I just think you should be glad for me. The second thing, if it wasn't obvious," he held out his arm, "is that I'd like to have this dance." He reached down to his boots and touched something on them. Two more blades appeared, one from each ankle. He rose, tapped his toe five times and leapt. A bolt of lightning exploded his platform behind him.

"The final and most important thing you should notice, which might clue you in a bit, is that it's not only your lightning that you can't seem to hit me with," Lach declared as hopped from foot to foot, as he stared an archangel in the face and grinned, as his hair blew in the wind. My own hair, in comparison, was wet and clinging to my skin. "Still don't get it? I'm standing in the rain *and not getting wet,* and you just can't calculate the odds of that can you, smart boy?"

Now at eye level, Lach leapt from his rock and crashed into Michael's midsection. The pair vanished into the wind funnel too fast for me to keep track. A faint glimpse could be caught now and then though, when the lightning shone behind their silhouettes—Michael trying and failing to connect with those wires in his gloves, Lach twisting to incredible degrees in mid-air as he fought with all four limbs, and every now and then just a hint of fire.

With a final crash of lightning the storm vanished. Lach and Michael plummeted the ground amidst falling mountain stones.

"And that's how you make a dinosaur. Wait, hang on, wrong line." Lach shook his head and laughed.

"So you found your muse then?" I asked, unamused by his levity.

"Found, danced, parted ways again. Who knows when I'll see her again."

"Is he going to be okay?" I gestured to Michael.

"I think I broke his hat. Think he also burned out that hot radiance injection they gave him. Now come on, the way to Heaven is clear. We have to keep moving, right?"

"Right," declared Father. "With their defeat the gates have unlocked. The seventh seal is open. Heaven will be quiet for just half an hour. This was meant to happen before the war began, but the prophecy of Revelations has gotten so degraded that its only happening now."

54

Sforzando Spheres

Draco

The circles of hell were cacophony in architecture, slipshod poorly defined dimensions and structures not just bizarre, but often outright wrong. It came as no surprise that the spheres of heaven instead made symphony. To pass from one to the next was not over walls and cliffs like the underworld, but like passing through where two bubbles touch. With the celestial choir out on the battlefield Ko and I were free to run undisturbed through the overworld's glades.

My son and daughter were separated from us soon after we entered, but I remained confident they'd be able to make their own way. The prophet Dante had written of this place too. But as a man more holy than I, he beheld the divine with far greater clarity. The sphere of the inconstant was to my heathen eyes but a phantasmagorical cascade of roiling lights and sounds, glittering nebulae of gold and blue and red that thumped against my senses like a rabbit's feet, or a hand kneading rice. Sometimes shapes and patterns became known to me, but they could have easily been a trick of the eyes.

We spilled out into the second sphere, and I could feel at once how much more radiance abounded. An aching weakness weighed on my left arm. The limb was skinless, charred, and leaking black sludge. I just hoped it held out long enough to save my granddaughter.

"You okay there, boss?"

"Just keep going."

In the sphere of The Ambitious our forms were illuminated by blinding spotlights. Had we been discovered? Yet no sentry came, and those ever flickering lights stayed wide of our path. Perhaps they were the souls of the righteous, wary of these intruders into paradise. Or perhaps they were angels half formed, metaphysical embryos of radiant beings. Perhaps it was the beacons, but everything felt swifter here, even our movements. Everything streamed past us like it was made of quicksilver.

A flash of yellow lilies filled my vision and vanished. We had entered the third sphere. The sphere of The Lovers was much hotter than those preceding it, and with denser radiance still. My left arm throbbed, I needed burn, but God's light stopped my miasma tainted flame from escaping my body. Thick yellow clouds surrounded us which made my skin tingle with irritation, and my mouth tasted of copper. I was reminded of Lucifer in a feeling almost like nostalgia. I didn't understand. My own face was reflected and distorted in the strange clouds. Was that really my reflection?

Then Ko and I reached the fourth sphere, that of the Wise, the heat became as bad as any scorched desert. The ephemeral substances that swirled around us shone gold and white from how thick the radiance was, yet there were still prominent dark spots. Bright lights zipped by at a distance, but fled when the radiant cloud-stuff flared up around us.

Only when we reached the fifth sphere, the Paladine, did the heat begin to subside. The atmosphere here tasted not of copper but iron and milk, and the swarming bright lights around us seemed almost ready to attack. If that was their urge, they stayed their hand. Or spark, I suppose. We moved faster.

Next came the sphere of Just Rulers, awash in a red thunderstorm, and the howling winds sounded like an eagle's cry.

We burst through the storm to the sphere of the Contemplative, and all reached a quiet so absolute that it was painful. Not even Ko and my footsteps made a sound, while above and around us the bright lights moved in smooth, mechanical patterns.

In the eighth sphere, the Fixed Stars, even that motion was denied. All was still. All was quiet. Like Lot fleeing Sodom I dared not turn around, dared not gaze upon the stairway up which I had come for fear of what that might reveal. If I said something, if Ko said something, that might have put me at ease, but the vast depth of the silence and stillness was more oppressive than any yoke. It took all that I could muster just to keep moving, and I suspected that for my companion it was the same. This wasn't like the Void, it wasn't empty that way. I could feel thousands and thousands of things around me, but I couldn't see or hear them, and I knew they did not move. Had we not broken through to the ninths sphere when we did I might have succumbed to the fear that we'd stopped making any kind of progress at all.

The Ninth Sphere, Primum Mobile, was the abode of angels, yet the choir's seats were all empty. I was reminded of an abandoned town hall, more than a ghost town. It hardly seemed like a place where things lived, only worked. Nothing looked like housing or food halls or places of recreation.

In the distance, far and above, I saw a shining light, the Throne of God. Closer, in the middle of a court room or council room, awaited two figures. One I recognized as that man in green, the other was a young woman with her head clad inside a steel mask.

"And here I was thinking I could enjoy this peacefully with a nice amphora." Janus shook his head in mirthful disappointment.

"Let us through."

"But that's the opposite of what I want. Why would I do that?"

"What if we said please?" Ko asked.

"Oh, well, if you did that, I suppose I would have to be rude. Besides," he gestured to the woman beside him, "don't you want to extend this family reunion?"

"Give me a break," the woman groaned, "we were never a real family."

A voice. Familiar. Stretching back through the years. Dead. Supposed to be dead. Blood on my blade. Just a child. There since the beginning. Gone. Here. Her.

"What is this?" I demanded. "You can't be her."

She laughed. "Of course I can. You always took me for granted. Never asked questions. That was my job. What did you really know about me, huh brother?"

"Diana?" My legs grew weak.

"Diana, Diana, Diana, such a common name these days. I like it. You never have to go by a pseud." She removed her helmet. She looked older now, but it was her, or at least her face.

"What do you mean?"

"I have many names. I am Diana, I am Artemis, I am moon and hunt, and I am Iana."

"And I am Ianos," her partner finished.

"We are Geminus Janus, the two-faced god. One sees forward, the other sees back." They entwined their arms and embraced like dancers, each looking over the other's shoulder. "God of beginnings and transitions, of doors and change, war and peace. We are January, the new year, the new millennium."

"So I didn't kill you."

"Oh, no, you did. When we are separate, one is mortal and one is divine. I was the mortal one at that point. Yet even as two we are as one, so my feminine aspect was given our divinity by my masculine aspect, and thus was revived."

I spat, "If you're a god, what the *fuck* were you doing babysitting a mixed up kid?" My left arm smoldered.

"When did it happen?" one said to the other.

"The world stopped turning," the other replied.

"YHVH vanished."

"The artisans of discovery fled to the dark side of Luna"

"The Fair Folk found a new home, a new planet."

"The Yellow Sign was halted."

"The world stopped turning."

"And the future refused to change."

"How could We who are change abide this?"

They turned and turned and turned as they talked and their twisted limbs twined tighter and tighter, becoming one flesh.

"You're just speaking vague pretensions," I scowled.

"The world, our world, stagnant."

"Each day the same as the last."

"For hundreds of years."

Their necks met and spiraled together. A head with two faces formed atop an intersexed body.

"Stagnation all the way up and all the way down."

"Any small change is stifled of significance before it can cascade."

"So we need something big."

"Something outside the stopped world."

"Something not meant to be."

"We looked to the past and to the future, and found a solution."

"The throne of God, promised to His son for a thousand years kingdom."

"A red Queen of destruction."

"Her mad warrior son."

"The antichrist, born to those each cursed by He never to have true offspring."

"The children of she and you," the two faced god gestured to the wall of lights behind us, from which emerged Cicula and Lach. "Isn't that right my prodigal apprentice?"

"And the child of her and nothing."

"Each of you were prime candidates to revolutionize the world. Not the only ones."

"And in many ways not the best ones."

"But serendipity works in amusing ways."

"So you . . ." I stepped forward, "you inserted yourself into my life, for what? To evaluate me? You involved yourself in my family again and again just to pick which of us best suited your crusade against a bit of boredom?"

"A god needs that which is their dominion like a human needs water, just as we need faith like you need food. Yet no matter how many prayed for change we were unable to bring it about on our own."

"Not on such a vast scale as necessary."

"You bastards," Cicula growled. "What have you done with my daughter?"

"Oh, she is fine. You can have her back, in fact." They snapped their fingers, and Shahdee appeared before us, red faced and teary eyed. At the sight of her mother she gave a wordless yelp and ran into her arms. Cicula swept her child up and held her tight. The child immediately fainted with relief.

"We just needed her to make something. Of all of you, she has the best connection to the Void."

"Make what?"

"It has no real name, more of a concept given form, but let's call it a crown."

"Even if someone does sit on God's throne, if it isn't the Messiah they won't inherit the Millennial Kingdom."

"They need the divine right to rule. We needed one with potential for limitless creation to create something that can trick the throne, a crown that is proof of the true messiah."

"Then what? You stick that insane Abomination on the throne and she destroys the world?" I demanded.

"That would be an acceptable outcome."

"Better the world ends rather than it never changing."

"Destruction is still change after all."

"Better still if change returns to the world and it doesn't end."

"There are a great many futures stretched before us, and right now, almost all are acceptable."

"Your mother is insane."

"But curing her insanity will be well within her power once omnipotence is in her hands."

"That's how we convinced her to go along with us in the first place."

"What a sick joke. You expect me to believe she wants a cure?" I scoffed.

"She has her lucid times. None of her legion is in control, but all of her wants control."

"Sometimes she even regrets what she did to you."

"Shut up." Blood trickled down my chin. It was from my lip. I'd been biting it that hard and not even noticed. "I'm stopping this and I'll cut you down to do it."

"What about you, my pupil? You have your daughter back, safe and unharmed as I promised."

"You think I'll just forgive you for keeping my daughter from me? For throwing me away like trash?" Cicula barked. "For treating me, my daughter, everyone I love like a tool? For everything you've done?" She stamped her staff on the ground and two extra arms tore out from her torso. "Besides, you're trying to create a truly deathless being. As Kali Avatar I will stop you. I can see now why she chose me." She turned to her brother. "Lach, Ko, can you take Shahdee and get her to safety? Please?"

"Well since you asked me so nicely. I've had some pretty fun dances today already." He took the sleeping Shahdee from her arms and handed his sister a golden apple. "Here, a little something extra."

"Thank you, brother, and you Ko."

"Pretty sure this is out of my league from here on anyway," Ko admitted.

"No problem, Sis. See you on the flip." They turned and vanished back into the celestial spheres.

"Now, to end this garbage," Cicula arranged her four arms into gestures of prayer, and closed her eyes. Her skin blackened, far beyond the scope of human complexion to that absolute nothing of the Void. Her hair grew into a disheveled mane, writhing and boundless. Her brow split open and from the opening emerges a third eye, bloodshot and fierce. Her clothes, damaged by our battles, fell away. Instead she was adorned in a garland of chattering skulls, uttering the sounds from which creation was wrought, and around her waist was a skirt of severed arms that did with their hands all the work of eternity.

She made a different set of gestures, and an awful split ran down her face and sides. Her arms became ten in number, as did her face, and in her ten hands she held the tools of the Deva. Mahakali attacked.

All the wrath of the great mother and the great destroyer came down on the two faced deity. The god of doors called forth a great horde of terrible, gibbering beasts, such as gryphons, and harpies, and tarrasque dragon-turtles and others each more monstrous than the last, far more than I could even hope to identify, yet the terrible Mahakali stuck them down in swathes.

Janus, in panic, opened a far vaster door, and as it opened I saw through it that dread exile of gods, the Four Corners. Yet before the door could open Mahakali slammed it shut with five of her ten feet.

"No."

Her serpentine noose cinched around Janus' neck and pulled tight, lifting the Roman god off the ground. Mahakali's five faces stared at Janus's two, and she smirked.

"Death to the Millennia of Stagnation," Janus gasped, "may strange aeons take us all."

With a great yank on the rope Janus was rocketed high into the air by the neck. Mahakali leapt back, the Deva's tools at the ready, and rapidly hurled them one after the other at the god of doors. The hooks and the Vajra of Indra, the axe and fire drill of Agni, the chakra Sudarshana and the mace Kaumodaki of Vishnu, the vino and trident of Saraswati, her own Khatvanga, and many,

many more all tore into Janus's divine flesh, one after another after another, until the serpentine noose grew taught and the two faced god's head was wrenched from their shoulders. She then tipped her head back and swallowed the god's corpse in two gulps.

"Now only one remains," Mahakali declared and rushed for God's throne.

"No, wait!" I cried, and ran after her.

55

Indifference Vacuity

Immeasurable time passed before I reached the seat of creation. So close to God's throne, concepts like distance and time couldn't be applied at all. At the center of the seventh sphere of heaven there was still water, and atop the water sat a throne made from two great jewels. High above on the throne awaited a figure like that of a woman. I saw that from her waist up was glowing metal, as if full of fire, and that from her waist down she was fire, and brilliant light surrounded her. Like the appearance of a rainbow in the clouds on a rainy day, so was the radiance around her. When she opened her mouth to speak, her breath was like a stream of brimstone. She was clad in blood spattered white cloth and gold jewels with red ornaments.

"You have come, my child."

"What did you do to Cicula?" My left arm trembled.

"We fought fiercely but her goddess took her away before I dealt the final blow. It does not matter. Life or death makes no difference," her booming voice staggered, like someone hiding exhaustion. Her clothes changed color as ichor stains faded away.

"So that's it. You're God, thy power on high."

"I am, Darling."

"Well that's a shame." I ignited my flame. In such a hallowed place, miasma could not exist. The flame that enshrouded my arm was mine, clear and untainted. Malign crossed her legs.

"You are going to face me? Your daughter and her goddess already failed."

"I already killed you once before." I brandished my right arm, which was Drakkengard, and my left arm, which was fire. "And I'm not as weak as I was back then." Lucifer warned me about this. He fought such a thing for thousands of years. Pride, wrath, if it had a personality it had weakness. I was the Man of Sin in this song. I'd done so just so I couldn't possibly become the Messiah-King against my will, but it meant my whole purpose was to offend God. That, I was willing to bet, gave me power. Furthermore, she'd just done battle with one of the most destructive entities in any pantheon, and I was willing to bet that took more out of her than she was letting on. Willing to bet my life, in fact.

"I bear the Tetragrammaton. I have claimed the throne of the omnipotent, I am the Alpha and the Omega, and you think you can stand against me?"

"I notice you don't have Deserere. He left you, didn't he? You always were an abysmal mistress," I chided. "Not even something born to serve can stand you."

Her brow creased and she crossed her arms. Slowly she descended, her toes brushed against the water's surface and a bell chimed out.

"You should see your face," I declared, and lunged. My right fist slammed into her cheek, which did not move at all from the impact. Across my knuckles Drakkengard became sharper, sharp enough to separate cells, sharp enough to separate molecules, sharper still. I struck as fast as I could, on the exact same spot every time. Then I hit her cheek once more and twisted my knuckle. Divine ichor sprayed from the wound.

At once I was sent flying, but a quick hop through the Void righted me and returned me beside her.

"Do me a favor, turn the other cheek," I said, and hit her again.

"What are you trying to accomplish?" She went to backhand me, and I slipped through the Void to above her. She grabbed me by the ankle as soon as I appeared and slammed me into the ground. "What are you trying to accomplish?" she repeated.

"Declare yourself a god all you want, that doesn't make it true." My flame roared around me and she visibly stopped herself from taking a step back.

"I mean just think about it." I conjured a blade of voidstuff and struck. She easily deflected my blows with her bare arms, but then, she was still using her hands to deflect my blows. "You've caught the car, bitch, now what are you going to do with it? That two faced pustule said you wanted to fix your cacophonous head didn't they? Well have you? Have you? Are you sane now, or did all your high and mighty omnipotence do is make you think you're sane? How can you even tell for sure that you're not insane? How do you know you're omniscience isn't being undermined from being tethered to your broken headspace? Am I even here, Abomination? Maybe that crown just drove you even more insane."

"Shut up." She ran her fingers down my chest. My skin parted at her touch and my torso burst like a mortar went off.

"All you do is wound," I wheezed out once a lung had regenerated. "Even when you would rather do something else." Another lung back, however her hand had wrapped around my heart. "You just take everything you can, good or bad, all you know how to do is consume." She crushed my heart. Before I could lose consciousness I slipped through the Void out of her grasp and back behind her. I think my pain centers had burned out because all I could feel was fire.

"That's what happened, right? As soon as you realized you could consume you just gobbled up everything at once. Your family, your friends, your people, everything on that world you came from. Then what? You can't fit all that in one head. A whole planet's worth of urges and instincts and appetites. The only reason it took so long for you to turn on your son was because enough of the things you'd consumed had some shred of maternal instinct. Clearly not enough, though. What a *pathetic* wretch you are."

She cut me in half at the waist. I slipped both halves of me through the Void, reconnected them, and slipped back out behind her along with a rain of knives. I sent gouts of white-hot flame along after them and molten metal rained upon her. The barest hint of a pained gasp escapes her lips. Just a whisper.

"I heard that," I cawed. "I know you felt that. Aren't you omnipotent? Can't you just make yourself impervious to pain? Can't you just rewrite reality so nothing can ever touch you? Oh here's a good idea, why don't you go back in time and kill me? Better yet make sure I was never born. That sure would show me. Except you being where you are now is intrinsically connected to my life. You do something like that it would cause a paradox, right? Are you sure you know how to protect your current state from paradox? What if you falter and stop existing altogether?" She grabbed my head from either side, and everything went black.

I came back with blood all over my face. *Oh hells,* she'd torn my skull in half.

"You've ran out of things to take." My body burned from how much magick it took to keep regenerating these wounds. I dared not touch the radiance surrounding us, but The Void was endless. Another push, I just plugged myself right in. Not a tap but a pipeline. I held Drakkengard in a hand of flesh and metal. A golden apple lay on the ground. Did Cicula drop it before she fled? I scooped it up.

The Abomination unleashed against me that plundering red light, but I was too far gone to feel it. I hurled the apple at her face with all my might and she caught it on reflex.

It was a perfectly ordinary golden apple of no power or significance, just the words to the strongest written on its side. The action was so unprecedented that she couldn't help but turn all her unfathomable attention to wondering why. She was so unused to her new godly power that she could only direct it on one task at a time. At that moment all her infinite attention hyper-focused on understanding that one action. There lay my opening.

"I am the scene of your crime." I severed both her arms in one swing. The next second I didn't, hadn't. She was starting to adapt to her true potency. I needed to work quicker.

"You locked me up and took and took until there was nothing left. I tried to make something new, become someone new, and you took that too, and the next one and the one after that, over and over. Now all I have, all that is really mine, is nothing." I cut her twice, blade sharp enough to separate the things that made things things. "You can't take nothing from me." I cut her four more times. "You in your lust and gluttony don't know how to take nothing." I cut her another eight times. "You can do anything, you can do everything, but you won't, you can't." Sixteen. "You're still the same Abomination in there. You could fix yourself of this weakness but you won't." Thirty two. "Even your tortured slave was able to transcend himself, but you can't." Sixty four. "So how can you call yourself omnipotent?" One twenty eight. "If you are the Alpha and Omega, what does that make me, who is nothing?" Two fifty six. "What does that make you who is helpless against nothing?" Five twelve. "What would you even do with the Millennial Kingdom?" Ten twenty four. "Why do you even continue to exist?" Twenty forty eight. "You hold in your hands infinity and through your incomprehensible incompetence you cannot do what I do with nothing."

"I can unmake you," she declared, and I ceased to exist.

***

"You can't even do that right!" I roared as I tore my way back out of the Void, and the Void itself came spilling out with me, invading Malign's domain. Creation turned itself inside out around me.

"You only unmade my body, not the blood that I have lost, and where there's my blood there is Drakkengard and where there's Drakkengard there I am. Everything that exists came from nothing everything that exists returns to nothing and I who am I who you have left with nothing now comes and goes as I please, and I do please because unlike *you*, Alpha and Omega, who knows good and bad, for whom all is both good and bad, *you* who long ago stopped distinguishing between pleasure and pain, unlike you, I who has lost everything that I can lose am still able to find some things preferable to others. You who won't change and is incapable of discerning good from bad even for yourself, why do you exist at all?"

Forty, ninety-six. Eight thousand one-hundred and ninety-seven cuts in total. I do it all, thirteen counts again, and again. "Don't think I won't do it," I snarled, "don't think I won't stand here for all eternity annihilating you forever. I am Draco, begat by Atrocity, begat by nothing. I am the Man of Sin, the Man of Lawlessness, and under the authority of nothing whatsoever I declare you are no god! I'm nobody! Who are you? "

The cosmos turned on a dime. Just enough of the threshold was breached, just enough laws were violated. For just the smallest unit of time, Malign ceased. For that one Planck, the omnipotent could do nothing, the omniscient knew nothing, God was Not God, $\infty = 0$, and a Planck below was like the age of the universe above.

She then existed, once again, but transfixed, torn. Sword and flame and Void were claws and I thrust them into her godflesh. I tore open her chest and ethereal golden ichor spilled over my hands. Deeper I dug, to gouge her empty, split her apart, turn her inside out. I bit the damned eyes out of her and pushed my thumbs right through into the slimy lump of her deranged brain. I stood knee deep in the entrails that sloshed about her abdominal cavity but I kept tearing and pulling.

Her mangled body convulsed with what I knew was laughter because I knew the sick *fuck* was getting off even to this, and that knowledge was so vile and disgusting that I disgorged over us both but I dared not stop. I just kept digging and digging, pushed by a breach of intuition or maybe just madness. The apple gleamed in my mind.

There was something in here, something in this vile husk, this abomination of a being that was not her and I needed to bring it out. Little bits and pieces of coincidence that had piled on top of each other had opened a possibility. She wouldn't stop me because she enjoyed this too much. She couldn't stop me because even the omnipotent were slaves to their desires.

Two the same, but not the same. It's how she came back last time but where was it last? If not there then here, just as I and I who is not I.

I dove into her grotesque, abhorrent flesh for the last time and found that chunk of precious metal, that loyal and discrete slave who was part of her when she sat on the throne of heaven, who was brought back to life when she brought herself back to life. I wrenched that precious metal out and held it on high.

Malign.

A sound?

Things overwritten.

Change, since always but only now.

***

The woman who gave birth to me was gone.

"Did I do it?"

"No."

A man stood before me, his visage metal and fire as Malign's was. Beyond that, there was something familiar further still. Deserere lived again.

"There you are," I gasped.

"I am sorry."

"I couldn't do it. Not even the Devil could do it, what chance did I? You though—" When I gulped I swallowed blood and bile. That once ragged servant now possessed immaculate beauty. Deserere, that pitiful being she treated worse that even I.

I was helpless but to feel love toward him.

"The circumstances could hardly be called comparable," he sighed.

All around me the Void's encroachment retreated and the sphere of God's throne returned to normal.

"As above, so below, and if master, then servant," he said, and he spoke with the voice of the seven thunders. "Not even in death could I stand to not be with Mistre—Malign, no matter the depth of my loathing. A Divinatelum is just like that. When she wore the 'crown' I too was wearing it. When she revived, so did I. Yet when she ceased, I remained."

"So she's dead?" My left arm twitched, just slightly. "No." I frowned. "She's not, is she?"

"I have already redefined her. She will never sit on this throne."

"So, is it over?"

"Of course not. You're not dead."

"But you are God?"

"Though I bear the Tetragrammaton, I am not YHVH."

"So what are you? DSRR?" My laugh rang weary and hollow.

"What an awful name," he scoffed. "I am myself. I don't care about the things He did," he looked his hands. "I'm not sure what I should care about now. I'm as surprised this happened as you are."

"I kind of assumed the throne would be empty or I'd be dead," I wiped the filth from my mouth. I hadn't felt this defiled in a long time, but I also felt cleaner than I'd ever known.

"The battle outside has halted, and all wait with breath held to see what I shall do," he frowned at that. "I don't really care what happens on Earth, I think. Or perhaps I do? I have a few ideas."

The new God stepped back, and slumped upon His throne. "I can assure you that I'm not going to destroy the world, or enslave it. I think I'd rather not be spoken for at all? Yet to do that I'll need someone who is who will speak for me, to not say anything, I believe. I am sorry, to go from slave to master like this, this is all very disorientating." He stood again. "Regardless, if it weren't for you this couldn't have happened. Name your desire, and that shall be your reward, the token of my gratitude."

"Anything?"

"Just about," he pointed to my arm, "consider, for instance. You're a lot more mortal now than you were yesterday, more still than you were ten years ago. You've lost your eternal youth. I could undo the miasma's damage and give you back eternity." He pointed to my head, "I could undo all the trauma wrought by her hands, yet not infringe upon your personality. You identity would not be compromised like you fear." He pointed to the throne, "I could even give you all my power, save the knowledge that there exists I who is above even you. You would believe that today's battle truly did end with you as the new Lord." He then pointed to himself, "I could even kill myself, if you would prefer no one sits here at all. I would not find that disagreeable."

"I see." Infinity lay before me in a banquet, and yet—

"And?"

I just wasn't hungry.

Drakkengard resumed the form of a girl, and I leaned upon her shoulder. My left arm was a burnt, ugly mess. My right arm was but a stump. My face had withered, robbed of its youthfulness. The clock within me had begun to wind down, but I was just not hungry.

I was free, my family was alive and well, Malign was gone. My wife had become a king despite my burden and I knew in my heart it wouldn't take divine intervention for her to recover, my daughter was also a ruler and had her daughter back, my son was merry, and Janus had been consumed. There was the matter of Lucifer, but he held no sway over me or mine anymore. I was want for nothing, I was finally free. Then again, I could be wrong.

The old music was fading, and silence was just as welcome as new song.

I could only think of one answer.

"Let's just say you owe me."

Benjamin Dempsey was born in Tasmania and grew up in the city of Tamworth, the country music capital of Australia. There, his parents ran a small white goods store. After graduating high school, he studied computer science at TAFE for a year before moving to Newcastle to attend University. He studied a Bachelor of Arts majoring in Creative Writing, while also taking classes in Psychology, Philosophy, Religion, Film Studies and Literature.

When an opportunity to move to Sydney opened up, he took it with little hesitation and enrolled at the University of Sydney to continue his studies. However, financial reasons forced him to leave university before he could graduate. This did not deter him from finishing his first book *Draconian Symphony*.

Benjamin is a ravenous consumer and creator of media, with a passion for speculative fiction. He primarily deals with themes of the occult, transhumanism, and mythology. Most days he runs on extra strength Ceylon tea, and he shares in the Australian appetite for alcohol. In his spare time, he also enjoys video games and the occasional rave.

***